THE FACET

MEMORY

HUNTER

FRANK MORIN

Memory Hunter
Book #2 of The Facetakers

This is a work of fiction. All the characters and events portrayed in this book are fictional, and any resemblance to real people or incidents is purely coincidental.

Copyright © 2015 by Frank Morin

All rights reserved.

ISBN: 978-0-9970233-0-5

A Whipsaw Press Original

Cover art by Christian Bentulan
(https://coversbychristian.com/)

Book design by Kate Staker
(https://katestaker.com/)

First Whipsaw printing: 2015

MEMORY

HUNTER

OTHER WORKS BY FRANK MORIN

Find all books on www.frankmorin.org

THE PETRALIST SERIES

Set in Stone, Book One

A Stone's Throw, Book Two

No Stone Unturned, Book Three

Affinity for War, Book Four

The Queen's Quarry, Book Five

Blood of the Tallan, Book Six
(release in late 2020)

When Torcs Fly, A Petralist Origins novella: Tomas and Cameron

Game of Garlands, A Petralist Origins novella: Anika

THE FACETAKERS SERIES

Saving Face, Book One

Memory Hunter, Book Two

Rune Warrior, Book Three

Aeon Champion, Book Four
(release in November 2020)

SHORT STORIES

"Odin's Eye," included in *A Game of Horns: A Red Unicorn Anthology*

"The Essence," included in *Dragon Writers: An Anthology*

"Only Logical," a purple unicorn story

"The Seventh Strike," included in *Cursed Collectibles: An Anthology*

ACKNOWLEDGEMENTS

Bringing *Memory Hunter* to life has been a long process, with input from many people. Taking the Facetakers into an alternate history fantasy spin had been one of several possible directions for the story, but proved to be the best one by a long shot.

As always, a huge thanks to my family, who believes in me even before there's solid proof that it's a good idea. My beautiful Jenny gave a lot of input into this one, with Kate and Kyle not far behind.

Special thanks to early readers of the story, who braved the script before it was polished. Carey Miller for extremely detailed feedback, James Morin for insights into military aspects, as well as Chinese cultural items I never would have figured out on my own. Phil Morin for helping me connect to the real vibe of New Orleans, and Joe Morris for in-depth discussions. Your feedback was more valuable than you can imagine.

Thanks to Joshua Essoe for another brilliant edit and Christian Bentulan for a fantastic cover that took our high-level discussions and brought them to life in breathtaking ways.

And thanks to all those who listened to the unique premise and didn't tell me I was a quack. I sleep better at night knowing other people agree this concept rocks.

CHAPTER ONE

No matter in what shape it comes, whether from the mouth of a king who seeks to bestride the people of his own nation and live by the fruit of their labor, or from one race of men as an apology for enslaving another race of simple mortals, it is the same tyrannical principle.

~Abraham Lincoln

One hour out from New Orleans, Sarah set aside her Louis L'Amour western and rose from her seat in the first class cabin of the airplane to use the restroom. The closer she approached the city and Tomas, the more her nervous excitement grew. She was eager to land, to escape the stale cabin air, even for the humidity of the deep south.

The bathroom was occupied and a heavyset woman in seat 2A proclaimed that she was next in line, so Sarah headed aft. As she slipped through the coach cabin, she considered the possible outcomes of her trip. Tomas had left the details of the vacation vague. He'd also been rather vague about why he was inviting her to join him.

He was clearly interested, and one of the reasons she'd accepted his invitation to meet him in New Orleans was that she was seriously considering exploring a relationship. He had saved her life, after all, had proven himself a remarkably capable man, one with a good soul that she could count on.

The fact that he was the key to her finding Eirene and learning more about that secret world of magic didn't hurt either.

A man seated in an aisle seat interrupted her musings by touched her arm as she passed. "Excuse me, miss, but didn't you work for Alterego?"

The man looked young, somewhere in his twenties, but dressed like he had accidentally left home with his grandfather's suitcase instead of his own.

"I did. I was a model there," Sarah said, forcing a smile.

Another reason she had accepted Tomas's invitation was for a chance to escape the media frenzy of Alterego for a while. She wasn't surprised that someone recognized her, but felt a flash of irritation anyway.

After the company's fiery collapse, she had received far too much media attention. They called her a hero, the girl who helped reveal the company's illegal activities. She'd slipped out of the limelight as soon as possible, her transition eased by her friend Jill's rise as the face of the disaster. Jill had been the number one top model, and she loved the attention. Sarah was grateful to let her have it.

"I knew it," the man said with a smile. He turned to the elderly woman sitting beside him and took her hand. "Gladys, dear, it's her. It's Sarah."

The old woman squinted through thick glasses. She reached out and Sarah took her gnarled, quaking hand. Gladys leaned toward her and scanned her head to toe. "Did Marilyn change back, dear?"

"No, this is my replacement," Sarah lied. Just her luck, getting stuck on a plane with friends of Marilyn.

"You look lovely, dear," Gladys said. "You could be sisters."

"I was very lucky," Sarah said.

The convict whose body had been stolen for Sarah hadn't been, but she was beyond Sarah's help. Sarah had escaped Alterego with body and soul intact by the narrowest of margins. Marilyn, the renter who had wanted to purchase Sarah's body, had ended up with the convict's very similar form. Marilyn was happy in her new-purchased youth, and Sarah retained her true identity.

"I'm glad someone was," the man muttered.

Upon closer inspection, Sarah noted the small signs of misalignment along his jawline. The skin stretched too tight in a couple of places, but bunched in unusual wrinkles right under his chin. His face fit the skull very well, and at first even she hadn't spotted the telltale signs that he was inhabiting a body that wasn't his original birthday suit.

If Sarah hadn't noticed, no one else would. She'd made hundreds of body transfers in her time as one of Alterego's top-ten female body donors. One of her hobbies had been studying how her face and those of the other donors fit the many temporary bodies they'd used while their own were being rented. Sometimes the fit was nearly flawless, while other times the effect was rather grotesque, as if their faces were but barely attached. Only later had Sarah learned the truth of the *facetakers* and their arcane powers that made the technology of Alterego possible.

"You were a client, weren't you?" Sarah asked.

"Walter," the man introduced himself, shaking her hand. "We both were."

"I had been renting 'A Night to Remember,'" Gladys said with a wistful smile. "So lovely. But they restored me. Poor Walter lost his body in the fire and was stuck in this one."

"I'm so sorry," Sarah said, crouching in the aisle beside him to keep the conversation a little more private.

'A Night to Remember' was Jill's body. Sarah's had been marketed as 'The All-American Girl,' and the wait-list of eager renters had stretched over two years. Her perfectly proportioned curves and loose brown curls had been glamorous enough to catch the eye, but not so much that they intimidated people.

Walter sighed. "It's a mess. Still dealing with lawsuits from this guy's family." He poked himself in the chest. "And arguing with four separate government agencies about whether I'm me or him."

Sarah felt partially responsible for the difficult position the couple were stuck in. In her fight to save herself, she'd helped destroy the evil concealed in the vault, down in the secret heart of the company. She still awoke in chill sweats sometimes from dark dreams in that vault, surrounded by soul coffins, facing Mai Luan and her arcane powers.

She didn't blame Walter for being unhappy. He and his wife had paid obscene amounts of money to rent young bodies, but always the plan had been to return to their original forms. When the company headquarters had imploded, many renter bodies had been destroyed. The dispossessed souls of the convicts whose bodies had been used as temporary replacement for staff and models were also destroyed, leaving bodies without anyone inhabiting them. The aftermath had been chaotic, the results an identity nightmare.

Her heart went out to this old couple, now separated in time. Walter was stuck in a different generation, and in the near future he'd be forced to watch his beloved wife die of old age while he was still young. Sarah had heard many similar tales of lives shattered by the company, and every one enraged her more than the last.

Sarah spoke softly, "Don't lose hope. I'm tracking a lead that might be able to help."

"Help how?" Walter asked. He sounded interested, but looked like he was trying not to get his hopes up.

She hesitated to say. One goal she had in visiting Tomas, in addition to a possible new romance, was to convince him to bring her to Eirene and beg her help in healing some of those broken lives. Sarah, Eirene, and Tomas were partially responsible for the mess, and although the technology was gone, Eirene was a facetaker. If Sarah could track her down, she was convinced they could find a way to help.

No one else knew about the facetakers and their strange soul powers, though. Sarah didn't pretend to understand it, but she'd seen it work, and she felt driven to understand the murky, arcane world she'd glimpsed.

So she said, "Alterego was destroyed, but there's a chance the secret to their work wasn't completely erased."

"That would be wonderful, wouldn't it, dear?" Gladys said.

Walter looked less inclined to hope for a miracle. "If you find it, let us know."

"I will," Sarah promised.

She took down their phone number, their need bolstering her determination to find Eirene and convince her to help. As she waited for her turn in the restroom, her eyes scanned the rows of passengers. She noticed a muscular man whose face did not quite fit. With her thoughts now focused on her goal to help the victims of Alterego, her gaze locked onto the telltale signs of misalignment.

He glanced up, saw her looking at him, and quickly ducked behind a magazine. Sarah turned the other way so he didn't feel uncomfortable. Some people still resented what had happened, and she didn't blame them.

On the way back from the bathroom, she looked for the man, but he wasn't in his seat. Before passing back into the first class cabin, she glanced back and caught sight of him sitting in a different seat, watching her with a scowl. When their eyes crossed, he ducked down again.

After she resumed her seat, she wondered about his odd behavior. Unlike Walter, his face had fit poorly. Most people still wouldn't notice the subtle mis-alignment, but she couldn't miss it.

Had he also lost his elderly body in the disaster? Lawsuits still raged across the country, and legislatures struggled to figure out the complex questions of identity left in the wake of the company's collapse.

Maybe the man's wife had rented Sarah's body? That might explain his reaction, especially if his wife had been restored to her aged self like Gladys.

So many wrongs needed to be righted. She'd convince Tomas to help, pitch her cause to Eirene, and together they'd make things right.

CHAPTER TWO

Anyone who doesn't take truth seriously in small matters cannot be trusted in large ones either. That is why there are so many rumors about the fountain of youth and so little real knowledge.

~Albert Einstein

Wake up, sleepyhead."

Gregorios pried his eyes open when Eirene prodded him a second time. As much as he longed to return to sleep, he smiled to see her. Her long imprisonment as a dispossessed soul had only sharpened his love for this woman.

When she appeared convinced he wouldn't drift off again, Eirene sat on the edge of the bed. "I need to review the plan for this morning's insertion."

She wore the athletic young body she'd acquired a few weeks prior when Tomas and Sarah had reincorporated her, and it fit her soul well. Gregorios had recently acquired his current form, a dependable, twenty-something body with excellent muscle tone. It was a temporary replacement. He looked forward to settling into a permanent model to begin another new life together with Eirene.

She spread a map of the ground floor of a hotel onto the bed. Instead of listening to her recite the insertion plan, Gregorios pulled her down beside him and gave her a lingering kiss. She didn't resist, returning the embrace with a youthful intensity that belied the many lives they'd shared together. Visiting some of their many descendants over the past couple of weeks had been good for her.

"Enough of that," she said eventually, sitting again and adjusting her shoulder holster. "One of us has work to do this morning."

"Well one of us stayed up most of the night doing surveillance," Gregorios countered. "The location's confirmed. She'll be there."

"Good." Eirene checked a pair of handcuffs, then slid them into the pocket of her blazer. "Tereza has a lot of explaining to do."

"I can come along," Gregorios offered, suppressing a yawn.

"No, dear." Eirene kissed his forehead. "I've got this. Tereza's no real threat, but if she gives me trouble, I'll need help carrying her out."

"Can do." He hadn't kidnapped another facetaker in a decade and looked forward to the chance. "You think she knows where Mai Luan's hiding?"

Eirene's expression turned serious. "I hope so. We have to track that monster down."

"You want to use the family to remove her?" Gregorios asked.

"No. I think it better to send the data to the council with Tomas. He'll take her down."

"Young guys get all the fun."

Eirene arched one eyebrow. "Is that so?"

It was going to be a good day.

"We'll talk about that when you get back," Gregorios said.

After Eirene left, he rolled over and went back to sleep.

Gregorios welcomed new dreams. It didn't matter whether they were exciting or mundane, he relished their freshness. He didn't dream new things often.

This wasn't a new dream. Gregorios had outlived most new dreams. The old ones would creep back into his mind and dredge up bits of memories that spanned the ages. Some were sweet and welcomed as cherished friends. Others reminded him of mistakes made or paraded past his mind's eye the countless masses of those he had outlived. Some offered lessons still to be learned or reminded him of hard-won truths that might have faded over time. He faced nearly all of them with calm acceptance. Danger lurked in railing against the past or refusing to see the truth in his choices.

Sometimes the alternative was worse.

The memory his thoughts returned to while he slept cast his mind back into a pivotal moment, one he avoided whenever possible. The dream folded around his mind like a glove full of splinters and triggered yet again the long-simmering anger as it tempted him to make a different choice. He didn't try to change how he felt. Embracing the anger was his best defense when forced to re-live that dark day when Berlin fell.

Gregorios headed south along the rubble-filled main thoroughfare of the Wilhelmstrasse as the dream memory coalesced into sharp reality. The whistling of falling mortar shells filled the air with high-pitched screaming, and explosions racked the city with constant rolling thunder. The scent of death hung in the air and clung to every surface, like the fine gray dust that billowed across the city in constant clouds.

Shouting and the chatter of small arms fire filled the brief pauses between thunderous concussions from the bombing. The stench of dust mixed with the smell of broken stone and gunpowder. Underneath the rest, fear and hopelessness clung to the streets, an invisible odor like distant burning trash. Every breath dragged more of the filth into his lungs, but he didn't plan to wear that body much longer, so its long-term health didn't concern him.

Few civilians ventured outside even there in the heart of the city. They hid all around, many seeking shelter in the imposing government buildings. Most were wise enough to avoid drawing attention to themselves in the streets flooded with the last of the city's defenders.

Some were just unfortunate.

As a squad of soldiers approached through the blowing haze, a woman scurried out from under a burned-out truck. She wore a wool coat that might have once been tan, but was layered with so much filth it looked black. With one hand she clutched a five-year-old girl close, and with the other she held a baby boy to her chest with fingers clamped over his mouth to keep him silent. Their fear-filled eyes stood out in sharp contrast to their smudged faces.

The woman nearly ran into Gregorios before she noticed him and yelped with fear.

"Find a place to hide," he urged, but she wasn't listening. As she sprinted away, Gregorios wanted to call out after her, to warn her to go the other way, but her fatal fear would drive her on regardless.

Behind her, one of the soldiers shouted, "Halt!"

She ran faster.

A ragged band of battered soldiers emerged from the haze, rifles at the ready, but they too paused when they saw Gregorios.

He adjusted his long, black trench coat and fedora, the unofficial uniform of the Gestapo. The soldiers scurried past like the woman had. Several glanced in his direction but looked away before making eye contact.

The obersoldat who had issued the challenge muttered a quick apology and followed his men without waiting for a reply. Abuses by the Gestapo were rampant and although the disguise presented some risk of getting shot in the back, it was so much better than the alternative.

In addition to his clothing, he wore the body of a perfect Aryan specimen, which added to his authority. No one would tempt fate by asking his purpose. If they did learn his plan, some would kill him on the spot. More would probably volunteer to help.

He glanced back at the ragged band. Many of the soldiers were boys drafted from the Hitler Youth Corps in too-big uniforms, their eyes shining white against dirt-streaked faces. Trailing them came old men who had stood valiant during the first World War, called to serve again in the hour of ultimate need. At the end of successful first lives, those men should have been allowed to die in peace.

He made a point of not glancing farther down the street to where the poor woman still ran, her bare feet leaving soft tracks in the thick dust. He might not have looked, but he couldn't block out the shriek of the descending mortar.

The explosion rocked the street and sent the soldiers diving for cover. A blast of hot air, sprinkled with stinging debris pelted Gregorios in the back. The wind moaned as it passed through the nearby husk of a truck and despite how many times he had heard it, he still shivered. It sounded like the final accusing breath from the tiny family just ripped from the world.

Gregorios turned off the main street and hurried around a towering office building pockmarked with shrapnel that left it looking diseased. At the bitter end, the city finally reflected the rot that had consumed its leadership.

His shame for having allowed that rot to fester for so long still burned as bright as ever. Gregorios allowed it to pulse through him, strengthening his resolve. The choice he was about to make would become a turning point in more than a single life. The cost would be high, but the only thing he regretted was not making it sooner.

He paused when he entered the expansive gardens of the Reich Chancellery. The distant sounds of fighting trailed away inside that oasis of tranquility set in the cancerous heart of Berlin. Gregorios allowed himself a deep breath to center his mind and to enjoy for the last time what had been his favorite place in the city.

Gregorios strode south across the carefully manicured lawns and threaded around craters of blasted dirt and splintered trees. Here the air smelled of green grass and scorched earth. He turned east again to face the rear of the Reichskanzlei and the Old Chancellery building. Situated just behind those white-walled edifices huddled a nondescript concrete cube of a structure. It spanned only twelve feet per side, with a single thick, iron door. To the right of the building stood a cone-shaped sentry pillbox.

Gregorios ignored the sentry outpost and made for the door in the cube building. The guard would recognize him from previous visits and Gregorios did not have time to waste.

To his right, just as expected, a dozen soldiers dressed in SS uniforms burst out of a concealing hedgerow a couple hundred yards to the south. They raced in his direction, led by Asoka, his long-time friend and soon-to-be betrayer.

The jaws of the trap were closing.

So be it.

Gregorios pointedly turned his back on the approaching threat and strode up to the heavy door. It served as the only entry to the underground bunker dug under the gardens. The door felt cold under his fingers. He brushed the layer of fine dust from the handle and pushed it open.

Darkness exploded out of the doorway in a physical wave that catapulted him off his feet. The unexpected blow consumed every sense and tore him from the dream.

Gregorios surged upright in bed, shocked awake by the startling ending to an already unpleasant dream. Sweat-soaked blankets fell from his torso as he blew out a long breath. It took a moment to dissipate the tension knotting his shoulders, and he used the time to rub at his throbbing temples.

He should have gone with Eirene. Beating up a rogue face-taker would've been so much more fun. He hadn't suffered that dream in months, and it had never ended that way before.

It was not a good omen.

CHAPTER THREE

When I despair, I remember that all through history the way of truth and love have always won. There have been cui dashi and tyrants and murderers, and for a time, they can seem invincible, but in the end, they always fall. Think of it—always.

~Mahatma Gandhi

Eirene entered the Queen's Court hotel with a casual stride. She paused in the beautifully restored lobby to admire the elegant salon. Padded chairs and fine couches clustered around expensive area rugs that floated on the emerald tile floor, forming little islands of tranquility without interrupting the flow of humanity.

She worked through the moderate crowd of hotel guests, curious window shoppers, and spa clients as she scanned for defensive measures. The basic hotel security systems were in place as expected, but those didn't concern her.

Wearing her fit young form, she blended right in. With her pretty face and thick brown hair, she could have easily headed for the spa or, with her business attire, accessed the offices.

A pair of men lounged near the elevators. They lacked the look of impatient husbands waiting for their wives and stood a little too far from the elevators to be waiting to board. The sports coats they wore were a little much for the heat of New Orleans even in the early autumn, and undoubtedly served the same purpose as her blazer.

Eirene slipped into a chatty bridal party that swept through the lobby, and easily reached the stairway unnoticed. Eyes in the main floor were pretty standard, but whoever was in charge of security didn't even bother to post another watcher in the stairwell.

She trotted up to the third floor, then took the elevator up to the twentieth. From there she returned to the stairwell for the final two flights.

It took only seconds to bypass the locked security gate blocking access to the top floor presidential suite. Still no guards. Sloppy. When she had been running operational security for Suntara, such lapses would have resulted in severe reprimands. Then again, it wasn't the most dramatic shift in the world since she had returned from years living in a box.

Although thick carpeting covered the last flight of steps, the stairway still smelled of cement dust and stale air. The fire door at the top lacked an alarm, but sealed tight all around. Eirene turned the handle with exquisite care and eased it open just a crack until she could slip a thin wire through the opening.

Using a small display connected to the other end of the wire, which held a miniature video camera, she studied the entrance to the presidential suite. A long, narrow entrance faced the stairs and nearby elevator. A pair of armed guards flanked the ornate wooden outer door of the suite.

Eirene had made no sound, and had moved the door so slowly that neither of the guards appeared to have noticed it open a fraction of an inch. That lapse was understandable, but they should have had video surveillance set up to monitor the stairwell. Were security breaches so rare these days?

Time to teach.

Eirene drew a double-barreled, semi-automatic dart gun from a shoulder holster. She dropped to one knee, braced her shoulder against the door frame, and used her leading foot to push the door open.

The guards noticed the door swinging wide and their hands moved to their sidearms, but they didn't draw until they saw her crouched, pistol aimed. The delay was more than long enough. Eirene caressed the trigger and the little gun made the tiniest whooshing sound as it spat chemical-filled darts thirty feet to the first target before his gun cleared the holster.

She shot the second guard as he was swinging his gun to bear. He was fast, but her darts worked faster. The first dart delivered an electric jolt that disrupted muscle control for a critical three seconds. The second delivered a fast-acting drug cocktail, including a paralytic and a tranquilizer that dropped the guards to the floor before the electric shock wore off.

Eirene slipped into the hall, gun trained on the motionless forms as she slowly advanced. She kicked their fallen sidearms out of reach. When neither guard moved, she patted their lower backs but found no telltale bulge of concealed soul packs.

She did not expect them to withstand the darts, but it always paid to be cautious. Although she appreciated the lax security, she hated such sloppy work. Enough facetakers had died over the centuries to prove the need for constant vigilance, and she cringed to see the new generation making the same stupid mistakes.

Before entering the suite, Eirene replaced the magazine with a fresh one. The marvelous little gun was quickly becoming her favorite tool. During the Great War they had thought the new drugs available back then incredible, but in those days they still needed precious seconds to incapacitate. Coupling potent modern drugs with compressed air technology was brilliant. The gun worked like a charm. The new equipment Gregorios had obtained completely changed the operational considerations.

Eirene cuffed the fallen guards with steel-mesh zip ties and gagged them. Although they showed no signs of enhancement, it always paid to keep a free avenue for escape. She doubted Tereza would give her much trouble, but she planned to enjoy this new life a long time. She wouldn't start by making foolish assumptions.

The door to the suite opened without a sound under her touch. Eirene slipped inside, gun at the ready, but found the entryway clear. The short hallway was hung with several pieces of art, including originals from local artists. She paused to admire the reproduction of Dance in the City by Pierre Auguste Renoir. She had always loved that one, and had told Pierre in 1883 when he completed it that he'd produced a masterpiece.

The suite opened into the living room and a gourmet kitchen. The dining room on the far side of the kitchen held an antique dining set and crystal chandelier. Italian marble flooring there triggered an unexpected sense of nostalgia for the long-distant home of her first life.

She passed the library and paused in the entryway to the grand salon with its museum-quality artwork and grand piano. Such opulence was standard for facetaker clients, who lived well and could afford to buy the risky miracle of another life. The floor plan she had studied before beginning her infiltration had shown the suite spanned three thousand square feet.

The salon was empty so she crossed to the wall behind the piano. The master bedroom shared that wall and she pressed a listening device to it. After the tiniest wave of static, clear voices spoke from her earpiece.

"I am happy you approve of the transfer vehicle." Eirene recognized Tereza's slight New England accent. Although their intel had been pretty solid, she always loved final confirmation.

"How does this work exactly?" a shaky old man asked.

"Just relax," Tereza said. It sounded like she was moving, probably getting into position behind the client. The transfer would begin shortly.

Perfect.

Eirene listened for another minute until Tereza began the transfer. A whisper of feeling across her skin like a distant breeze confirmed the woman had embraced her nevra core, the heart of her soul powers.

Eirene tucked the listening device into her pocket, checked the pistol, and drew a Taser. After a slow count to five, she moved to the bedroom door, gently turned the latch, and slipped into the room.

CHAPTER FOUR

You only get one life—unless you can afford a second.
~Hernan Cortes, conquistador, 1542

The master bedroom was huge, with an enormous bed, vaulted ceilings, and a full sitting area. Tereza stood near the bed, behind a reclined chair upon which lay the fat old client.

Tereza's eyes blazed like amethysts, and purple fire rimmed her hands as she drove burning fingers into the skin along the old man's jaw. His expression looked serene, his body slumped absolutely still. She had already severed the soul points linking him to the host body and begun removing his soulmask.

The client's face began pulling away at the jaw. Skin sloughed off to either side as it leveraged higher, revealing the shimmering soulmask underneath as it separated from the underlying bone structure. It came free abruptly with a wet, sucking sound like a boot lifting out of the mud.

The soulmask of the old man was the tangible manifestation of his soul. It was shaped like his face, but as it rose above his skull, it flattened somewhat. The translucent soulmask shimmered with internal light. Streamers of rainbow smoke floated below it, dangling in wispy coils.

Tereza threw her head back in silent ecstasy, embracing that singular moment experienced only by facetakers taking another's soul.

The skin of the client's skull settled into a smooth sheet, like a shopping store mannequin. It stretched in a blank canvas but for a tiny slit where the nose should be. The bone structure remained in place, although a little less pronounced than before. When embedded into the skull, the soulmask meshed into the bones, shaping them to fit its profile.

Like Eirene, Tereza possessed the rare ability to embrace her nevra core, the active power source of her soul, and direct the energy generated by it, known as nevron, to overpower the soul of simple mortals. Removing another's soul by extracting their soulmask was the heart of the facetaker powers, and a service that wealthy clients had paid handsomely for throughout the ages.

On the bed lay the body of a fit young man, the transfer vehicle, its mannequin-blank face revealing that its previous owner's soul had already been removed. Tereza would fuse her client's soulmask into that host, restoring the client to mortality to enjoy a new life, a new youth. It was a good match. The client would look quite natural there. At least some aspects of the modern day operation still ran smoothly.

Tereza blinked a couple times and the glow of her eyes faded. She noticed Eirene standing in the doorway, but instead of looking surprised, the mousy little woman greeted her with a curt nod.

"I'll be with you in a moment." Tereza glanced at Eirene's weapons. "You won't interfere with council-sanctioned work, will you?"

That was not the response Eirene expected.

She didn't need centuries of finely-honed instincts to recognize that her carefully planned surprise had been expected. The most galling part was that the woman was still grounded in her first life, for love of the gods.

Eirene squashed her surprise. "By all means, finish what you've started."

As Tereza turned toward the bed to complete the transfer process, Eirene nearly triggered the Taser. It would have felt good, but if Tereza really was working on a council-sanctioned transfer, Eirene couldn't afford to incur any more of their wrath.

So she turned and bolted for the exit. She would plan a different interrogation scenario later, but first she had to extract. Tereza must have back-up ready, and Eirene didn't want to meet them. She crossed the suite without encountering resistance, but the two guards she had left outside near the elevator were gone.

Not good.

The elevator chimed.

Before the doors opened, Eirene sprinted for the stairs. She caught a glimpse of several armed men piling out of the elevator before she crashed through the fire door into the stairwell. Voices shouted an alarm, and she plunged down the stairs at a full sprint. At least two of the newcomers wore tactical vests that left their muscular arms bare. The dark runes tattooed there had shone against their pale skin.

Eirene felt flickers of fear. The entire situation had been a trap and she had walked right into it. Maybe her long absence from the real world had left her rustier than she thought.

She could beat herself up about the mistake later. The enhanced warriors were most likely enforcers. It wasn't a surprise she hadn't recognized any of them. She'd been gone for too long. But she understood all too well their deadly skills. Had Tereza played her hand with a little more care, Eirene would have lingered a few more fatal seconds in the suite.

Eirene reached the security gate separating the top-floor suite from the rest of the stairwell and burst through just as the fire door above crashed open and heavy bodies began thundering down the steps.

Eirene left them far behind.

They started shooting. Bullets ricocheted off steel and concrete, and painful echoes reverberated through the stairwell. None of the shots came close, and the security gate slammed shut behind her, blocking their aim.

The enforcers continued down, shouting loudly, and started shooting as soon as they passed through the security gate. They couldn't hope to hit her.

They were herding her.

If she could just reach the fifth floor, she could implement the primary escape plan. Getting that far would be the challenge. The stairwell door below her flew open and three armed men rushed inside, guns up.

With less than a full flight of stairs between them, Eirene launched herself at them, every ounce of momentum focused on the heel of her foot. It drove into the first man's head hard enough to crack even an enhanced skull. The impact rattled her all the way up to her hip.

It also knocked the enforcer into his two companions. Eirene tucked her body tight and hit them like a cannon ball. The brutal impact jarred her to a halt and left her head spinning, but the men fared far worse. One tumbled right over the rail, and barely caught himself, hanging over the open drop eighteen floors down.

The other two landed beneath her and cushioned her fall. Only one of them tried to move, so she kicked him in the head. After the second kick, he collapsed beside his unconscious partner.

Eirene took off down the stairs again, delayed exactly three seconds by the encounter. That was pretty good, even for her.

For the next fifteen seconds she flew down the steps, every muscle attuned to the need to run faster. Nothing mattered but the blur of steps, the pounding of her heart, and the thrill of the downward plunge at the very cusp of losing control.

Stray bullets and the frustrated shouts of pursuers faded to silence as she focused exclusively on the tricky technique of running down the stairs at a full sprint. Even the hollow thudding of her feet on steel and concrete barely registered.

Eirene almost ran right past the door to the fifth floor. With a grin she flung it open and leaped through.

She skidded to a halt and her confidence shattered.

Waiting for her in the hallway, barely ten feet away, stood eight black-clad men with silenced pistols already aimed in her direction. Mai Luan stood to one side, a pleasant smile on her lovely face.

Even as Eirene snapped her weapons up toward the hated woman, the men fired. They were using the same specialized pistols that she carried. Sixteen darts drove into Eirene's abdomen and chest. Pain rippled through her torso in disproportionate magnitude to the tiny impacts, and she rocked back as agony thundered through her.

As soon as the initial electric shock subsided, Eirene embraced her nevra core and severed sensory input from her body, but she had taken too much damage. Her arms became numb, dead weights and her weapons slipped from her fingers despite her efforts to pull the trigger just once.

Eirene focused all her nevron on maintaining a single nerve connection and blocking the effects of the paralytic drug. Her body wobbled like a newborn and her vision turned fuzzy. Her chin fell forward, but none of that mattered. Through the growing haze, and with agonizing slowness, she pulled the sleeve of her right arm up past her watch to reveal a second device strapped to her forearm. It looked a lot like a watch, but with no face. Simplicity itself, it sported only three buttons.

She tried to push the red one.

She failed.

Her body collapsed to the floor and that last vibrant connection snapped. If she had worn a body with more bulk, it might have withstood the drugs another half second, just long enough to send the signal.

As the fast-acting tranquilizers shut her body down, Mai Luan leaned over her. "By all means, let's send for Gregorios."

Mai Luan pushed the yellow button.

CHAPTER FIVE

Yes, at times I did provide new lives to those who could afford them, even when they didn't deserve them. Most of the time though, I focused on ridding the world of heka, of tyrants, and of those who lived one life too many.

~Gregorios

As the plane made its final approach for landing, Sarah forced worries of body renting and Alterego aside. She would enjoy herself, she'd secure the meeting with Eirene, and she'd keep an open mind about Tomas.

New Orleans airport was strangely empty when Sarah stepped off the plane, full of nervous excitement. With nothing but carry-on luggage, she exited the secure area and descended an escalator toward parking. At the bottom of the escalator stood a tall statue of Louis Armstrong, the famous jazz musician, blowing his trumpet. As she passed, she noticed his face looked strange. It didn't fit right.

She stopped to look closer, wondering if maybe she was just obsessing a bit, projecting her worries about her recent harrowing experience. No, the statue's face was just odd.

"Sarah!"

She turned to find Tomas jogging toward her, and rushed to give him a hug.

"Welcome to New Orleans," he said grandly and gave her a peck on the cheek.

What was that supposed to mean? No attempt to steal a real kiss, and his hug was more like a brother's than a hopeful boyfriend.

"What's with no people around here?" Sarah asked. "I thought this place would be packed."

He shrugged as he took her roller bag. "No matter how busy it gets here, it always feels kind of empty. Not the strangest thing about New Orleans."

"What do you mean?"

"Wait till we get into the city."

He led the way toward the exit, but did not take her hand. Sarah studied him as they headed for the short-term parking garage. He was average in build and stood only a couple inches taller than her five-foot-eight. His hair was straight and brown, his face rather unremarkable. She was happy to see him, but didn't feel the anticipated thrill of emotion to think of him as a potential boyfriend.

Although still not yet noon, it was already hot and humid. She was glad she had packed warm weather clothes and wondered why he had insisted she bring something for cooler temperatures.

Tomas had saved her life, helped her escape Alterego with soul and body intact, and for that she owed him a debt she could never repay. At the same time, he had introduced her to the terrifying reality of Alterego's secrets. Facetakers and runes and freaky soul coffins and Mai Luan. Part of her wished she could leave all that mind-bending baggage behind for good, but that was wishful thinking. She needed to know more, and she needed Eirene.

For that, she needed Tomas. So even if the romance fizzled, she'd enjoy herself, and she'd focus on her other goals.

They climbed into his Honda Accord and although he held the door for her, he made no other advances. As they headed for the parking lot exit, Sarah caught another glimpse of the man with the mis-matched face from the airplane. He was hurrying across the parking lot toward a nearby row of cars and vans, and he glanced several times in her direction.

Poor guy. She hoped he'd let the past go.

As Tomas paid the parking fee and took the long ramp that arced high over several buildings toward the highway, she wondered if she'd mis-read his intentions. Although he looked rather plain physically, he bore himself with confidence. He seemed older than he looked, and had demonstrated some remarkable abilities during their escape from Alterego. He'd broken into the vault and confronted Mai Luan and Mr. Fleischer more like a trained fighter than a medical tech.

Mai Luan had looked like a normal, petite Chinese-American woman before she tried to kill them with archaic rune magic. Then she'd shrugged off several mortal wounds and somehow imploded the entire corporate headquarters in on herself.

Tomas had helped Sarah escape that nightmare. There was more depth to him than anyone she'd ever met, and she found that immensely attractive. With her famous good looks, there was no shortage of handsome guys to date, but Tomas offered the possibility of something more. At the moment he looked relaxed, happy. That was a good sign. He glanced at her and smiled.

She felt comfortable in his presence, just as she always did. It was that good-hearted dependability that she had first grown to appreciate. She trusted him, and looked forward to getting to know the real Tomas.

Traffic picked up as he accelerated onto Highway 10, heading east toward the city, but he merged without any trouble. She asked, "So I'm here. Tell me about the plan."

He grinned. "We have a lot of ground to cover. One day is not nearly enough to explore New Orleans."

"What do you mean? You told me to plan for at least two weeks."

"But not here."

She punched his shoulder. "Fine. Be all mysterious, but give me a clue."

"You brought your passport, right?"

"Yes, but I didn't need it to fly to New Orleans."

"You'll need it when we leave for Rome."

"Rome!" Sarah laughed. "You've got to be kidding."

"I take it you're pleased." He glanced in the rear-view mirror.

"I've always wanted to go to Rome." She squeezed his hand. She had wanted to travel for a long time, but had not managed to get away much in the past couple of years. She had left Alterego a wealthy woman and could go anywhere. Rome would be the perfect place to start.

Most guys thought flowers were romantic surprises. She liked how Tomas thought bigger than that. "So what do you have planned for tonight?"

"We're going to the French Quarter."

"Sounds like fun."

"It'll be great. I guarantee it."

She stared past him at glimpses of the huge Lake Pontchartrain north of the highway. This vacation definitely had possibilities. Now she just had to get that meeting with Eirene set up.

Tomas glanced in the rear-view mirror again and frowned. "I hate to sound like a bad TV show, but we've got company."

Sarah scanned the traffic behind them, expecting to see a news van. Leave it to the media to interrupt her vacation. But there were no news vehicles anywhere in sight.

Tomas said with a tone of disgust. "They're even driving a white van with tinted windows. How cliché can they be?"

She spotted the van coming up in the left lane, but it didn't look remarkable. "I don't understand."

Tomas changed to the far right lane and accelerated. "Either they're following you to settle scores from Alterego, or they're following me. That would be . . . bad."

"What do you mean?" Surviving Mai Luan's freakish attack and the fireball of the imploding Alterego building had been bad according to Tomas. Fear she had thought permanently buried started clawing back to the surface.

"You made some powerful enemies who might have discovered your involvement in the company's collapse, despite everything I did to hide it. They're not the kind of people to just forgive and forget."

"Who would be following me?"

He hesitated. "People working for Mai Luan."

Sarah shivered to hear that name spoken. Although Tomas had warned her that Mai Luan might not have died in the disaster, she had not wanted to believe it. With more than a little worry, she watched the white van for another couple minutes as they passed the Metairie suburbs, but nothing looked suspicious.

Sarah started to wonder if Tomas was making the whole thing up. They had become close through a time of conflict and danger. Did he think he needed to manufacture more of that to keep her around? Could he be that insecure?

Tomas looked calm, but alert, not freaked out by the thought of someone following them.

"Is this some kind of joke?" she asked.

Before he could respond, the van accelerated and swerved into the middle lane to come up beside them. The side door slid open to reveal the same man from the plane, secured in place with a harness, and wielding a military style rifle. It looked like one of those AK-47 rifles the terrorists always carried.

The man leaned forward and fired.

CHAPTER SIX

A room without books is like a body without a face.
~Marcus Tullius Cicero

Sarah screamed as Tomas slammed on the brakes. She lurched forward against the seatbelt as bullets tore into the road right in front of the car.

The van braked and the gunman swung against his restraining harness, forced to stop firing as his rifle swung wide. The brakes on Tomas's car squealed, and he swung in behind the van. Other vehicles around them swerved and blared their horns. A compact collided with an SUV that skidded into its lane. The car crumpled and the SUV rolled right over it, sending bits and pieces flying, and forcing all three lanes of traffic to grind to a halt.

The van slowed further and began swerving from side to side. Tomas stayed in their wake, matching their every move.

Sarah shouted, "What are you doing? Get us out of here!"

"He's trying to shake me loose so the gunner can get another shot," Tomas said, sounding remarkably calm.

"What about the rear door?" she asked, surprised no one had started shooting at them from there yet. Her hands shook and she fought down a ridiculous notion that she was in a bad dream and just needed to wake up.

"I've got it. Cover your ears."

He extracted a huge pistol from under his seat. Sarah recognized it as a forty-five caliber. It looked like an H&K USP. She'd had a boyfriend who'd loved that gun, but the double-stacked magazine made the grip too big for her. Tomas rolled down his window, transitioned the gun to his left hand, extended it out the window, and fired.

Sarah clapped hands over her ears just in time, but the concussive booming of the gun just outside his window still hurt. The window in the van's left rear door shattered and the van swerved hard to the left. Sarah doubted she could have hit anything with a one-handed, left-handed shot while driving and swerving.

Tomas accelerated, and the plain-looking Honda had a lot more power under the hood than Sarah expected. The sudden acceleration drove her back into her seat.

"Watch out!" she shouted as they pulled even with the right side of the van, barely ten feet from the gunner.

Before the man could bring his rifle to bear, Tomas fired again. The bullet tore into the gunner's chest, and blood splattered the van's interior as he sagged in his restraining harness.

Another man leaned around the gunner, a pistol in his hand. Tomas ignored him and continued accelerating. As they pulled even with the front of the van, he fired again. The passenger window exploded all over the man seated there.

The van braked hard and swerved away.

Tomas continued to accelerate. When it appeared the van would not immediately give chase, he rolled up his window and holstered the gun back under his seat.

"I think they were following me," he stated.

Sarah craned her head around to stare at the van falling farther behind. "How did you do that?"

Her heart still raced and fear that had not had time to really grab hold spiked to near-panic levels. She wanted to slap him for looking so calm.

"Just take deep breaths," he offered. "You faced worse in the vault."

"But they had guns! They were trying to kill us."

Tomas laughed. "Sure, if they had caught us by surprise, it wasn't a bad plan. But they're just human."

"We have to stop, have to call the police."

"That wouldn't help."

"Why not?" She focused on the conversation as an anchor for her thoughts.

He chuckled. "The NOPD usually manages to arrive only after emergencies are over. They're also notoriously corrupt, so there's a pretty solid chance they're already on the payroll of whoever hired those hit men. Wouldn't help."

"But that's not supposed to happen these days." Why did everyone always say to call the police first if the police wouldn't help?

Tomas laughed. "Are you serious?"

Sarah took a couple of deep breaths, trying to bring her pounding fear under control. She hadn't had police help at Alterego. They'd had to figure things out on their own. They could do it again. In her mind, she heard her parents ridiculing her as they so often had when she was younger. They would tear down her choices and try to force her into a useless life with no dreams, no ambitions. She had plenty of practice overcoming challenges, so she centered herself like she did when facing their criticism, and regained control.

"Tomas, the guy with the rifle. I saw him on the plane."

He considered that for a few seconds before saying, "That's why I didn't spot any tails on the way to the airport."

"Why would you even be looking?"

Instead of answering, he cut in front of an eighteen-wheeler and took the Carrollton Street exit. Sarah didn't see the white van as he merged into light traffic, then turned left to circle the campus of Xavier University.

After a minute she dared begin to hope and said, "I don't see them. Are you sure we should have left the highway?"

"They had fallen behind, but might have had a second team waiting for us." He took several rapid turns, and when the van did not appear behind them, Sarah started to relax a little.

He circled back to the campus and pulled into a student parking lot. "I think we're clear."

"So tell me why you were watching for tails on the way to meet me," Sarah said.

He hesitated before speaking. "I had hoped you wouldn't get caught up in everything else."

"Now's not really the best time to be vague," she warned. "Tell me what's going on, Tomas?"

"Remember when I told you Eirene was still searching for Mai Luan?"

"I hoped you were wrong about her."

"I wish I was, but I guarantee Mai Luan is still alive."

"How does Eirene's search for Mai Luan connect to a guy from my flight trying to shoot us?"

"You're sure it was the same guy?"

"Positive. His jawline showed signs of misalignment, just like I used to see at Alterego. I couldn't miss it. I saw him again in the parking lot before we got into your car."

Tomas frowned, looking annoyed, and a little worried. "So they were following you."

"What does that mean?"

Tomas stepped out of the car and she did the same. He collected her bags and led the way toward the street. "Those people I mentioned you might have upset after Alterego? They're very powerful, but I had hoped they'd overlook your involvement. They've been hunting Eirene and her husband for decades. Now that she's free, I figured they'd focus on her."

Sarah didn't like hearing that Eirene was being hunted too. She had only known Eirene a short time, but she felt a connection with the woman. The thought of Mai Luan and those gunmen hunting Eirene terrified Sarah as much as the thought they had followed her onto the plane. If she didn't need Eirene so badly, she'd suggest they take the next flight to Rome and leave this crazy town behind. Mai Luan terrified her more than anything, and she didn't want to be anywhere around the woman.

"Wait a minute. Decades?" Sarah asked as the rest of what Tomas had said sank in.

"It's a long story."

"And it includes her husband?"

He nodded. "Gregorios."

He had mentioned that name in the vault when he had first extracted Eirene's unincorporated face from its little coffin.

"Who is he?"

Tomas' phone rang. He glanced at the caller ID and grunted. "That's him."

CHAPTER SEVEN

Live because you will die tomorrow. Learn because you will live forever.
~Mahatma Gandhi

Tomas flagged down a cab and told the driver to take them to the downtown business district. He looked relaxed during the drive. The cab driver turned out to be one of the chatty types, and between the two of them, the men spent the drive pointing out landmarks and explaining the rich history of the area.

Sarah struggled to match Tomas's outward calm. She held her hands in her lap to disguise the tremors that still shook her from the near-shooting. How Tomas could act so casual after killing a man was another mystery, one she wasn't as eager to delve into. He'd saved her life again, but who drove around town with guns under their seats and fought off machine-gun-wielding criminals?

Sarah had long wanted to visit New Orleans, so she tried to enjoy the ride, despite her lingering fear that gunmen would appear around every turn and shoot them all while they sat helpless in the cab. In her mind, she kept seeing the gunman sagging in his harness, covered in blood. Her hands shook again from delayed shock. Tomas took them in his and rubbed her shaking fingers.

"Thank you," Sarah said, surprised by how much his touch helped calm her.

"Welcome to the Big Easy," he said.

"Not so easy," she chuckled, and more of her tension eased.

"We're on Canal Street," he said, pointing to beautiful old buildings on each side.

"Skirting the French Quarter now," the cabbie piped in. "Basin Street over there is where Louis Armstrong grew up." He pointed out a couple of famous theaters with huge, neon marquee signs, as well as the street cars running up the center of the street.

As they moved deeper into the area, Sarah felt a growing excitement. There was an energy in the air that thrummed against her hyper-alert nerves. It was coupled by a renewed feeling of wanting to look over her shoulder constantly.

They passed a brass band playing on the corner of Canal and Bourbon, surrounded by an enthusiastic crowd. That feeling of excitement intensified, but Sarah's shoulders itched like she was being watched.

Tomas caught her glancing back. "You feel it don't you?"

"I feel something," she admitted. "I thought it was just me."

The cabbie laughed. "No, ma'am. That's the vibe of New Orleans you're feeling. Gets even stronger near the river."

Tomas nodded agreement. "It's part of the city. You get used to it pretty fast, but you'll notice it every time you return."

The cab pulled to the curb near a parking garage for Harrah's Casino. Sarah had heard of that landmark before. She thanked the cabbie as Tomas paid the bill, and the man wished them luck at the poker tables.

Instead of heading for the casino, Tomas led her into the parking garage. "You know, there's a great local band playing tonight I'd like to catch after dinner."

She'd noticed several groups playing at street corners. Music seemed to be a huge part of New Orleans. Usually she'd be thrilled to explore that, but today the idea felt surreal.

She worked on matching his calm as she followed him up to the second level of the parking garage. When they exited the stairs, he took her hand and walked the long line of cars. A man stepped out of the shadows behind a dark SUV five cars away, and Sarah tensed, ready to dive to the ground or run for the exit.

Tomas squeezed her hand and continued toward the stranger. "It's all right."

Sarah studied the man who at first looked unremarkable. Young, with curly hair, probably in his twenties. She had only known Eirene for one afternoon, but such a young man couldn't be her husband.

As he drew closer, she realized her initial appraisal was wrong. His face looked too mature for his body, although it fit pretty well. Only when she thought to look for it did she notice the tiny signs that he was not wearing his birthday suit. The skin along his jaw was stretched a little too tight in some places, bunched up in extra wrinkles in a couple others. A shadow at the corner of his chin could easily be mistaken for a spot that needed shaving, but it wasn't. None of those little marks would mean anything to anyone else, but she knew what they meant.

"Sarah, I'd like to introduce Gregorios," Tomas said simply.

Gregorios took her hand and bowed over it in a manner that might have been popular a very long time ago. His dark eyes were deep and piercing.

"I've heard a great deal about you, Sarah." His voice was rich, and although he spoke softly, she sensed great strength in him.

She actually blushed. "Thank you. It's a pleasure."

He didn't look worried, even though Tomas had suggested Eirene might be in danger. Gregorios popped open the SUV's rear hatch. The tinted windows reminded her of the van they only recently avoided, and goosebumps rippled down her arms in a fresh wave of unease.

Gregorios handed a dark blue, lightweight jacket to Tomas. "Eirene's car is one level up."

"Any sign of surveillance?" Tomas asked as he donned the jacket.

"None. We'll scout on foot."

Tomas checked the big pistol he'd taken from his car. He slipped it into a simple holster that he tucked into his waistband. Gregorios handed Tomas another holstered pistol that he slipped into his jacket. The two men checked ammunition with practiced efficiency, and Sarah's forced calm started to crack. They were preparing for another armed confrontation, right there in the parking garage.

Tomas handed her a small can of pepper spray. "This is the brand you prefer, right?"

"Yes. How'd you know?" she asked as she took the can. Its weight felt reassuring, but still felt pitifully inadequate compared to their guns.

"I pay attention," Tomas said with a little smile.

"Stay behind us and try to keep quiet," Gregorios said, giving her a reassuring smile as he slammed a magazine home. "It'll be all right."

Then he and Tomas led the way up the sloping ramp toward the next level. Sarah trailed them by about ten feet, not wanting to draw too close in case they needed to use those guns, but not wanting to fall behind in the dim expanse of the parking garage either.

The two men walked casually and drew no attention to themselves. The drivers of the few cars that passed focused almost entirely on Sarah anyway. She was just happy the glimpses she caught of the passing motorists revealed nothing threatening.

When they reached the third level, they slipped behind a lifted pick-up and spent ten minutes staring down the length of the parking bay. Whenever the area was clear of pedestrians, they used binoculars and even a heat-sensing scope.

"Which car is hers?" Sarah asked.

"Silver Toyota," Tomas replied.

It sat most of the way down the garage and looked completely unremarkable. Eventually Sarah got bored with the whole clandestine surveillance. "Maybe she just got delayed?"

Gregorios shook his head. "She triggered a distress signal from a nearby hotel, but the transmission cut off after less than a minute."

"Not good," Tomas said.

Gregorios added, "I monitored the building for over an hour before you arrived but saw nothing to suggest they've moved her."

Sarah asked, "Do you think she's . . . ?" She couldn't finish the sentence. It was just too awful.

"Unlikely, but if her body was fatally damaged, under most circumstances she could sever her link with it," Gregorios said.

Despite living the lie of Alterego for so long, Sarah knew so little about the real world of these people. Gregorios seemed to consider the idea of his wife dying little more than an inconvenience. Sarah hadn't realized facetakers could abandon their bodies at will, but there was so much still to learn. What other aspects of facetaker powers did she need to understand if she was going to talk Eirene into helping her restore those victims of the company they'd helped destroy?

How many times had Eirene abandoned her body in the past?

How old were they?

Alterego had made billions selling access to temporary youth, but for the first time, Sarah really considered the fact that facetakers could just take another body when they grew old, sick, or injured. Barring something catastrophic like getting squashed by a runaway train, was there any limit to how long they could keep it up?

She glanced at Gregorios again and he suddenly appeared far more mysterious than he had a moment ago.

How did Tomas fit in? He was no facetaker, but he was also not the medical tech he had pretended to be at Alterego. The two men clearly had experience working together. One more mystery she vowed to unravel when they got to Rome.

Tomas spoke. "We need to insert, determine if she's been dispossessed."

"Agreed."

The two men headed for the stairs and Sarah hurried to catch up. She took Tomas's hand as they returned to the SUV. "You're going to enter a building where you're pretty sure something bad happened to Eirene?"

"Yes."

"Shouldn't we call the police?"

He shook his head. "We talked about that. Even if we got them to respond soon and they're not already working for the people responsible, they'd likely run into resistance in there."

"That's exactly why we should call them."

"I know this is hard to deal with. I had hoped to spare you getting further involved, but you remember what Mai Luan did in the vault?"

She shivered. "How could I forget?" Even after getting blown up, tased, and stabbed, the woman had kept coming.

"What do you think would happen to normal police officers walking into a situation like that?"

"You don't think she's in there, do you?"

If Mai Luan might be in the hotel, Sarah really worried for Eirene's safety. She still had nightmares about the freaky woman.

Gregorios said, "Unlikely. She would pose an exceptional risk, but chances are slim to none we'll encounter her. She's not the only threat out there, though."

Tomas said, "All reasons we can't call the police, and that's why you should probably stay here until we get back."

Sarah began shaking her head before he finished speaking. Parking garages felt spooky on a good day. With the strange New Orleans vibe setting her already-jittery nerves twitching, there was no way she was going to stay there alone with murderous gunmen wandering around.

The shooter had known to follow her onto the plane. What if they had tracked her somehow to this place? Alone she wouldn't stand a chance. She planned to stay close to Tomas until she understood what was going on and why someone wanted to kill her.

Just as importantly, she feared for Eirene. If the attack on Eirene was tied to the recent gunman in the van, helping Eirene would also help her find answers.

"I think it's better if I stay close."

"It'll probably be dangerous."

The comment triggered a surprise flash of anger. She had not risked her life to escape Alterego and regain her own body just to have some nameless thugs kill her. Let her useless brothers live lives of anonymity, too afraid to take any risks in life. She refused to accept that fate.

"Tomas, you said yourself the same people who tried to kill us are probably the ones hunting her. Do you really think I'll be safer anywhere else?"

Gregorios said, "It'd be better to introduce you to our world a little more gently, but you're already a target. We don't have time to waste arguing about it. We can use your help anyway. Follow my lead, and we'll try to make this as quick and simple as possible."

"I wish we had a full team," Tomas said.

"If wishes were omelets . . ." Gregorios said.

Sarah didn't get that one.

Tomas shrugged. "I'd feel more confident if we had our battle suits."

"That I can agree with," Gregorios said. Then he turned to Sarah. "Have any nice outfits in that bag of yours?"

"Uh, yes. Why?"

"Time to play tourist."

CHAPTER EIGHT

If you want to know what a man's like, take a good look at how he treats people during his second life.

~Elvis

Sarah entered the Queen's Court hotel, and for a moment excitement pushed back the tension knotting her shoulders. She knew it was stupid, but assaulting such a gorgeous hotel somehow helped her feel more confident. Whoever they were after had great taste.

Dressed in a form-hugging skirt and matching blouse, she attracted lots of attention. With Tomas half a step behind, she passed through the elegant salon, taking her time to appreciate the artwork and draw as many eyes as possible.

She was good at it. She had not been Alterego's number five top-rated model for nothing. With her perfectly proportioned curves, smooth skin and thick hair, she'd been marketed as 'The All American Girl.'

No one paid any attention to Gregorios, dressed in a delivery uniform and wheeling two large roller bags behind Tomas as she led the trio toward the elevator. Inside, they rode to the ninth floor.

"Why the ninth?" Sarah asked.

"Always been my lucky number," Gregorios said.

"I thought seven was lucky."

"Not for me. Some lives are better left un-lived."

After exiting the elevator, they found an empty hall. Gregorios knocked on one door and, when there was no answer, he produced a small silver box with a hotel key card extending from the bottom. He inserted it into the lock. A light turned green and with a soft click the door unlocked.

They slipped inside a comfortable suite. Thankfully it was empty, with two suitcases in the extensive closet and clothing belonging to a couple with terrible taste in colors.

"This feels weird," Sarah said. She had suggested renting a room but Tomas had explained they didn't want to leave a paper trail.

"We're not staying," Tomas assured her as Gregorios opened the roller bags and started extracting gear.

"We should. I mean, some other time." When he glanced at her, eyebrow raised, she shrugged and added, "I like this hotel."

While the men donned bulletproof vests, strapped on double shoulder holsters, and covered it all surprisingly well with a pair of custom leather jackets, Sarah slipped into the bathroom and changed into slacks. When she emerged, Tomas was loading one holster with an odd, double-barreled pistol.

"I've never seen a pistol like that. What model is it?" she asked.

"Insurance."

Gregorios donned a similar set of weapons. "Customized design of ours to deal with the special nature of the threat. We call it the Final Transfer."

Sarah approached and touched the odd weapon. "I've done a fair bit of shooting, but I've never seen anything like it. What caliber is it?"

Tomas handed it over. It was lighter than she'd expected from the size of the barrels. It bore no manufacturer stamp or serial number, just a strange symbol. It looked like a stick figure of a man with no legs.

She touched the symbol. It looked familiar. "You draw on your toys when you get bored?"

"That's an Egyptian hieroglyph. Ankh. It's the key of life."

"Strange symbol to mark on a gun."

"It'll make sense some day." Tomas dropped the magazines from the unique weapon and showed her the strange darts they held. "It shoots a non-lethal mix."

The first dart was black and felt like rubber. "This one delivers a powerful electric shock. Wrecks muscle control for a few seconds."

He pointed to the second. "This one pumps out a potent mix of fast-acting drugs. Paralytics, tranquilizers, and sleep agents." It was red, and Sarah declined to touch it.

She frowned. "How do you know you get the right dose?"

"The only people we shoot with these can handle it."

"Well let's hope you don't have to shoot anyone up there," she said.

"Best to be prepared." Tomas took the weapon back and slammed the magazines home. "Or it could be us getting the final transfer. We'll use non-lethal first."

Then he tucked his original H&K pistol into the other holster. "But always keep the forty-five as back-up."

After they loaded more gear into various pockets, Tomas handed Sarah a slender canister about the size of a bottle of hair spray, along with a pair of silicon ear plugs.

"What's this?"

"Bear spray. About ten times more potent than that mace you carry. Just in case. This one's been modified to only spray a few feet so it's not so dangerous to use indoors."

"You're so thoughtful."

Her flippant tone sounded weak even to her and she tried to keep a tight rein on her growing tension as she slipped it into her deep coat pocket.

"Never say I don't give you things," he grinned.

Did she really volunteer to join these two? They were preparing for pitched battle in a high-class hotel. The whole situation was beginning to feel like a crazy dream.

He'd better give her lots of answers after they got out of there.

Tomas helped her wedge the slender ear plugs into her ears. "These'll block any loud noises but not interfere with normal hearing."

They left the room after less than five minutes and stashed the empty bags in the nearby vending area. They returned to the elevator and after Sarah confirmed it was empty of other passengers, the heavily-armed men joined her. Gregorios inserted his black box card impersonator and punched the top floor.

"Shouldn't we take the stairs?" Sarah asked.

"Eirene had planned to. Didn't help her much."

Tomas nudged Sarah to one side and drew his weapons.

The elevator beeped and Tomas blew out a breath. "Here we go."

CHAPTER NINE

No matter which life you're living, it is better to be hated for what you are than to be loved for what you are not.

~Andre Gide, author and Nobel Prize winner
for literature

Gregorios followed Tomas quickly out of the elevator on the twenty-second floor, and Sarah slipped out a couple seconds later. The entryway faced a single, ornate door but was otherwise empty. Gregorios used his card device to open the door, and Tomas led the way carefully inside. A slight scent of incense floated in the air.

As the men moved silently down either side of the entry hall, weapons at the ready, Sarah trailed behind, gripping her bear spray so tight her fingers ached. She focused on trying to keep her breathing calm and avoid breaking into a loud pant. Every muscle felt tense and a little shaky. Sweat trickled down the back of her neck, and her hands shook.

What were they doing breaking and entering? How much did she really know about Tomas anyway?

He'd saved her life twice. How much more did she need to know?

As they stopped at the threshold of a large kitchen that shone with stainless steel and granite surfaces, a woman's voice called from deeper within the expansive suite. "In the salon."

Sarah jumped and took a step toward the exit, expecting the men to retreat now that their cover was blown.

They didn't. Tomas glanced at Gregorios, who shrugged. Then they continued their careful advance, efficiently swept the kitchen and living room, and moved into the hall on the far side.

When Tomas ignored Sarah's silent waving, she wanted to scream at them to back up and think about it. Obviously someone knew they were coming. Continuing into the suite had to be a bad idea. If the paintings weren't so clearly expensive, she'd have snatched one off the wall and hit Tomas over the head with it. That would get his attention.

They passed a plush library, and paused in the entrance to a grand salon that could have been taken from any palace. Several overstuffed chairs and a long couch took up the center of the room near a gleaming black grand piano. More antique wooden chairs were positioned around the perimeter of the room, along with ornate little tables.

Tereza sat in an overstuffed chair near the piano, facing the doorway. A large black canvas roller bag stood nearby. She had been one of Mai Luan's assistants, one of the women Eirene had been hunting. That did not bode well. Worse, Tereza looked unconcerned by the pistols aimed in her direction.

"You're late. I expected you at least half an hour ago."

Gregorios shrugged, "You'll wish I'd taken longer soon enough."

"One of us will," she replied with a little smile.

Sarah followed Tomas into the room, each step a struggle. She wanted to leave, but she felt more scared for Eirene than ever. If Tereza had hurt Eirene, Gregorios would take her apart, Tomas would stomp flat anything that remained, and Sarah would volunteer to burn the remains. She focused on her anger, using it to quell some of her fear.

Tereza glanced in her direction. "Sarah, my dear. So glad you're alive and well." Her tone made the words a lie. She gestured at a nearby table with tiny sandwiches and several little bottles of fancy water. "Won't you join me?"

"I think we'll take it to go," Gregorios said, advancing farther into the room, Final Transfer dart pistol trained on Tereza. "On your feet."

"You do realize I'm sponsored by the council in today's activities?"

"All of them?"

She smiled and tapped her crystal glass twice with a tiny silver fork. "Absolutely."

The bedroom doors on either side of the salon flew open and men dressed in street clothes charged into the room.

Gregorios reacted with startling speed, pivoting to face the three men emerging from the left, and drawing his forty-five. Even as Sarah was still digesting the unexpected assault, he shot the first attacker in the chest with the Final Transfer.

The gun made a surprisingly gentle whooshing sound that merged with Tomas' first shot. He had moved just as fast as Gregorios and turned toward the three men charging from the right. His twin projectiles caught the lead attacker in the face, and the man collapsed with a scream that became a garbled, inarticulate cry.

Sarah watched in terrified fascination as the man Gregorios shot staggered under the electric shock, but did not fall. He was a grotesquely muscled giant and the knock-out drugs apparently were too weak to drop him.

He slowed and picked the darts out of his skin as his companions continued past, then said with a wicked chuckle, "That tickled."

The man Tomas had just shot also started struggling back to his knees. Sarah retreated and expected the men to join her racing for the exit.

They did not.

Gregorios called out in a surprisingly calm voice. "Enhanced."

"Not enforcers," Tomas snapped.

Things started happening almost too fast for Sarah to follow.

Gregorios emptied the magazines of his Final Transfer pistol into the closest of the advancing attackers while at the same time repeatedly shooting the second with his forty-five. The sharp cracking of the pistol sounded soft and distant through the ear plugs she wore, and Sarah was grateful for them.

She'd heard pistols fired up close at the shooting range, and they were so loud they hurt even in open spaces. She wished she had vision filters to block the image of the man staggering under the onslaught, blood spraying with every impact.

Both men slowed, then collapsed almost close enough to touch Gregorios feet.

His guns clicked empty just as he turned them on the third attacker. The giant lunged and punched Gregorios so fast his hand seemed to blur in the air. The fist slammed Gregorios in the chest and sent him flying past Sarah to crash into the wall.

The attacker raced past Sarah even as she raised her bear spray and fumbled with the safety. Just as Gregorios rose shakily to his feet, the man swept up a heavy, overstuffed chair and threw it.

Gregorios managed to get one arm up before the chair smashed him back into the wall so hard he cracked the wood paneling.

The big brute lifted him out of the wreckage, and Sarah was horrified to see the bone of one of Gregorios' arms protruding from his broken flesh. Instead of screaming in pain, Gregorios calmly kicked the attacker between the legs.

Even that brute couldn't ignore a kick like that.

Gregorios slipped out of the huge man's grasp as the giant staggered, clutching at his groin.

Sarah shoved the bear spray into her pocket, swept up a broken chair leg, and clubbed the brute in the back of the head. It thumped off his skull, but didn't seem to bother him.

He started to turn in her direction, but Gregorios punched him in the throat. That finally dropped him to the ground where he writhed and gagged for breath

A shouted curse drew Sarah back around to where Tomas had been firing both guns at one of his attackers. The man had collapsed into an unmoving heap. The last man had paused and Sarah was shocked to see him cutting into his leg with a slender knife, slicing right through his pants.

Tomas dropped the spent magazines and slammed home fresh ones just as the bleeding marks on the man's leg began to glow with blue-white light. The man leaped forward and blurred across the room in a super-fast rush.

Somehow Tomas anticipated the move and threw himself to the floor. The fast-running attacker couldn't stop in time, tripped over Tomas, and tumbled past Sarah all the way to the far wall.

Tomas chased him down and when he rose, Tomas beat him over the head with an ornate chair.

Then the first man Tomas had shot rushed past Sarah and tackled Tomas so hard he drove him right through the wall and into the library. Books thundered down off the disrupted bookshelf, and drywall dust billowed into the room.

The sight of Tomas fallen, blood on his face, shocked Sarah out of her frozen fear. With a scream of mingled terror and anger, she jumped onto the back of the attacker. Her weight knocked him forward, but he didn't fall. Instead he spun and heaved on one of her arms. She lost her grip on his shoulders and tumbled back across the room toward the piano.

She came to a painful stop close to Tereza, the soft carpet saving her from broken bones. Tereza put down one of the tiny sandwiches and mocked her with a clap. "Valiant effort. Stupid, but valiant."

The woman pulled out her phone and started snapping photos as the men fought and shouted and cursed in close hand-to-hand combat. The man who had thrown Sarah across the room went after Tomas, but something hissed loudly from the library, sounding like compressed air, and the man staggered back, clawing at his eyes and bellowing in pain.

Gregorios, who had just knocked the last of his assailants to the ground, slammed a fresh magazine into his Final Transfer and fired all fifteen shots into the screaming brute's back.

Gregorios looked battered, with blood running down one cheek and soaking his broken arm, but none of that slowed him as he turned toward Tereza. He focused on her with a look of such anger that Sarah cringed away.

Tereza snapped another photo. "Best show in the house."

While Gregorios advanced, he grasped his broken arm with his good hand and, with a smooth, steady pull, set the arm. The sight of the jagged bone slipping back into his flesh nearly made Sarah sick. Gregorios didn't even flinch.

Several of the fallen attackers began to stir, despite the beating they'd just taken. Tomas rushed from one to the next, clubbing them in the back of the head with his pistol. He also pulled up the backs of their shirts. Most of the men had dully glowing red symbols tattooed onto their skin.

He calmly shot each of them with his Final Transfer dart pistol repeatedly. With each double strike, the glow from the tattoos faded. He stopped firing when the marks changed to black.

Instead of tattoos, the giant and the man who had knocked Tomas through the wall both wore slender black packs strapped to the small of their backs. Tomas ripped the packs off and tossed them away. The giant's grotesquely bulging muscles deflated to half their size, and the other man slumped unconscious to the floor.

"We've got a couple of Occans and a bunch of Charlies," Tomas said.

"That's very interesting," Gregorios said as he approached Tereza. "And you still claim to be working with council sanction?"

Sarah looked from one to the other, confused by the strange actions and the cryptic conversation.

Tereza, looking less sure of herself, lifted her camera. "One more shot."

"Oh, shut up." Sarah sprayed her in the face with the bear spray. It emitted an orange cloud that enveloped her head and seemed to cling to her. Sarah caught a whiff of the acrid scent, and scuttled farther back, coughing.

Tereza shrieked and tumbled from the chair, rubbing at her eyes and coughing violently.

Tomas kicked her back to the ground as she tried to rise.

Gregorios ignored the screaming Tereza, stepped past Sarah, and knocked over the large black roller bag she'd noticed when they first entered. He shoved it under the piano, then extended a hand to Sarah. "Are you all right?"

Tereza shouted from the ground where she still clutched at her face, "I'm not through with you yet!"

She raised her phone again and pushed the button. A thunderous boom shook the room and the piano rocked off the floor with a discordant jangle. A cloud of dust billowed up into the room from under the piano, smelling of gunpowder and wood polish.

Sarah cried out in fear and stumbled away from the new disaster.

Tomas emerged through the thick haze and took her hand. She wrapped her arms around him and asked through a coughing fit, "What was that?"

"Military-issue weighted net, propelled with an explosive charge," Gregorios said. "In that roller bag I pushed under the piano."

"How could you possibly know that?" Sarah asked.

He shrugged. "The placement was suspicious and I've seen them used before."

Tereza shouted something that sounded like a curse, but in a language Sarah didn't know. The woman's face was red, her eyes nearly swollen shut in reaction to the bear spray, but she seemed to be already recovering. That dosage would have disabled most people for an hour.

Gregorios grabbed Tereza by the chin. "Enough games. Where's my wife?"

"I'm not privy to that information. Now unless you want me to file formal charges with the council—"

He punched her in the nose.

Gregorios leaned close and growled in a low, dangerous voice, "To every level of hell with the council! Answer me or we'll see how you like living in a box for the next century."

That cowered her, but the outer door to the penthouse crashed open and the sound of many running feet echoed through the trashed room.

"You're out of time, old man," Tereza said with renewed confidence.

He punched her again, hard, on the side of the head. She fell unmoving to the floor.

Then he turned to face the approaching enemy.

"I'm starting to get annoyed."

CHAPTER TEN

There are only two ways to live each life. One is as though nothing is a miracle. The other is as though everything is a miracle.

~Albert Einstein

A s booted feet clomped against Italian tile in the kitchen, Sarah reluctantly released Tomas so he could face the new threat. She wanted to scream that they should instead be running. Tomas had said they expected to face resistance, but this was insane.

"Flash-bangs," Gregorios said as he and Tomas stepped forward beside a long couch in the center of the room.

The two men pulled grenades out of their pockets and Tomas glanced back at Sarah. "Best to close your eyes but keep your mouth open a little."

They threw the grenades as Sarah dropped to one knee behind the couch and followed Tomas' directions.

Just as harsh voices began shouting in the doorway, several powerful concussions thundered through the room with enough force to shatter windows. She couldn't help but flail around for Tomas. All she felt was dust and empty carpet. When she opened her eyes, she could barely see across the room to where heavy smoke billowed around a bunch of shadowy forms.

Those forms stumbled into the room, sharpening into dark-clothed men in tactical vests, carrying shotguns.

Tomas was waiting for them.

He had already crossed the room and stood pressed to the wall on the right side of the entrance. He exploded into their midst, dropping one man with a well-placed kick, and snatching the man's shotgun out of his hands. He clobbered the second black-clad commando with the butt of the weapon and dropped to the ground under the barrels of two of the other men as they fired. The shots shredded furniture, knocked holes in the opposite wall, and caught one of their companions in the shoulder, spinning him off his feet.

Gregorios grabbed Sarah's arm and pulled her to one side to the cover of one of the couches. As they moved, he fired his H&K pistol into the dark shapes in the doorway. The booming concussions sounded distant, but still filled her with terror.

Tomas pumped round after round into the men clustered around him. Despite their flak vests, at that close range, shots knocked them off their feet and into their comrades, spraying blood. Under the concentrated barrage, all seven attackers fell in seconds.

Sarah watched in horror, hands pressed over her ears, and eyes watering from the smoke. She didn't want to see anyone hurt, but what else could Tomas do? Who filled penthouse suites with squads of armed men?

Who was Tomas? He looked like a rather plain man, but he fought like a special-forces commando.

Before the echoes of the gunfire faded, Gregorios propelled Sarah toward the door. "Go!"

"What about Tereza?" Sarah asked as he pushed her along. She caught a glimpse of the unconscious woman lying near the shattered piano. An overstuffed chair, with the stuffing blasted out from a stray shotgun round, lay across her torso.

"She's not the one responsible for all this," Gregorios said.

"We need to go," Tomas shouted from the doorway.

Sarah rushed over and wrapped her arms around him, hardly believing he had survived that insane fight. His eyes blazed from his grime-covered face, and he grinned at her.

"Amateurs." He spoke the word with a distinct British accent.

"Go," Gregorios repeated as he slapped a fresh magazine into his Final Transfer pistol and checked his forty-five.

They ran from the shattered suite to the elevator and Tomas said, "I'm glad that second group wasn't enhanced."

"That would've been more surprising than finding a council-sanctioned facetaker running a heka cell," Gregorios said as he pulled a long roll of bandage out of a jacket pocket.

The elevator door opened, revealing an empty car. Tomas left Sarah to help Gregorios tie the bandage in place on his bloody, broken arm while he stepped inside, pushed a button, then returned to the hallway. As the elevator closed and began its descent, the three of them took the stairs down three flights. They then took a different elevator down to the ninth floor where they collected their roller bags and found another empty suite. They changed out of their battle gear and washed off the worst of the smoke and grime. Ten minutes later, they were back in the elevator, looking more or less presentable.

Sarah realized something. "Why aren't the alarms going off?"

"The penthouse is pretty isolated," Tomas said.

"But the smoke?"

"They would've disabled the detectors before we arrived," Gregorios said.

"Someone would've noticed windows exploding."

"Undoubtedly," Gregorios agreed. "All the more reason to leave immediately."

"But who were those guys?" This was real life, not the set of a huge-budget action movie. People didn't hold pitched battles in expensive hotels, and no one got back up after getting beaten hard enough to put normal people in the hospital for weeks.

Gregorios said, "The identities of those men don't matter. Only their handler is important, and anyone who can field a team like that deserves to be approached with caution."

They arrived at the third floor and skirted a wedding reception party. They left the hotel via a side stairway that led out a back door.

"That doesn't tell me anything," Sarah said.

"Right now we have to focus on getting out of here," Gregorios replied. He led the way at a brisk walk, outwardly calm, but constantly scanning in all directions.

"You want me to drive Eirene's car?" Tomas asked.

"No. Skip the garage. You know better than to leave the same way you arrived."

"What then?"

Gregorios led the way across the street and into Harrah's Casino. The busy casino consumed the enormous main level, but they wove through the crowd without slowing. The smoky haze that filled the gambling hall reminded Sarah of the smoke-filled suite, triggering a shudder from the memory of the recent fight. She suppressed it as they exited the building on the far side.

Traffic was heavy, with street cars and vehicles packing the area and the sidewalks crowded with people.

"What's the occasion?" Sarah asked as she followed Tomas through the crowds.

"It's always crazy down here near the river."

Across another busy street, they faced the abandoned New Orleans World Trade Center. It looked like it used to be quite a place, but Tomas explained that it hadn't been reopened since Katrina. They passed near it, entered the Riverwalk, and crossed Spanish Plaza.

Tomas pointed out the huge fountain, surrounded by benches, outdoor seating, and mosaics and information about the Spanish occupation of New Orleans. The crowds were heavy and a band was just finishing a catchy tune. Everywhere Sarah looked, people were enjoying themselves, oblivious to the dangers passing through their midst. Plunging into this energized area so recently after the deadly fight in the hotel left Sarah feeling strange, as if she were in some kind of sur-real nightmare.

"Wish we had more time," Tomas said, a little smile on his face as he studied the area. "This is a nice place to visit."

"Next time," Sarah said. She just wanted to find a quiet place to regain her composure.

They slipped onto a ferry at the riverbank just as it prepared to depart.

"That was good timing," Sarah said.

"Why do you think we made Tereza wait so long?"

"You planned to use the ferry?"

Gregorios shrugged. "Always have a back-up plan or three if you want this life to last a while longer."

They moved to the wide windows of the main deck. With the crowds packed around the ferry, Sarah had expected it to be full, but it was half empty. They had plenty of room to find a quiet, open space.

Tomas nodded out the window. "They recovered quickly."

He pointed out two men from the penthouse running across the square toward the ferry. They missed it by twenty seconds.

Sarah sagged against him and let tension ease from her muscles. She gave him a weak smile. "We got away."

"They'll try to cut us off on the other side."

"Don't worry about it," Gregorios said. "I've timed it to Algiers Point. We'll disembark at least sixty seconds before they can reach the terminal at best speed."

The Mississippi was wide and seemed to be running fast. During the short ferry ride, Sarah worked to calm her racing heart. After washing again in one of the bathrooms, she sank into a soft seat and leaned back, just breathing. She felt a little faint, but didn't feel sick like she had after learning the truth about Alterego. The brutality of the fight still shook her. She could scarce believe they had survived.

As the ferry reached the center of the river, she felt the current vibrating against the hull. It really was moving fast. She forced herself to her feet to join Tomas near a window where he scanned the river. "How did you learn to fight like that?"

"Lots of training."

The problem was, he didn't look like a trained warrior. Maybe a trained accountant.

"Well, you're going to have to teach me some."

"That's a very good idea."

He slipped an arm around her waist and pointed out the window. "I've always loved New Orleans from the river."

"It's a fabulous view." She leaned against him, happy that he seemed more comfortable sharing a little more intimacy. Did beating down a bunch of armed men make him feel romantic?

"And magic doesn't work over open water very well."

Sarah perked up at that. "What do you mean magic?"

"Why do you think Tereza picked this city to host that transfer? New Orleans has long been a stronghold of the *heka*."

Again with the weird word. "You're talking about those men. You called them enhanced. What are they?"

"Dangerous. Around here, if they're locals, they're part of the broader voodoo culture."

"Really?" First gunmen trying to kill them on the highway, then the gun battle in the penthouse, and now voodoo? Sarah wanted to crawl into a dark hole and hide. She'd known the world of the facetakers was dangerous, and was starting to second-guess her decision to pursue her goals and learn more about them anyway. "Is that why the city feels so strange?"

"It's part of it. Most voodoo's a bunch of fake tourist-trap nonsense, but there are a few with real powers. Those, the ones with real *rounon*, are heka, even if they don't know it."

"Isn't ronin what they call rogue samurai?"

"Rounon, not ronin." He exaggerated the pronunciation. "It's an old word, Greek, referring to their rune powers."

"How could they not know they have special powers?"

"The ones we fought today did, but not everyone discovers the truth. Many untrained heka get confused by legend and myth."

"Is that why those men were so hard to knock down?"

"It's related." He paused and considered her for a moment, holding her gaze with his. "You know, I hadn't really intended to get you involved in this."

"But I am."

"You don't know what you're getting into. Once you know, your world will never be the same."

"My world's already not the same. Without you and Eirene, I'd have been lost." She thought back to the struggle to escape Alterego, with Mr. Fleischer maneuvering her to agree sell her body. If Tomas hadn't helped her escape and win herself back, she'd be . . . well, maybe nothing.

"If you stay with me and learn the truth, you may never be found again."

Sarah leaned against him, considering his words. She was afraid, should probably take the next plane as far from Tomas and Gregorios as possible, but found that she couldn't. She needed to know what she was facing. Only then could she decide how to act.

So she drew Tomas away from the window to some seats apart from other passengers. "Tomas, I get it, and I appreciate your concern, but I want to help find Eirene, and I need to know who these people are trying to kill me. Talk."

Tomas smiled, taking her hands in his. "I've always loved your spirit, Sarah."

"Don't get mushy. Those men weren't normal. Why not?"

"Because they're heka."

"I still don't know what that means. Are you saying they're some kind of voodoo priests?"

"No. Voodoo is a misnomer. Heka is a blanket term we use for anyone with a rounon gift, or those who serve them."

"Explain rounon."

"You saw the man cutting into his leg?"

Sarah shuddered. That had been freaky. "Yes."

"He and the big guy had rounon gifts. He was marking a rune, a special symbol, into his leg. That's why he was able to suddenly move so fast."

"And the other guy's huge muscles?"

"Another rune."

"Why did he deflate like that?" It had looked like someone had poked a hole in an inflatable toy.

"I removed his soul pack."

"That fanny pack thing?"

"Exactly. It contained a dispossessed soulmask."

"Why would they do that?" Tomas's weird actions were making a little more sense.

"Because heka rounon powers are linked to human souls. Human souls have real power, lots of power, and heka can tap into the power of souls to fuel their runes. The evil ones usually prefer to drain the force from other people's souls."

Sarah recoiled at the idea. She'd experienced hundreds of body transfers, although she'd only understood what was going on the last couple of times. The moment when her soulmask was lifted free of her body was surreal and scary. The loss of most sensory input, the complete helplessness. It was horrific to think of someone kidnapping her at that moment, using her in some arcane ritual.

"So they're like cannibals?" she asked.

Tomas nodded. "That's a good way to look at it. Most of the time, heka can't gain access to dispossessed souls and have to resort to draining strength from the fully incorporated living. It's harder to do, and they can't draw as much. The human body naturally provides excellent shielding. That's where a lot of magic rituals come from, attempts to hide the runes. But when they can get their hands on the dispossessed, that's when they become most dangerous."

"Tereza gave them souls," Sarah guessed.

"Most likely. No facetaker in good standing would do that, though."

"What does that mean?"

Tomas grimaced. "The situation's more complicated than we thought. We'll discuss her involvement later. The important thing is that they had soulmasks. With dispossessed souls, heka with an active rounon gift can apply various runes to draw upon the force of those souls and enhance themselves."

"What happens when the soul runs out of power?" Sarah whispered.

Tomas shrugged. "Depending on the magnitude of the rounon gift, they might drain the soul entirely until it cracks and dies. Weaker rounon can drain the dispossessed to the point they never recover, even if they were restored to a host. Those people linger with broken minds, lacking the spirit to recover."

"That's terrible."

"Agreed. The runes grant the heka a lot of power though. Those two in the hotel had the weakest form of active rounon. They needed physical contact with the dispossessed soul to power their runes."

"That's why the packs," Sarah said, understanding.

"Exactly. When I removed the packs, they lost connection and their runes fizzled. We call those heka Occultists, or Occans."

That explained part of his cryptic statement in the hotel. "You also mentioned Charlies."

"Charlatans. The other fighters had been enhanced, but lacked active rounon gifts. Those runes you saw on their backs were marked and activated by the occans. Some time earlier today, they drew power from a dispossessed soul through those runes. It's a way for non-gifted people to fuel an enhancement for a short period."

"So they use other people like rechargeable batteries?" That was gross.

"Something like that. The runes they wore were basic symbols increasing strength and providing rapid healing. That's why they could absorb so much damage. The soul force they'd absorbed earlier was spent healing them."

"That's why you kept shooting them," Sarah said, feeling a little sick.

"Exactly. When the runes are first activated, they glow bright red. As the soul force is exhausted, the glow fades to black."

"So heka are voodoo priests," Sarah repeated, trying to get it straight in her mind. "They can be occultists or charlatans."

"Not just voodoo. You'll find heka in every culture. Voodoo is just what they call it here. In other places they're labeled devil worshipers, witches, wizards, shamans, or any number of names related to the occult arts. When they tap the power of human souls, which is by far the greatest source of supernatural power in the world, they're all heka."

"But you'd think people would notice dispossessed souls," Sarah protested.

"Not necessarily. They're easy to conceal, and some heka have stronger powers. They can mark their runes on the souls they plan to drain, activate twin runes on themselves, and fuel them remotely."

"Like wireless power sources?"

"More or less. It's a higher level power, with pros and cons we can discuss more later. We call those heka Channelers."

"And they're the worst?"

"They're more than bad enough most days. There are others, but they're far more rare. I think we've covered enough. It's a lot to take in."

That was the understatement of her life. She had come to New Orleans hoping to enjoy some time with him, talk Eirene into helping her, and begin the process of returning to a normal life.

Normal had left them behind in Oz.

She leaned her head on his shoulder, drawing strength from the solid feeling of his presence.

He sighed. "I suppose we'll miss that jazz band tonight after all."

Sarah managed a weak laugh and snuggled a bit closer. "We'll think of something."

CHAPTER ELEVEN

Educate and inform the whole mass of the people. . . . They are the only sure reliance for the preservation of our liberty against facetaker manipulations or heka abominations. Greater powers may be terrifying, but only through knowledge may they be overcome.

~Thomas Jefferson

G regorios led the others off the ferry, scanning for threats. He saw none. The heka hadn't managed to call any other support units. He'd suspected they wouldn't, but appreciated getting something right today.

They escaped the ferry terminal without issue, caught a cab to a car rental agency, and headed west out of the city with Tomas at the wheel of a rented SUV. Sarah sat in the passenger seat and Gregorios reclined in the back, a fresh bandage on his broken arm.

Although he had blocked sensory input from the damaged limb, the flesh had suffered significant trauma. It hampered his ability to function. The temporary body had served well over the past few weeks, but he would need a change. With the threat of heka operatives, he needed optimal performance. If only they had time to detour and claim his favorite battle suit.

Tomas's girlfriend slumped in the front seat, looking exhausted. She had performed well for an untrained civilian. Eirene had told him a little about her. The girl showed promise, but she had jumped into dangerous waters. He'd drop her off at the next exit if he thought it would improve her chances of escaping the brewing conflict, but she was already a target. He needed to understand how she fit into the picture.

So many questions. So few answers.

Above all else, he needed to track Eirene down. She had survived her long dispossession remarkably well, but he shuddered to think of the trauma she'd suffer if returned to another lead-lined box. Tereza's involvement with the heka had caught him by surprise. The fledgling facetaker was but a pawn, but of who? She claimed good standing with the council, but also consorted with heka. Such a conflict of interest should not be possible.

Was she still working for Mai Luan? More important, what did the council know? Questions multiplied in his mind as the miles slipped by and Tomas took a complex, zig-zag route toward their destination. It increased the distance many times, but gave him ample opportunity to scan for pursuit.

Eventually Tomas glanced in the rear-view mirror and made eye contact. "If Tereza really is on council-sanctioned business, they'll track your credit cards."

"All the traceable ones. The one I used for the car is new, something Eirene worked up just the other day."

"What is this council you keep talking about?" Sarah asked.

Gregorios hesitated. The more he revealed, the less chance she could ever walk away.

Tomas glanced in the mirror again. "She should know."

"The situation is complicated enough. Do you really want her drawn in that deep?"

"I'll make that choice," Sarah said with brave stupidity. "I owe Eirene, and Tomas owes me a vacation."

Gregorios sighed. "Don't say I didn't warn you. Tomas has told you a little about facetakers?"

"I've seen face transfers, the real ones without the machines," Sarah said. "I saw Mai Luan and Tereza pull people's faces off. Tomas told me they're facetakers, people who can transfer souls to different bodies by swapping out the soulmasks. I've experienced it firsthand."

"That's a good start."

"Eirene is a facetaker too," Sarah added, as if wanting him to argue the point.

"As am I."

Sarah turned to Tomas. "You're not, though."

"No. We work together." Tomas glanced over at her long enough for Gregorios to worry about the vehicle starting to drift.

"What kind of work do you do?" she asked.

Good question, Gregorios thought. The girl was sharp.

"Specialized security."

"So, you're a mercenary or something?"

"Not exactly."

They drove in silence for a while as Tomas completed his circuitous route and took the Crescent City connection bridge eastbound. He eventually pulled off the highway near the airport.

"So tell me about facetakers," Sarah prompted finally.

Gregorios explained, "There are other facetakers in the world. Most of us have come together into a loose organization."

"Ruled by this council?"

"Essentially. They're known as the Suntara Group."

"Why?"

"It's a long story."

"Everything's a long story with you guys."

She had no idea.

"This Suntara Group doesn't like you right now, do they?" Sarah asked.

"Correct." Another good question. Gregorios approved her perceptive mind.

Tomas added, "Worse, they're apparently working with heka for the first time."

That worried Gregorios the most. The evidence pointed in that direction, but he couldn't imagine what might have driven the council to make such a crazy change in policy. Destruction of all heka was a millennia-old rule for a reason.

Occasionally heka could prove useful, but each time one was turned, the decision to try was a calculated risk. The choice to power enhancements through the destruction of other souls was a cancer in the hearts of the heka, corrupting them and turning the vast majority of them into enemies of society. They posed a threat to the world order, an order the facetakers had spent centuries shepherding into existence.

Exterminating heka with active rounon was a necessary part of maintaining a stable world. Gregorios had led the team responsible for removing such threats for a long time. He'd been labeled a rogue decades earlier, though. As an outsider, he knew too little of the current inner workings of the council to understand why they would take the extreme risk to involve heka in their operations.

"And wasn't Mai Luan a coo-something?" Sarah asked.

"Cui Dashi," Gregorios said with a grimace. "She's involved somehow, but the council would never involve itself with such a monster."

"So tell them the truth about Tereza's connection," she suggested.

"It's not that easy."

"But they have Eirene."

"Perhaps," Gregorios said as Tomas pulled up to a weed-choked lot not far from the airport.

It looked like it had stood abandoned for a while, its appearance decrepit even in comparison to other nearby industrial buildings. The lot was surrounded by a chain-link fence topped with razor wire, which did still look in good condition. A small parking lot held only a single pick-up facing the simple two-story building. It looked like a worn, metal box, a hundred feet on each side, with rust-sprinkled shutters concealing all the doors and windows.

Everything looked exactly as it should.

Tomas jumped out to unlock the gate, so Sarah slid to the driver's seat and pulled the rental into the parking lot close to the side door. When Tomas led them inside and flipped on the lights, Sarah paused and stared in surprise at the comfortable living room that greeted them. Twenty-foot ceilings with soft lighting illuminated the room. The walls were painted in warm colors. Thick carpet covered the floor. Comfortable couches and chairs faced either a cold fireplace or one of the two flat-panel television sets. The air smelled fresh, so the exchangers were still working.

A chef-worthy kitchen opened off the living room, with granite counter tops and stainless steel appliances. The cupboards were stocked with enough food to last the three of them for months.

Sarah trailed him into the room. "What is this place?"

"Safe house," Tomas said. "There are dozens scattered around the world." He turned to Gregorios. "Won't the council look for us here?"

"Unlikely. Eirene used to work logistics, and she confirmed this one hadn't been used for decades before we moved in a few weeks back. We haven't seen any sign that anyone's aware we're here."

This place had been the closest thing to a home for them in far too long. He'd find her and they would start another life together. By all the forgotten gods, anyone blocking him would face his wrath. He rarely let himself get angry, but he could feel his rage stirring. This time, he didn't feel like snuffing it out.

"She's a good housekeeper," Sarah said.

"A hired service checks in periodically and keeps it stocked and cleaned. The money's handled automatically and many of these safe houses get forgotten for a while. We make sure we're not around when they're scheduled to clean. They've never seen us, and I doubt any other facetaker beside Eirene remembers this one even exists."

Tomas showed Sarah around and she chose one of the available suites upstairs.

"Plenty of hot water?" Sarah asked, moving toward the bathroom.

Gregorios said, "Yes, but that can wait. I have to do something, and you'll want to see it."

"What's going on?" Sarah asked as he led them down to the medical bay in the basement. The cool air smelled stale, the soft hum of machinery the only sound. Every surface was stainless steel or white cloth.

"You want to be a part of this, so you can help Tomas prep for my transfer."

He ignored the treatment and operating rooms and headed for the long cooler, similar to ones used by morgues. He selected the third door and slid it all the way open to reveal the hibernating body, his current home suit. The body looked healthy and ready to go. In its mid-thirties, it was toned and fit, stood exactly six feet, with several tattooed enhancement runes in strategic locations. The hair was black, Eirene's current favorite choice. It wore only boxer shorts.

Tomas and Sarah transferred the body to a gurney while Gregorios lay down on the empty bed of the cooler tray. He shivered at the touch of the cold metal, which reminded him of his own long dispossession so many centuries ago. Tomas moved to stand by his head and signaled he was ready. It was so much easier with competent help.

Gregorios embraced his nevra core, his soul center. When transferring the souls of others, or when forced to transfer himself without help, he worked through his hands. With a trusted assistant, all he had to do was sever all ties with the host body and set his soul free. He directed his nevron against the soul points that anchored his soulmask to the host body.

Located along the jawline, under the nose, and behind both eyes, they were intangible to anyone not possessing a nevra core. That core was the center of his soul, the well from which sprang his soul force. The fuel cell, so to speak. The nevron was the energy pouring out of that core, the power of his soul that he manipulated now to perform the soul operation.

His senses contracted, draining away until he felt nothing but his face. "Do it."

Tomas grasped him just under the jaw, and Gregorios focused his nevron again, severing the final connection to his host. Purple flames rippled along the edges of his face as Tomas lifted.

Gregorios's soulmask pulled away from the skull with the wet sucking sound he had grown to hate. Flesh slipped free as his soulmask disengaged from the underlying skeletal structure. As it emerged, Tomas lifted him higher. His vision altered until everything looked black and white and strangely angular. His sense of smell vanished, and his hearing expanded tenfold.

With experienced precision, Tomas carried Gregorios over to the body waiting on the gurney. To Tomas, his soulmask would look like a shimmering face mask trailing rainbow smoke. Tomas positioned it and pressed it onto the new host.

Sarah stood nearby, one hand raised to her mouth, eyes

wide. She'd experienced more soul transfers than any mortal, but she'd been drugged prior to most of the sham operations. She'd seen a couple honest soul transfers, but she needed to be here, to witness it again. This was the world she was entering, and mortals usually found it unsettling in the best of times. She couldn't afford hesitation if she was called upon to help in the future.

Gregorios connected with the body and his soulmask plunged through the skin. His nevron sealed the connection and restored the soul points, linking each sense to the host. Since no soul had inhabited the host, it welcomed him without resistance.

Flesh flowed up over his soulmask as it bonded with the bone structure of the host skull and began to subtly alter it to fit his facial profile. His senses expanded as he fused with the new host, and every molecule of the new body clamored for attention. Despite the countless times he had transferred, he shook under the flood of sensation and his body rattled on the gurney.

Tomas leaned over him, holding him down until the tremors subsided. Sarah joined him, bracing Gregorios's legs. The longer the dispossession, the more traumatic the experience. Since he had only been dispossessed for seconds, and had worn this particular body for years, reconnecting came swiftly.

After seven seconds he drew in a steady breath. "Stable."

Tomas helped him up and he donned a set of clothes from a nearby shelf. "It's good to be home."

"So this is your real body?" Sarah asked, glancing from him to the suit he'd left on the cooler tray.

"It is the primary host for this life." Gregorios gestured at the one he'd just abandoned. "I took that one from a man who had helped steal the body of a young woman for another to use."

"Oh." Sarah looked satisfied.

One of the functions the council oversaw was managing host bodies and transfer vehicles. The world could be an ugly place, and there was always a demand for healthy young bodies, but they avoided targeting unwilling mortals as much as possible. Occasional rogue facetakers wreaked havoc by aggressively taking souls and were put down before the public became aware of the existence of their kind. Facetakers possessed great power, but mobs of angry mortals had destroyed more than one careless facetaker through the ages.

"I think it's dinner time," Gregorios said.

"After I shower," Sarah said, heading for the door, looking eager to escape the room.

Tomas helped clean up. The group who serviced the safe house would see to healing the broken arm of the empty host. It'd be ready for him in a couple of months if he needed it again. Empty host bodies fell into a hibernation-like stasis, alive but able to linger for many months with little to no care if properly stored. That state slowed healing, but allowed them to maintain a ready stable of specialized suits.

"I can't wait to get back to Rome," Tomas said as they headed for the stairs.

"Have you told her?"

"Not yet."

"She needs to know."

"I'm planning on it," Tomas said a little defensively. "Alter-ego left scars. I'm trying to do it gently."

"Don't wait too long. It'll only make it worse." Sarah was proving to be interesting for a mortal, but Tomas was not doing himself any favors by keeping secrets.

They returned to the kitchen and Gregorios cooked a full meal of steak and au gratin potatoes. He left the hood fan on low until the room filled with the mouth-watering aroma of grilled beef.

He closed his eyes and breathed deep. This was Eirene's favorite meal. He'd cooked it for her countless times, using every imaginable form of fire. He could imagine her sitting at the table, calling to him not to burn the steaks, even though it'd been lives since he'd last made that mistake.

The room seemed far emptier when he opened his eyes.

Tomas returned from his room, dressed in jeans and a loose t-shirt. Sarah joined them just as Tomas finished setting the table. She had changed into a comfortable pair of shorts and a soft, cotton blouse that looked fantastic. Of course, just about anything she wore would look good. Tomas gave her a little kiss on the cheek and Gregorios noted her expression. She didn't look satisfied with that reserved show of affection.

Tomas definitely needed to tell her soon.

She closed her eyes and drew in a long, slow breath, savoring the scent. "That smells amazing."

Gregorios appreciated people appreciating his cooking. "It's sort of a specialty. You look lovely, my dear. Now that we've all changed, let's eat."

After eating quietly for a few minutes Sarah asked, "What now?"

"Now I talk with an old enemy."

CHAPTER TWELVE

The army enhanced with my runes is the true nobility of our country.
~Napoleon Bonaparte

After dinner, Gregorios fetched a soul coffin out of a closet where he had left it two days before. He hated the little prisons, but they served a necessary purpose. So he forced down the memories of dark imprisonment they always triggered, even though his had been a different form of incarceration.

"Let's see if we know the right questions now," he said as he placed it on a table in the living room.

"Wait, who's in there?" Sarah asked.

"A facetaker I captured on a remote island," Gregorios said. "Involved in a clandestine soul gathering operation. She and one of her assistants got in my way. That's where I got that temporary host. I believe her activities are somehow tied to Mai Luan."

He flipped the coffin open to reveal two soulmasks. They had been dispossessed only a few weeks, so were almost full size. They had faded from shimmering translucence to gray, but the rainbow mist hadn't withdrawn. It still floated with only slightly muted colors. Over time, dispossessed souls would shrink, eventually to the size of china dolls, their misty tendrils drawn inside as the soul faded into a hibernation-like state. People were not intended to live dispossessed, and most minds broke down quickly in the forced solitude of soul coffins.

Sarah grimaced and rubbed her arms. Gregorios knew she had seen coffins like this before. It was a good sign that she already disliked them.

Gregorios set aside the soulmask of the man he knew only as Curly, whose damaged body he had just left in the medical bay. The soulmask felt cool and unresponsive. As Sarah and Tomas leaned closer, he set his internal defenses, then carefully extracted the second soulmask. The rainbow mist of her soul latched onto his arm and her nevron slammed against his, but rebounded against his already activated core.

Dalal was a dangerous adversary, but in her dispossessed state she could not hope to overpower him. After the initial assault, her will subsided and she hung docile in his hand.

"Who is that?" Sarah asked.

"A bad person," Tomas whispered, then motioned her to silence.

"Well Dalal, how are you feeling?" Gregorios asked.

"*You know better than anyone how I feel.*" Her shrunken lips twitched and her voice sounded no louder than a high-pitched whisper. Although lacking the physical form needed to produce speech, soulmasks held the power to project limited sound.

"Indeed. How long you get to enjoy that state is up to you."

"*What do you want?*"

"Information, of course. How much does the council know of your activities?"

"*Give me a body and I'll explain everything.*"

"You'll remain dispossessed until I believe you've shared in good faith."

"*Then you get nothing.*"

"So be it."

He moved her over the coffin and she quickly added, "*Know that my actions were sanctioned.*"

"Including your involvement with the heka?"

"*Why such an interest? I told you I didn't have Eirene.*"

"She turned up elsewhere."

"*Where is she? I haven't seen her in decades.*"

"That's what I'm trying to find out."

Soft, helium-high laughter rang from her soulmask as it expanded slightly. When she spoke her voice came stronger. "*You've lost her again so soon?*"

Gregorios forced down a flash of irritation. "Where would a council-sanctioned facetaker acquire a couple occans and a gang of charlies?"

"Surprised, no? That must tear at you like daggers. So much work to find her and now the council has taken her away again."

"So it was on council orders?"

Curly, who had lain quiet on the table, twitched and his face brightened a bit. His whisper-voice spoke for the first time. *"The council does not command everything."*

"Silence, you fool," Dalal said.

Gregorios banged her soulmask against the side of the coffin in warning and focused on Curly. "You assume to know the will of the council?"

Curly's laughter rippled into the air. *"Those old fools think they're in control. They see only shadows of truth."*

"Your lies are making matters worse," Dalal snapped.

"I'm tired of sharing that prison with you," Curly replied. *"I will speak on condition of freedom. They cannot stop us anyway."*

More and more interesting, Gregorios thought.

Sarah spoke up. "You said 'we' let them believe they're in control. You're not referring to Dalal, are you?"

"Dalal is but a tool of the master like the rest."

"Shut up," Dalal's voice was almost a shout and her will struck at Gregorios again in a futile gesture of anger. Something Curly was saying terrified her.

Sarah leaned a little closer. "You're heka, aren't you?"

"How can you know that? Who are you?"

Tomas looked just as surprised as Gregorios felt. Sarah was a new player, how did she figure it out before the rest of them? Curly's body had not worn power runes and Gregorios had dismissed the man as a simple servant.

Gregorios lifted Curly's soulmask to look into his half-sphere eyes. "Tell me what your group's done with my wife, or I swear you'll suffer like no embodied soul ever has." He directed a pulse of his nevron against the soulmask and purple fire danced along the outer edges of the floating rainbow mist. It jerked and coiled up closer to the soulmask. Even the dispossessed could feel pain.

"It wasn't us," Curly assured him quickly.

Sarah shook her head. "Now you're contradicting yourself. First you said the council doesn't know, that your group is secretly in control. Now you're saying you're not responsible after all."

"You cannot speak of this," Dalal shrieked. *"Gregorios, your threats are meaningless. Eirene was taken recently, no? After we were imprisoned here. We know nothing of current events. You must speak with the council."*

"I plan to," Gregorios replied. "And I'll discuss with them the full extent of your activities. They may decide to ask a few questions themselves."

With that threat hanging over them, he returned both soul-masks to the coffin and latched it shut.

Tomas hugged Sarah. "You were awesome."

"I don't like liars."

Tomas said, "I think you ended the interrogation early. We should pull everything out of them."

Gregorios shook his head. "We don't have time. I've heard enough. There's always heka plotting against the council or trying to unleash plague on the world. Our top priority is finding Eirene, and I got the clues I need." He forced calm over his growing fear for her. "I cannot allow them to lock her away again. You don't know what that does to a person."

He trailed off as shadows of remembered horror shook him, but those were not his worst fears. Heka could do far worse to Eirene than kill her.

"Then what will you do?" Sarah asked.

"Somehow the council's involved. That's where I need to find the answers."

"You can't go to them. You're still most wanted on the rogue list," Tomas said.

"I can go to one."

"Who?"

"The one they'll never expect me to approach." He took a deep breath, focusing on the need to find Eirene. That need settled his thought, firmed his resolve.

"We're going to Los Angeles."

CHAPTER THIRTEEN

No one can make you feel inferior without your consent, especially when you wear the rune I do.

~Eleanor Roosevelt

At the wheel of a rented sports car, Gregorios approached a gated estate in the hills above Los Angeles, with views of the distant ocean and Santa Monica beach. He passed the main entrance without slowing and turned at a secondary drive. A solid steel gate blocked the road, but he pulled up to the keypad and punched in a sixteen-digit universal facetaker code.

He held his breath as he pressed the pound key to submit the code. It had been valid just weeks prior, but the codes changed every two months. If a new code was in play, a warning would trigger inside the estate and he'd lose the element of surprise.

Tomas and Sarah waited back at the hotel. If this visit went poorly, he didn't want them caught in the crossfire. He trusted Tomas to continue the mission to find and free Eirene if he was taken or incapacitated.

After an eternal two seconds, a green light blinked on and the gate swung silently open. A fraction of his tension eased and he accelerated up the winding drive to the sprawling estate atop the hill. He passed several armed security guards who saluted but did not interfere. Unless they received orders to the contrary, they allowed every facetaker with the correct code unfettered access to the main grounds.

He parked in front of the huge white, Caribbean-style mansion that reared four stories high with wings that swept back in gentle arcs from the circular drive. He left the car with a valet and entered the building where an aged, tuxedoed butler stood waiting for him.

"How may I assist you, sir?" The man spoke with a British accent as stiff as his starched collar.

"Please take me to Meryem."

"Should I call ahead, sir?" Even though protocol dictated that Gregorios announce himself, he ignored the tradition.

"No. We're old friends and I want to surprise her."

"She does like surprises," the old man said and turned to lead the way into the complex.

Although the old butler was very subtle, Gregorios caught the shift of one arm between strides. Most likely, the old fellow was alerting security. Good. Gregorios hated unprofessional help.

The butler led him to a sprawling patio surrounding an Olympic-sized swimming pool. A wide portico shaded the area, with inset stained-glass skylights that cast rainbows of light across the water. Half-reclining in a plush poolside chaise and wearing a surprisingly modest swimsuit, sat Meryem, a voluptuous woman with thick, dark hair that spilled past her shoulders. A couple of shirtless assistants who could have posed for men's health magazines sat nearby taking notes on laptops.

The woman glanced over and gasped when she recognized Gregorios. She rose gracefully to her feet with a dazzling smile. Gregorios knew that face all too well and recognized her sensual movements although he'd never seen her wearing that form. It was unusual for Meryem to hold onto a body very long. He'd never known her to look over thirty. Although still alluring, her body was well into its forties.

"Gregorios!" She glided across the patio to embrace him.

"Hello, Meryem," he replied with genuine warmth as he allowed thousands of pleasant memories to bubble through the back of his mind. "It's very good to see you."

She retreated a step to scan him with an approving grin. "You're looking great. That's a new model, isn't it?" For a second, a look of terrible hunger flitted across her face before she concealed it.

He pretended not to notice. "You look beautiful."

She laughed, her rich voice caressing his ears, and took his arm to lead him back to her chair. She waved the assistants away and ordered the butler to fetch food and drink. Then she settled onto the chaise and slid a hand down her flanks. "Always the gentleman, Greg. I'm fat and old."

He settled into a seat beside her, not bothering to look around for the telltale signs of security forces watching him through the sights of their rifles. Her adopted form no longer pleased her, so why did she not make a change?

A pretty young serving girl arrived with a tray heaped with drinks and finger foods. Gregorios ignored it but Meryem selected a tropical drink and took an appreciative sip. "You're not one for rash moves, my old love. Why risk coming to see me now after so many years?"

"You know why I'm here. Tell me about Eirene."

She made a childish little pout and sipped again. "Here I thought you'd turned over a new life and come to start another affair."

"Not yet, I'm afraid."

"But you could," she said suggestively and leaned a little closer. Even wearing that form, she moved with the same seductive grace she always had.

He said gently, "We made some good memories, but Eirene's still my wife."

"For now," Meryem said without rancor. "Until you move on to a new life, just like you did when you left me all those lives ago."

He leaned forward and cupped her face with one hand. Fear flickered in her eyes and her fingers tightened around her glass, but she did not pull back, did not embrace her nevra core. So a little trust still lingered.

Gregorios let his fingers caress her warm cheek and his heart quickened with remembered passion.

She began to smile and leaned into his hand.

He wrapped his fingers around the edge of her jaw and tightened his grip. The fear returned to her eyes.

"Now's not the time for us," he said firmly. After tugging gently against her jawline, he released her. Meryem couldn't quite hide her relief.

"Now tell me where Eirene was taken and why she was targeted."

"There's much going on, Greg," Meryem said, leaning back out of reach and sipping again. "Projects half a century in the making are culminating. It's an exciting time." As she spoke, her eyes glowed with that same hunger.

"I don't care about that. I just want my wife."

"You'll care eventually. You recently risked another transfer. How are you feeling?"

"Impatient." He allowed a hint of anger into his voice.

Meryem saluted him with her drink. "You and your iron will." Then her smile faded. "Even you aren't immune. The day will come when you'll need us."

"Today I just need my wife. Don't make me ask again."

"I'm not a central player right now. Too much work with the consignment team."

"I'm not surprised. Some of the world leaders are getting old."

"Old and rich," she agreed with a smile. "Just the way we like it."

"I'm glad you're busy, but don't change the subject."

"Oh Greg, you've been out too long. You should see what we can do with face recognition software these days."

"Not interested."

The consignment team, which Meryem had led for centuries, was responsible for scheduling soul transfers for wealthy clients. They maintained a database of potential clients and suggested body donors. In days of old the preferred transactions were those where rich clients supplied their own transfer vehicle, usually a young relative. When they lacked a suitable host, the consignment team would find and abduct one.

In the last century, Meryem had started buying donors or, when that was not possible, paying out a large sum to the family of those taken. Disguised as life insurance payments, no one ever complained, even when they had known nothing about the policy.

The activities of the consignment team had created one of the rifts between Gregorios and Meryem during the short life they had shared together. In his opinion, many of their wealthy clients weren't deserving of new lives.

First-life abuses were usually compounded in later lives. Those who lived long enough and accrued enough wealth for multiple lives sometimes purchased one life too many, suffering mental breakdown as the repeated soul transfers led to soul fragmentation. The resulting broken minds or fractured spirits often led to atrocities that Gregorios's team had been assigned to deal with. Jack the Ripper was one example, as were several of the more notorious mass murderers.

Over time he'd become more and more dissatisfied with the system, but Meryem wouldn't agree with him that things should change. She was proud of her work. It was the way of the world and she would not be ashamed of it.

"Very well," Meryem said, drawing him back to the present. "Be stubborn. It was always one of your qualities I found most aggravating. And most alluring."

He waited.

She took a big bite out of a huge strawberry, caressing the fruit with her full lips before giving him a wide smile.

"If you want Eirene, you need to go to Rome."

Gregorios's heart sank. He'd been afraid of that.

He rose. "Thanks."

"You owe me," she said as she also stood. She slid one finger down his cheek and leaned closer. "I always collect."

He pulled away. "Good-bye, Meryem."

"Don't dawdle, Gregorios," she called after him as he strode for the exit. "I don't know the details, but I doubt Eirene will enjoy what they have planned for her. Lab rats rarely do."

CHAPTER FOURTEEN

Nothing in life is to be feared, it is only to be understood. Now is the time to understand more, so that we may fear less. And yet, I have failed to determine the underlying principle fueling Nobel's runes. I am one of those who think like Nobel, that humanity will draw more good than evil from new discoveries, but what to do with a power source that defies nature? I am left to conclude that perhaps the secrecy imposed by the government regarding these runes may be necessary until further study can be performed.

~Marie Curie

Rome.

They were really in Rome.

Sarah could scarce contain her excitement when they landed on a late evening flight. She had wanted to see Rome forever and, despite the gravity of their mission to track down Eirene, she was thrilled to see the city.

Not that she'd get to see much of it right away. While Tomas headed straight for the Suntara Group headquarters, Sarah was forced to join Gregorios in driving to a safe house in the city. Gregorios was a decent tour guide, but when he talked about the important landmarks lying so close by, but invisible in the darkness, she wanted to tell him to shut up. Better not to know how close she was while still unable to see anything.

She did get to see the Colosseum. Traffic passed surprisingly close to the ancient home of the gladiator games, and Sarah eagerly studied the ruin with its three levels of stone arches. Although only part of it remained, she could imagine it in all its ancient glory, and the sight took her breath away. She'd seen many photos, but seeing it in real life inspired he so much more. She leaned against the open window, simply soaking in the awesome sight.

Gregorios surprised her by making an obscene gesture out his window as they left the ancient wonder behind.

"What was that for?"

"Tradition." He gestured toward another monument they were just passing. "That's the Arch of Constantine."

The huge, freestanding triumphal arch would have looked imposing anywhere else but in the shadow of the Colosseum. Sarah wished they could get out and inspect its three giant arches and the statues standing atop columns flanking the openings.

One more sight Tomas needed to show her. A little while later, she caught a glimpse of St. Peter's Basilica in the distance and that just fueled her thirst to sight-see as soon as possible.

The safe house ended up being a typical Italian three-story home with salmon colored walls, wooden shutters over the windows, and a garden on the roof. It was clean and comfortable inside and since they had little baggage, it only took minutes to settle in.

After fixing some dinner, Gregorios turned on the television, looking bored. Sarah spent the next hour fretting until Tomas returned. She tried to keep herself distracted by exploring the safe house. It looked like a normal home with a few additions. The doors and windows were set into steel frames, and she didn't doubt they were a lot more solid than they looked. A stainless-steel door with a keypad lock blocked access to the basement and she decided not to ask what was kept down there.

Gregorios revealed that the council owned the safe house, although so close to the headquarters, it was rarely used. That didn't entirely make sense to her, and he hadn't sounded as confident about the location's security as he had about the place they had visited outside New Orleans. The most puzzling mystery was how Tomas could just walk into the headquarters building and search for Eirene without arousing suspicion.

"I'm in good standing. Don't worry," was all he had said.

She did worry. She couldn't help it. Tomas was her anchor in this frightening new world she'd plunged into. Without him, she'd feel completely lost and too frightened to push ahead. His calm strength had saved her once, and she relied on it until she understood better the dangers they faced.

At just past one in the morning, Tomas strode in the front door and declared, "She's here!"

Gregorios's mask of calm vanished and he rose as quickly as Sarah did.

"You're sure?" Gregorios pressed.

"I couldn't risk gaining access to see her in person, but I'm sure she's being held there."

"So the council was responsible after all."

"Maybe." Tomas dropped into an overstuffed chair. "From what I gathered, she was actually taken by Mai Luan."

That appeared to trouble Gregorios more than Eirene's capture had. It terrified Sarah. She rubbed her arms against a sudden chill. The thought that Mai Luan might still be alive had scared her, but it sounded like the terrifying woman was actually in Rome with them. Returning home to the States suddenly sounded like a very good idea.

Gregorios growled, "That doesn't make any kind of sense. The council has to know what she is."

"I think they do," Tomas confirmed. "No one said cui dashi aloud, but the way they talked about her, it was clear."

"No matter what they want Eirene for, what would drive them to permit any contact with a known cui dashi that didn't involve big guns?"

Sarah settled onto the couch close beside Tomas's chair and said, "Mai Luan is terrifying, but there's more, isn't there? What's a cui dashi?"

Tomas placed a hand over hers. "Sorry, of course you need to know what we're facing."

Gregorios said, "Cui dashi are a melding of bloodlines. They are the extremely rare individuals who inherit the heka rounon gift as well as the active nevra core of the facetaker."

"Nevra core?" Sarah asked. She hadn't expected to need to learn so many new terms, but she was stepping into a shadowy world, kept secret from outsiders.

"It's our center, our soul force," Gregorios explained. "Think of it as the fuel cell of our powers. We have the ability to tap our nevron, or the energy generated by our core, and leverage the force of our souls in ways no mortals can."

Sarah understood why Tomas just called it magic at first. If she hadn't experienced facetaker powers and witnessed soul transfers and shimmering soulmasks, she wouldn't have understood what he was talking about. "So that's why Mai Luan was so strong?"

Tomas squeezed her hand. "Yes. When those bloodlines merge, the two different powers magnify each other exponentially. Cui dashi can enhance themselves beyond anything the rest of us could hope to match, and they can overwhelm the souls of even experienced facetakers."

Gregorios added, "If our nevra core is a fuel cell, hers is a nuclear reactor."

Sarah shuddered. Although Mai Luan had looked like an unremarkable, slender, Chinese-American woman, she had possessed incredible strength and survived injuries that should have been lethal.

Gregorios added, "The bigger problem is that the vastly magnified power of the cui dashi usually lead them to view the rest of the world as lesser beings. The next logical step is wanting to take control."

"They become dangers to everyone. Every single one has turned bad," Tomas said.

"That's why we've always united against them. Until now," Gregorios said.

Tomas grimaced. "It gets worse. Mai Luan is scheduled to appear before the council tomorrow. She's going to use Eirene in some kind of experiment."

"Oh, no," Sarah breathed. She couldn't imagine what Mai Luan's plan might be, but the thought of that vile woman torturing Eirene left her shaking with terrified rage.

Gregorios's expression hardened, his eyes glinting with points of purple light.

"We'll see about that."

CHAPTER FIFTEEN

It is our choices that show what we truly are, far more than our physical forms.
~Tomas

Sarah eagerly stepped out of a little bus taxi that Gregorios had hired to take them the short drive to Vatican City. She grabbed Tomas's hand and drew him out of the vehicle to stand beside her.

The air was warm and the street packed with the funny little cars popular in Rome. Swarms of scooters and bicycles wove around each other everywhere, and crowds jostled past on the sidewalks.

"This is awesome." She turned in a circle, trying to take everything in at once. The buildings looked old, and a weight of history hung over the city. After the freaky excitement of New Orleans, it felt wonderful, as if she were dipping her toes into a timeless pond. She had felt it the moment they arrived, but the bright light of day magnified the feeling.

The air smelled of exhaust and fried street vendor food, all overlaid over the scent of weathered stone. Beeping horns and hundreds of small engines made a constant background noise, punctuated by scores of voices talking in many languages. Loud American tourists mingled with English visitors, while French and German accents sounded nearby. All of them were surrounded by the sing-song words of the local Italians. It made a wonderful din, so unlike anything she heard in the States.

Sarah wore designer jeans, a green silk blouse and a light jacket. Tomas was dressed in khaki pants, polo shirt, and a sports jacket, while Gregorios dressed like a tourist with cargo shorts, yellow shirt, and a typical backpack.

"Quite a sight, despite how many times I see it," Tomas agreed.

Sarah had decided not to ask about the coincidence that their planned vacation destination just happened to be the location of the secret facetaker council headquarters. She had ulterior motives for joining him in New Orleans, so she didn't begrudge him little secrets.

Once they found Eirene, she dared hope they could free her and convince the council of the danger Mai Luan posed. It sounded like they possessed the resources to deal with the cui dashi. Of course, that meant they had the resources to deal with Gregorios, Tomas, and Sarah too. Sarah's nervousness had intensified as they had approached the Suntara headquarters. She hated how scared she felt of the shadowy council she'd never met.

If only everything worked out. She had to believe it would, somehow. She'd love to celebrate with dinner at a nice restaurant and see some of the town without worrying about heka or cui dashi or anyone else chasing them. She couldn't imagine enjoying the sights with Eirene still prisoner. She'd never handle the guilt.

Gregorios didn't bother staring at the sights. His wife's peril had left him grim-faced. His intensity scared her a little and she reminded herself again never to get on his bad side. She and Tomas had helped free Eirene only recently, and it sounded like she'd remained in that tiny coffin for years.

Sarah swore to do everything in her power to help Gregorios save her from suffering a similar fate again. Gregorios's commitment seemed super human. Who sacrificed so much for their spouse these days? Most people would've filed for divorce and moved on.

That single-minded devotion helped Sarah overcome her nervous caution around Gregorios. She decided she liked him. Despite the very real dangers they were likely to face, she couldn't leave now. She didn't understand everything he and Tomas had shared with her, but she wasn't sure she could handle any additional truth yet.

Just focus on today's task. That was enough.

Once Eirene was free and they were out of danger, she and Tomas could consider a new vacation. Sarah only hoped the gunmen who had followed her to New Orleans were connected with the plot against Eirene. Wouldn't it be nice if resolving the current conflict secured her own safety? She doubted things would wrap up so neatly, but held onto hope until she was proven wrong.

Gregorios led the way into the crowds and merged with the loud tourists and the vendors clamoring for sales. Sarah followed, still holding Tomas's hand and trying to see everything. She'd been surprised to learn the headquarters of the shadowy council was right there in the heart of Rome, surrounded by millions of tourists.

Gregorios pulled them past the long lines of people waiting outside the entrance to the Vatican museum and turned down a mostly deserted side street. He and Tomas compared watches.

Tomas said, "Time to go."

Sarah hugged him, and he kissed her cheek.

"Be careful," she urged him.

"I told you, I'll be fine. I'm expected."

She still worried. Tomas was living the dangerous life of a double agent. He'd told her the night before that his connection to Gregorios was secret, and that he officially worked for the council.

"No one cares that you've been gone for days?" she pressed.

"I'm an enforcer. We come and go a lot."

"Oh, an enforcer. So you do have a title. I thought you were just a mercenary who won't talk about his work."

He actually leaned forward and kissed her on the lips. He barely brushed them, but it was an improvement. "I'll explain more when I get back."

"You bet you will."

With a final reassuring smile and a wink, he slipped back into the crowds. He had pointed out a nearby, unremarkable building of aged stone as the Suntara Group headquarters, but she wondered if he might be lying. It didn't look like the home of a super-secret, powerful sect of soul stealing kidnappers. More like the headquarters for a law firm or a bunch of accountants.

The building was not far from the museums, situated at the edge of the Vatican gardens. The tourist map Gregorios had given her listed it as some type of government administration building. What better place for them to hide than a building so easily ignored compared to the famous landmarks all around?

"Let's go," Gregorios said. He shouldered his simple backpack and led the way down the narrow street to a side entrance of the museum.

Sarah followed, a little nervous. The door was locked and a bored-looking guard stood outside. Gregorios had insisted they could easily get in without having to wait in line for hours with the tourists at the main entrance around the corner. She hoped he wasn't planning to attack the guard.

He didn't. He just walked up to the guard and showed an identification card. The man saluted and opened the door for them.

That was too easy. With all his talk of soul powers, she'd expected him to pull an Obi-Wan move and mind control the guard. She cast one last look around, taking in the beautiful gardens and the view of the dome of St. Peter's cathedral in the distance, then followed him inside. Hopefully they weren't walking into some kind of trap.

No one jumped them as they traversed a long, dim hallway of age-blackened stone. The passage was cramped and smelled of dust, and slightly of mold. Tiny windows, spaced too far apart, let in only a little light, and dust-motes danced in the feeble beams. Sarah was not impressed. Wasn't everything in the Vatican museum supposed to be awesome?

Then they exited a simple wooden door and slipped into the crowds pouring into the Sistine Chapel.

That *was* awesome.

Sarah gawked at the incredible paintings spanning the entire ceiling and most of the walls. A complex architecture of beams and trusses spanned the ceiling, surrounding the panels of awe-inspiring paintings that filled every inch of the space with vibrant color.

She was stunned to learn from Gregorios that the ceiling was actually quite flat and the three-dimensional effect was an optical illusion. Her nerves calmed under the incredible sight and for a moment she forgot her worry for Eirene and her fear of the shadowy council. She wished Tomas was there to enjoy the view with her.

Fifteen minutes passed in a blur, then Gregorios tapped her arm and motioned toward the exit. Time to go.

He was no longer carrying his backpack.

"Five minutes," he said softly as they followed other tourists out the exit.

Planting the backpack was all they needed to do besides wait for Tomas to make his move. His was the critical mission.

Gregorios turned toward the distant safe house where they'd wait for Tomas, but she pulled him in the other direction. "Can we go through Saint Peter's Square?"

He gave her that intimidating look of his, but she held her ground. "I hate waiting, and it won't take that long, will it?"

Seeing the Sistine Chapel had calmed her nerves. Hopefully St. Peter's would accomplish the same thing. She hated enjoying herself while Tomas was in danger and Eirene's fate unknown, but the thought of sitting in the silent safe house, with nothing to do but wait only magnified her fears.

Gregorios sighed and turned the other way.

Sarah took his arm. "Thanks for being flexible."

He managed a tight smile, despite the worry in his eyes that reflected the fears she was barely controlling. "I hate waiting too."

Just as they reached the famous square, Gregorios checked his watch. "Smoke distraction should be detonating any second."

They made it halfway across the vast square before distant sirens began to blare. Police cars soon raced past, lights flashing. A moment later, a flood of tourists poured into the square from the direction of the museum, and Sarah caught bits and pieces of excited chatter about a bomb in the Sistine Chapel.

Stage one complete.

It was all up to Tomas now.

CHAPTER SIXTEEN

What spirit is so empty and blind, that it cannot recognize the fact that the foot is more noble than the shoe, and skin more beautiful than the garment with which it is clothed? How much more the beauty of the soul than the clay that houses it?

~Michelangelo

Eirene awoke abruptly.

Consciousness returned like a splash of icy water rippling through her mind, too fast to be anything but the result of a drug. Every sense clamored for attention, almost like the intensity of a new bonding. She didn't know how long she'd been unconscious, but she sensed it was quite a while. Although she appreciated that she didn't awaken confused or slow-witted, she wondered what else the drug might be doing to her.

Even before she glanced around at her surroundings, she embraced a fraction of her nevra core and loosened the connection between her soul and the body she wore. It insulated her against any other influences on her mind.

She sat in the facetaker council chamber in the Suntara headquarters, strapped into a high-backed leather chair facing an enormous polished-wood table and six council members who sat quietly watching her. Not good. She had often reported to the entire council body so sitting before half of them didn't intimidate her. What did shock her were the looks of cold, clinical detachment with which the elderly facetakers regarded her.

They were old. That fact struck with startling force. One of the benefits of being a facetaker was abandoning an aging or sick body to take another life. All of the council members had always preferred young, healthy bodies, often abandoning them far earlier than Eirene usually did. Now they looked old, in their sixties or seventies. She couldn't imagine what might have driven them to cling to these lives so long.

They had expected her. The attack on her really was sanctioned by the council. Did they also understand Mai Luan's true danger?

Asoka sat closest to her right. The aged leader of the enforcers wore the same body she'd last seen him in prior to her previous imprisonment. He looked unhappier than normal, although his anger did not seem directed toward her.

He always looked grumpy, ever since the life he spent serving as a cardinal. It had been his efforts that had secured them permanent ownership of their headquarters. The fact that he had lived for centuries as a Buddhist monk had prepared him for a life of religious service and by all accounts he had done a remarkable job. His contacts in the Vatican still benefited the council, but he seemed to still begrudge that life.

John and Aline sat across the table from Asoka, but were turned away, talking quietly together. Zuri wore an overweight body whose sagging, ebony folds more than filled her chair. The diamond necklaces piled around her throat glittered with reflected light as she leaned forward, intense gaze locked on Eirene. Harald lounged beside her, grossly fat and bald.

Shahrokh, the leader of the council, looked aged and frail. He sat at the head of the table, directly across from Eirene, and studied her with such an intense hunger it unnerved her. She had never positioned herself at odds with the council in any matter of import besides refusing to help them destroy her husband. For the first time, she feared what they planned for her.

Mai Luan stepped into view beside her, dressed in a simple, white lab coat.

"Welcome back."

"How . . . ?"

Which question to ask first? How could Mai Luan be standing at ease in the council chamber? How had they not yet ordered her termination? How had the council broken millennia of tradition to allow the presence of the cui dashi? How . . .

Mai Luan pressed a thick piece of tape over her mouth.

"Now that you've chosen to join us, we can begin," the slender woman said in a pleasant tone, belied by the ice in her gaze.

"About time," Shahrokh said with an irritated grunt. "Get on with it."

"Of course," Mai Luan said with the tiniest of bows.

She presented a demure, harmless face to the council. Could they not know what she was? The slender Chinese-American had benefited from both ancestries. She wore her silky, black hair long, tied back to accentuate her delicate features. Her face looked more American than Chinese though, and she stood average height, with a petite, athletic build.

Eirene wanted to curse them all as fools. No matter what Gregorios might have done to them, allowing Mai Luan into their midst was pure lunacy. She didn't bother to struggle to free her mouth. They clearly intended for Mai Luan to be present, and wouldn't listen to anything she had to say.

Mai Luan lifted a blocky metal helmet from under the table, trailing dozens of wires. Its thick, raised faceplate looked a lot like an optometrist's phoropter, but with jagged knobs and viewports.

Whatever that thing was, Eirene didn't want it on her head. She struggled weakly, shaking her head, but Mail Luan only chuckled and slipped the contraption over her head. She strapped it down tight, but left the faceplate raised.

"Comfy?" Mai Luan asked with a little smile. She turned Eirene's chair just a little to allow her to glimpse a machine positioned behind her.

It stood on steel casters, locked in place, and its simple rectangular base stood three feet tall and two feet wide. The shining steel of the outer shell was unmarked except for bright red letters emblazoned along one side that read *Sotrun III*. Atop the steel base sat a small monitor, turned away from Eirene. Tereza, also white-coated, sat on a stool, staring intently at the monitor, fingers tapping occasionally on the keys.

It looked a lot like the machines Sarah had described from Alterego, the ones used in soul transfers, but adapted to use the helmet and Frankenstein phoropter faceplate.

The situation was making less and less sense. She'd been hunting Tereza partially to learn the details of the machine and its supposed technology, and partially to confirm whether or not Mai Luan had survived. She hadn't visited the council headquarters since her escape from Alterego. She'd hoped to learn from Tereza who might have been involved in orchestrating her capture beside Maerwynn, and if it was safe to return.

Apparently it wasn't.

What made no sense was why Mai Luan would openly reveal the secret to them? Tereza was in league with Mai Luan, but was the council complicit also? It seemed hard to believe.

Mai Luan flipped a switch on one side of the machine and the helmet on Eirene's head began to hum with electrical current. Eirene could accept that the council might order her dispossessed again as leverage against Gregorios. Despite the terror that thought triggered, she understood the reasoning. But why use the machine? Why allow Mai Luan into the chamber?

Another white-coated tech, this one a young man, extracted a second helmet from a padded case. He plugged its wire bundle into another slot on the machine and placed the helmet onto an empty chair to Eirene's left.

Mai Luan placed a soul coffin on the table.

Eirene began to thrash in her chair despite her resolution to face her fate with calm. She didn't doubt for a second that Gregorios would track her down and set her free again, but the sight of the soul coffin filled her with panic.

She couldn't face that again.

She tried to scream at the council to release her, to allow her to fight for her freedom, to issue a formal challenge, but the tape only allowed vague mumbling. She could never defeat Mai Luan, but their honor should require them to allow her to try.

The cold gazes of the council members didn't change.

Mai Luan ignored her futile struggles. "Esteemed patrons, I thank you for agreeing to witness in person the first test of the completed prototype."

Eirene slowed her struggles to listen. Something else was going on, something unexpected. The council members listened eagerly, anticipation on their faces.

"We will commence the experimental calibration utilizing this *volunteer*." She made a mocking gesture toward Eirene.

Then she flipped open the soul coffin and extracted a soulmask. The male tech secured the soulmask into a web harness that he placed on the table in front of Eirene. She noted tiny runes inscribed onto each harness strap. They were utilizing heka runes in the council chamber and no one cared?

Asoka finally reacted, leaning forward and frowning at Mai Luan. Despite his age, his frown still carried a weight of danger few could ignore. "Can't you leave your rounon rituals outside?"

Mai Luan met his stare with perfect calm. "Certainly, if you're volunteering to power the machine with the force of your soul instead?"

Asoka huffed and muttered something grumpy under his breath, but settled back into his chair with no further complaint. Eirene watched him in shock. As head of the enforcers, he was a legendary fighter. He might not be able to hold his own against a cui dashi, but she'd never seen him so easily cowed. All he had to do was make a single gesture and the room would flood with security forces.

He did gesture, but it was nothing more than a brushing motion of an impatient old man. "Get on with it then."

Mai Luan startled Eirene further by taking the seat beside her and slipping on the second helmet.

Tereza drew the faceplate down over Eirene's face, and the jagged clamps dug into the flesh around her eyes and along her jaw. It blocked out all light and the electrical hum intensified. Eirene fought down a fresh wave of fear and embraced her nevra core. She vowed by all the gods of her many lives that Mai Luan would not find her an easy target.

Tereza leaned close and spoke softly. "Just relax. This will feel weird."

She wanted to shout curses accumulated from a dozen centuries at the woman. Did they really think she'd submit like a sheep? She'd fight with the same fury that had granted her victory over the mightiest of the heka warriors of ancient Rome.

A telltale ripple of power caressed her face as Tereza directed her nevron into the machine. Maybe that was why Mai Luan had donned the other helmet, as a way to combine forces with her against Eirene.

Still, she would fight.

Eirene braced herself for the first assault and prepared the full force of her nevron for an overwhelming counter-attack.

The assault never came. Something was wrong. Instead of the fiery heat of another's power trying to rip her soul from her host body, the force humming against her skin vibrated with a secondary source.

The dispossessed soul.

Before she could even figure out how to fight it, a hole opened in her mind and sucked her consciousness down like a whirlpool.

After a breathless moment of panic and soundless screaming, she awoke.

In Japan. In 1944.

CHAPTER SEVENTEEN

It does not do to dwell on lives and forget to live.

~Gregorios

Dressed in one of her favorite bodies, Eirene trailed a diplomatic entourage into the high-class residence of a Japanese general. His name no longer mattered. She climbed the stairs with a spring in her step even though a distant worry tugged at the back of her mind. Something was wrong, wasn't it?

She pushed the distraction aside. It was ruining the moment.

Just inside the doors, she scanned the crowd of well-dressed party goers and picked out the face she sought. He stood taller than most of the other guests since he was not Japanese.

His dashing good looks and suntanned face stood out from the crowd. His cover was that of a member of the Hungarian consulate team and he was an exciting secondary mark. After she finished scouting the heka cell supposedly operating in the area, she would give him her full attention.

With a start, Eirene realized she was re-living a memory. She'd visited this memory many times through dreams, but never in this state. She felt the pull of the memory, like an invisible undertow, pushing her to live the moment as she always had. For the first time, she felt as if she could break from that remembered sequence, consciously alter her memory.

As she turned a slow circle, amazed by the startling clarity of the moment, it ended abruptly, replaced by a rapid succession of memories, like a slide show rippling through her mind. In seconds images passed of her meetings with high ranking Japanese officials and didn't even slow when she met in absolute secrecy with the emperor himself.

One aspect of her tri-fold mission to Japan had been to negotiate deposits for potential soul transfers for several top officials in case the war went badly. The questions of honor and responsibility were complicated, but still they chose to meet with her. Enough of them preferred the idea of escaping justice for atrocities committed during the war that they gladly handed over large deposits of gold to secure their spots. Should the need arise, they could abandon their old lives and start anew with additional piles of hoarded wealth to enjoy.

The lure of a second life was hard for anyone, any culture, to withstand.

Time didn't slow again until she crouched on a hillside outside of Tokyo. It was night and clouds blocked the moon and stars. She lay in the darkness as she studied an innocent-looking compound of ramshackle houses through a pair of powerful binoculars. She had tracked the suspected cell of heka operatives there and had studied their movements for several nights. The next day she planned to call in the strike team of enforcers to eradicate them.

She swung her binoculars to the north and, after a moment of careful study, picked out her secondary target. The man supposedly from the Hungarian consul crouched far closer to the compound than she, peering through his own binoculars. She had spotted him the night before and enjoyed watching him. His people were not Hungarian, and they referred to the heka as kashaph. She would learn to love how that word rolled off his tongue. He was eager, brave, and foolish.

She could manipulate those qualities. She had.

The next day she would arrange to run into him by chance and strike up a conversation. His name was Ronen, and he was a hunter.

Her memories began skipping forward again in rapid succession. A montage of images flashed past of their courtship, his proposal, and the wedding. She tried to linger on that one, but the memory was ripped away by an external force.

Only then did she realize that another presence participated in her memories. Another will controlled the images. It was that presence that leapfrogged through her life as if sifting through an old scrapbook.

It was a tenuous feeling, difficult to pinpoint, and hard to focus on as every shifting moment pulled at her focus. She tried to fight it, tried to concentrate, but then her mind locked onto that one fateful night.

She stood in a darkened room near the window overlooking a three-story drop, invisible from outside. A shadowy figure moved just beyond the window and hands grasped the sill. She focused on those hands, one of which held a gun.

Then the memory lurched forward again and she stood above a too-familiar body that lay on the floor, face crushed, and bloody, and unrecognizable. Those same hands she had seen at the window, now her hands, held a fire extinguisher dripping with blood.

Footsteps approached from the hall.

She rushed for the window, already preparing to block out the wail of anguish she knew he would make when he found his beloved wife lying dead in their room. That part always hurt. As she crouched on the window sill, ready to plunge to the ground, it was not howls of anguish that filled the room but screams of agony.

Something was wrong. He wasn't supposed to be hurt, just heart-broken. More screams, followed by crashing sounds of brutal struggle.

With a great effort, she resisted the pull of the memory that drove her to make the leap as she always had. Instead she rushed across the room, ignoring the dead woman lying on the floor, and flung open the door.

A huge wolf, wearing the face of Mai Luan, stood in the shattered living room holding a limp, bloody Ronen off the ground. He looked old, far older than he should have the day he found his beloved dead.

Mai Luan grinned through long, canine teeth.

Then she ripped his throat out.

Eirene screamed and lunged, enhanced hands reaching to rip the monster apart. The Mai Luan wolf swatted her aside with a laugh, and she crashed head first into a thick wooden door post.

Her entire body convulsed as she snapped awake, once again in the council chamber. She sagged against the chair that still held her restrained, shaken from the memories and sweating with fear.

What had just happened?

And why did her face hurt so much?

CHAPTER EIGHTEEN

I love mortals. They consume the power of their souls with such exuberance.
Even better, their industry has invented so many wonders in recent decades.
I salute them, for I will enjoy the fruits of their labors for centuries to come.
                                        ~Zuri, facetaker council member

M ai Luan pulled the jagged faceplate away and dragged one
fingernail down Eirene's throbbing face, grinning just like
the wolf in the dream. Eirene flinched away, hating herself
for the weakness but unable to stop the reaction.

The council members sat right where she remembered, leaning forward, studying her closely. Why had they sanctioned the
bizarre test? Did they know the machine somehow granted Mai
Luan access to her mind? It had to be Mai Luan filtering through
her memories, using the machine and the strange helmets.

Eirene's head still spun and she felt exhausted. Her thoughts
moved too slowly to make sense of the situation, but new fear
blossomed. If they let Mai Luan continue these experiments,
what secrets might Mai Luan dredge from her memory?

Asoka said, "Take that tape from her mouth so we can ask
her some questions."

Eirene was eager to speak with them, to raise the voice of
caution. She knew nothing of what they hoped to gain by allowing Mai Luan into their midst, but whatever she had promised
them was surely a lie.

Instead of obeying, Mai Luan disconnected the dispossessed
soul used to fuel the machine. It looked smaller, weaker, with
fine cracks running across its surface. The rainbow smoke of its
soul strength had faded to gray.

They had consumed almost all of its life force.

Mai Luan placed the soulmask on the table, looked across to Asoka, then casually smashed it with the heel of her hand.

"Her feedback is of no assistance. I've seen her mind and she will only lie."

"You can read minds?" Shahrokh asked from across the table.

"Not exactly, but I caught glimpses of some of the memories she visited, enough to make it clear she will do anything to thwart your success."

That garnered hard stares from the council. Eirene tried to focus her muddled thoughts, tried to organize them into a coherent list. First, she realized Asoka had made no move to destroy Mai Luan for shattering that soulmask. Such an act was forbidden, but none of the council even appeared to notice.

Second, Mai Luan was concealing the truth of the machine's capabilities from them. Finally, they appeared completely ready to accept the word of an outsider, a hated cui dashi, over one of their own. Even if she could get the tape off, she realized they'd never believe her warning.

A wailing of sirens began outside the building. It was loud enough that a large number of police and fire vehicles had to be congregating in the street nearby. A few seconds later, the head of building security entered the room.

"I'm sorry to disturb your meeting," the powerfully built, middle-aged man said, "but some kind of explosive device just detonated inside the Sistine Chapel."

A collective gasp from every throat echoed Eirene's own shock. They knew this area better than anyone. She remembered the long years spent building, then painting the chapel. Such a wonder of the world, such a part of her heart.

She had personally handled the soul transfer of Michelangelo, rewarding him with a second life for the remarkable work he did. The thought of anyone harming that unique chapel filled her with indignant fury.

Asoka growled, "What's the world coming to? No respect for anything." He finally looked angry, although it irritated Eirene that it was a threat to the nearby landmark that enraged him the most.

Mai Luan spoke. "It appears there may be other matters you need to attend."

"Nonsense," Shahrokh protested.

"It's just as well," she said smoothly. "My team and I must analyze the results of this test and verify optimal calibration of the machine."

"Did it work?" Aline asked, her voice a raspy croak. Aline lived large and loved her vices. This long life was taking its toll.

"It appears to have been a great success," Mai Luan assured them. The council relaxed, all grinning like fools. "The test proved that the concept is sound and the underlying technology is ready for final tuning."

"When can we try it?" Aline asked, her lined face intent.

"Soon."

The first tiny bit of understanding clicked into place. The council members planned to submit to Mai Luan and her machine.

Why?

She puzzled over that as the meeting broke up. A pair of burly enforcers released her from the restraining straps, although they left her hands chained.

Instead of leading her to the holding cells in the sub-basement, they took her to the far end of the building on the same level as the council room and pushed her into a small waiting room with only a single padded chair. It appeared her reprieve would be short lived.

The moment when they stopped and waited for one of the men to unlock the door would have been the best chance to make a break for freedom, but she knew these enforcers. They were some of the toughest men in the force, with many enhancing runes. Her body felt shaky and her head throbbed. Not an ideal time to test herself against them.

Besides, help was coming. Her muddled thoughts were finally beginning to clear and she recognized Gregorios's flair for the dramatic in the supposed bombing of the Sistine Chapel. If he really did cause any damage, she would rip his face off and leave him dispossessed for a month.

Once inside the improvised holding cell, she dropped onto the chair. She centered her mind and tried to focus her thoughts on everything that had just happened. The truth was there, she just had to find it.

Twenty minutes later, the door swung open and Tomas stuck his head in and asked, "Ready to go?"

Eirene smiled and rose to her feet, extending her hands for him to unlock the chains.

"Good to see you. We have one stop to make first."

CHAPTER NINETEEN

We rob banks! What else you want us to do? Bonnie's got a gift, I tell ya, a real gift. She draws them pictures on my skin and it's like magic. I get strong and fast and can't hardly miss when I shoot, see. Let 'em come and try to take us.

~Clyde Barrow, of the Bonnie and Clyde gang

When they emerged from the temporary holding cell, Eirene found the halls empty. That upper level where the council met was rarely used for other purposes. She didn't bother to ask what he'd done with the other enforcers. He wouldn't have permanently damaged them or risked exposing his true allegiance.

"Where to?" Tomas asked.

"I need to study that machine."

"They moved it to the smaller conference room."

"Is it accessible?"

"I think so."

Eirene squeezed his hand. "Good work." Then she frowned. "It's Mai Luan."

He nodded, expression grim. "I heard. Madness."

"They can't understand the danger."

"I don't think they'll listen to me either."

"We'll figure out a way. For now, I need a closer look," she said.

They slipped back along the hall and down a cross corridor. The distraction of the bomb would wear off all too soon, but she figured they had a few minutes before they absolutely needed to be away. The greatest risk was running into Mai Luan.

They reached the small conference room and Eirene motioned Tomas to wait. She pushed open the door and peeked inside. The table had been pushed to the far wall near the barred window. The machine sat in the middle of the room, with Tereza perched on a stool, typing on the keyboard.

Eirene slipped through the door and advanced. Tereza looked up when she was six feet away. The woman's eyes widened in shock and she opened her mouth to cry an alarm.

Eirene lunged and slammed Tereza's head onto the top of the Sotrun machine. The steel case made a surprisingly musical tone from the impact. Tereza's eyes rolled up and she fell unmoving to the floor.

Eirene resisted the urge to kick her a couple of times. She'd remove the woman's soulmask before they left. Tereza had a lot of questions to answer.

She ignored the tempting little screen, borrowed Tomas's phone, and began snapping photos of every component. She noted more tiny runes engraved into the inside of the helmets, and snapped several photos of those.

"Hurry." Tomas had remained near the door. He had shifted to the wall on one side, pulled a satchel off his shoulder, and was fiddling with something inside.

"Almost done. They've inscribed runes all over this thing. These symbols are new."

The door crashed open and Mai Luan stepped into the opening. "Of course they're new. No one's seen those runes in millennia."

Eirene's heart sank. With Mai Luan standing in the only exit, they were trapped.

Tomas shifted to the right along the wall away from Mai Luan until his shoulders struck the corner. She ignored him and took a confident step into the room.

The satchel Tomas had left beside the door belched an enormous gout of flame and a heavy projectile. It caught Mai Luan in the ribs. Bones shattered as it tore into her torso, creating an astonishingly huge hole.

Then the projectile exploded inside of her.

The blast threw her off her feet and smashed her halfway through the wood-paneled wall. Most of her guts sprayed across the room, and she hung limply, her torso shredded.

Eirene bolted for the door.

Mai Luan leveraged herself out of the broken wall, her expression livid. She tried to speak, but only bubbles of blood dribbled out her mouth. She lunged toward Eirene, but her legs buckled.

Eirene paused in the doorway to glance back. Mai Luan's gaping wounds were already closing. In seconds she'd be mobile again. Eirene had faced cui dashi a couple of times, but this level of regeneration was impressive even for them.

As they ran down the hall, Mai Luan's voice chased them, penetrating the ringing in Eirene's ears from the recent blast. "I'm not through with you, Eirene. Your soul is mine!"

Tomas dropped a couple of smoke bombs onto the floor behind them, and threw another far down the hall in front. The sharp reports of their detonations sounded muted to Eirene. Her ears still weren't working right.

Thick smoke billowed into the hall, obscuring everything. Three seconds later, the fire alarm began wailing and sprinklers blasted them with water.

"What did you hit her with?" Eirene asked as they ran for the stairs.

"Latest gadget from Quentin. He calls it the mini-mortar."

"I love that man."

They descended to ground level, paused to compose themselves, then exited the stairs into the main lobby. That was the most dangerous part. If anyone recognized her, enforcers could drop them before they escaped the lobby.

They needn't have worried.

The huge open space with domed ceiling, tiled floor, and museum-quality statues lining the walls was filled with shouting people. It was the one semi-public place in the building and some of the people forced from the nearby Vatican museum had come there to loiter near all the excitement. The klaxon alarms triggered a near panic, and Eirene and Tomas slipped unnoticed into the crowd pouring out of the building onto the street.

With so many emergency vehicles already in the vicinity, police and firefighters were converging on the building, probably worried it was a second terrorist attack. The bedlam made the perfect cover for a getaway.

Only when they were safely in a cab did Eirene allow herself a sigh of relief. "Thank you."

She'd known Tomas since his first life, and thought of him as one of her many sons. Today he'd made her proud.

"Consider one of the many debts I owe you paid in full."

"You know your cover is probably blown."

He grimaced. "I need to return at least one more time."

"You'll need your battle suit for sure," she agreed. "What did they do to you?"

"I'm not entirely sure, but it's nothing good."

He leaned back against the seat. "I can't believe they let her in the building."

"It's even worse than that."

"How can it be?"

"I don't understand it all yet, but it's clear Mai Luan's maneuvered the council into a trap. She has some leverage over them that's blinded them to the truth about her."

"She'll annihilate them," Tomas said.

"I'm afraid you're right. What worries me more is what she might be planning to do afterward."

CHAPTER TWENTY

The tree of liberty must be refreshed from time to time with the blood of patriots and tyrants. At other times, it must be carved with runes of enhancement.
~Thomas Jefferson

s soon as Eirene entered the safe house, Sarah gave her a big hug. It had really worked! She was so thrilled to see Eirene safe, so relieved that she was free. Riding the high of the moment, she wrapped her arms around Tomas's neck and gave him a big kiss.

He actually kissed her back. The day was definitely looking up.

"You really did it," she gushed.

He smiled. "Piece of cake."

She turned to ask Eirene a question, but the words died on her lips. Gregorios and Eirene stood close together, not speaking, but joy glowing in their eyes. He held her face cupped in one hand, and she closed her eyes. They just stood like that for a moment, radiating love without having to move.

After a long moment, Gregorios removed his hand and she cupped his face in like manner while he closed his eyes and leaned a little into the singular embrace. Only after she dropped her hand did they finally kiss each other.

Sarah squeezed Tomas's hand. She felt privileged to witness the tender moment.

Then she realized they'd been holding each other's faces exactly the way they would had they planned to call upon their powers and remove each other's soulmasks.

Tomas took her arm and pulled her into the kitchen.

"That gesture . . ." she began.

"We probably should've left. That was a private moment."

"It was more than just a caress, wasn't it?"

"You're a quick study. It's a sign of complete trust and devotion, a surrender to another facetaker. It's how they renew their bond."

So romantic, she thought. She gave him a sly look. "So what do you non-facetaker enforcers do to renew your bonds?"

He grinned. "First, we go out tonight to see some of the sights."

Sarah kissed him again. "I agree. Let's celebrate!"

There was so much to see. She was just getting really excited about all the possibilities when Gregorios and Eirene entered the room, holding hands.

"How's the perimeter?" Eirene asked.

Tomas said, "Stable, but given our proximity to the headquarters, there's risk. I've taken precautions."

Eirene seemed satisfied with the vague answer and motioned them all to sit around a high wooden table. She explained some of the bizarre experience in the council chamber and Sarah agreed that the modified machine Mai Luan was using sounded a lot like the ones used at Alterego.

"What did you mean that someone was driving your memories?" Tomas asked.

"Like she was controlling what I saw."

That was freaky and nothing like what the machines were used for at Alterego. Then again, Sarah and the others who submitted to the machines without knowing what was really going on were always drugged prior to the transfers. Had Mai Luan and her assistants sifted through Sarah's memories while she slept?

She didn't think so, but the idea disturbed her at a fundamental level. Just thinking of such a violation of a person's inner self left her feeling dirty.

"Mai Luan was in your dream?" Gregorios asked.

Eirene nodded. "It felt like she was looking for something, searching my memories."

"For what?"

She shrugged. "Nothing I saw in that dream would be useful to her."

"You said that she told the council you were the trial run," Tomas said, his brow furrowed as he considered the puzzle. "But she concealed from them the truth of what she was doing in your mind."

Gregorios said, "In that case, it sounds like she plans to search their memories too."

"I think she plans more than that."

Eirene explained about the runes in the helmet and showed the photos to Gregorios, who frowned over them. "I've never seen runes like these either."

"According to Mai Luan, no one's seen them for millennia."

"What does that mean?" Sarah asked. Tomas had said the occultists used runes to steal life force from victimized souls, but that didn't sound like what was going on with the machines.

"Either she has access to secrets hidden from most of the world, or those runes were only recently rediscovered," Tomas said.

Sarah was getting lost. "But what do they do?"

"Runes are symbols of power," Eirene said.

Sarah took Tomas's hand. "This is different than the runes we talked about after the hotel in New Orleans, isn't it?"

"Yes. Runes can be used in different ways by heka with higher level rounon gifts."

"Or cui dashi," Gregorios added.

"Right," Tomas agreed. "Some heka can bond runes to sacrificed souls but not need to remain in contact with them to fuel their enhancements or other types of spells. Those heka are channelers."

Eirene said, "The runes were on the machine, the helmets, and also on the harness connecting the soulmask with us. They drained its life force to help power the machine. Coupled with Tereza's nevron, it provided Mai Luan access to my mind and control over my memories."

Sarah frowned. "It sounds like make believe."

Gregorios shrugged. "Make believe often starts as truth. Lots of fables start that way. For example, where do you think the child's game 'got your nose' really came from?"

That was more than a little disturbing.

Eirene rolled her eyes. "Don't get him started. He loves discussing how legends date back to actual events."

"So how do you know what the runes do? I mean, for sure?"

Gregorios said, "That's the question. Each rune has a specific purpose. There are quite a few, but many have been lost over the centuries."

He explained that in ancient history there were powerful runes lost during times of upheaval of great empires dating back to Rome, Greece, and all the way to biblical times in ancient Egypt.

"Those were some strange times," Eirene muttered.

Sarah stared. How old were they, really? She didn't quite dare to ask.

"Perhaps that's what she's looking for. Other runes," Tomas suggested.

"Perhaps," Gregorios agreed slowly. "But if she already has access to lost runes, does she need more, or is she looking to mine secrets from the council members' minds?"

Eirene asked, "Why are they allowing it? They're looking old, but they can't be senile yet."

"That bothers me as much as anything," Gregorios said. "I've only ever known facetakers to actually grow old when they're hoarding lives."

Eirene nodded slowly and glanced at Sarah. "The machines help prevent mental dissipation. Sarah, you're living proof of that."

"That's why I could transfer so many times without going nuts, right?" Sarah asked. The machines had helped block most of the weird memories from the bodies she'd inhabited, although she'd made enough transfers by the end that some shadows of memories were starting to slip through.

Gregorios nodded. "No mortal can handle very many transfers, guaranteed. But the dangers are more extensive than simple mental dissipation. That's the gradual loss of identity as the different hosts begin breaking down your mental stability. The resulting holes get filled with bits of lingering residue from the hosts' previous owners. But even with your mind intact, you should've suffered severe soul fragmentation."

"What's that?" Sarah asked.

"Every time a soul bonds with a host, part of its essence is spent establishing the connection. Each transfer costs a little more life force, and more is left behind with each subsequent dispossession. Mortals don't have the strength to manage more than a few. The machine must somehow shield the soul from that fragmentation."

No one had explained all the risks so clearly. Sarah shuddered to think what Mai Luan had helped do to her and the other donors. The cui dashi terrified her, but for the first time her fear was tempered with growing anger.

Gregorios continued. "The problem is that the council are already dealing with the issue. I guess preventing it from getting worse is still a big win."

"Perhaps Mai Luan's convinced them the machine can actually reverse the process," Eirene suggested.

Gregorios nodded. "That's the first thing that makes sense. It'd be a miracle, a promise they couldn't ignore. The only thing any of us really have to worry about is soul fragmentation and mental dissipation from living too many lives."

"Why can facetakers handle more than the rest of us?" Sarah asked.

Eirene said, "Our nevra core. Our soul force is far stronger and we control it exponentially better than mortals. We can prevent loss of nevron during transfers because we recognize the danger and possess the tools to combat it."

Gregorios added, "We can delay the inevitable, but if the machine could reverse the degradation, facetakers could live forever."

It sounded like they already lived pretty long to Sarah.

"You might have it," Eirene said.

"Let's see if we can get any confirmation," Gregorios said. He fetched the soul coffin holding the imprisoned souls of Dalal and the other man he called Curly.

"Now that we know better questions to ask, let's see what we can learn."

He popped open the face coffin and peered inside. With an exclamation of surprise, he drew out the two soulmasks.

They were closely locked together, and he had to pull hard to pry them apart. Dalal's soulmask glowed brighter than before, almost as bright as the LED-like lights that blazed in facetaker eyes when they called upon their strange powers. Curly's soulmask looked small and gray, more dead than alive.

Gregorios lifted Dalal's soulmask high and his eyes glittered with power. The brilliant rainbow streamers of her soul gripped his lower arm and for a moment Sarah worried the woman was going to hurt him.

Dalal's whisper-voice came stronger than in the past. "*You will know pain.*" The streamers of her soul power clawed up his arm.

Gregorios's eyes burned brighter, and whispers of purple fire rippled along his hand. He growled, "You've stolen much of his soul force, but you cannot defeat me while dispossessed."

Dalal shrieked in high-pitched frustration as the advance of her rainbow tentacles slowed, ending with a shower of brilliant green sparks that left them convulsing. The glow faded as the rainbow streamers retreated and Dalal's living mask dulled to a normal shimmering translucence.

Eirene fetched a hammer from a nearby cupboard and brandished it. "Shall I crack your defiance a little, my dear?"

Dalal settled down.

Sarah realized with a start that she no longer found it strange to see someone holding a dispossessed soulmask. She'd already slipped so far into their world, but felt like she understood so little. Dalal would have ripped off Sarah's face had she been the one to lift the woman's soulmask from the coffin. What other unknown dangers had she not discovered yet?

"What happened?" Sarah asked.

Tomas slipped an arm around her waist and she leaned against his solid presence. "She tried to kill that poor wretch."

"Can she do that when she's just a mask?"

"It's difficult, but possible given enough time," Gregorios said.

"Good thing we checked in on them when we did," Eirene added. She gently took up the ghostly face of Curly and stroked it with a lightly glowing finger. Under her touch, the face began to glow and become more opaque, and the sickly mist coiled under it grew longer and shifted into subdued rainbow hues. "He's deeply wounded."

Gregorios gave Dalal's soulmask a shake. "If you want any hope of ever possessing a body again, tell me why."

Her helium-high whisper-laugh sounded like fingernails dragging on a chalkboard. "*If I'd kill to keep a secret, do you think I'd willingly divulge it?*"

"Eventually," he said in a cold, hard voice.

Eirene cut in. "But since this fellow isn't dead, perhaps he can shed some light on the mystery."

She regarded the soulmask for a moment, head cocked to one side. "Tomas, we'll need a host for this fellow to help him recover."

"On it." He strode from the room.

Gregorios began questioning Dalal on what she might know of Mai Luan's plans, but she refused to provide any useful information. Their conversation circled around several useless times without getting anywhere. Gregorios grew frustrated, but that only seemed to encourage Dalal to deny his requests.

She tried to change the subject by congratulating him on recovering Eirene, but then taunted her. "*Do try to stick around a little longer.*"

Tomas returned in less than half an hour with a dirty beggar fellow who was passed-out drunk.

Eirene directed him to place the man on the floor.

"You're not planning what I think you are?" Sarah asked. Would they really just kill someone out of hand like that?

"Only temporarily, my dear," Eirene assured her.

Tomas added, "He's drunk enough that he'll assume it was just a weird dream. He'll never know the difference."

Sarah still didn't like it. She had fought hard to retain her identity. It disturbed her to see them rip another person's away with barely a thought.

Tomas must have read her concern. "Plus, he'll be thrilled to find a hundred dollar bill in his pocket when he wakes up."

That helped, but she still felt uneasy. "Just make sure you put him back."

Gregorios asked, "Why the sudden squeamishness? At Alterego you underwent more transfers than perhaps any of us have."

"I know, but I volunteered."

"We'll be gentle," Eirene assured her, then positioned herself over the sleeping man's face while Tomas efficiently bound the man's hands and feet.

Sarah wanted to look away, but couldn't. For most of her time at Alterego, she'd been fooled by the unique technology, never understanding that it alone could never accomplish the miracle of moving a soul from one body to another. She'd never really considered why her face swapped along with her consciousness.

Now she knew the truth, had witnessed several transfers, including Greg's self-induced transfer outside of New Orleans, but she still struggled to really believe it was real. She watched in sick fascination as Eirene wrapped glowing fingers around the jawline of the sleeping drunk. Her eyes burned like amethysts, and purple fire flickered along her hands as they sank into the skin of the jaw.

Then she pulled. The face began lifting, starting at the jaw, with that wet, sucking sound that gave Sarah nightmares. It sounded like a boot coming free of thick mud, and she stuck fingers in her ears to block it. As the face lifted higher, flesh fell away to allow the shimmering soulmask to pull free of his body.

Eirene lifted it high, but her expression reflected none of the ecstasy that Sarah had seen from both Mai Luan and her assistant when they removed souls. That helped a little.

The skin of the abandoned skull flowed together and rippled like waters of a pond before settling into a smooth expanse of skin, unbroken but for a tiny slit where the nose should be. The soulmask in Eirene's hands flattened and shrank, the eyes compressed, and the rainbow smoke of his soul coiled just underneath.

The entire process took barely twenty seconds.

Sarah rubbed her arms and suppressed a shiver. She couldn't allow herself to lose it over one face getting ripped off its body. Hopefully Curly could tell them how to do the same to Mai Luan.

CHAPTER TWENTY-ONE

Despite all the centuries I have studied them, I still cannot imagine what it must be like for mortals, limited to just one life as they are.

~Shahrokh, head of the facetaker council

irene slipped the dispossessed face under a cushion on a nearby couch.

"He won't suffocate?" Sarah asked.

Dalal laughed. *"You never used to keep fools around, Gregorios. You're growing soft."*

"Shut up." He banged her face on the edge of the table.

With eyes still burning purple, Eirene pushed Curly's still-pale soulmask onto the body. It sank into the skull and flesh flowed up over it to seal it into position. For a moment, the face shook like Jell-O as the soulmask bonded to the bone structure and altered it slightly to better fit the contours of its profile. Then the entire body began convulsing as the new soul connected.

Sarah remembered that part all too well from the time Dr. Maerwynn had transferred her soul from the body of a china doll. Every transfer before that, she'd been drugged, awakening in the new host.

That first moment when every cell, every nerve, connected with her consciousness had nearly overwhelmed her the one time she'd been awake for it. Tomas had explained that the longer the soul was dispossessed, the greater the shock. She had no idea how long Curly had been away from a body, but he recovered from the shock quickly.

The man lay quietly and appeared to be sleeping. Sarah had worried he'd start screaming or struggle against the bonds, but he made no move. Gregorios dropped Dalal's soulmask in the soul coffin and locked it.

Tomas checked Curly and said, "I think the alcohol in that host is going to be a problem."

Eirene placed fingers along Curly's jawline, under his eyes, and in the center of his forehead. Her eyes glowed softly purple and she held her fingers there for several seconds. Curly gave a start, and his eyes blinked open.

"I've blocked some of the input links," Eirene said. "His muscles will still perform sluggishly, but his mind should function."

They gave Curly a few minutes to recover while Eirene repeatedly checked his vitals. Finally, she said, "He's as stable as he's going to be without weeks of rest."

Gregorios crouched next to the man, who they propped against the couch. "Can you hear me?"

Curly started to laugh, a manic sound that raised goose-bumps along Sarah's arms. His face might have looked handsome on a better body, but at the moment it looked a bit lopsided, as if not quite working properly.

Gregorios and Eirene took turns prodding him with gentle questions. After several minutes of crazed laughter and incomprehensible babble, he began to sound a little more coherent. He rocked back and forth without seeming to be aware of the movement and started to speak in broken sentences.

They learned that he was indeed an occultist, who had worked with Dalal on the island project researching runes of enhancement. Sarah didn't know what island they were talking about. She'd ask Tomas about it later.

Eirene showed him the close-up photos of the runes on the machine. Curly stopped moving, his eyes widened in fear, and he clamped his mouth firmly shut.

"Tell me about the runes," Eirene pressed.

He shook his head violently.

Gregorios leaned forward. "Very well. If you won't talk, we'll put you back in the box with Dalal."

Curly screamed a long, tortured sound, then snarled at Gregorios, "You're unworthy to see them, to touch them! The runes of ancient power are sacred."

"Why?"

Curly's voice dropped to a hissing whisper and his eyes bulged in their sockets. "The grand masters will destroy you all!"

Gregorios slapped him. That shocked him back to something almost resembling sanity.

"Talk," Gregorios growled, his expression turning so grim that Sarah feared what he'd do to Curly next.

Curly shrank back from Gregorios's wrath, whimpering with fear.

Eirene moved between them, her expression kind. "I know you've suffered a lot. Tell me what you know, and I'll make sure the suffering stops."

Curly sagged with relief and whispered, "The runes enhance the machine."

Gregorios shifted farther back while Eirene continued the interrogation. His rage vanished and he winked at Sarah.

After almost an hour of questioning Curly, who repeatedly slipped into incoherence, Eirene leaned forward and placed glowing fingers on his face again. "Thank you. Why don't you sleep now?"

His eyes drooped as he succumbed to the influence of the alcohol in his system.

Eirene sat back. "He won't wake up any time soon."

"Did that make sense to you?" Sarah asked.

"Some."

Gregorios said, "Either those runes can actually affect the reversal of at least some soul fragmentation, or Mai Luan's convinced the council that they can."

Eirene said, "More interesting were the tidbits about accessing memories. He more or less confirmed my theory that the person wearing the second helmet can drive back through the memories of the person wearing the first helmet. I believe Mai Luan was using me to fine-tune the process. When she perfects it, she'll control access to the victim's entire life history."

Tomas said, "Two functions blended, but the council only sees one."

Sarah asked, "So what's the danger to the council if the promise is a lie?"

"Severe soul fragmentation. Even with mortals, that gets ugly," Gregorios said.

"The ones we don't put down right away usually end up making a huge mess," Tomas agreed.

Gregorios said, "Even facetakers feel the effects eventually."

"Like strange memories in your head?" she asked.

"Exactly. Those are early symptoms."

"Usually degrades to psychosis. Think Jack the Ripper," Tomas added.

"Just like Irina's nervous breakdown." Sarah thought back to one of the models she'd known who'd disappeared from the program.

Tomas nodded. "Yes, she snapped and had to be put down. The same should have happened to you, but it looks like they improved the technology enough to keep you going longer."

"Now they've perfected it," Eirene said.

Gregorios frowned, looking immensely frustrated. "I should've recognized the danger. I had just put down the last council member who broke the consistency barrier before Asoka set me up."

"What's the consistency barrier?" Sarah asked, struggling to keep up with the flow of new information.

"It's the point where the integrity of the soul passes the point of no return. It's the point where mental dissipation and soul fragmentation leave a person broken, with too many gaps filled with bits and pieces of lives from their hosts' previous owners. At that point, be they mortal or facetaker, they have to be put down."

"You think they've been hovering at that point since the nineteen-forties?" Eirene asked.

"It has to be. I would've seen the signs. It was my job to remove them when they broke down. They saw me as a threat. That finally explains Berlin."

"They've hunted you for the past century, colluded in sealing me in a coffin for years, and gave their souls into the keeping of Mai Luan all out of a desperate attempt to prolong their final lives," Eirene said angrily.

"I think so," Gregorios said softly, his expression grim.

"So you think the new machine can actually reverse the process and restore their mental health?" Sarah asked.

"Potentially. It must do enough to appear convincing," Gregorios said.

"If it really can . . ." Eirene said, voice tinged with awe.

"There's nothing stopping us from living forever."

Tomas said, "The only problem is that Mai Luan's cui dashi. It's clear she's concealing the second function from them."

Gregorios nodded. "She needs something from them. She has access to the council. If she wanted to hurt them she could just detonate a bomb."

"No, she wants to strip their minds first, take every secret." Eirene said. "Then she'll kill them."

Sarah asked the biggest question they all seemed to be ignoring. "So?"

"What was that, dear?" Eirene asked.

"Why are you so worried about it? I mean, aren't they trying to kill you? Why do we care if they do something stupid and Mai Luan kills them?"

She surprised herself more than a little with the callous tone of her voice. She feared Mai Luan more than any living being, and she knew the cui dashi scared the others too. It made no sense to risk their lives for the council unless the council could eradicate Mai Luan for them.

Gregorios shook his head slowly. "It's not so easy. First, the council is involved in other things, and destroying them would have negative consequences on a global scale."

"Plus, I guarantee Mai Luan is worse," Eirene added. "Blocking whatever knowledge she seeks to gain through this elaborate scheme will prove well worth it for our own well-being."

The logic made sense, but it still felt like they were taking on more risk than they should. It seemed unfair they worried about the safety of people who had treated them so badly.

"There has to be more to those runes than Curly told us," Tomas said.

Gregorios sighed. "I agree. That's the key to the entire question, but it presents a problem."

Eirene grew very serious, her gaze fixed on Gregorios. "You're suggesting we take a terrible risk."

"What?" Sarah asked. She still felt like she hadn't understood half of what they were saying.

"We? Are you really sure you want to go there after all these years?" Gregorios asked.

"I had hoped to put it off another century or so."

"At least."

Eirene said, "But we need to know, and they're the only source of information."

"Who?" Sarah asked again, starting to feel frustrated.

"The Hunters."

"Like the NRA?" Sarah asked.

Gregorios barked a laugh and Eirene cracked a smile.

"No," Tomas said through his own grin. "Different type of hunters. Best rune experts in the world. If anyone knows what those markings mean, they will."

"Why is that a risk?"

"They've sworn to kill us," Eirene said.

"Well, me in particular," Gregorios added.

Sarah wasn't sure she wanted to ask why again. It seemed everyone who knew Gregorios wanted to kill him eventually.

"You'll need to offer them something notable to survive long enough to ask their help," Eirene said.

Gregorios smiled. "I have just the thing."

"That's your favorite toy," Eirene said, sounding surprised.

"I don't see another choice." Gregorios rose. "It's settled. We're going to Jerusalem."

"By way of Sweden," Eirene added.

Sarah crossed her arms. "I'm not going anywhere until you explain what you're talking about."

CHAPTER TWENTY-TWO

Being deeply loved by someone, no matter which life you are living, gives you strength, while loving someone deeply gives you courage.

~Lao Tzu

Sarah didn't have to go anywhere.

The two facetakers left within the hour, however. Sarah and Tomas would stay in Rome while the others went to find the hunters. She tried not to think about the fact that Mai Luan was in the same city. Tomas had said the safe house was secure so she'd trust him.

Besides, the best camouflage she could think of while in Rome was visiting all the historical sites along with millions of other tourists. She asked Tomas about the hunters Gregorios and Eirene were going to see.

"They're a tight-knit group based out of Jerusalem."

"They're Jewish?"

"No. At least, I don't think so. But they've lived within the Jewish community since the nation was restored. They have ties with the Jews that date all the way back to the time of Moses."

"How is that possible?"

He smiled. "With everything you've seen, you still wonder about things like that?"

"How long have you lived?"

"I'm not a facetaker. I'm not on my first life any longer, but I'm not nearly as old as they are." Admitting even that much seemed to be difficult for him.

"Have you ever been married?" She tried to keep her tone casual, but the words came out a little tense.

"I thought we were talking about the hunters?" he said with a smile that didn't quite hide the worry in his eyes.

She let him change the subject. For now. "So tell me about them."

They sat together on one of the couches and he explained that the hunters were descended from the family that founded the order way back in ancient days. Their primary purpose was to hunt the heka, or kashaph, as they called them. They considered it a divine calling to rid the world of those evil powers. They were a secretive, patriarchal order, whose family line was one of the oldest in the world.

"That's incredible," Sarah said. She felt deeply curious about the hunters as she considered Mai Luan. Ridding the world of people like her would indeed be a worthy life cause, albeit a dangerous one.

Tomas explained that they had developed contacts and alliances all over the world. They were well-trained, exceptional fighters, skilled in dealing with the devilry the kashaph conjured through their rounon symbols.

"So if facetakers hate heka too, why do the hunters want to kill Gregorios and Eirene?"

"Well, they also consider facetakers to be devils incarnate, possessed with an evil power that needs to be eradicated."

"Oh." That made things difficult.

"They're not always at open war with the facetakers. It's a complex relationship, but in the last century it's soured, particularly where Gregorios and Eirene are concerned."

"Why?"

"Eirene's issues with them date back to the second World War, and I don't know the specifics, but they swore vengeance on Gregorios after a hunter failed to assassinate him."

"Wait a minute, if they were trying to assassinate him, where do they get off getting angry when he killed the guy trying to take him out?"

"Gregorios didn't kill the hunter. He returned the assassin's soulmask to Jerusalem in a box."

Sarah grimaced. Those were the people Gregorios was going to see?

"So why risk it?"

"They're experts at runes. No one, not even most heka, know so much. If anyone can decipher what Mai Luan is planning with that machine of hers, it'll be them."

Sarah thought about that for a minute, but only worried more than ever for Gregorios's and Eirene's safety.

"So I guess we're stuck in Rome for a couple days," she said to change the topic. She'd love to enjoy a little down-time with Tomas, just be tourists for a couple days and not deal with arcane problems until the facetakers returned.

"What would you like to do tonight?"

Sarah beamed. "You're the local. Surprise me."

They dressed up and headed out for a sumptuous dinner at La Pergola restaurant, located at the elegant Rome Cavalieri Hotel. The interior was gorgeous, with antiques and famous works of art. Tomas somehow scored a table near one of the enormous windows with breathtaking views as the sun set.

Sarah drank in the sight of the city, with St. Peter's glowing in the distance, then gave Tomas a wide smile.

"Will this do?" he asked.

"It's amazing. I'm surprised we were able to get in."

"There's usually a long wait list, but I know the owner."

"Really? How?"

Tomas dipped a piece of soft bread into olive oil and saluted with it. "It's a long story. I helped his grandfather out of a tight spot a while back. I've been friends with the family ever since."

"How far back?"

His smile faded. She could tell he was nervous about talking about his past, but he'd have to find the courage to discuss it if he wanted their relationship to go anywhere. For now she'd enjoy the evening. Maybe once he relaxed more he'd be willing to share.

The meal was delicious. By the time they left a couple hours later, Sarah was so full she could barely move. So they decided to walk for a while and took a slow tour through some of the downtown landmarks. She didn't comment on the fact that the waiter hadn't asked Tomas for any payment.

The Trevi Fountain took her breath away. It was bigger than she had imagined, and the soft lights illuminating Neptune and the sculpted horses concealed much of the wear they'd suffered through the centuries. She could imagine herself standing in ancient Rome, enjoying the same spectacular view.

Then a police car passed, siren wailing. The sound reminded Sarah of the dangerous situation they were still embroiled in, triggering a rush of fear. It brought to mind the unexpected, violent attack on the highway in New Orleans, the shock she'd felt at the brutality of the close combat with enhanced heka in the hotel, and worry for Eirene's safety. They'd rescued Eirene, but the danger was far from gone. Mai Luan moved in the same city. She could be anywhere, could be watching them that moment.

Sarah suddenly felt exposed. They shouldn't be walking the streets of Rome, pretending all was well when it so clearly wasn't. Everywhere she turned, she glimpsed another ancient pillar or church that dated back to the Middle Ages, or older, but she couldn't recapture the sense of wonder she'd felt earlier. Nowhere in the States that she had ever visited radiated such a weight of history, but she wished they'd stayed in the safe house. She couldn't enjoy it now.

They paused on the Spanish Steps, and she forced herself to buy a gelato, fulfilling a lifelong dream dating back to the first time she ever watched Roman Holiday. She barely tasted it.

She leaned against Tomas while they sat on the steps. "It's been a good night, hasn't it?"

"I think so," he said, but his voice sounded distracted.

She turned to him, but found him scanning the crowd, a little frown on his face.

"What is it?"

He pulled her to her feet and led the way up the long stair. "We're being followed."

She knew it. This was such a bad idea.

Before she could turn and look around, he wrapped an arm around her shoulders and whispered to keep going. She enjoyed having him hold her, but the motivation was terrible.

At the top of the steps, he flagged down a taxi and they piled in. He changed the destination four times, which sent them criss-crossing the city before he finally asked the annoyed driver to pull over at the corner of a shadowed piazza. He gave the man a big tip, but the taxi still sped off with a spin of tires.

"Are you sure we should get out in a place like this?" she asked. The shadows seemed longer than they had in the taxi, and the relative quiet and lack of other people heightened her sense of fear. Wasn't the cardinal rule of traveling to always stay around other people for safety?

Tomas led her at a trot down a shadowed path through the piazza. Instead of continuing to the far side, where lights from another busy road beckoned to Sarah with the promise of safety, he turned off the path.

"Where are you going?" Sarah asked as Tomas approached a darkened building. Like so many others in Rome, the three-story structure sported a columned portico. Tomas pulled her into the pitch darkness behind one of the columns where they would remain invisible but could still view the piazza.

"I need to know who's following us," he whispered.

On a normal date, he'd have lured her into the darkness for a little romance. If only this was a normal date. She hated the fact that she was wearing a skirt and heels. If they had to run, she'd kick off the useless shoes, but slacks would have been a better choice.

"How do you even know they didn't lose us?"

"I wouldn't have."

"Who do you think they might be?" she asked, trying not to sound as scared as she felt.

"Either they're enforcers or heka."

"Then why would you want to hang around?" Sarah demanded. He had proven he possessed remarkable fighting skills, but this didn't seem like a smart place to plan a showdown.

"To see which group it is," Tomas explained. "If it's the enforcers, that means my cover's been blown and the council's assigned a strike team to remove me."

He said it with such calm acceptance. Sarah admired that, wished she shared his unbreakable calm, and wanted to slap him to get more of a reaction.

Tomas continued. "If it's heka, then Mai Luan's coming after us."

"What if it's both?" Sarah hated asking the question. Why suggest things could get worse?

"I doubt it. She's playing them, and no doubt they've convinced themselves that they're using her. They won't work together, not for something like this."

"So what happens when they show up? Did you bring a gun?"

"A couple," he admitted. "But I don't want to confront them yet, just gather intel."

"Did you bring a scope? That way we could gather intel from farther away."

He chuckled. "Good idea, but no, I left the scopes at home."

A white passenger van stopped in the same place their taxi had moments ago. Several figures jumped out and jogged across the piazza.

Sarah's pulse quickened and every muscle tensed as she pressed herself against a nearby column. She tried to breathe, but found it hard to get any air.

The shadowy figures passed not far from their hiding place without slowing. When they reached the road on the far side, they spread out. A moment later, the same van stopped and they all jumped back in.

After the van sped away, Tomas said, "Heka."

Sarah asked, "How can you tell? I couldn't see any details."

"Didn't need to. Enforcers train as a team. They'd have moved through a place like this in a more organized formation. Those guys moved like a gang. No discipline, no cover. Heka for sure."

"What does that mean?" Sarah asked.

"Mai Luan's on to us. We'll have to be careful, and probably move our base as soon as Gregorios and Eirene return."

Mai Luan was chasing them. Sarah crossed to him and wrapped her arms around his waist. He held her, his head leaning against hers, his gaze locked on the piazza. She suddenly wished Gregorios and Eirene hadn't left. She felt vulnerable.

There had to be a way to change that.

"How do we fight her?" she asked.

Tomas turned to face her. She couldn't see his expression, but his arms tightened around her shoulders. "If it comes to that, we'll pick the time and place. She's dangerous, but not immortal. We've defeated cui dashi before."

"Good." She embraced the anger she felt at Mai Luan for so casually destroying so many lives. Hopefully the shared resolve to defeat her would provide enough motivation for the hunters to help. They needed all the help they could get.

Tomas waited in the shadows ten more minutes. Sarah remained close beside him and they silently held each other in the darkness. It wasn't the romantic moment she might have hoped for, but it was the best they could manage.

Eventually he led her back out to where the taxi had dropped them off, and flagged another one. The entire time they stood exposed at the curb, Sarah scanned nearby shadows, jumping at every sound. A gray van passed, and she clutched Tomas's hand nervously until it faded into the night.

Tomas ordered the taxi to take them to St. Peter's. There they mingled with the crowd while he watched for anyone following them. Sarah scanned the crowds and spotted several suspicious people, but none of them seemed to worry Tomas.

They took four more taxis, each to a different popular attraction, and repeated the process of blending and scanning.

Finally Tomas said, "I don't see anyone. If they're still on to us, they're better than any heka I've faced in decades."

"How many decades?"

Tomas sighed. "Please not now."

"Fine, but don't avoid it forever."

"I won't. I promise. I need to show you something first. Then we'll talk."

She could handle that.

When they returned to the safe house, it didn't feel so safe. What if they'd been followed, despite all Tomas's efforts to confuse any trackers?

Tomas shared her concern, insisting on monitoring the perimeter through a bank of security camera feeds.

Sarah found some pie in the fridge and served up a couple slices. She sat with him for a mind-numbing hour watching the images flip past, and chatting about little things. She realized she'd never just hung out with him. She asked him about places he'd visited, and got more than she'd planned. He'd traveled just about everywhere, and talked easily about different cultures and countries and peoples. He spoke eighteen languages. That was a little intimidating.

He asked her about her family. She didn't like talking about her past, but found herself telling him about her insanely religious parents, their condemnation of any lifestyle that didn't include marriage and as many children as she could handle, all while living on a modest, lower middle class budget.

Tomas gave her an appraising look. "And you overcame that upbringing to become one of the top five body models at Alterego?"

"I got into modeling as a form of rebellion," Sarah admitted. "I wanted to prove to them that I could make my own choices." She tried not to think about the fact that her choices had nearly lost her the only body she'd ever owned. She hated to think anything her parents had browbeaten into her might have had a seed of truth.

So she told Tomas about her three brothers. The two older ones with their large families and blue-collar jobs, and the younger one who was a priest in a protestant church.

"Do you speak with them often?" Tomas asked.

"Not much," Sarah admitted. "I sent money a couple of times. I felt bad to hear about all their bills with those kids. But mom and dad found out and got real angry. They asked me to stop."

"When this is over, you should call them," Tomas urged.

"Why? They don't understand me."

"They're family," he said softly, his expression growing intense. "You won't always have them."

The conversation turned to Eirene and Gregorios. Tomas revealed that Eirene had taken up SCUBA diving and was planning extensive ocean exploration expeditions.

"I've never been diving. Sounds like fun."

"It is. Eirene's traveled the globe many times, but she's never set foot on the bottom of the ocean. The thought appeals to her."

"What about Gregorios?"

"He loves technology," Tomas said with a chuckle. "He's like a little kid with new gadgets. He's getting into mobile app development."

Sarah laughed. "Really? He wants to develop the next Angry Birds or something?"

"No, he's got bigger plans than that," Tomas said, but wouldn't elaborate.

Sarah enjoyed the conversation as it turned to less meaningful topics. Spending time with Tomas like this was really nice, but as the night wore on, the stress of the day caught up with her and her eyes started to droop.

Tomas noticed. He kissed her forehead. "I'm glad dinner wasn't ruined at least."

"I enjoyed it. Thank you," she said, cupping one of his cheeks in her hand and kissing him lightly on the lips. He might not be her boyfriend yet, but he was a good friend, and that left the door open to all sorts of possibilities.

For tonight, that was enough.

CHAPTER TWENTY-THREE

I'm not afraid of death; I just don't want to be there when it happens.
                                        ~Meryem, facetaker council member

Gregorios walked up to a fortified gatehouse in front of a walled compound on the outskirts of Jerusalem. He wore a wide-brimmed hat, a black T-shirt, and commando pants over a powerful young body that had just arrived via special air freight from Sweden. That proved far more efficient than traveling all the way across Europe to pick it up personally.

The wall that stretched away to either side reared over ten feet, made of thick blocks of stone topped with razor wire. He spotted several cameras monitoring the outside. Melek was as paranoid as ever. One of the reasons Gregorios liked him more than most of his ancestors.

The two armed guards at the gate eyed him suspiciously as he approached and one stepped forward to meet him while the second stayed back to cover him. When they demanded identification, he simply extended both hands, palms up, to display tattoos on his forearms.

The man stared in shock. "Reuben?"

Gregorios tipped the brim of his hat up to reveal his face. "I'm here to see Melek."

The guard stumbled back and both he and his companion snapped weapons up to the ready position but didn't fire. Gregorios allowed himself a slightly deeper breath.

First hurdle crossed.

The second guard spoke quickly into his throat mic in Hebrew, but the barrel of his rifle never wavered.

Seconds later the outer gates swung open and two dozen heavily armed men swarmed out to surround Gregorios, military carbines ready. He stood unmoving in the middle of the kill zone. He suppressed the urge to cough. The sudden noise might just trigger a hail of bullets even his enhanced body couldn't absorb.

Eirene spoke into his earpiece. "I can't shoot all of them if they decide to become hostile, love."

He said nothing, but the twitch of his lips into a half smile triggered a chorus of shouted commands to stay where he was. The creaking of leather sounded loud in the night air as the men leaned into their rifles, ready to fire. They were as touchy as he expected.

A solidly built man wearing camouflaged khakis stepped through the crowd. His salt-and-pepper hair was cut military short and although he had to be pushing fifty, he still radiated strength.

"Hello, Melek," Gregorios said.

Melek stopped three paces away, his expression calm but his eyes burning with hatred. He spoke in an angry growl. "How dare you come here?"

"I want to make a deal."

"Then why do you wear the body of my son?" Melek demanded, leaning forward as if on the verge of lunging. "Where have you kept it hidden, demon?"

"In a safe place. It would've been a huge waste to destroy such an excellent specimen."

He hated the idea of handing the body back over to the hunters. It was his favorite battle suit, branded with twelve beautifully customized runes. It was simply one of the most completely enhanced forms Gregorios had ever experienced.

Of course, getting attacked by it had been singularly unpleasant. He wondered if Melek understood just how close his son had come to accomplishing his mission. No one had come closer in almost two thousand years.

With his own body critically injured in the fight, he had taken Reuben's and been thrilled with how well it performed. Since then it became his go-to battle suit, kept in cold storage in Sweden when not in use, concealed in a facility he owned.

"What crimes have you committed while posing as my son?"

Gregorios protested, "I've taken excellent care of this body. I should bill you for the maintenance."

Melek drew a pistol. "And now you come here to taunt me. Did you really think I would allow you to escape, especially while desecrating my son?"

Eirene's voice spoke into his ear, "Not looking good, love. Try something different."

"Listen, we can stand here threatening each other, or I can restore your son. Up to you."

Melek hesitated, pistol by his side. "Why would you offer this after leaving my son in purgatory for so long?"

"In my defense, Reuben attacked me. I spared his life."

"Better to die," Melek said softly.

"I offered him a chance to back down, but he refused."

"Don't you lie to me!" Melek raised the pistol.

"You don't have to believe my version of what happened that day, but believe me when I tell you I didn't come here to fight. I come in good faith, with an honest offer to restore Reuben if you agree to give me a few minutes of your time."

That surprised Melek enough to lower the gun again. "What new devilry is this?"

The man was getting repetitive. "Listen, if I wanted you dead I could've just strapped a bomb to my chest and taken all of you with me."

That triggered a nervous shuffling among the surrounding men.

He continued. "But clearly I didn't do that. We have a bigger problem now. Time to move past the old hates."

"Easy for you to say."

"You think it's easy for me to walk up to this gate and let you surround me?" He smiled. "I appreciate your faith in me."

"Enough of your lies," Melek hissed.

Before Melek could again raise his pistol, Gregorios advanced a step and leaned close to Melek. The man did an impressive job of not retreating but couldn't hide the flicker of fear in his eyes. All the surrounding men leaned forward, fingers on triggers.

"Stop wasting my time," Gregorios growled. "You have a choice to make. Restore your son or kill your enemy. What's it going to be?"

Melek's expression mirrored his internal struggle as reason battled intellect. Thankfully, reason won.

He spoke through clenched teeth. "Come then. Restore my son." He motioned toward the open gate.

Just then, a young man rushed out through the gate, still donning his jacket. He looked to be in his mid-twenties. Tall, dark haired and in excellent condition. "Let me kill him father!"

Eirene's voice whispered into Gregorios' ear, "So much like his great grandfather."

"Not yet, Alter," Melek said without turning.

Alter raised a pistol he carried in his right hand. "Why not? He's right there! I'll do it."

"He's wearing Reuben's body."

Alter gasped, then snarled with rage, "He's mocking us and you stand there doing nothing? Kill him!"

"Son, wait—"

Alter settled into a shooting stance, pistol aimed at Gregorios head, finger already pulling the trigger.

The gun snapped out of his hand and he yelped in pain, clutching his bleeding hand to his chest. They never heard the report from Eirene's suppressed rifle.

Gregorios said, "I would've expected a son of yours to show a little more discipline, Melek."

Alter took an angry step forward, but Melek motioned him back. "Stand down, Son." Then he turned to Gregorios, "I trust there will be no other injuries."

"That's up to you."

Alter approached Melek. "Father, why don't you kill him?"

"He's going to restore your brother."

"He's a liar, Father. Don't believe him."

"He claims to have come in good faith. We will prove him." Melek gestured to Gregorios, "Come, I'll take you to my son."

Gregorios chuckled. "Not like this."

"I told you! Give me a gun," Alter cried.

"You will keep your word," Melek said angrily, "or you will die right now."

"I always keep my word, but I cannot restore your son to this body unless I have another available to transfer to, can I?"

"What do you have in mind?" Melek asked slowly, expression and voice radiating distrust.

"Like I said earlier. I'm here because we have a greater threat to deal with."

"Like what?"

"When's the last time you faced a cui dashi?"

Another murmur rippled through the crowd. "Those demons were exterminated."

"Apparently not. And this one is more dangerous than most."

"Why is this our problem?" Melek asked.

"You're hunters. It's what you do."

"And your council fields teams of enforcers. Or are they too busy still hunting you?"

"There are other complications. I need your help."

That generated more whispers, and hunters exchanged incredulous looks. Gregorios cautiously pulled a bundle of photos from his pocket and extended them. Melek accepted them and risked a glance. Then he looked again.

"Where did you get these?"

"They're inscribed on a machine."

"What machine?"

"Like I said, complications. I'll give you the details when we meet to restore Reuben."

"Meet?"

"You're a man of honor, but I think it prudent to meet at a more neutral location. I restore Reuben and you tell me about those runes."

Alter interrupted. "Don't let him go, Father. We'll never see him again."

Melek looked torn. He glanced from Gregorios to the photos again. "When?"

"Tonight. Northeast side of the city. Near the Hebrew University is a cozy little garden." He extended another piece of paper. "Specific directions. Come alone."

Melek took the paper. "If you betray me in this, every resource we possess will be dedicated to the single task of destroying you and everyone you love."

"Get your homework done. I'll see you tonight."

He winked at Alter. The young man snarled, hands balled into fists, but a warning look from his father kept him in his place. Gregorios walked away. The circle parted and he forced himself to move confidently, despite all the rifles pointing at his back.

In his ear, Eirene whispered, "You think they'll try to double cross us tonight?"

"I'd be disappointed if they didn't."

CHAPTER TWENTY-FOUR

A growing worry has been plaguing my sleep these past months. We have stood against the tide of evil threatening to consume the world for forty centuries. Yet still I fear we may not be enough to keep the world from tipping over the brink. A new evil lurks in the shadows, a threat laughed away for decades.

I cannot shake the chill certainty that we have allowed it to grow until it is too strong to stop. We will fight it with the strength of our very souls, but will it be enough?

~Melek

Gregorios hated waiting.

It shouldn't have bothered him anymore, but it did. Despite so much experience, he still found himself growing impatient. Some things just didn't get easier with time.

He stood beside a simple cot set up in a small garden on the outskirts of Jerusalem. Night had settled over the city, cloaking the world in shadow, although enough light reflected from nearby buildings to keep the area in perpetual twilight. The garden was a private oasis surrounded by city, with clear visibility to all avenues of approach.

Gregorios wore his regular body again. He hated swapping out of the battle suit because everything else he wore always felt weak and slow for the first few hours afterward. Reuben's body lay on the cot.

Eirene's voice spoke into his ear. "Incoming. Single male. Not Melek. Looks like Alter."

They didn't wait long to spring the first surprise. He wondered how they would justify the double-cross. The hunters were implacable enemies but held to a strict code of honor that could usually be counted on.

Alter approached on the paved path leading to the garden, carrying a box about the size of a soul coffin, and a manila folder. His hand was already healed.

Good rune work. His soul was probably already bonded to almost as many runes as Reuben's had been.

"Where's your father?"

Alter faced Gregorios proudly. "I stand for him. We cannot risk him alone with a demon."

Typical foolishness. "Are you qualified to explain those runes?"

"I am one of the leading runesmiths in the clan."

"Hard times, huh?"

Alter bristled. "Restore my brother or I'll kill you now."

"Show me what you brought."

Alter flipped open the manila envelope to reveal enlarged photos of the runes, with typed words beside each one. "I have the information you seek."

He snapped the envelope closed but didn't hand it over. "You get it once Reuben is restored."

"Fair enough." Gregorios resisted the temptation to snatch the envelope away from Alter, but then they'd fight and he might have to resort to removing another of Melek's son's soulmasks. It wasn't worth the hassle.

"Some of these runes are very ancient," Alter added, his voice a little less belligerent. "Where did you find them?"

"Let's deal with your brother. Then we'll talk about the runes."

Inside the box rested Reuben's soulmask. It was partially shrunken, but the rainbow mist still glowed with vibrant colors.

"You've taken good care of him."

"He is blood."

"Good. That improves his chances for full recovery."

Gregorios lifted the soulmask and it triggered a flood of mostly unpleasant memories. "Hello, Reuben. You're looking well, all things considered."

The whisper voice drifted up to him. "*I will kill you, demon.*"

"Relax. I'm restoring your body tonight. You'll be a little shaky at first, so don't try anything taxing. We have a truce at the moment, so don't make me regret it."

Alter said, "You've damaged my brother's honor enough, demon. Don't taunt him again."

Gregorios said, "I spared his life when I had every right to take it. Don't ever forget that."

He sometimes wondered why he had spared Reuben. The young hunter was arrogant, a deadly enemy. But he descended from an honorable family line, and Eirene would have urged Gregorios to show mercy. The things he did for his wife.

Alter opened his mouth to make another angry reply but Gregorios cut him off. "Hush now. I have work to do."

He positioned the face over the blank head and embraced his nevra core. His eyes and hands began to glow, and under the influence of his nevron, the soulmask expanded slowly and the rainbow mist started to pulse beneath it. He glanced at Alter and found the young man leaning forward, fists clenched, as if barely containing the urge to leap upon him. If the boy made a rash move, Melek would lose a second son.

As Gregorios began to press the soulmask into place, Alter asked, "What rune are you using?"

Gregorios didn't pause, but spoke even as the skin began flowing over the soulmask to seal it to the body. "I don't use runes, boy."

Alter approached. "What are you doing? It's masked well. I can barely feel it."

"You probably feel something triggering in his body. He has more runes than most."

Impressive that the boy could sense anything at all. Gregorios would not directly trigger the runes. That would happen as Reuben's soul sealed with the body and reactivated the runes. He wouldn't have expected anyone to sense anything so quickly or without physical contact.

"No, it's not that," Alter protested.

Gregorios glanced at Alter again. Maybe they could find time later to discuss what he was feeling. It wasn't normal, and anything unusual where the hunters were concerned was worth investigating. As the skin settled and Reuben gasped his first breath, Gregorios snapped, "Take his legs, quick."

He used his weight to pin Reuben's torso and hands.

Alter reacted a little too slow, still protesting about the runes. Reuben's body convulsed as his long-dispossessed soul connected with a physical form for the first time in years. Every muscle shook and his legs shot out and caught Alter in the stomach. The boy grunted but didn't go down. He threw himself back on top of his older brother and held on tight.

The spasm passed after only about twenty seconds. Gregorios didn't bother pointing out to Alter how unusual that was. Better the boy didn't think about it. As Reuben's body quieted and his breathing settled to a normal rhythm, Gregorios retreated a couple of steps.

Reuben sat up clumsily and Alter embraced him. "Welcome back, Brother!"

"You've grown so much, little brother."

Reuben hugged him back, but his arms were not working very well yet. After such a long dispossession his limbs would feel stiff and asleep. Many people couldn't handle being restored after years, but Reuben had been cared for very well by his family. Gregorios gave him a fifty-fifty chance of regaining his full faculties and not just flipping out into a psycho.

Then again, maybe he was just optimistic.

Reuben shattered the tender moment by speaking in what he probably hoped was a whisper but came out as a shout. "Come, Brother, together we can kill . . ."

His words trailed off into a garbled whisper and he slumped back onto the stretcher.

Alter shook him and called his name but got no response. "What happened?"

"Oh, he'll be all right," Eirene said brightly as she stepped out of the shadows of a tree not far away. She dressed in form-fitting black pants, hair tied in a simple ponytail, just a hint of make-up, and a royal blue shirt with a scoop neck. The outfit was calculated to make men like Alter underestimate her even though she carried a dart gun loosely in one hand.

From the look on Alter's face, it was working. He stared at her, clearly confused. Was she an enemy or a lost college student?

"Who are you?"

"Insurance." She pulled a small dart out of Reuben's leg. "The box I got that dart from says he'll sleep for a few hours. Might have a headache when he wakes up."

Alter frowned. "A single dart wouldn't affect him."

Eirene patted Reuben's head with a gentle touch. "He's a tough one, is he?"

Gregorios refused to laugh and ruin Eirene's work, but it was a struggle. She had completely thrown Alter off balance.

"Your brother's been dispossessed for quite a while," she said. "It'll take a few hours for his soul to fully connect with his body and bond anew with all those runes. He'll be fine."

Eirene stuck the dart gun into the front of her pants and extended a hand that Alter took out of pure reflex. "It's a pleasure, Alter." She cocked her head to one side. "Has anyone told you lately just how much you look like your great grandfather?"

"How could you possibly know that?" Alter looked her up and down, still holding her hand. "You can't be more than twenty."

Eirene laughed and patted his cheek. "You're so sweet. Your family is not unknown to me."

"I would've remembered meeting you," he said with a warm smile.

"I last saw your great grandfather long before you were born." Her eyes grew distant and her smile faded. "I am far older than I look."

"Who are you?"

She gave him a dazzling smile. "I'm Eirene."

Alter snatched his hand away as if stung and stumbled back with a cry of surprise. "You can't be. Not the Mistress of Darkness!"

"Oh, I like that." She beamed at Gregorios. "We should add that to our Christmas cards this year."

She pulled out a smartphone and started typing away like crazy.

Alter frowned. "What are you doing?"

"I'm updating my profile with that right now. Do you have any idea how incredible social media is? I'm out of the loop for a few years and suddenly the world gets connected."

"Uh, I don't use any social media," Alter said slowly, craning his neck to see what she was doing, without drawing any closer.

"Good for you," Eirene said, fingers still flying. "Your father is a very wise man. If he let you on those sites, you'd have new girls knocking on your door every day."

"Really?" Alter perked up.

Gregorios interrupted. "While Reuben's napping, why don't you tell us about those runes? We have a long way to go and not much time."

Alter lifted a radio. "I'll summon my cousins to bear Reuben home. I'll explain about the runes while we travel."

So he did have some more surprises of his own.

Gregorios shook his head. "Your job is only to explain the runes."

"No, my job is to study them. I'll explain what I can of these that you brought, but I must gain access to the machine."

"I don't think that's a good idea," Gregorios said.

Alter stood his ground. "You warned us a cui dashi has risen. Armed with these runes, they could do much harm. I need to know what their plans are if we are to stop them."

"We?"

"As you said, you need help. I'm it."

CHAPTER TWENTY-FIVE

To the well-organized mind, death is but the next soul transfer.

~Queen Elizabeth I

S arah slept in and found Tomas had prepared an impressive breakfast when she woke.

"Good morning," he greeted her enthusiastically. She doubted he slept much the night before, but he looked more chipper than he had in the past few days. "What would you like to do today?"

"Not get chased," she said hopefully.

He saluted with a glass of orange juice. "I'll do my best."

His good humor was infectious and by the time they finished breakfast, she was willing to risk another excursion on the town. The sights of Rome were too tempting to resist for long. They started by visiting the Colosseum, and Sarah could have spent half the day at the ancient arena. It was bigger up close than she had anticipated, towering over them and instilling a sense of awe. Those weathered stones held such a wealth of history, she wished she could explore even the restricted areas.

"Maybe another time," Tomas had said.

"Really?"

"We'll see."

As they passed the Arch of Constantine, Tomas made an obscene gesture at the beautiful arch just as Gregorios had the first night they arrived in Rome.

"Why do you all do that?"

He shrugged. "It's a tradition Eirene takes very seriously. I just do it to support her."

So Sarah flipped off the Arch too.

They visited the Parthenon next and then the catacombs. She wished he had chosen something besides those creepy tunnels lined with dead people, and she gladly moved on to the Roman Forum. She loved the forum, although she felt a little sad walking through the skeleton of what must have been an incredible sight in its day.

Tomas said, "We'll have to get Eirene to show us around another time. She can tell you all about the ruins."

"She didn't actually live in Rome, did she?"

"You sure you want to know?"

Sarah hesitated for just a moment. "Yes."

Tomas nodded. "She was born in the early days of the republic."

"That's like two thousand years ago," Sarah whispered.

"More. The republic started in the eighth century B.C. and she lived through most of it, and from there right through the empire."

"I can hardly believe it."

"It takes a while. Gregorios is even older."

Sarah wondered about that as they continued the tour. What must it be like to have lived for so long? There were so many interesting historical figures. How many of them had they met? Did they meet Jesus Christ, or Julius Caesar, or Queen Elizabeth? The possibilities seemed endless. She and Eirene needed to sit down and talk for a month when the facetakers got back.

They returned to the safe house after lunch at an open-air cafe and Sarah gave Tomas a long kiss. "That was a great morning."

"I'm glad you enjoyed it."

Then he got that nervous look in his eye again and her plans for the afternoon began to look shaky. "What's wrong?"

"Nothing," he lied. "It's just, there's something I need to show you."

"Good. Show me." He had said that after he showed her 'something,' he'd tell her about his past. She was looking forward to that conversation.

He surprised her by taking her hands and saying, "First I have to run to the office."

"The Suntara headquarters?"

"Yes."

"Are you crazy?"

"I'll be fine," he assured her. "It won't take long but it's really important."

"How can you say that? You said yourself your cover's probably blown, and there's no one around to help if you get into trouble."

"It's a risk," he admitted. "But it has to be done."

"Why?"

He hesitated. "It'll make sense when I get back."

She wondered if she'd ever understand him. "I don't think it's a good idea."

"I know, but it's necessary."

"So you keep saying." She hated thinking of him walking into a potentially dangerous situation, but it was clear he was determined. She kissed his cheek. "Well don't take too long."

He squeezed her hands a final time and left. Sarah dropped into a padded chair and flipped on the television. She found a great tourist channel discussing all the best tourist sites, and started taking notes on other places she would make him take her. She would hold him to his promise or they were in for a very rocky day.

Occasionally, she glanced at the soul coffin that held Dalal. That woman was a piece of work. They had sent the drunk on his way the day before and stuck Curly's face in one of the closets under a pile of towels. She tried not to think about how wrong it was that those facts didn't even bother her any more.

Barely an hour later, Tomas rushed back in through the door. She had expected him to take a lot longer.

He looked worried.

As soon as he spotted her he called, "Grab your bag. Hurry."

She chased him into the kitchen where he pulled a keyboard out of a recessed cupboard and began typing furiously, his face intent as he scanned the security monitors.

"What's wrong? Did the facetakers figure out it was you?"

"No. Never made it to the office. I spotted a tail and circled back around."

"You led them here?"

"I think I lost them, but I wanted to make sure you were safe." He gripped her hand tight. "If they knew where to start tailing me, they might've come for you too."

"You think it's Mai Luan's guys again?"

"Most likely. We have to hurry. This location may be compromised."

That was a terrifying thought, confirming Sarah's fears from the night before. She rushed to her room to grab up her belongings and returned to the kitchen four minutes later with everything packed.

Tomas was there, a couple of bags at his feet as he again focused on the outside monitors. One bag was his backpack, and the other was a large black duffel packed with weapons, cash and a bunch of other gear. The sight of it drove home just how serious he considered the risk.

"What about Dalal and—"

A loud beep cut her off and a flashing light appeared on his monitor.

Tomas muttered a curse. "Grab the coffin. Hurry!"

She rushed into the living room and snatched it up. Tomas shoved it into his duffel. The monitor showed a view of the enclosed courtyard just outside the front door. A group of tough-looking men were entering the courtyard, pulling out weapons. She'd spent enough time at shooting ranges to recognize automatic rifles with suppressors.

Tomas typed a command and slapped the Enter key. On the screen, orange clouds of smoke suddenly billowed into the courtyard from three sides, enveloping the men.

"If they're not enhanced, that'll stop them," he said.

"But they're probably enhanced?"

He nodded and the worry already knotting her stomach spiked to full-blown fear.

Tomas typed a couple more commands and nodded with satisfaction. "Let's go."

Instead of heading for the back door, he led her into the bathroom.

"I don't think hiding in the bathtub is a good idea," she said.

"Trust me."

He pushed on the sink. It rolled aside, lower cupboard and all, like it was set on hidden wheels, revealing a dark, narrow stair leading down. He grabbed a pair of flashlights attached to the wall, handed one to her, and led the way down.

The sink rolled back into place behind them.

"What is this place?"

"Back door."

They followed the stairs down quite a ways to a long tunnel lined with stone. He stopped at a series of lockers recessed into the wall and punched in a combination. One of the doors popped open and he extracted a shotgun that was so short it had to be illegal. He hefted it and pulled a bandoleer of extra shells over one shoulder.

"Ever use one of these?"

"Not that model, but I've shot shotguns. I don't like the recoil."

"KSG. Fifteen rounds. Best weapon for close encounters."

It probably kicked like a mule. She was relieved she wouldn't be the one carrying it. Tomas extracted a pistol from the locker and handed it to her along with three spare magazines and a paddle holster to clip to her belt. "Forty-five. Can you handle it?"

"If I need to. Have any Tasers?" She preferred something non-lethal, but took the handgun when he shook his head. She was comfortable with guns, but had never dreamed of actually needing to shoot anyone. With the weight of the gun dragging at her belt, she prayed they could escape unseen.

A muffled *wump* sounded behind and above them. She felt it through her shoes as much as her ears, and dust drifted down from the ceiling.

"What was that?"

"They're enhanced. Breached the main door. The apartment is set with explosive charges. Hopefully that'll slow them long enough for us to get away."

They'd been sleeping surrounded by explosives? No wonder he had a hard time relaxing.

The fact that explosives were only enough to *slow* their pursuers ratcheted her fear higher. She clutched Tomas's hand as he led her along the dim passage by the light of their flashlights. Thankfully it only took another minute to reach the far end of the tunnel that ended in another staircase. A steel door blocked the top, and Tomas typed a code in a keypad set in the wall. A small terminal glowed to life, showing both sides of a narrow alley.

"Looks clear. Let's go."

He pushed open the door and led the way into the alley, shotgun at the ready. Sarah followed close behind, carrying the heavy bags. They slipped along the stifling alley that reeked of heater exhaust and rotting trash.

Sarah tried not to pant, but her heart was racing and her hands felt clammy on the straps of the bags. She silently urged Tomas to hurry.

Just before they reached the end of the alley, four men rushed around the corner in front of Tomas. The two in front skidded to a halt and raised carbines, but their companions collided with them and threw off their aim. Bullets tore chunks out of the wall near Sarah's head.

They were carrying AK-47s with the stocks and barrels chopped to illegal lengths, and suppressors screwed onto the barrels. The rapid-fire reports still sounded terribly loud so close and in the confines of the alley.

Tomas was already returning fire.

He fired his stubby shotgun so fast the gun made a continuous roar that pounded against Sarah's ears so hard she shrieked, dropped the bags, and clamped hands over her ears. The hail of buckshot blasted the first two attackers into their companions. Even as the second pair tried to return fire, Tomas flicked a little lever on the shotgun and resumed firing until all four men lay sprawled and bloody on the ground.

The entire confrontation took barely five seconds.

Sarah stared at the grisly mess as Tomas kicked the men over and pulled up their shirts. The men all wore slender packs, which he yanked off and tossed down the alley.

"Are they dead?"

"No. They're occans, so their fueling souls would've already started healing them. They should stay out for a while."

Sarah snatched up the fallen bags while Tomas paused just long enough to shove more shells into the twin loading tubes at the base of the stubby shotgun. Then he led the way around the corner into the backyard, gun held low and ready.

A huge fist knocked the gun aside and a second one smashed into Tomas's face. The shotgun fired wildly into the back fence as it flew out of his hands. He tumbled to the ground, knocked right off his feet.

A giant of a man came around the corner and kicked Tomas in the ribs before he could rise. Tomas managed to get his legs up to block, but the blow sent him rolling several feet.

Before the huge attacker could close on him, Tomas lunged to his feet, a long knife in his hand.

The big fighter drew his own knife. It was long, with a serrated upper edge.

Sarah shot him in the back.

He staggered, and she kept firing, her arms locked into the shooting position she'd practiced so many times. She screamed as she fired, hating the sight of blood spurting from the man's back as she gunned him down.

The slide of her gun locked back, empty. She hadn't realized she'd fired so many times. While she fumbled for another magazine, Tomas kicked the huge attacker to the ground and removed his soul pack. When the man groped for his leg, Tomas kicked him in the head a couple of times.

"That was amazing," he said when he turned to her.

Sarah managed to holster her pistol without dropping it, despite the shaking of her hands. She felt sick by what she'd done. Knowing she hadn't killed the man helped, but she couldn't believe she just did that.

"Aren't you full of surprises?" The familiar voice spun her around.

Mai Luan stood at the corner of the alley, flanked by four more armed heka.

CHAPTER TWENTY-SIX

I shall not do more than I can, and I shall do all I can to save the government, which is my sworn duty as well as my personal inclination. We must stand against the enslavement of human souls, regardless of the justification of those who would profit from it. I shall do nothing in malice. What I deal with is too vast for malicious dealing.

~Abraham Lincoln

Sarah stood frozen in fear as she faced Mai Luan, who stood barely ten feet away.

Tomas started shooting.

He stood farther from the corner than Sarah, so his first shot passed so close to her that she felt the whoosh of air and ducked away.

Blood blossomed across Mai Luan's chest from the first round of buckshot, and she stumbled back a step into one of her men.

Tomas kept firing, pumping the little shotgun so fast it sounded like it was shooting on full auto. Only one other shot struck Mai Luan, ripping into her stomach.

Then she burst into motion, dodging to the side with super-human speed. Tomas's rounds drove into the heka who had been standing behind her. Tomas turned, firing after her, but she moved too fast.

Sarah dropped to the ground as he swung the weapon toward her, and he fired over her head. She rolled over to see if he'd hit Mai Luan, but the cui dashi had continued across the yard, snatched up the fallen knife from the giant heka they had dropped earlier, and threw it at Tomas.

The blade struck the shotgun with such force it knocked it out of Tomas's hands. He reached for his knife, but Mai Luan closed with a rush and punched him in the chest. The blow threw him off his feet. He soared eight feet and crashed into the wall of the nearby house.

Two of the heka rushed him, guns up.

"Don't kill him yet," Mai Luan said calmly as she brushed a stray lock of her long, silky black hair from her face.

Tomas rose slowly, hands raised, and the two heka flanked him with rifles aimed at his head.

Sarah also rose, and Mai Luan approached, a frown on her lips. A speck of blood marred the smooth skin of her face. Through bloody holes in Mai Luan's blouse, Sarah could see she'd already healed.

Mai Luan stood shorter than Sarah, but the very fact that she looked so non-threatening made her all the scarier. Sarah considered drawing her pistol, but Mai Luan could break her in pieces before she ever aimed it.

"I had hoped you'd prove a bit more resourceful," Mai Luan said. "Defeating you this easily won't do anything to restore my reputation."

Sarah said, "Give me Tomas's shotgun, and I'll shoot you in the face a few times. That might make you feel better."

She had known Mai Luan only on a superficial level at Alter-ego. She hadn't known anything about facetakers or cui dashi until she ventured into the vault with Tomas in his hunt for Eirene. She was surprised Mai Luan addressed her instead of Tomas, as if . . ."

"You sent the gunmen in New Orleans," Sarah said, putting the pieces together.

"Useless," Mai Luan spat. "I'm glad they failed, really. Removing you personally is a slight improvement, but not much."

"What do you have against me?" Sarah asked.

"How dare you ask that?" Mai Luan growled, lunging across the distance to Sarah in a blink and seizing her by the throat. Her tiny hand lifted Sarah easily off the ground, her fingers like bands of iron.

"I don't understand," Sarah gasped, barely able to breathe.

Mai Luan lowered her to the ground, pulling her face down until their eyes were level. She hissed, "You broke my spell. You, a helpless mortal, a brainless donor. You destroyed everything I'd built there and forced me to flee in disgrace."

She flung Sarah away.

Sarah rolled several times, but her thoughts spun faster. In the vault, she'd thrown the dispossessed soulmask of Dr. Maerwynn in an act of pure desperation. It had somehow activated the rune circle Mai Luan had been drawing, triggering an explosion that had allowed them to escape. Mai Luan had destroyed the entire Alterego complex after that, and Sarah had assumed she'd killed herself when it all imploded.

"I didn't know what I was doing," she protested.

Mai Luan clenched her fists, her face reddening. She stalked toward Sarah, murder in her eyes. "That only magnifies the dishonor. Do you have any idea how long I worked on that project, perfecting that technology? You destroyed so much. You!"

She stood over Sarah, shouting now. "Do you have any idea how hard it is to succeed when you're always treated as second-best?"

Mai Luan had pretended to be one of Dr. Maerwynn's assistants. Sarah hadn't realized the relationship had been so rocky.

"Of course I do," Sarah snapped, her fear fading under a flash of anger. "I only ever made it to number five." She wouldn't tell this woman about the constant berating she'd grown up with.

Mai Luan laughed. "You think your petty model rankings matter to anyone?"

"They did to the people I worked with," Sarah said. She stood and her height advantage bolstered her confidence, even though she knew it was a fake superiority. "How many lives did you destroy in your work?"

The Chinese-American looked genuinely surprised. "Who cares? They were only mortals. Their sacrifice was a small price to pay."

"Not to them," Sarah retorted. Images of all the lives left broken after the destruction of Alterego fueling her anger.

"You're so naive," Mai Luan said.

Before Sarah could retort, Tomas sprang into action. He snatched the rifle out of one distracted heka's hands, clubbed the man with the stock of the weapon, and opened fire on Mai Luan. The suppressed AK47 spat a full magazine at her.

Bullets tore through her skin, from stomach to neck, stitching her torso and spraying blood into Sarah's face. She recoiled, and drew her pistol.

The bolt on Tomas' rifle locked back on an empty chamber, smoke drifting out of the barrel. The air smelled of gunpowder and blood.

Mai Luan straightened her shirt. "Do you mind? We're having a conversation here."

Sarah said, "My turn."

She shot Mai Luan in the face.

The bullet, fired from a distance of eighteen inches, drove into Mai Luan's eye, snapped her head back, and dropped her to the ground.

"Shoot her again," Tomas shouted, leaping upon the nearest heka. The two of them fell to the ground, grappling for the weapon. The other two heka looked torn between helping their comrade or staring at Mai Luan's fallen form.

Sarah shot Mai Luan seven more times, every one of the forty-five slugs striking her in the head. The slide locked back and she looked down to find the release to drop the mag and replace it with a spare.

When she looked up again, Mai Luan was standing in front of her, face bloody but unbroken, her shattered eye glaring.

She spat two flattened bullets at Sarah.

Sarah recoiled, but brought her pistol up again. Mai Luan snatched it out of her hand and pressed the barrel against Sarah's temple.

"At least you put up a fight before the end," Mai Luan hissed.

"Leave her alone," Tomas shouted. The three heka fighters had restrained him and held his arms behind his back. "She's barely a part of this."

"Oh, no," Mai Luan whispered into Sarah's ear. "You're neck deep and sinking."

She pushed Sarah stumbling, then crossed to Tomas and waved the heka aside. "You want me to focus on you instead? You who betrayed our trust?"

"It was my pleasure," Tomas said, standing unarmed but unafraid as he faced her.

Mai Luan glanced at Sarah and a wicked grin spread across her face. "Sarah, I won't kill you yet. You made me suffer. I'm going to give you the chance to suffer some too."

She grabbed Tomas by the shirt and lifted him off the ground. He kicked at her torso and arm to no effect. She took a long knife from one of the heka.

"Come here, Sarah," she beckoned with the knife.

Sarah approached on shaky legs. "Let him go."

"I release him into your care," Mai Luan said.

She lowered Tomas to the ground. Sarah took a hesitant step forward. Would Mai Luan really let them go?

The evil woman drove the knife to the hilt in Tomas' side.

He gasped, eyes wide with pain, but didn't seem to be able to make any sound. Mai Luan released him and he dropped to one knee, clutching at the hilt sticking from his side, a groan escaping his lips.

"No!" Sarah rushed forward, but Mai Luan pushed her back.

"You can have him in a minute." She gave Tomas a critical look. He knelt before her, one hand on the hilt of the knife, his face pale. She reached down and twisted the blade.

A scream tore from his tight-clenched lips.

Sarah rammed her shoulder into Mai Luan, but rebounded from the smaller woman. "Leave him alone!"

"There," Mai Luan said, looking satisfied.

She turned to Sarah. "He's got an hour to live, my dear. I'm very good at judging these things."

Sarah started to cry. She hated herself for it, but the tears came. She faced Mai Luan, filled with rage at the woman's casual cruelty, and horror at what she'd done to Tomas.

Mai Luan patted her cheek. Sarah recoiled, but Mai Luan grabbed a handful of her hair. "Stay put till I'm through with you, or I'll twist that knife again."

Sarah froze, quivering with the need to destroy this woman, but at a loss for how to do it.

"Here's the game we're going to play," Mai Luan said in a conversational tone, as if Tomas wasn't dying just feet away. "You watch Tomas die. No hospitals, no doctors, just you and him. Otherwise I'll make him scream for weeks."

"I hate you," Sarah whispered.

"Good." Mai Luan smiled wide. "That might give you the strength to prove a little more interesting. Take good care of him, but when he dies, don't forget to run."

"I'll kill you," Sarah said.

"I do hope you try. But remember to run. When I'm finished with this project, I'll find some time to hunt you down." Her good humor faded. "When I find you, you'll wish I'd kill you as quickly as I did Tomas."

She turned away, but called over her shoulder. "Make it fun, Sarah."

Mai Luan motioned one of her men to scoop up the bags Sarah had dropped, stealing her one hope of finding medical supplies.

They left Sarah and Tomas alone.

CHAPTER TWENTY-SEVEN

All you need is love. But a little chocolate and a new rune now and then doesn't hurt.

~Zuri, facetaker council member

Sarah rushed to Tomas and dropped to her knees beside him. His body shook with agony, and sweat dripped from his bowed head. His eyes were clenched shut, and he breathed slow and shallow. His skin looked pale, and felt cool and clammy when she touched him.

"Oh, Tomas, I'm so sorry," she whispered. Seeing him in such pain, dying, tore at her heart.

He tipped his head up and opened his eyes. "I don't feel so good."

She wasn't sure if she should laugh or cry, so she kissed his cheek. "What do I do?"

"We have to get out of here," he mumbled as his head sagged toward the ground again. "Police will be here soon."

"We need help," she said. "Maybe—"

"No," he interrupted. "You heard her. She'll kill us both."

"We have to do something," she cried. She refused to accept Mai Luan's order that she sit around and wait for Tomas to die.

"Yes," he whispered, face clenched against the pain. "But not that. Help me up."

Sarah pulled one of his arms over her shoulder and heaved him to his feet. He groaned through clenched teeth and every breath hissed with pain as the movements tore at his wound.

"Should we remove that?" Sarah asked, pointing at the knife.

"Not yet. I'd bleed out faster."

Sarah tried to move slow, smooth, but Tomas was heavy, unwieldy, and his feet stumbled along, barely helping her keep him upright. Every wince he made heightened her worry, but they had to move. If he fell, she'd never lift him. It seemed to take forever to cross the small back yard to the gate in the high wooden fence.

"Where to?" she asked through panting breaths.

Sirens wailed in the distance, coming fast. For the first time she noticed smoke in the air that didn't smell like gunpowder. The explosion at the apartment must have started a fire.

"The police are coming," she said.

They could provide medical help. The temptation to rush around the building and flag them down was nearly overwhelming. They could help save Tomas. Only Mai Luan's threat of inflicting even greater torture on him if she did that kept her from trying.

"Keep going," Tomas grunted through gritted teeth. "Not far."

She nearly dropped him before she managed to open the gate, and he bit back a cry of pain when he lurched and nearly fell. He smelled like sweat and blood, and his blood coated her clothing and hands. It was hot and sticky, and if she wasn't so worried, she would've shrieked from the feel of it.

"There," he said between breaths. "Silver SUV. Carport."

She hadn't known they had access to a car. The parking spot wasn't adjacent to the house, so she hadn't paid it any attention.

Thankfully it was parked close behind the rear gate and no one was around. The local residents were either all out gawking at the fire, or at least smart enough to avoid the area of so many gunshots.

She found the key in Tomas's pocket and helped him into the back seat. She was terrified they'd knock the knife against the seat and hurt him even more, but he managed to lie down with the handle sticking up. The vehicle's darkened windows would conceal him from anyone outside.

He looked more comfortable. She couldn't have held him up much longer, but she wasn't sure what to do next. Dying in the car wasn't much of an improvement over dying out in the yard.

Tomas coughed, then winced, a long groan slipping through his tight-pressed lips.

"We have to get this bloody knife out," he said, his voice slipping into a British accent.

"You said you'd bleed out if we do."

"Not if you help," he panted.

She followed his gestures and ripped away the remnant of his shirt. She nearly puked at the heavy scent of blood that filled the vehicle. Blood leaked out of the wound. The torn skin was puckered around the blade and Sarah choked back a cry of despair to see the steel standing from his side. He really was going to die. Fresh tears streamed down her face and her mind went blank. She didn't know what to do, but tried to control herself. She had to be strong for him.

Tomas took from his pocket a small folding knife and handed it to her.

"What do you want me to do with this?" He couldn't be hinting at what she feared he might be. She wouldn't do it. She'd take him to the hospital first and take their chances there.

He surprised her by tracing a pattern onto the skin of his side with his own blood. His hands shook, but he managed a remarkably precise image. It looked a lot like the runes they had studied from the machine. The specifics of the symbol were different, but it had to be some kind of rune.

Tomas gestured weakly at the knife and then fell back, exhausted. "Mark pattern."

"What are you saying?"

"Cut that into my skin around the wound. Knife in the middle."

"You're crazy."

"Enhancement," he breathed. His voice was fading. "Might save me."

"Tomas, how can this help?"

He didn't respond.

They were out of time.

Sarah gritted her teeth and opened the knife. Using part of his ripped shirt, she wiped the blood from the wound and laid the blade onto his skin.

Horrified by what she was doing, she made the first cut.

The little knife was as sharp as a scalpel, and it cut deeper than she intended. He didn't even twitch.

She could no longer hear his breathing. She wanted to shriek that Mai Luan promised he'd live an hour. It hadn't been that long. She couldn't lose him yet.

Sarah bit her lip with concentration, and tried again. The blade sliced through his skin far too easily. It sickened her to see fresh blood welling up from the cuts, merging with blood leaking from the knife wound. Between the two of them, she and Mai Luan were killing him.

She wiped the blood away, but had to cut faster.

Sarah leaned over him and tried to hurry, but he winced from one mark and she snatched the blade away. Knowing she was hurting him even more nearly drove her crazy.

"I can't do this," she shrieked.

Tomas slowly twisted his bloody right hand into a thumbs up. "You must."

Then his hand went limp. Hopefully he was passed out again and wouldn't feel any more. Sarah decided to finish the rune and then rush him to the hospital. What else could she do?

She focused again on tracing the intricate pattern into his skin around the blade. She hated cutting him, but as she worked she felt drawn to the rune despite her revulsion. Its complex beauty called to her and as she worked on it, she found that somehow it made sense. Well, almost all of it did. A couple of the lines he made with his shaky fingers were sloppy.

He had made a mistake.

How she knew that, she couldn't imagine, but she was sure of it. She should copy it exactly the way he indicated, but somehow deep down inside she knew that was wrong, that it would break the rune.

So she changed it.

If she was mistaken, she was killing him.

She made the final mark with a confident stroke even though she wanted to scream with fear, even while she desperately prayed the rune would work. As soon as the blade connected the last two lines, the pattern began to glow with a soft blue light. She sagged against him, suddenly exhausted. The light intensified for several seconds until it filled the interior of the vehicle. The bloody marks faded away, leaving the rune clear and bright against his pale skin.

Tomas opened his eyes and lifted his head to look down at the rune. "You did it."

"Don't look so surprised." The attempt at levity failed.

"Pull the knife out," he ordered.

"No, I can't. You said you'd bleed out."

"Not any more. The rune helps with healing, but not until the knife's gone."

Sarah grasped the handle. It was warm from his body heat, sheathed securely in his side. "Please, don't make me do this."

"Do it, Sarah," Tomas whispered, gripping her other hand. "Or I'll die."

With a cry of revulsion, Sarah yanked the blade out in a single, convulsive heave. Tomas gasped, his face white, and his body arced off the seat with a spasm of new pain.

Sarah tossed the knife to the floor of the vehicle and pressed his shirt against the open wound. Blood was pouring out now that the blade wasn't plugging the wound.

"I thought you said this would help," she cried.

"Give it a minute." His voice was soft, weak. His eyes closed and his hand slipped off the seat.

The brightly glowing rune faded to black.

"No no no," Sarah muttered, pressing the improvised bandage harder against the wound. With her other hand, she prodded the rune. It had faded to a black mark that looked a lot like a tattoo. She suspected that was a good sign, but why would the glow fade? Had she broken it? Should it have kept glowing? She peeked under the bandage and the bleeding had slowed. A scab covered the wound.

That was fast. Maybe the rune really was working.

She couldn't remain there any longer. The sirens were very loud. If the police cordoned off the block, she and Tomas might get trapped and discovered. Someone would inform the authorities of the gunshots, and she needed to leave before they began a search.

Sarah shook Tomas gently. "Tomas, where should we go?"

He didn't respond.

"Useless," she muttered, trying to rally her spririt.

She packed additional padding across his side with a spare shirt she found in the back and secured the whole sloppy bandage with her belt. Then she wiped her bloody hands on his shirt, climbed into the driver seat, and pulled onto the street.

At first she just wanted to get away from pursuit and potential arrest. Tomas had blown up the house and they'd shot several men. She doubted the heka had died, but were any of them still lying in the alley? Either way, she had fired a whole lot of bullets at them. How long would the police put her in jail for that? Would they believe it was self-defense?

Hiding in a jail wouldn't slow Mai Luan for long, Sarah could imagine her slaughtering a precinct full of police and breaking through steel bars to wreak her promised vengeance. Mai Luan would kill Sarah long before she got a chance to testify.

If she tried to explain, tried to tell the truth, she'd get locked in a loony bin for life. No one would believe the secret existence of the facetakers and their ancient powers or Mai Luan and her enhanced fighters. Sarah barely believed it herself. She didn't doubt that if she tried to reveal the secrets to the authorities, council-assigned enforcer hit squads would race Mail Luan to silence her.

That left her feeling desperately alone. She wasn't sure how to reach Gregorios or Eirene, didn't know where else to turn.

After fifteen minutes of driving, her hands began to shake so badly she barely managed to pull off to the side of the road. She sat there for several minutes, just trying to breathe as her heart raced and her body reacted to the stress of the recent battle.

Once she managed to calm herself a little, she checked on Tomas. He was still alive and actually seemed to be sleeping better. The scab looked stronger, the bleeding stopped. Hopefully that meant the rune was working. She rummaged in the back of the vehicle and found a blanket to cover him.

She also found a light jacket that was only two sizes too big for her. She slipped it on to conceal the blood smears on her shirt. When she returned to the driver's seat, she noticed for the first time the Colosseum in the distance. Was it only that morning that they had visited it?

She glanced back at Tomas. "You're a rotten date, you know that?"

He surprised her by opening his eyes. "I thought nursing me back to health would spark a little Florence Nightingale Effect."

"You wish." Seeing him responsive was such a relief she wanted to climb back there and kiss him.

"You did good," he said, his accent American again. "The rune saved my life." His voice was weak, and he looked surprised, like he couldn't quite believe he lived.

"How?"

"I'll explain later." He glanced down at his blanket-covered form and muttered, "Carl's going to be angry."

"Who's Carl?"

"Doesn't matter. Let's get out of here."

"Do you have any idea where we can go?"

"Yes."

Sarah felt so relieved to have a direction, a promise of hope again. Tomas gave her an address and passed forward his smartphone. She found the address on the other side of town.

"Is this another safe house?"

"No. A friend."

"I hope they have some medical supplies."

"He does. We'll be safe there."

Sarah grunted. She doubted it, not with Mai Luan planning to hunt her down. She realized there was only one way she'd ever feel safe again. Either she or Mai Luan had to die.

She voted for Mai Luan.

Tomas added weakly, "One more thing. Don't say anything about Gregorios or Eirene."

"What am I supposed to tell them?"

Tomas didn't answer. He had passed out again.

CHAPTER TWENTY-EIGHT

Success is not final, failure is not fatal: it is the courage to continue even in the face of enhanced Nazis that counts.

~Winston Churchill

God bless the makers of GPS.

It took an hour to escape Rome and drive up into the low hills on the outskirts of the city. Sarah followed the directions to a large estate with a guardhouse and high, iron fence. Seeing the armed guards made her very nervous and she became intensely aware of the pistol holstered under her jacket.

With no other alternative, she drove up to the gate and forced a confident expression on her face. Most men reacted well to her smile.

The guard leaned a little closer than strictly required and actually smiled when he asked her business. She hadn't figured out a clever way to explain it so she rolled down the back window and gestured over her shoulder.

"I've got an injured man here. Says you folks know him and can help."

As the guard advanced to peer in the window she added, "His name is Tomas."

The man apparently recognized Tomas because he made a wild gesture to a second man seated in the gatehouse, jabbering loudly in Italian. The gate began swinging open immediately.

"What happened?" the guard asked.

"Worst date of my life, that's what."

He looked surprised. "You didn't . . . ?"

"No. Some kind of gang, I think."

"I'm glad you're all right," the guard said sincerely. "Take him up to the house."

She thanked him and accelerated up the winding drive. The house was actually a huge mansion set on a sprawling estate, surrounded by several outbuildings. Two huge, square towers flanked the main entry, and everything was yellow stucco or rough-hewn stone. Ivy crept up one wall, adding a splash of green to the Mediterranean style. Red brick tile led her up the circular driveway and under the covered entrance.

Four people rushed out to meet her, carrying a stretcher piled with bright red boxes marked with the white cross of medical supplies. Two wore white coats and she hoped they were doctors. Even before she turned off the engine, they threw open the rear doors and began assessing Tomas's injuries. Their obvious professionalism and the fact that she didn't understand half of the terminology they spoke rapid-fire between themselves gave her the first real feeling of hope since the brutal fight in the alley.

"They will take very good care of him."

She turned to find a mature gentleman in a finely tailored, gray suit standing behind her. His hair may have been graying, but his shoulders were broad and he exuded a sense of strength. He carried himself with a military air, but his ice-blue eyes radiated warm concern that helped ease her worries.

"Bring me hourly reports," he directed the medical staff who were already shifting Tomas onto the stretcher. He spoke with a cultured, British accent.

Sarah followed them toward the building, but the man in the suit placed a gentle hand on her arm. "Leave them to their work."

He extended a large hand and shook hers with a firm but not overpowering grip. "I am Quentin. Welcome to my home."

Sarah suddenly became aware of how terrible she looked in her bloody clothing and bedraggled hair. Hopefully he hadn't seen the gun on her hip under her over-sized jacket. She wasn't making a good impression.

He seemed to understand her anxiety. "It appears you've had quite an eventful day."

She laughed softly, and that flushed the lingering terror. "You could say that again. I'm Sarah. Thank you for helping us."

"It is an absolute pleasure, my dear." Quentin smiled and she noted the many laugh lines around his eyes and mouth. She barely knew him, but her first impression was positive. She hoped she was right about him.

He took her arm and led her into the beautiful entry hall paved with peach-colored tile, and lined with archways. "What happened?"

She might instinctively like him, but Tomas's warning suggested the wisdom of caution. "Some crazy guys with guns jumped us on our way to dinner."

"Are you injured?"

"No, just a little shaken. Tomas put up quite a fight, but they hurt him pretty bad. Knife wound."

Quentin grimaced. "Those are never good, but my medical staff are among the best in the city."

He led her into a luxurious salon and Sarah paused to stare at the expensive tile, the graceful arches in the doorways, and the comfortable furniture.

"I love your house. Doesn't look like a hospital."

"Thank you. May I offer you a place to clean up?"

"That would be lovely. But how do you know Tomas?"

Quentin said, "He and I are very old friends. I could tell you stories about him that you would never believe."

"You're on. I'd believe a lot."

He inclined his head a little. "I accept the challenge, my dear. It sounds like you know Tomas well."

"Sometimes I wonder." She wasn't sure how much to reveal about herself, but Tomas had cautioned her against revealing their connection to Gregorios and Eirene, so that prevented her from discussing anything they'd done recently.

He chuckled. "And you are American. Did you meet here in the city?"

"No. We've known each other a while."

Quentin didn't seem bothered by the vague answer. "Perhaps after you're refreshed, you would enjoy a tour of my estate?"

"Yes, thank you."

He rang a little bell on a nearby table, and a black-haired woman in a white and blue uniform entered from the next room. "Please show Sarah to a room where she can freshen up." He took her hand again before she left. "Thank you for bringing him here."

"I'm glad you were home."

Quentin smiled. "After our tour, allow me to host you in the dining room. I am a poor replacement, but I offer my services until Tomas is up and about again."

"Thank you, and I'll hold you to the promise of some good stories."

Sarah followed the maid across the room and up a curving grand staircase with mahogany rails. She glanced back once. Quentin had not moved, and was watching her with a serious expression on his face. He smiled one more time and only then did he turn and stride swiftly out of sight.

CHAPTER TWENTY-NINE

It takes a lifetime to grow up and become who we really are. For some, it takes several lifetimes.

~Dalai Lama

T he maid led Sarah to a huge suite. Beyond the private sitting room was a bedroom complete with balcony overlooking a huge pool. She also found a large private bathroom that had both a shower and a jet tub bigger than many Jacuzzis, already filled with steaming water.

Even better, the solid wooden outer door sported a heavy brass handle with a lock, plus a separate deadbolt.

She showered first. The shower had an entire wall of jets that enveloped her in a pulsing column of water. She started to grin as she spun slowly under the massaging streams. Then she noticed the blood running off her and disappearing down the drain.

At the sight of it, her fear of Mai Luan returned. This time, however, it was tempered by anger and the resolve to stop the cui dashi. Mai Luan had made the fight personal. Sarah had never been a violent person, but Mai Luan's cold brutality forced her to face the reality that she had to fight. Some people couldn't be reasoned with.

Some people just had to be put down like a rabid dog.

As scary as the situation was, she was grateful she hadn't abandoned Tomas in New Orleans. She might have enjoyed her ignorance for a while.

Until they killed her.

Mai Luan would have hunted her down. At least this way she could draw upon powerful allies and fight for her life. The world was far deadlier than she'd imagined, filled with shadows she had yet to explore. She lacked Tomas's fighting skills, but she could learn.

Sarah toweled off as she considered that. She could either choose to be a victim, or she could fight. She vowed to find a way to turn the tables on Mai Luan. With Tomas, Eirene, and Gregorios, they'd find a way. She'd make Mai Luan wish she'd killed them when she had the chance.

The newly made resolution helped restore her confidence as she raided the bathroom's impressive stock of beauty supplies. In the walk-in closet she found a man's dress shirt that looked passing fair with her dark slacks. She wouldn't wear the bloody blouse again.

Mai Luan's theft of their bags rankled. Such a petty gesture. Sarah would've preferred meeting the well-dressed Quentin wearing something a bit more formal, but at least she no longer looked like she worked in a slaughterhouse. She found a shoulder bag to use as a purse and dropped the pistol inside.

Quentin was waiting for her downstairs in the salon. "You look splendid, my dear."

"I hope you don't mind that I borrowed a shirt."

"It never looked so good," he said with a warm smile.

He was quite a charmer. She liked him more and more.

Sarah took his arm and he led her on a tour of the mansion. It was incredible. Too many rooms to count, and everything was decorated with exquisite taste. Each room reflected a different theme or time period. Ornate furniture, rare paintings, suits of armor, and fine statues were scattered throughout.

She decided she wanted one.

Sarah hadn't really enjoyed her recently acquired wealth and had a lot of money available. A nice mansion would be just the thing.

They passed quite a few servants but no one else. For such a huge building, that seemed strange. Quentin looked relaxed, but each time he entered a room or reached an intersecting hall, he paused for a second to scan their surroundings. He disguised the action by asking her questions or pointing out details of the area, but she picked up on it anyway.

One entire wing was set up as a hospital ward. There they inquired after Tomas. He was in surgery but the early prognosis was good. The doctor, who stood at attention while delivering his report, raised his hand in salute.

Quentin waved him away, then glanced at Sarah. "He used to be a soldier. Some habits die hard, I guess."

"Why do you have such an extensive medical facility in your home?" Sarah asked.

"Our work often requires medical assistance. Treating my men here is far more efficient and avoids the questions we'd face in a public hospital."

That was interesting and a little unnerving.

"What exactly is your work?" Sarah dared ask. Quentin had been a gracious host so far, but she wondered how he'd react to her prying.

"Tomas didn't tell you?" He considered her closely, his eyes calculating.

"No. He just said you could help."

"I'm glad you brought him here." His ready smile returned and he held out his arm for her again. When she took it, he led her back into the hall. "I beg your indulgence, my dear. We'll discuss my business once Tomas awakens. What of your family? Will they be worried?"

Sarah shook her head. "Not likely. My parents and I aren't exactly close. Will I get to meet your family today?"

"I am afraid not. My children all live overseas, and my wife passed away four years ago."

"I'm very sorry."

"She did not suffer, and her soul is at rest now," Quentin said quietly, but old sorrow reflected in his eyes for a moment.

It passed quickly, and he led her out of the hospital wing. They bypassed another entire wing on their way back to the main building.

"What's in there?" Sarah asked.

"Nothing interesting. That wing is undergoing extensive remodeling."

She didn't hear the sound of construction, but maybe the workers had the day off? She decided not to press him. She needed his help and couldn't risk antagonizing him.

They finally returned to a long dining room that sported at least two dozen paintings on the wall. They were high-quality works that would have looked completely at home in a museum of art. Two places were set near one end of the polished table that could have easily sat twenty.

Quentin motioned Sarah to sit and helped slide her chair in. "I hope you don't mind dining here in the art gallery," he said as he seated himself across from her. "The formal dining room is a bit too much for the two of us."

"This is beautiful."

Several servants entered bearing the first of several courses on silver platters. The meal was divine. They started with fresh fruit that refreshed her without filling her up. A spicy dip followed, served with warm pita and olive bread. It smelled freshly baked, and the aroma lingered in the air.

She sampled dolmas, made of grape leaves stuffed with herbed rice. She wanted to fill her plate with that single course, but when she finished her small portion, a waiter replaced it with a traditional Greek salad. By the time the main courses arrived she wondered where she'd fit them.

The yogurt-marinated chicken fell off the bone, it was so tender. Roasted lamb followed, with gemista, which was roasted peppers and tomatoes stuffed with rice, raisins and herbs. She was glad she hadn't stopped at the dolmas. Everything was cooked perfectly, and despite how much she had already eaten, each new dish tasted so good, she eagerly dug in.

Quentin explained each of the dishes and spoke at length of the foods grown locally in Italy. "I hope you don't mind my choosing the meal for you," he said as they sipped on Cupido soft drinks. "But I thought you might enjoy a traditional Mediterranean feast."

"It's absolutely delicious," Sarah said. She hadn't realized how hungry she was, but she ate far more than she usually allowed herself. Quentin didn't seem to mind.

As she raised a fork full of potatoes he asked, "What about our friend Gregorios?"

She paused for just a second in surprise but used the pretext of finishing the mouthful before answering. She frowned, "That jerk told me his name was Tomas."

Quentin laughed and slapped his thigh with one hand. He looked younger like that, and must have been extremely handsome in his prime. She had thought she did a pretty good job with that one, but he was not fooled.

"Very good. Where did Tomas find you? Not only are you beautiful and resourceful, but quick witted."

"Thank you, but I already have a date. Well, I did, but you've already managed to supplant him for dinner. Are you planning to take his place for the rest of the evening too?"

She actually got a little flush of embarrassment out of him.

He raised his glass in salute. She clinked to it and he said, "Let's leave that part of the conversation out until Tomas can join us."

She wasn't entirely sure if he meant the questioning about Gregorios or the bit about him taking Tomas's place as her date.

She could believe it either way.

After the servants left with another stack of plates, Quentin spoke quietly, his expression serious. "I hope you will come to realize I am trustworthy, my dear. Although I trust all of my staff implicitly, your caution is well advised around them. It is always possible anything overheard could travel beyond the walls of this house.

"So is that why we're dining alone?"

"Yes. That and the fact that I rarely have a chance to enjoy an intimate meal with such a beautiful woman whose company I so much enjoy."

"Other than your daughters, perhaps?"

He winced at the jab at his age, but his smile didn't falter.

Their conversation turned to less delicate subjects and when he learned she was new in Rome he launched into very entertaining descriptions of the best tourist attractions. He shared nuggets of history he assured her she would never learn from normal tour guides.

As deserts were being served, a butler entered from the far side of the room. "Pardon me, sir. You have additional guests."

"Very well. Show them in."

Quentin did not look surprised. He should have warned her. He had made her feel comfortable in his presence but she wasn't really dressed for company.

The door opened and Gregorios and Eirene entered the room. Gregorios grinned when he saw them seated at the table.

"What's for dinner?"

CHAPTER THIRTY

No matter how many lives I live, a perfect sunset is a special moment that still holds the power to replenish my nevra core. Every soul needs to discover beauty and love, for they fuel the soul and keep us young.

~Eirene

Relief nearly made Sarah giddy as she leaped to her feet and rushed over to embrace Eirene and then Gregorios. "I'm so happy to see you."

"Are you all right?" Eirene asked.

"Fine. Tomas is hurt though."

"He is expected to make a full recovery," Quentin added as he joined them.

A young man trailed the others into the room. When she turned to say hello, he actually bowed over her hand and pressed his lips to her knuckles.

"Hello. I am Alter." He spoke English with a slight accent she couldn't quite place but found very pleasant. He was tall, with dark hair and eyes, and deeply tanned skin. His face was quite handsome.

But the greeting was still weird. "I'm Sarah."

He seemed willing to hold her hand for a while, but she pulled it away. He needed to tone down the advance. They weren't on hand-holding terms.

"How did you find us?" she asked Gregorios. "You didn't go to the safe house did you?"

"No. We tracked Tomas by his GPS."

Sarah wondered if there might have been a way to send a message to them sooner. It would have helped if she'd known Tomas had a trackable GPS.

She said, "I'm glad you found us. I wasn't entirely sure this was the best place to go."

Quentin made an exaggerated look of hurt. "Sarah, how could you say that after our lovely dinner?"

Alter frowned, "Miss, are you here under duress?"

"Well, it's certainly not the best of times."

He surprised her by assuming a dramatic pose. "I pledge my service to guaranteeing your freedom."

"Uh, thanks." She glanced at Eirene. Was this guy for real? Eirene shrugged, her expression long-suffering.

Sarah placed a hand on his arm to calm him down. "No, it's nothing like that. Quentin has been a perfect gentleman."

Quentin chuckled. "I only just managed to supplant Sarah's last date, and you're already trying to move in and take my place?"

"I think I've had enough dates for one night, thank you." She appreciated his attempt to keep the conversation light. With Gregorios and Eirene back, she felt a little more secure than she had all afternoon.

Alter looked a little disappointed.

Quentin added, "I must admit I am surprised to find a hunter in my home, not aiming a gun at me, and in apparent cordial company of two of my oldest friends."

"You know me, sir?" Alter asked, surprised.

"Your family is not unknown to me."

"And you, Mister Quentin, are known to me," Alter said with a noted lack of warmth. "I cannot claim it's a pleasure to be a guest in your home."

"Perhaps I'll surprise you."

"You aid and abet these demons in their work. You don't want to surprise me."

Gregorios interrupted before a real argument could brew. "What happened to Tomas?"

Sarah glanced at Quentin and raised an eyebrow. He made a little bow, closed the door behind the group, and slid aside a concealed wooden cover on the wall to reveal a recessed keypad. He typed in a code and a low-pitched hum began rumbling softly around them.

"The room is secure from any active listening."

Sarah had to be sure. "Gregorios, can we trust this man?"

"I like you more all the time," Quentin said. He didn't look the least bit offended.

"Quentin is an old friend and perhaps the only person I trust in the facetaker organization right now," said Gregorios.

"Then why did Tomas warn me not to speak of either of you to him?"

Quentin said, "In case others overheard, I suspect. Our positions require delicacy at times."

"What position is that?" Sarah asked.

"I oversee the armory and special projects for the council," Quentin said.

"He makes the best toys," Gregorios added.

"You'll have to give me the rest of the tour," Sarah said.

"As soon as it can be arranged," Quentin replied.

She nodded toward Alter, who was watching them all with unguarded distrust. "And how about him? I thought you couldn't trust hunters."

The young man bristled, but Eirene patted him on the shoulder. "You could learn something from Sarah about being circumspect."

"I'm not that bad."

"Keep working on it, dear."

They sat around the table and Sarah related the important points of her ordeal with Tomas. When she told them about the confrontation with Mai Luan and how she shot the cui dashi in the face, Alter gaped. His first impression was going to be completely skewed.

When she finished, Eirene gave her a hug. "I'm sorry we weren't there to help."

"I swear to destroy this cui dashi and save you from her wrath," Alter proclaimed.

"That would be nice," Sarah said. She'd take any help she could get, even from an overzealous hunter.

Gregorios looked thoughtful. "She's targeting you personally. That's unexpected."

"She blames me for wrecking her work at Alterego."

Eirene said, "I can see her point, but it seems an overreaction to me."

"It sounds like she's not operating alone," Quentin said. "Her comments to you suggest she's part of a larger organization."

"And that her standing was damaged by that fiasco," Eirene said with a nod.

Gregorios grunted. "Not good. Bad enough to have a cui dashi alone. We already knew she had a team, including Tereza, but if she has a broader support base to draw from, that changes the situation somewhat."

Alter interjected. "Not entirely. Kill the abomination first. Dismantle her organization second."

Sarah liked how he thought.

She answered quite a few probing questions from the group, then Quentin called for a servant to provide an update on Tomas's condition. When they learned he was stable and awake, Sarah rose.

"I need to go see him."

"Let's all go," Eirene said.

"Just wheel him down here," Gregorios said, gesturing at the platters of baklava and yogurt parfait waiting on the table. "We can eat while we wait."

Eirene hauled him out of the chair. "Take one to go."

CHAPTER THIRTY-ONE

I like to be a free spirit, but I can't do this. I know I signed the contracts, accepted the payout, but there has to be a way to avoid surrendering this life to another. Meryem promised to find me a replacement, but whose life would I be stealing?

I don't want expensive gifts; I don't want to be bought. I have everything I want. I just want someone to be there for me, to make me feel safe and secure. I pray the hunters can provide the answer in our upcoming meeting.
~Princess Diana, August 1997

Tomas's face was still pale, but he looked alert sitting in his raised hospital bed. His loose-fitting clothes concealed the bandage, and Sarah breathed a sigh of relief to see him looking so much better.

Sarah greeted him with a kiss on the cheek and a gentle embrace. "I'm so glad you're feeling better."

"All thanks to you." He squeezed her hands gently and his eyes spoke volumes.

The threat of losing him had driven home to her how much she cared for him. It looked like he'd come to the same realization.

The others packed into the hospital room and Quentin ordered the staff to maintain a security perimeter. Eirene greeted Tomas with a hug. Gregorios waved his parfait spoon. Alter mumbled something vague and looked a little sullen.

They chatted for a couple of minutes until another butler arrived carrying enlarged photocopies of the runes Eirene had photographed on the machine. They passed the copies around for everyone to review, then turned the discussion over to Alter.

He began to speak slowly, as if considering every word. He looked decidedly uncomfortable teaching anything to the assembled company.

"These runes are powerful. Some are known to us and date back over two thousand years. Others we've never seen before."

From the grave looks on everyone's faces, Sarah realized she was missing something. "That's important, right?"

"Of course," Alter snapped, but immediately added, "Sorry. If we've never seen them, then no one has."

"Uh, I saw them," Eirene said.

"Well, usually," Alter corrected.

Sarah said, "I don't know much about runes. I'm glad you're here to teach us."

Alter stood a little taller and spoke to her as if they were the only two in the room. "The demons were right to come to us. No one knows runes better than we do. My family has maintained the master rune catalog for over forty centuries."

"Wow." It boggled the mind to think of that much history. He was talking about works started in biblical times. Sarah knew nothing of her family beyond her great grandmother on her father's side. It seemed impossible to trace a family line that far back.

"I knew it." Gregorios broke into the intimate conversation. "There *is* a master book."

Alter cringed and looked like he might stop talking altogether. It was clear he was attracted, so Sarah pushed him a little. "What did you learn about the runes in the photos?"

He barely hesitated before explaining. From his initial study and from what he learned from Eirene about the machine, he felt confident her initial assessment was correct. The runes allowed the person wearing the secondary helmet, assuming they were either heka or facetaker, to see into the mind of the person wearing the primary helmet and drive through their memories.

Eirene said, "That confirms our theory, but with so many runes involved, there has to be something else going on."

He shrugged. "I don't know enough about these other runes yet. I can probably figure it out with more study, but for now we're guessing."

"You can figure out what a rune does?" Sarah found the rune symbols fascinating, and was eager to learn everything she could about the topic.

"Usually. They're generally built around known symbols from ancient languages. Most common are Egyptian hieroglyphics or ancient Chinese pictographs."

"You understand all that?"

"I've studied it all my life."

She had not even managed to learn Spanish.

Tomas spoke for the first time. "Whatever those other runes mean, the threat's obvious. With the information Mai Luan could glean from the council members, she could overthrow the entire operation. She could learn everything."

Gregorios nodded. "She'll know as much as anyone. More even. She can remove them and step into their place without missing a beat. They're signing their own death warrants, and they're doing it willingly."

"Won't they stop when they learn the truth?" Sarah asked. She felt no love for the mysterious council, but even she saw the danger in granting Mai Luan more power. Once she consolidated her position in place of the council, she'd hunt Sarah and the others down.

Quentin sighed. "No. They see only the promised reversal of their advanced soul fragmentation. She's got them by the throat. Without her, they're at the end of their last life."

Alter perked up. "So they're going to die either way? Perhaps we should put them out of their misery now and thwart Mai Luan at the same time."

"Nice try," Gregorios said with a chuckle. "You'd go down in history as the hunter who decapitated the entire council."

"For the good of the many, it may be time to reward them for their evil ways." Unwavering fervor burned in his eyes. He absolutely believed they were evil.

Sarah could be convinced where the council was concerned, but Alter lumped Gregorios and Eirene into that same group. Their powers were unnerving at best, and always terrifying, but she didn't believe they were evil.

"Let's hold that option for a last resort," Eirene said.

Sarah was a little surprised when Alter reluctantly agreed with her. He had looked ready to argue all day with Gregorios.

"Timing is bad," Quentin said to move the conversation along again. "There's some high profile soul transfers scheduled soon. The King of Thailand is due in just a couple of months."

"Queen of England will probably make another transfer sometime next year," Tomas added.

"What?" Sarah looked from one to the other, but neither of them made any sign they were joking.

Tomas shrugged. "The queen's jumped before. She probably can't handle more than one more though, not unless the council gets their hands on one of those machines."

"You've got to be kidding." Sarah wasn't sure if the thought of the Queen of England utilizing the facetaker services troubled her more than the idea of the council gaining the ability to glean state secrets from her mind through a machine.

"She's a lot older than you think," Tomas said.

Eirene said, "She should've transferred a few years ago. We had it all scheduled to use Diana as the transfer vehicle but her premature death derailed those plans. It's taken a few years to orchestrate the right pieces to try again."

"You can't be serious!" Sarah had loved Princess Diana.

"Of course we are, dear." Eirene actually looked surprised by her shock. "It's tradition to prepare a suitable host. The queen is a little more particular than some, but she can't just transfer into any commoner. She'd lose access to her power and wealth."

"I can't believe I'm hearing this." She refused to ask what they had planned to do with Diana after stealing her body. They were casually discussing identity theft on a level the world couldn't comprehend.

Alter watched her with interest. "You knew nothing of the activities of these demons, did you?"

"I'm new."

"You should leave. They speak the truth in this case. My clan has worked for millennia to eradicate the kashaph and to block the worst of the facetaker plots. They've corrupted the souls of some of the world's greatest and created monsters we usually have to put down."

"That's a bit of an exaggeration," Gregorios said.

"I speak the truth," Alter declared. "European royalty in particular have long embraced the dream of eternal youth. If not for the safe havens they provided you demons we would have eradicated you centuries ago."

"First-life optimism is always refreshing," Gregorios said. He smiled at Sarah and added with a shrug, "Everyone needs to make a living."

Alter barked a laugh. "You corrupted entire royal lines. You introduced the weakness that drove them from the throne."

Gregorios said, "I blame inbreeding. We tried warning them about that, but they just couldn't seem to grasp the concept."

"We're getting off topic," Quentin said.

"She must understand the company she keeps," Alter said. He focused on Sarah. "The Hundred Years war was fought primarily over which country would maintain rights to facetaker transfers. Much of the Spanish gold from the new world was siphoned off to pay facetakers so royalty could purchase extended lives."

"I can't believe it," Sarah said. No one was even denying the allegations. Everything she knew about world history was apparently wrong.

"Nice one-sided lesson," Gregorios said. He didn't look the least bit rattled by Alter's accusations. "You just left out the fact that your self-righteous clan murdered quite a few royals in your attempts to interfere."

"Your acts are an abomination!" Alter shouted.

"You've got plenty of blood on your hands," Gregorios countered. "Your murders triggered World War One. What's more abominable, allowing those who can afford it to purchase extended life or triggering a conflict that killed millions?"

"Whoa!" Sarah cried. "You're saying the hunters assassinated the Archduke of Austria?" She'd studied the Great War in high school, and was proud that she actually remembered that part.

"He was kashaph," Alter said.

Gregorios said, "That was only the last straw. The hunters had made several attacks in preceding years, and their heavy-handed attempts to influence world powers set the stage for world conquest and then triggered the war."

"You cannot justify your abomination by pointing out the blame of others," Alter cried. "It's not right for the wealthy to take the lives of the poor."

Gregorios said, "Life isn't fair. It never has been. What we do is no worse than what anyone else does. We try to find willing donors and provide for their families. You can't say that for your clan."

"The English princess was not willing."

"How would you know that?" Eirene asked.

Alter lost some of his bluster and stammered, "Well, she didn't look willing."

"You set up that accident, didn't you?" Gregorios asked.

"I refuse to answer your questions." He began to blush.

"Self-righteous hypocrite," Gregorios muttered.

"Your family killed Diana?" Sarah asked, horrified. "How could you?"

"Her life was forfeit," Alter said, blushing under her accusing gaze. "This way she died at peace, not sacrificed to the demons' abomination."

"Don't pretend you know what it's like," Tomas said angrily. "You took the choice out of her hands."

Alter glared at Tomas. "I won't stay here. I cannot work with the likes of you."

"Relax Alter," Eirene urged, but he backed toward the door. It opened behind him and he bumped right into a female doctor as she entered.

The woman stumbled and grabbed Alter to keep from falling, and the two of them banged into the doorframe together. Alter spun violently, shaking the woman off and jabbing out with a blindingly fast punch.

He pulled the punch short so close to the startled doctor's face it looked to Sarah that his knuckles were actually brushing her skin. The doctor stared at Alter's fist with wide-eyed shock.

For his part, the young hunter stammered, "I'm so sorry. You surprised me." He looked like he couldn't decide if he should retreat from her, or try to steady her, and ended up frozen by indecision, fist still raised to the woman's face.

She gently pushed it down, and Sarah was grateful to see amusement twinkling in her brown eyes rather than fear or anger. "I apologize for startling you. I work around enough fighters, I should know better."

Quentin approached them and frowned at Alter. "I must insist you not harm the help, or we may end up disagreeing after all."

Alter looked like he preferred taking up the challenge evident in Quentin's voice, but after glancing at the doctor again he retreated another step and said, "I will be more careful."

"See that you do. Doctor Sofia, are you all right?"

The woman nodded. "I'm fine, thank you. Just checking in to see if you need anything." Like most of Quentin's staff, she appeared competent. She looked to be in her thirties, with a trim figure and classic Italian features.

"We're fine," Quentin assured her.

Doctor Sofia nodded, but before she left she said to Alter, "Try not to be so hasty, young man. Everything will be all right."

The brief encounter seemed to have broken Alter's anger. Sarah still wanted to yell at him, maybe slap him for condoning the death of Diana. She'd been the storybook princess that all the girls loved. The revelation that she'd been a victim in the secret world of facetakers and hunters disgusted Sarah.

But Mai Luan's threat loomed over everything else, so she swallowed her anger. "Alter, please. We need you." He hesitated until she held out a hand. "Please, help us. Not everyone sees the world the same way, but we have to deal with Mai Luan."

He slowly returned. "I'll use whatever information you divulge to aid my family's efforts in thwarting you."

Eirene patted his arm. "It's all right, dear. I am sure your family is already monitoring the high profile transfers. If they didn't know about them, I'd be very disappointed in your father."

As the group gathered around Tomas's bed again, Eirene paused to look after the doctor.

"It's not time for your check-up, love. Don't get distracted," Gregorios teased her, pulling her back to the group.

Tomas said to Alter, "We expect your family knows about the high profile transfers, but there are always standing precautions against interruptions. We know how to deal with your assassination attempts."

"You know nothing," Alter snapped, staring down at Tomas. "No hunter would remain invalid like this. If you cross my brothers, they'd destroy you."

Before they could start arguing again, Eirene said, "Alter needs more time to study the runes, but we know enough to start making plans. The council must change course and bring their resources to bear in removing Mai Luan."

Alter said, "We should just call in my family. We'd remove the cui dashi."

"Not a chance," Gregorios said. "Any hunter strike in Rome would lead to open warfare, especially now with the council committed to her. They'd see it as an attempt to kill them all."

"We are not afraid of them," Alter declared.

Eirene said, "You should be. There hasn't been outright war between the facetakers and the hunters since before the days of your great-grandfather. You have no idea how many people would die in a conflict like that."

"Besides, the enforcers monitor the hunters as standard procedure. If a strike team headed for Rome, they'd find the full might of the Tenth waiting for them," Tomas said.

Alter opened his mouth to argue further, but Eirene made a placating gesture. "Let's leave your clan as a last resort."

"We may want to begin positioning some of our own assets," Gregorios said.

Eirene considered that. "Carefully. Any big moves will tip off the enforcers."

"Best to convince the council of the danger and unleash the enforcers on Mai Luan," Tomas said.

"They want the machines too badly," Quentin disagreed.

"But if they recognize the threat, they can at least use the machine without allowing Mai Luan access to their minds," Gregorios said.

"He has a point," Eirene said.

"I could bring the information to Asoka," Tomas volunteered.

Quentin grimaced. "That would reveal your true loyalties. I'm afraid his anger at the betrayal would overrule any logical consideration of the information you tried to bring to light."

"How can they not know you freed Eirene?" Sarah asked.

"I was careful. The enforcers I disabled never saw me coming, and I avoided the video cameras."

"Mai Luan saw us," Eirene said.

Quentin said, "She hasn't revealed his part in your escape. I would've heard about that."

"Probably because she wanted to kill you herself." Sarah took Tomas's hand. "She nearly succeeded."

Quentin added, "It's still a bad idea. You won't convince Asoka, and might make matters worse."

"I could try Meryem," Gregorios suggested.

"She's scheduled to arrive in Rome late tonight, so she's a good choice," Quentin said.

Sarah wondered what would happen to Quentin if the council learned of his involvement with Gregorios. His only concern seemed to be for Tomas.

"Are you sure?" Gregorios asked.

"All of the council are gathering for the results of the tests with the machine."

"Very well. I'll pay her a visit. I just saw her a few days ago."

Eirene frowned. "I don't like it. I don't trust her."

"She didn't try to kill me last time."

"So you think you'll get lucky twice in one week?"

Gregorios grinned. "I feel lucky, and my goal is to get lucky every day."

Eirene's frown faded. "You wish."

The banter helped ease some of Sarah's renewed nervousness. Some of what she had learned disturbed her deeply, but seeing the depth of their bond helped reassure her they were still good at heart. She'd learn the full truth eventually, but her trust in them wasn't misplaced. She glanced at Tomas and he winked.

Alter frowned at the two. "I don't believe in luck."

Could he really be so clueless?

Eirene gave Alter a warm smile. "You will, dear. One day you'll meet the right woman."

"What does a woman have to do with luck?"

Gregorios said, "Let's stop while you're behind." Then he asked Eirene, "Can you think of anyone better to speak with?"

She considered for a moment before shaking her head.

"It's settled then. In the morning, I'll pay Meryem a visit and share what we've discovered."

"Do you think it'll help?" Tomas asked.

"Perhaps not, but it's all we can do until we find where Mai Luan is hiding."

"We'll have to fight her directly if the council won't do it," Sarah said. The thought terrified her, but it'd be necessary. Mai Luan had made it all too clear that she planned to kill them all. There was only one way to respond to a threat like that.

"It's either the council or it's us," Eirene said.

"I've wanted to take down a cui dashi for years," Alter said, fists clenched.

"Be grateful you haven't had to face her yet," Eirene said.

Gregorios added, "If we can ferret out her lair, with careful planning we can neutralize her."

Sarah doubted it would prove that easy, but she'd stand with them. Mai Luan would regret making the fight personal.

CHAPTER THIRTY-TWO

Be yourself; everyone else is already taken.

~Oscar Wilde

Gregorios paused across the street from the main entrance to the Suntara headquarters and smiled. Tomas had outdone himself.

Gregorios had asked for a diversion to allow him time to pass through the semi-public foyer of the building and avoid detection by the enforcer spotters. The secondary entrances were all monitored and even with the right codes, he couldn't hope to pass without getting intercepted. Usually that was the case with the main entrance too.

Not today.

Crowds of people of all ages clamored outside of three of the four doors to the lobby, jostling for their chance to get in. Guards stationed around the last entrance struggled to keep eager civilians back. Over and over they repeated that those doors were reserved for workers with security clearance.

Gregorios timed his approach for when an overweight foreigner tried to rush past the guards and it took three of them to wrestle him back. When Gregorios flashed his badge, the distracted guard waved him through with barely a glance.

Behind him the overweight foreigner screamed, "Tell the Pope I'm worthy!"

Inside the foyer was even worse. Frantic people packed the area around the main desk, jostling for their chance to make their case before the overwhelmed staff. Their voices echoed through the vaulted room in a deafening roar.

Tomas had leveraged a Vatican email address to begin the rumor that the Pope was planning an unscheduled visit to the building. He suggested that the Pope planned to grant special blessings to a handful of lucky believers. All they had to do was present themselves at the main desk and convince the attendants that they were the most deserving. The catch was that the attendants would deny any knowledge of such a visit unless a person convinced them they were worthy.

Surrounded by cries of, "I'm worthy" in a dozen languages, Gregorios slipped around the edge of the crowd to a simple, unmarked door locked with a code panel. Although normally monitored, every available staff member would be diverted to deal with the unexpected rush on the building.

Gregorios entered the code and, after one last appreciative glance across the tumultuous room, took the stairs up.

Meryem's office was located on the fourth floor with the other council members. Gregorios made it to her door without alerting anyone to his presence. He slipped inside without bothering to knock.

Meryem sat at her desk. After a brief look of surprise, she gave him a dazzling smile. "Gregorios my dear, even I'm surprised by your audacity."

"We need to talk."

She pouted as she rose and came around the desk. "Why waste such a romantic gesture with talk? After showing such ingenuity to get to me, I'd hoped for something more."

"Here's something more. Did you know Mai Luan is cui dashi?"

Meryem's smile vanished and she recoiled. "You lie."

"Not about this."

She regarded him for a long moment before responding. "Impossible."

"You're all in grave danger." He took her hand, which triggered an instant smile from her. "I don't want you getting hurt."

"Oh, Greg. That's so very chivalrous." She leaned in to give him a little kiss on the cheek.

At the same time, she pricked his arm with a little pin.

The double-crossing . . .

Eirene had been right about her. Again. She'd bring it up over and over for the next half century.

He staggered toward the door and tried to block the effects of the fast-acting drug as it burned through his system. He managed to mumble, "I was trying to warn you."

"I know." Meryem took his hands in a firm but gentle grip and easily restrained his attempts to draw a weapon.

He swayed and she leaned close to whisper into his ear. "But it's far too late for that."

Gregorios's legs gave out and he collapsed to the floor. The last thing he saw through gathering darkness was the door swinging open to reveal Mai Luan, followed by Asoka and a pair of enforcers.

CHAPTER THIRTY-THREE

The fear of death follows from the fear of life. A man who lives every life fully is prepared to die at any time.

~Mark Twain

Gregorios awakened, strapped to a chair in the council chamber. Several of the council members were already seated around the long table. Despite the warnings from Eirene and Quentin, the sight of how old and frail they looked shocked him.

He hadn't seen them in far too long and had underestimated the severity of the situation. If they were so far gone, they'd never listen to him over the one who held the key to their restoration.

Asoka sat closest to him and smiled when Gregorios regained consciousness. "You led us on quite a chase, Gregorios. I never expected it to end right here in our own offices."

"You always lacked imagination."

Without losing his smile, Asoka back-handed him across the face. The blow rocked him against the seat, but the throbbing in his cheek paled against the cold certainty that Asoka meant to kill him. Meryem, who sat across from him, looked uncomfortable, but the others just looked on with open distrust.

Gregorios said, "You're weak, and you've been hunting the wrong person."

"You betrayed us," Asoka snarled.

"I was always true to our overriding mission."

Asoka cackled and the abrupt change disturbed Gregorios more than his earlier anger. His strange laughter faded almost immediately and he looked around the table, eyes unfocused, as if confused.

Aline, who sat on the other side of the table, pointed toward Gregorios. When Asoka looked in his direction, he stared for ten full seconds before blinking in sudden recognition.

He smiled. "You led us on quite a chase, Gregorios. I never expected it to end right here in our own offices."

He'd broken the consistency barrier. If the rest of the council was this far gone, they might need to call in the hunters after all.

Before they had branded him traitor, it was Gregorios's job to euthanize council members pushed beyond the breaking point. Apparently the aged council had made sure no one else had assumed that role.

That was exactly why they had set him up in Berlin. Even back then they had realized the danger and determined to remove him in a preemptive strike. So many years wasted. It sparked a fresh wave of anger. He'd known these people for thousands of years, and for most of that time, he'd considered them the best souls in the world. They had fallen, and the scope of the tragedy was as depressing as the burning of the famous library of Alexandria had been.

Shahrokh sat across the table, looking tired and worn. He spoke for the first time. "Your arrival was fortuitous. We needed a subject for the final test."

"You're all going to die," Gregorios said, driven to make a final plea, despite the truth of their condition. "The machine's a lie prepared by the cui dashi to gain access to your minds and destroy everything you've built since Rome."

"Brilliant lie," Mai Luan said as she entered the room, followed by Tereza and a male assistant wheeling the machine.

The council members perked up at the sight of the machine. Even Zuri, who was old and fat and barely recognizable, slouching in a huge chair that must have been brought in special for her.

Mai Luan regarded Gregorios coldly. "With that little lie you could cloud the entire arrangement, sow discord, and delay the critical testing of our breakthrough technology." She gave him a mock bow of respect. "So at last we meet the famous Gregorios."

"Mai Luan. I have to admit, now that we meet in person, I'm underwhelmed."

She punched him in the chest, her hand blurring through the air. The blow tumbled him to the floor, chair and all, and cracked at least one rib. He slid all the way past Asoka to the wall on the far side.

"See? Cui dashi," he grunted.

At least Meryem finally looked a little uneasy. From his position he couldn't see the faces of any of the other council members.

As the male assistant pulled Gregorios back into place, Mai Luan said, "I apologize for my anger. Like your enforcers, I have applied runes of enhancement."

"Why didn't you tell us about this?" Meryem demanded.

"Did you share all your secrets with me?"

Meryem was always a shrewd one. More important, she always looked out for herself. "Perhaps Gregorios's warning was not so foolish a thing."

Gregorios fought back a groan. Every breath triggered searing fire in his chest. That woman packed a terrible punch. But maybe the pain would be worth it.

Then again, maybe not.

Mai Luan laughed softly. "So quick to doubt."

She surveyed the other council members. "Very well. We will withdraw until you decide you can trust us again."

Before she and her assistants could so much as take a single step away, Asoka rushed to block them, moving faster than a man in his condition should be able to.

Shahrokh spoke above the other council members, who all started shouting together for Mai Luan to stop. He called her back and gave Meryem a withering look. "Please ignore Meryem's foolish words. Her heart has never been right where Gregorios is concerned."

Incredibly, Meryem didn't fire off the retort Gregorios expected, but slumped in her chair. She looked torn, but clearly wouldn't risk her chance at the machine by taking a stand against the others.

The machine might not have stolen their secrets yet, but the council had already surrendered to Mai Luan.

Unbelievable. He had never seen anything like it. Those old men and women were the closest things to living gods on the earth and they were cowed by a single brilliant woman. They had to know she planned to kill them when she finished with them.

And still they did it.

He had never looked forward to dying, but had flirted with death enough that he had resigned himself to the inevitability of it. Apparently the other facetakers had not. They feared the one enemy they couldn't defeat on their own, but in their scramble to escape their fate they were guaranteeing their fall.

With no further arguments, Mai Luan and her assistants got to work. They secured the helmet to Gregorios, and Mai Luan donned the secondary unit. The soulmask they extracted from a nearby coffin looked familiar. It was Curly, who had told them of the runes. Gregorios wondered if Mai Luan had reincorporated Dalal yet.

Tereza smirked down at him before closing the jagged faceplate with a hard snap. He tried to keep his breathing calm. He had felt a cui dashi's power once and knew he could not withstand them. Mai Luan might look slight, but her power far outstripped his own. Magnified by her rounon gift, her nevra core could bring to bear entire magnitudes more soul force than he could, despite centuries of discipline.

That didn't mean he planned to give up.

He had helped destroy more than one of the monsters, and he vowed to find a way to defeat Mai Luan too. Their strength led to arrogance that could be turned against them. Somehow.

Mai Luan's voice echoed faintly through the constricting helmet. "This test will confirm final calibrations are correct and verify that Eirene's tampering did not damage the delicate components. After completion of this test, I expect to begin scheduling sessions with members of the council."

"Get on with it then," Asoka said.

The machine hummed to life and Gregorios felt its power pulsing against his face, fueled by the dispossessed soul. Eirene had warned him about what came next, but he still embraced his nevra core and prepared to defend himself.

It didn't help.

CHAPTER THIRTY-FOUR

It's the possibility of not having another one that makes each life interesting.
~Rasputin, rogue facetaker

Eirene and Alter sat at the long dining table in the art gallery, studying printouts of the runes, with Sarah looking on. She found the entire subject very interesting, especially after her experience with the healing rune she cut into Tomas's side.

She felt driven to learn as much as she could about them. The table around their work area was piled with finger foods, fruits and half a dozen pitchers of juices. A gentle fragrance filled the room, a mixture of warm, baked goods and the clean scent of fresh fruit.

Under Alter's direction, Eirene had arranged the runes as best she could in the order they had appeared on the machine. "I think that's it," she said finally. "As close as my incomplete set of photos allows."

"It's a good place to start," Alter said as he leaned over the runes, his expression intent.

He really did seem to know what he was talking about. His belligerence faded while working on the runes, replaced by honest enthusiasm.

"Why is the order important?" Sarah asked.

Alter glanced up from his study. "Like I said earlier, the runes are built around ancient forms of writing. Because of that, the order's important. They build upon each other like crude sentences."

"Fascinating."

"It really is. For example, I could say, 'I love to teach you new ways to think.' But with the same words, I could say, 'I think to teach you new ways to love.'"

That was a good one. He seemed to realize just how bold he was being because he looked away and actually flushed.

Sarah smiled. "I see what you mean." If she'd met him first, she might have been tempted to give him a chance. He lacked the depth she found so attractive in Tomas, but made up for it with good looks and enthusiasm.

Eirene chuckled. "Yes, he made his point very clear."

Alter pointed to the rune closest to him. "The problem is, they're using ancient runes that have fallen out of use. It's like trying to write in Old English. The word use is different, and some may not mean what we think."

Sarah slid a little closer to see what he was pointing at. He glanced up and his gaze lingered on her face a second longer than necessary. She pretended not to notice. She was already busy trying to figure out one relationship.

Right on cue, Tomas entered. He wore casual clothes and actually walked under his own power. His color had returned, and he looked ten times better than just the night before. Sarah met him with a warm hug, which he returned before she led him to the table and explained what they were doing.

"Good idea. What have you learned?" Tomas asked.

"Still figuring that out," Eirene said.

"Does it matter that the ones that look more Chinese are mixed in with the ones that look more Egyptian?" Sarah asked.

Alter said, "It is a bit unusual."

"But that's how they were ordered, as best we can tell," Eirene said.

"Isn't it harder to build sentences in two languages at once?"

Alter nodded. "It is. The nuances of the characters used as foundations for the runes often allow for multiple focuses, depending on the interpretation. Chinese symbols in particular can be extremely tricky. Mixing them in with Egyptian-based runes really confuses it."

"Which ones have you seen before?" Tomas asked.

Alter pointed to several of the runes and they were all ones based around Egyptian looking characters. "These are all very old, but the others are unknown to us." He picked up a picture of one of the Chinese-based runes. "We know so little about runes dating this far back in China. Very little knowledge trickled out of that half of Asia."

Eirene leaned back in her chair and sipped a red fruit drink. "We never got much out of China either. We know there were heka active there at times, and got hints of facetakers but never managed to make solid connections."

"I thought the council ruled all the facetakers," Sarah said.

"Just the ones we know about. Over time we discover more of them and encourage them to join."

Alter grunted. "Your enforcers are nearly as ruthless in removing the rogues as my clan."

Sarah looked from one to the other. "You kill them? Why?"

"The council helps maintain a stable world order," Tomas said.

"Stable for you," Alter interrupted.

"Rogue facetakers pose a threat just as real as active heka cells," Tomas explained.

"Are the heka that much of a threat to you?" Sarah asked.

"To us personally, not so much. We know how to deal with them," Tomas admitted.

Alter interjected. "If allowed to mature, kashaph can form cults that pose a threat to the unsuspecting world. We remove every rune we can, but if they're allowed to learn to master their rounon gift, and if they acquire sufficient runes, they can wreak terrible damage."

"Worse is when they team up with a rogue facetaker," Tomas said. "Like the Black Death, the plague that swept the world in the fourteenth century."

"Heka started that?" Sarah asked.

Alter said, "They did. They used a uniquely crafted series of runes. Their leader was extremely clever."

"She was a rogue facetaker," Tomas explained. "Gathered a following of well-trained heka disguised as monks in a monastery. With those runes and seven dispossessed souls, they triggered a pandemic that killed over one hundred million people. Slaughtered over half the population of Europe."

"Why would they do that?" Sarah asked. Everyone had heard of the black plague, but she'd never imagined it was triggered intentionally.

Alter said, "They were targeting my people, but the disease spread out of control. We destroyed that cell, and we've kept the secret of those runes from the world ever since."

"You still have the runes?" Sarah asked.

"We keep all runes we discover."

"Why? What if someone tried to use them again?"

"We protect our rune lore as our greatest treasure. Most of the world doesn't even know it exists. But if another group of kashaph attempt something similar, we can leverage that gathered rune lore to block and even undo much of the damage."

"It's still scary to consider," Sarah said.

Tomas said, "Be grateful major world powers don't know about the existence of that book. They already tamper with building stronger diseases to use as weapons, and some of them are actively exploring the use of heka strike teams."

Alter grimaced. "We destroy all those we can, but it's difficult when they're protected by governments."

"Rogue facetakers present other problems," Eirene took up the thread of the conversation. "Most people don't know we exist and don't want to know. Over the centuries, we've been classified as many things from witches to devils to vampires."

"As you should be," Alter grumbled.

"Your family has sparked enough riots through the centuries just to execute facetakers that you shouldn't play the righteous card," she said. When he made no other comment she continued. "Given the dangers of exercising our powers openly, we've developed a rigorous set of procedures that help ensure the safety of both ourselves and our clients."

"Rogue facetakers don't have that discipline. They make a mess, and we just talked about how bad things get when they fall in with the heka," Tomas said.

Alter added, "Merging of bloodlines spawn the cui dashi. One more reason to block those unholy alliances. In this my family's in agreement with your council."

"That's why we do it. The downfall of the Tsars was a direct result of the meddling of another rogue facetaker," Tomas said.

"Really?" Sarah asked. The conversation was disturbing, but fascinating.

Eirene nodded. "Gregorios couldn't stop Rasputin before that chain of events spiraled out of control."

"Rasputin was a facetaker? Why haven't people heard about any of this?" Sarah asked.

"One of the council members heads a department dedicated to ensuring we're written out of history. We've been remarkably successful."

"You change history?" That was more appalling than anything else she had heard.

Eirene gave her an apologetic smile. "A little. It gets twisted around enough on its own, but we do nudge it at times to make sure the world remains ignorant of our activities."

Sarah sat back in her chair, considering what she'd learned, and not happy about it.

"We could discuss these dangers all day," Eirene said. "But I think Sarah understands enough for now. Let's not lose track of our task."

"Thank you for explaining it to me," Sarah said. She needed to ask Alter more when they found more time. The subject interested her as much as the revelation of how runes could be used for evil purposes horrified her. She yearned to know how else they could be used for good.

Alter declared, "We must stop this Mai Luan before she wreaks untold damage with the knowledge she plans to steal from the council, and with her unique runes. The world order may be less than it should be, but we don't want to plunge it into chaos."

"Agreed," Eirene said. She gave Alter a warm smile and he managed a weak smile back.

He pointed at the runes he had indicated earlier. "These support Eirene's experience. They'll assist in focusing the recipient's mind back in time and magnify the memories, making them more powerful, more . . . realistic."

After a moment he frowned. "But that's not all of it. There's more going on here. I can see how it's possible they're being used to grant control over those memories to the passenger, but the interpretation is tenuous."

"Meaning?" Tomas prodded when Alter paused again.

"Meaning that unless there are other runes reinforcing that interpretation of the runes in the machine, it may be possible for the primary to fight that control."

"That would be good," Eirene said.

Alter nodded. "It's fascinating. I've never seen runes applied in such a way to memories." He leaned over the table, scanning the symbols, muttering to himself.

"Are they applied in other ways to memories?" Sarah asked after a moment, when it looked like he had forgotten anyone else was still in the room with him.

He started. "How did you . . . Never mind. That's not important."

"So they are?"

"It's not something we speak of."

Eirene said, "It is today. We can't have you holding back. What do you know about runes and memories?"

Alter sighed, rubbing a hand over his face. "It's possible with proper training to hunt through one's own memories to pivotal moments in your life. When immersed in such a memory, a hunter may discover a rune representing the truth of that moment."

"How does that work?" Sarah asked.

"The rune manifests the deepest truth of that moment, fueled by the power of the memory. It's revealed to the hunter as a burning symbol. Those personalized runes, when applied to that hunter's body and bonded to their soul, become powerful enhancements that trump standard runes."

"Enhancements? You mean like the rune I cut into Tomas's skin to save his life?"

Alter stared, looking astonished. "That's impossible. Only those possessing rounon gifts, such as the heka or my clan, can engrave a rune with the power to bond it to a soul."

"Show him," Sarah told Tomas. He obediently lifted up his shirt to reveal the tattoo-like rune on his side. The wound looked much smaller, totally scarred over, as if it had happened weeks ago.

Alter studied the rune and then looked from Tomas to Sarah. "You said you're new to runes. How did you know to do this?"

"I drew it first," Tomas said.

"I just marked it," Sarah added.

Alter studied the rune. "This is a non-standard rune."

Tomas craned his neck to study it, and Sarah crouched beside him. Alter pointed to the marks she had changed.

Tomas shrugged. "That's not how I planned to draw it. I was in pretty bad shape though, so I guess I messed up."

"You don't just mess up and accidentally create a higher rune." Alter sounded insulted.

"He didn't. I made the change when I was cutting it."

"You?" They asked in unison. Their shocked expressions nearly made her laugh. Maybe now they wouldn't think she was a completely helpless observer.

She shrugged. "The lines were a little blurred, and the way you drew it didn't feel right."

"What do you mean?" Alter asked, his face intent.

"I can't explain it." The attention was making her nervous. "While I was marking the rune, it seemed to make sense to me. But those two lines didn't. I just went on gut instinct."

Alter looked at her like she had just grown a second head.

"What?" she asked.

"Who are you really? No one develops that level of sensitivity without years of training and practice."

"I've never seen a rune in my life."

Eirene said, "Perhaps there's something we're missing. Runes draw upon the force of a soul. Heka sacrifice other souls, while hunters and our own enforcers use enhancement runes bonded to their souls and powered by that force alone."

"Agreed. So?" Alter asked.

"So facetakers move souls between bodies. The manifestation of rounon gifts and nevra core are different, but they all tie back to the soul. Sarah has experienced more soul transfers than any but the eldest of the facetakers."

Alter recoiled from Sarah as if she had just turned into a viper. "Impossible. No mortal soul can withstand so many."

"They were using a prototype of the machine," Sarah explained. "I didn't know what was going on. I thought it was some kind of technology that moved our consciousness, but Eirene's right. I've transferred hundreds of times."

Eirene said, "That has to be it. She has a discerning soul. I sensed that immediately. I suspect she developed a sensitivity to soul-based powers. That would explain why the runes make so much sense to her."

"Wow. You've got a super power," Tomas said with a grin.

"Saved your life," she retorted.

"Since Tomas's soul is experienced bonding with enhancing runes, that may have also contributed to their success," Eirene added.

"Did you know about that when you asked me to do it?" Sarah asked.

"No." Tomas admitted. "I was dying. I knew chances were slim, but we had to try something."

Sarah took his hand. She'd known that she'd almost lost him, but hadn't realized his life had hung on so slender a thread.

"We have to study this further," Alter said. He drew a little closer and considered her with a slightly disturbing intensity. "Do you have any runes?"

"Like my own tattoos? No."

"You should."

"Maybe I will."

No way she was going to carve herself with a knife until she learned more about it. Still, the idea took hold in her mind with such power she knew she'd try it eventually.

Eirene said, "Later. We still need to determine how the other runes tie in. Do they affect memories too? With our nevra core, facetaker memories are exceptionally sharp. Wearing that helmet, things felt almost as real as when I first lived them."

"Until we understand Mai Luan's plan, she holds the advantage," Tomas said.

They needed to flip that advantage to their favor, and soon.

CHAPTER THIRTY-FIVE

We have only one task, to stand firm and carry on the racial struggle without mercy. What an elegant solution to both of our problems, destroy the Jews and remove the hunters in one fell stroke. With our enchanters working with archaeologists to uncover lost runes, we'll soon control a power greater even than the supposed splitting of atoms. We will prepare here in the fortress of Europe, an army unlike any the world has ever known. We will sweep our enemies from the world and impose true order.

~Heinrich Himmler

Berlin.

Filled with the same anger the memory always triggered, Gregorios strode up Wilhelmstrasse with mortars whistling overhead, machine guns chattering in the distance, and clouds of heavy black smoke drifting across his path. He was angrier than normal, or maybe just angry about something else. He couldn't quite remember, but felt sure he shouldn't be there.

The air stank of dust, broken stone, gunpowder, and fear. Every breath dragged more of the filth into his lungs and, had he planned to wear that body much longer, would have left him fearful of contracting lung disease.

The dirty woman and her children scurried past, faces filled with fear.

Gregorios shouted, "Don't go that way!"

She ran faster, unwilling to avoid the fate hurtling toward her and her children. The knowledge that he couldn't stop the coming tragedy fueled Gregorios's rage.

Then time lurched forward and he found himself in the gardens of the Reich Chancellery, facing the rear of the Reichskanzlei.

He ignored the sentry outpost and made for the door in the cube-shaped building. To his right, a dozen soldiers dressed in SS uniforms burst out of a concealing hedgerow a couple hundred yards to the south. They raced in his direction, led by Asoka, who looked more eager for the upcoming confrontation than normal.

The jaws of the trap were closing around him again.

For the first time Gregorios paused and looked closely at the onrushing soldiers. He wanted to confront Asoka and rip out his soul, but that wasn't supposed to happen yet. The dream memory pulled him back toward the steel door and he allowed himself to slip back into the familiar movement.

The door opened into a small entry room with stairs that led down into the underground Fuhrerbunker. That was his ultimate destination.

Usually he woke at this point. That much he did remember.

This time he didn't wake up.

A woman waited inside. She sat in a chair on the far side of the otherwise empty, concrete room, dressed in a crisp uniform of the German military intelligence. The brim of an unusually large hat covered her face.

She had never been there before.

He approached the long stair leading down into the bunker where Hitler awaited him. The dream drove him in that direction, but proximity to the ultimate target sparked a rebellious anger.

Gregorios stopped.

For a second everything froze, as if the dream was a movie he had just paused. He had never done that before, had never realized he could. Never before in a dream had he stepped outside of the moment while still in it.

The frozen second passed and the dream tried to exert control and force him to follow the prescribed path, but he resisted. It was like trying to stand in a fast-flowing river while the waters tore the stones away from under foot. With agonizing slowness, he turned away from the stairs.

The strange woman had risen and stood behind him. She tipped her hat up until he could see her face.

Mai Luan.

"You're not part of my memory."

She smiled, showing her bright, even teeth. "I am whatever I choose to be here."

"But it's my memory." He was struggling to think against the pull of the memory, but his thoughts were sluggish.

He hated her, didn't he?

She lifted a hand toward his face and although her smile never faded, her eyes grew cold. "This dream is now mine."

Gregorios slapped her hand away.

His thoughts might be muddied, but he knew enough to keep her hands away from his face. How dare she interrupt his dream, especially this one? That day had been the end of much and the beginning of many things, none of which was her business.

"Get out," he growled.

"Once I find what I seek." She gestured toward the stairs. "Get back to it."

The pull of the dream on his mind intensified and his feet began moving toward the stairs. His mind blanked and he forgot why he was struggling. Just go down there and get it over with.

No.

It took every ounce of concentration to stop his foot that was already swinging out over the top step. It hovered in the air, quivering with the internal struggle. Then ever so slowly he brought it back to the floor and again turned.

"You lack any right to be here," he growled at Mai Luan, whose calm fled before his wrath.

She hauled him off his feet and punched him so fast he never saw her fist coming. The blow smashed him across the room and out the exterior door. He lay blinking stupidly up into the smoke-filled sky as waves of agony radiated from his bruised chest.

He slowly rolled to his knees. The SS soldiers were getting close and Asoka wore a snarl on his face. He'd never actually seen them approaching before. How could he know what they'd look like?

Then something dark and scaly lunged out of the shadows of the sentry pillbox. It moved with startling speed and yanked two of the soldiers back into the shadows. Blood and screams sprayed out over the rest of the squad, who all turned toward the unexpected threat and fired into the darkness.

Something with a terrifyingly deep voice howled. It sounded like a wolf that had swallowed an amplifier.

That was definitely not part of the memory. It was twisting into a nightmare. The creature reminded him of the shadow of another nightmare he once had, the dark memory of a barely remembered threat.

Whatever it was, it distracted him from the real danger.

Mai Luan again lifted him off the ground with one hand and threw him back into the bunker. He bounced once on the smooth cement floor, crashed through the chair she had been sitting in, and slammed into the far wall.

Despite the pain, he forced himself to his feet and reached for his sidearm. Confused, he glanced down.

It was gone.

He always carried a gun in this memory.

Mai Luan sauntered into the small room. Gregorios grabbed up two of the legs of the broken chair and attacked her with them. She might be cui dashi, but he had trained as a fighter for more centuries than he cared to count.

He attacked with every ounce of power he could muster and threw every trick of stick fighting he knew at her. She was inhumanly fast and far stronger than he, but she lacked his depth of training. He landed enough solid hits to slow her down and avoid her grasping hands.

The enclosed room smelled of cement dust, and soon of sweat. They fought across the smooth floor and he beat on her with ever-increasing tempo, trying to drive her over the edge of the stairs, but she twisted away. The move left her open and he beat both sticks into her face so hard his hands hurt from the impact.

She gasped, an expression of shock on her bruised face, and Gregorios laughed. This was his memory and by the forgotten gods, she'd wish she'd never entered here.

He avoided a two-handed lunge and tried to break her teeth. As the two of them fought back and forth across the small room, more howling echoed from outside, followed by more gunfire and new screaming. It distracted him just a little.

A little was enough.

Mai Luan slugged him in the face so hard she nearly took his head off. The blow drove him back into the wall. He struck with such force that he probably left a dent in the concrete.

It also knocked him right out of the dream.

Gregorios awoke in the council chamber, rocking back in his chair so hard it almost tipped over. His face screamed with pain and he coughed up blood. His chest ached and every gasping breath felt like a knife between his ribs.

He blinked against the pain and tried to center his thoughts. What had just happened?

Clearly Mai Luan had dragged him into his dreams, but did he choose that one or did she? The dream had been exceptionally clear, but he'd recognized that he was dreaming. What about the strange monster?

He couldn't think through the pain. He hadn't hurt that much in a long time. One thought struck him with as much force as Mai Luan had. Everywhere she hit him in the dream hurt in the real world.

How was it possible?

Tereza lifted the jagged face plate, then removed the helmet. A gaggle of voices finally registered and drew his attention. The council members were all speaking at once, hitting Mai Luan with a barrage of questions about the test. How did it go? Why was Gregorios spitting blood and looking so battered? Why was her face bruised?

Mai Luan had removed her helmet and sported a bruise on her lovely face right where he had clubbed her with the leg of the chair. So he was not the only one who could bleed in the dream world.

She glared at him and he winked back. She didn't need to know how much she terrified him.

It took several minutes for her to calm the council. She fed them a bunch of blather they never would have accepted if they weren't so desperate to gain access to the machine.

Mai Luan leaned close to Gregorios as she returned her helmet to Tereza. "Your soul is mine, along with everything I decide to take from your mind."

"You're such a—"

She didn't even let him finish, but shoved a Taser into his ribs and triggered a double burst. Before the jolting electricity subsided, Tereza jabbed him with a tranquilizer.

On most facetakers, the electric shock would disrupt their focus long enough for the tranquilizer to put them out like any mortal. Gregorios and Quentin had developed the idea decades ago. It was the same concept as his double-barreled pistol, and he had trained himself to withstand exactly that deadly combination.

It was still hard, but all that painful training kicked in and he managed to embrace enough of his nevra core to partially sever the link between his soul and his body in time. As rattled as he was, he barely managed to surround his mind with enough nevron to block the effects of the knock-out drug.

Mai Luan whispered into his ear, "Know that I'll track down your wife soon. She too will fuel my rise to power."

"I'll kill you," he mumbled.

She patted his cheek. "I'll break your spirit, just like I broke Sarah. You'll beg to die before we're through."

Gregorios didn't respond, but slumped forward in his chair and dragged his eyes closed as if the drug had worked. It would still shut his body down for a bit, but far less than expected.

Shahrokh spoke. "The test is completed. You promised this one would prove the final calibrations were dialed in. Did it work?"

"We identified one glitch that must be resolved," Mai Luan assured them. "I calculate the adjustments will take no more than a day. We'll test Gregorios one more time, and then move on to scheduling council members."

"Is that why he was spitting blood?" Meryem demanded.

"Yes."

"How can the machine cause damage like that?" Asoka demanded. "You said this was all a mental exercise."

Mai Luan explained. "Gregorios attempted to interfere by embracing his nevra core. He hurt himself by trying to damage the machine from within."

Shahrokh said, "We shouldn't allow him to test it again. It's not worth the risk."

It was hard not to laugh in their faces. There were so many other questions they needed to ask, but she was deadening their minds with the promise of salvation. They heard what they wanted to hear.

Mai Luan said smoothly, "On the contrary. Once we confirm we can succeed even with a resisting subject, that will prove the safety protocols are correct."

Why did she want to test him again? There had to be something in that memory that she wanted.

The council and Mai Luan discussed the schedule for the next test for a few more minutes. No one paid Gregorios any more attention, which was exactly what he needed.

CHAPTER THIRTY-SIX

You can never be overdressed or overeducated.

~Quentin

With the test completed, the council members quickly dispersed. A pair of enforcers were assigned to lift Gregorios from his chair and drag him to a holding cell in the basement. His legs were unshackled and left to drag behind, but they kept his hands cuffed behind his back.

Asoka spoke as they were dragging him away. "Gregorios has gone soft."

Gregorios yearned to punch Asoka in the mouth, but resisted the urge. Asoka might inhabit an old form, but he was no fool. That was a classic test that often worked on even experienced operatives.

Gregorios remained limp until the enforcers paused to unlock the cell door. As soon as he heard the cell door begin to swing open, he lunged and knocked the lead enforcer into the cell. They might be powerfully enhanced soldiers, but even they could be knocked down when taken by surprise.

Gregorios threw himself against the second enforcer, but the half-second delay was plenty of time for the man. He knocked Gregorios against the wall next to the cell door and punched him twice in his already hurt ribs. Gregorios hissed with pain and tried kicking the man's knees with no luck.

The fellow threw another punch but Gregorios twisted away and the man hit the corner of the door frame. He yelped and Gregorios kicked him between the legs.

As the man went down, the enforcer Gregorios had knocked into the cell jumped onto his back. The two of them stumbled across the hall. Gregorios spun wildly and bit the arm wrapped around his neck. The enforcer slipped off and Gregorios twisted free.

Both enforcers faced him in the hallway. Battered as he was, with his arms still chained behind his back, he was going to have a very hard time of it.

Then one of them suddenly pitched to the floor where he lay twitching.

The second enforcer snarled, "What did you do?"

"Magic."

Then the second enforcer jerked in shock and fell to the floor, arms and legs flailing.

Quentin stood ten feet behind the enforcers, double-barreled pistol still raised. "Magic?"

"Keeps them guessing. Besides, kept that guy still for another second."

Quentin frowned as he removed the cuffs, "The day I can't hit a moving target at ten feet is the day you bury me."

"I'd trust your aim for at least a couple days after that." Gregorios gripped Quentin's shoulder in silent thanks.

"Sloppy not to watch their backs anyway," Quentin said as the two of them tossed the unconscious enforcers into the cell and locked the door.

Even as Gregorios dropped the key into his pocket, he heard muttered curses inside. That was pretty good recovery.

Gregorios accepted the pistol from Quentin. "You'd better make yourself scarce before someone sees you."

Quentin saluted. "I need to get back to the toy shop anyway. Working on non-lethals for heka takedowns today. Some exciting breakthroughs recently."

"Anything new against cui dashi?"

"That's on tomorrow's brainstorming schedule."

"Good. Think fast. See you later."

Gregorios headed the opposite way of his old friend. He stopped at Asoka's office and threw open the door without knocking.

Asoka sat in a padded chair behind his huge desk. He recovered from the shock of the unexpected intrusion with remarkable speed for an old guy and jumped to his feet.

Gregorios shot him in the chest with the double-barreled pistol. The blow knocked him back into his chair. While Asoka twitched under the double tap of electric shock and fast-acting drugs, Gregorios tied him up with his own shirt. Then he donned Asoka's fine wool overcoat and signature wide-brimmed hat.

Before the drug shut down Asoka's mind, Gregorios gave him a mock bow. "You know, I've always liked this hat."

"I'll kill you," Asoka growled.

Gregorios punched him in the mouth. "Payback is always the best part of my job."

"Kill me, then."

It always infuriated him when fools tried to assume the role of martyr.

He leaned closer. "I was never your enemy, you idiot."

Asoka struggled against the restraining shirt, but his strength was fading under the effects of the sleep drug. Gregorios leaned close.

"Listen carefully. Mai Luan is cui dashi and the machine grants her the ability to travel through your memories. She's going to strip your mind and destroy you all. She's never going to restore your soul."

"You lie," Asoka muttered, growing drowsy.

"Think about it. You're the one who betrayed me, but I've never lied to you. Ever. We have differences to resolve, but Mai Luan's a bigger threat than any other. You're smarter than you've been acting. Defend yourself."

Asoka mumbled something too soft to understand, then his eyes drifted closed.

Gregorios stood over him for a moment, torn. By all rights, he should remove Asoka's soulmask and shatter it, but all he saw was a broken old man seated before him. He hoped Asoka would consider the warning when he awoke. It was all Gregorios could do for him and for the council.

He'd lead his small team against Mai Luan, but if the council didn't act in their own defense, they would fall and there was nothing Gregorios could do to save them from the fate they were walking into.

CHAPTER THIRTY-SEVEN

There are more beautiful people living in the world today than ever before. I know, I've cataloged them for centuries. The consignment team has never had such an easy job finding excellent transfer vehicles and it's never been easier to find delicious boys to attend me.

~Meryem, facetaker council member

Sarah moved across the polished hardwood floor of the exercise room in a series of kicks and punches. Tomas, who rested in a comfortable chair nearby, called out the moves in an ever-increasing tempo and she struggled to keep up.

The door opened and Alter entered. Sarah's concentration wavered and she stumbled.

"Focus," Tomas urged.

"In a minute," Sarah panted. She rested hands on knees and sucked in several deep breaths. Then she walked to the wall of mirrors for a drink from her water bottle. She was enjoying the strenuous workout.

The exercise room was located on the main floor, with wide windows overlooking the pool. The room smelled of wood polish and faintly of chlorine. Sarah planned to take a swim after the workout. As a top model for Alterego, she kept in excellent condition, but her muscles burned from the unfamiliar fighting moves.

"What do you think?" Sarah asked.

Tomas said, "You have great natural talent. You're taking to the basic forms really well. In a couple days when I'm back on my feet we can begin sparring."

"What are you doing?" Alter asked from the door.

Sarah wiped her face with a small towel. "Tomas promised to teach me some self-defense. I think I'm going to need it."

"No doubt," Alter said as he crossed the room to join them. "Have you had any training before?"

She shrugged. "Not much. Just a couple evening classes at the local gym."

"Well, you can't learn self-defense without a sparring partner. Come, I'll take you."

"I don't think that's a good idea," Tomas said with a frown. "You hunters use a different style. I don't want to confuse her."

"We'll start with the basics," Alter assured him although he never looked away from Sarah. "That won't cause any harm."

"Oh, I'll cause harm," Sarah promised with a smile as she faced off with him.

Tomas didn't look happy to have his role as teacher supplanted, and she knew he probably hated the idea of her getting physical with Alter. Well, he'd have to deal with it. She needed to learn, and he needed to learn to trust her. They were either going to make a relationship work, or they weren't. Getting jealous wasn't going to help.

They had already faced heka twice, and both times she'd felt terrified and unsure how to defend herself. She couldn't count on luck keeping her alive in the future, especially once Mai Luan decided to come after them. She needed to learn everything she could, and she'd take that knowledge from anyone offering it.

Before she and Alter could begin, the door opened again and Gregorios swept inside, his long coat billowing behind, most of his face concealed by a wide-brimmed, leather hat. Eirene walked by his side.

Tomas looked relieved and Alter irritated.

"Nice hat," Sarah said.

Gregorios made a little bow and Eirene said, "Don't encourage him. He always liked that hat."

"What happened?" Tomas asked.

"They're farther gone than we feared," Gregorios said. He tossed the hat onto a bench against the wall and Sarah gasped to see deep bruises on his face.

"You about done here?" he asked.

"Sure. We can finish later," Sarah said.

She pulled on a light jacket to cover her sweat-soaked exercise top and followed the group back to the gallery dining room. Quentin had returned and waited for them there, sitting at the head of the table laden with an assortment of snacks and drinks.

He greeted Sarah with a tiny bow and helped push in her chair. She sat between Alter and Tomas, and they mirrored similar expressions of surprise at Quentin's chivalrous move, followed by chagrin that they hadn't thought of it first.

Quentin leaned close. "I hear you're interested in training to fight?"

"I am. Tomas and Alter both volunteered to teach me."

"Excellent, my dear. Please add me to your card."

"My what?"

"Your schedule," he said with a little smile.

"Are you sure you want me trying to hit you?" Sarah asked, surprised. He still looked to be in excellent shape, but he was easily twice her age.

Quentin chuckled. "No, you go ahead and punch the young men as much as you like. There are a few things I can teach you that they haven't mastered yet."

Tomas said, "He's the best. Quentin was recruited from British special forces to run the armory. He's our mad genius weapons inventor."

"Careful with laying on so many compliments," Quentin warned. "Or one might assume you are trying to ingratiate yourself with your boss."

"Wait, you're Tomas's boss?" Sarah exclaimed.

"Technically, yes. For the past eighteen months, on paper at least, he reports to me as a special operations asset."

"Couldn't really tell them I was working with Gregorios, could I?" Tomas asked.

Sarah said, "You could've told me sooner. Quentin, I'd be honored to train with you."

She was comfortable around guns, but welcomed a chance to practice with an actual soldier.

"It will be my pleasure," Quentin said.

While they dug into the snack food, Gregorios told them what happened to him at Suntara. Sarah wanted to ask lots of questions about his memory of Berlin, but he didn't look like he was in a mood to share more details. The fight with Mai Luan sounded brutal, and by the stiff way he sat in his chair, she could tell he was in a lot of pain.

"It's interesting that Mai Luan pushed you back to World War Two like she did with me," Eirene commented.

"She flat out said she's searching for something."

"Her name is a lie," Alter interjected.

"What?"

"You said she's Chinese or Chinese-American. That name doesn't work in Chinese. It has to be some kind of alias."

"It sounds Chinese to me," Sarah said.

"The sounds are, but Chinese names are very important, and are chosen carefully. Those sounds, and the characters they form don't flow well and don't produce the effect a good Chinese name seeks."

Gregorios saluted with a muffin. "Interesting point. I'll ask her about it the next time I see her."

"Good." Alter missed the sarcasm. "Knowing her family line might be important. There has to be a reason she'd choose a name like this."

Eirene said, "We'll see what we can learn. Whatever she's looking for must be from the war. The memories coincide."

That gave Sarah a thought. "Do you have any shared memories she might find interesting?"

"I hadn't considered she might be interested in memories like that," Eirene said with a grin.

Gregorios laughed and nearly snorted fruit juice right out his nose. He started coughing, which made him wince in pain. Tomas slapped him on the back a few times, probably hurting him more.

Sarah blushed. "I mean shared memories of the war?"

"Most of the world shared in those events one way or another," Gregorios said when he caught his breath.

Alter, who had been frowning again, rocked back in his chair. He looked shocked.

"What is it?" Sarah asked.

"Ah, nothing."

"That excuse didn't work last time. Spit it out," Tomas said.

"It's nothing," Alter insisted even though he still looked rattled.

Eirene said, "Dear, you've lost every chance of hiding whatever it is you just realized. Now don't insult us all by pretending we didn't see what we just did. You have a terrible poker face."

"I don't play poker."

"Don't. You'll lose your shirt," Gregorios said.

"What did you realize?" Sarah asked. She wouldn't mind seeing him lose his shirt.

Alter folded his arms, his expression unfriendly. "It's not something we talk about."

Gregorios growled, "You insisted on coming along so you could share your knowledge with us and help us bring down Mai Luan."

"This is different."

"Then it's exactly what we need to hear."

When he still didn't speak Gregorios added, "Either explain, or you're on the next flight back to daddy."

"You cannot force me away!"

"Wanna make a wager?" Tomas asked. The threatening tone would have worked better if he wasn't still mostly confined to a chair.

That approach wasn't working, so Sarah placed a hand on Alter's arm. "Mai Luan promised to kill me. She'll do it if you don't help us."

Alter's anger faltered under her steady gaze and he swallowed hard. He spoke softly to her, again as if the two of them were alone. "When you brought up the shared memories, that's when I knew."

"Tell us." She squeezed his arm. He really did have excellent muscle tone.

"You know how we were discussing runes yesterday and how we can pull special ones from our most powerful memories?"

"Yes."

"This is related, but far more powerful."

"How?"

He spoke with great reluctance. "All of the runes we've discussed so far are runes that draw from the power of individual souls, but that's not the only type."

"Some runes aren't appropriate for personal enhancement," Eirene said.

"Like the rune webs enchanters can fashion," Tomas added.

"Enchanters?" Sarah asked.

He said, "The highest form of heka rounon power. Channelers can power their runes remotely by bound dispossessed souls, but the runes still work the same way they do for occultists. Fully trained enchanters can link several soulmasks into a spell, a rune web that's far more powerful, with broader effects, sometimes covering an entire area instead of an individual heka."

"Those are a higher form of rounon spellcasting," Alter said. "But there's a higher form still. Only the most trusted rune experts in my family know about them."

"That's why you hesitated," Sarah said.

He nodded. "We call them master runes."

CHAPTER THIRTY-EIGHT

If you're gonna have two lives at least make one of them pretty.
~Marilyn Monroe

I've never heard of master runes," Gregorios said.

"Like I said, they're a closely guarded secret and for good reason."

Everyone leaned closer since he spoke so softly, clearly torn between the desire to explain and the need to keep the secret. Sarah's touch finally won out. "You must swear to keep this knowledge secret and share it with no others."

Gregorios said, "Agreed, unless that knowledge is necessary to bring down Mai Luan."

When everyone nodded agreement Alter continued. "The memory runes we've discussed before represent personal truths that resonate with a person's soul. They produce far greater enhancements for those individuals than generic runes because they're attuned to that individual soul. In the same way, there are runes attuned to pivotal moments in history."

"How does that work?" Tomas asked.

Alter shrugged. "It just does. Important moments in history, those pivotal moments where large segments of the population are focused on the outcome of the event, are attuned to the souls of those thousands or even millions of people. As a result, those moments are imbued with incredible power."

"I can hardly believe it," Eirene whispered.

Alter said, "They are rare, and extremely difficult to access. It can be done only by one who is connected with that moment, who is trained properly, and who is gifted with sufficient power. They must travel their memories to that moment and embrace a truth of the event.

"A truth?" Sarah asked.

He nodded. "Such a moment will likely link to many truths. A moment of great victory for one is also the moment of crushing defeat to another. Which truth the memory walker embraces will shift the rune to reflect that truth."

Memory walker. Sarah liked the sound of that.

Gregorios leaned back in his chair, expression thoughtful. "This is new territory. I've lived moments like that, events where the course of history lay in the balance."

"Those would provide the most powerful master runes," Alter said.

"So you're saying that those moments link to the souls of those involved, and can draw upon that power even now?" Quentin asked.

Alter nodded. "It's a higher form of power, only ever accessed twice that I'm aware of. Most people lack the training, the individual self-mastery, and personal experience with such a powerful historical moment. For those few who do though, they may gain a glimpse of the master rune attuned to a truth of that moment."

"So it could be done by a well-trained heka?" Tomas asked.

"Unlikely. They rarely develop the depth of skill or discipline. The life expectancy for such a kashaph is short, for we'd become aware of them and hunt them down."

"If we didn't get them first," Tomas said.

"A cui dashi like Mai Luan could do it," Eirene said.

"Perhaps," Alter said thoughtfully.

Gregorios slapped the table. "But she's not doing it. She doesn't have the memory. She's developed her machines to search through the memories of the only other people who could do it."

"Facetakers," Sarah said in unison with Quentin.

Gregorios nodded. "One of the effects of manipulating our nevron is exceptional memory clarity. If anyone could grant her access to a master rune, it's the minds of the facetaker council."

"If she has indeed learned of the existence of master runes and actually gains access to it, she could unlock terrible power," Alter said, his expression grave. "We've never faced such a threat."

"How? I don't understand," Sarah asked.

Alter explained. "This subject delves into theoretical metaphysics. Little is known of the power of history."

"Especially when it's changed," Sarah muttered.

Eirene asked, "Are you saying history represents real power? I've seen it motivate for good and evil, which is why we have to keep the truth of history secret at times."

"It's more than a motivational force," Alter said, warming to the topic. "Think about it. If one who's been properly trained can draw great power from important moments in their life, there's something there. The personalized history runes are real. We've documented the sharp increase in the effectiveness of those enhancements."

"I believe that much, but how does that translate to broader history?" Gregorios asked.

Alter said, "Pivotal moments. Those are the only moments we're talking about. Think back to times you've lived where the outcome was so critical that nations committed their whole resources to supporting their goals."

"Stalingrad," Gregorios said somberly. "Both Germany and Russia committed everything to that battle. Nearly two million people died as a result of that campaign. It was one of the turning points of the war."

"You were there?" Sarah asked. He spoke like he had first-hand experience.

"I was. The Germans had fielded a unit of highly enhanced heka channelers during that offensive. They had hoped to shatter the Russian defenses with those superhuman troops."

"You fought against them?" she asked.

Alter said, "Not hardly. Gregorios worked for the Germans. My family destroyed that unit. One of my uncles died in the fighting."

Sarah could scarce believe it. Gregorios had worked for Hitler?

Gregorios read her expression. "I worked on assignment, although I disagreed with the mission."

Alter said, "You can't apologize for what you did. There's too much blood on your hands."

"Did you ever ask yourself how your family learned about that heka unit?" Gregorios asked softly. "Or how they obtained so much detailed intelligence regarding the specifics of the enhancements being employed?"

"My great-grandmother Elizabeth captured the information."

Eirene said, "It was arranged that way so your great-grandfather Ronen would believe the report. Otherwise he would've led your family into a slaughter."

"I don't believe you," Alter said.

Gregorios said, "Believe what you want. I positioned assets there that your family never knew about. They turned the tide of that fight from the shadows. In fact," He nodded toward Tomas. "I'm not the only one who—"

"Who's getting off topic," Tomas interrupted. He kept his expression neutral, but Sarah noted the tightening of his eyes. He was nervous about something Gregorios had been about to say. She wanted to ask about it, but maybe it was a point that would only anger Alter more.

"Perhaps I am," Gregorios said after a brief hesitation. "Stalingrad was a moment that affected millions of lives directly, and the entire world indirectly. How would a moment like that fuel real power that someone like Mai Luan could leverage?"

Alter looked like he wanted to argue more, but reined in the impulse. "Stalingrad is a good example. If we returned to a memory of one who lived through it, we might gain access to a master rune. That rune represents a deeper truth. For example, it might tap into the commitment from the soldiers on both sides to sacrifice for the greater good of their mother countries. Millions of souls were focused on that moment, and many of them died for a cause they believed in. There is tremendous power in a soul dedicated to such a cause. When so many souls unite for the same cause, that moment in history is imbued with residual energy."

"You're saying that if Mai Luan gained such a master rune, she could access the lingering force of all of those souls focused on that moment?" Eirene asked.

"Yes. The rune is the key to unlocking a power source mightier than anything the world has ever seen. That's why this is such a closely guarded secret."

"That's it," Tomas declared. "It has to be."

He pulled Sarah into a hug which broke her hand away from Alter. She returned the embrace, appreciating his creativity.

Gregorios nodded. "It's the first idea that actually makes sense. Everything fits."

"So Mai Luan could take that master rune and use it as a personal enhancement?" Sarah asked.

Alter shuddered. "Such a thing has never been done. It would be an abomination to corrupt such a rune for her personal enhancement."

"But it's possible?" Eirene pressed.

He hesitated as he really considered the idea. "I'm not sure. To try might well destroy her."

"But if she succeeded?" Sarah asked.

"She would become a force such as the world has never known. I don't think we could kill her if she was powered by such a force."

Gregorios said, "She's hard enough to kill without master runes, but what if that's not her plan? What else could she do with it?"

"If she could configure it properly, she might be able to couple it with the runes she's already discovered. Amplified through that machine of hers, she could probably break the minds of anyone hooked up to it. She could re-shape their wills and turn them into her willing slaves."

Eirene grimaced. "I hadn't thought things could get worse. She's not just trying to steal access to those memories. She's planning on complete domination of the council."

Tomas said, "That's bad. With the contracts coming due over the next few years and with a little patience, she could gain control over several heads of state."

"She would rule from the shadows and no one would know," Gregorios said.

Alter scowled at him. "Don't look so surprised. Your evil ways had to backfire eventually. Your organization might very well have laid the foundation for her to take over the world."

"Now you're just being melodramatic. She hasn't gained the master rune yet. We can still stop her," Eirene said.

"We have to," Gregorios agreed.

"If we can't stop her immediately, we must destroy the council," Alter pressed.

"Perhaps. She has to be stopped. Let's agree on that for now," Gregorios said.

"And how long do you think any of us would live once she gained control over the might of Suntara?" Eirene added.

They didn't have to answer that. Mai Luan had already promised to hunt Sarah down, and that was before she gained access to a super rune that might make her invincible.

As the conversation faded into discussion of the ramifications of what Mai Luan could do if Alter's fears proved correct, Sarah found it hard to focus. She let the others discuss questions about the master runes and timing of important upcoming soul transfers. It seemed impossible that such evil could be committed on such a global scale. She squeezed Tomas's hand and looked to him for comfort.

He looked grave, but gave her an encouraging smile. "We'll figure it out."

Then he rose. "I'm heading back to the council headquarters. I'll see what intel I can gather."

Sarah stared in disbelief. "You're crazy. Mai Luan nearly killed you last time. If she learns you're alive, she'll finish what she started in the alley."

"There's a couple of things I have to do," he said, trying reassure her. "I have the element of surprise. I'll slip in and out before anyone's the wiser."

She looked to Eirene for support but the facetaker surprised her by saying, "It's a calculated risk, but Tomas is right. He has to go."

"At least wait until you're better," Sarah urged.

"This is the best time," Tomas insisted.

Quentin also rose, dabbing at his mouth with a creamy white napkin. "I also must return to Suntara. I assure you, my dear, that I can get Tomas into the building safely."

Eirene added, "There are things Tomas has to do, things he must restore."

"You're still hiding stuff from me," Sarah accused him.

"I'll be back before you know it. Everything will be clear then. He gave her a kiss on the cheek and left with Quentin.

Sarah watched after him, terrified she might never see him again. She trusted Quentin, but why would they all agree to send Tomas on such a dangerous mission so soon after Gregorios's disastrous infiltration of the council building?

Gregorios and Eirene left a few minutes later to visit the medical wing.

Alter gave Sarah a warm smile. "If you're not busy, how about we get back to that self-defense training?"

"Good idea." She eagerly followed him back to the exercise room.

She really needed to hit something.

CHAPTER THIRTY-NINE

The Swedes embrace devilish runes that grant their soldiers strength and rapid healing. But for this advantage, I would have conquered Charles' armies long since. Gregorios informs me that a group of hunters may be amenable to removing Charles' heka supporters and open the way for successful conquest. The only catch is that I cannot reveal to them my involvement with the facetaker, who they consider a different form of evil. This is a simple requirement. I would offer far more to obtain my second life.

~Peter the Great

All evidence of the hysteria surrounding the supposed papal visit had been erased by the time Tomas arrived at the Suntara building. Gregorios's description of the bedlam his ruse had caused made him wish he'd seen it. Maybe he'd take a few minutes to look up the security recordings.

Tomas bypassed the main entrance and approached an unmarked solid wood door on the side street. He swiped his ID card and pushed the door open.

A bulletproof glass wall greeted him on the far side of a plain entrance vestibule. To pass through the second gate set in that wall required a second card reader, plus a retinal scan. An armed guard sat at a monitor on the far side. Tomas had met the man a couple times, but hadn't seen him in over a year and couldn't remember his name.

Quentin, who had just passed through the security gate, stood chatting with the guard.

Tomas swiped his ID again and leaned over the scanner so it could check his eye. He maintained a calm expression, despite his fluttering nerves. If Mai Luan had revealed his connection to Gregorios to the council, warning lights would begin flashing in other parts of the building, triggering an immediate response by heavily armed enforcers.

The door buzzed to allow him through. Tomas glanced at Quentin as he reached for the door. His old friend wore a slight frown, but didn't make the wave-off sign that would send Tomas bolting for his life.

The guard didn't look alarmed. "Tomas, it's been a while."

"Sure has."

"I heard you were dead."

"I'm not finished with this life just yet," Tomas said with an easy smile.

"Welcome back," the guard said, then gestured toward his monitor. "I've got a note for you. Priority one. Shahrokh wants you in his office."

"Does it say why?"

"No, but he's cranky today, so don't delay. The system will have already notified his office."

"Thanks."

He saluted Quentin, who fell in beside him. When they passed out of earshot of the guard, his boss said, "I checked the security board. You're not on it, but this summons can't be a coincidence."

"No, it can't, but they know I'm here. I can't dodge the meeting without arousing suspicion."

"Be careful," Quentin said, then stepped into the elevator that would take him into the bowels of the earth beneath the building where his workshop was located.

A moment later, the other elevator chimed and the doors slid open.

Tereza stood inside.

Tomas couldn't avoid her, so he hid his frustration at running into one of Mai Luan's confirmed lackeys so soon and stepped into the elevator. He'd hoped to complete his objectives with a minimum of interaction.

"How did you survive?" Tereza didn't hide her surprise.

"Mai Luan made a critical mistake," Tomas said.

Tereza tried to exit past him, but he shifted to block her way. He leaned close, enjoying the flicker of fear that crossed her face despite the fact that she was a facetaker and he only an enforcer.

"You picked the wrong side, Tereza, but it's not too late to fix this."

Her nervousness evaporated with a soft laugh. "You should've started running as soon as you woke up, blockhead."

"I'm not going to let you destroy the council. On my honor, I swear you're finished."

His glower didn't faze her. "Save your silly honor. You can't stop this. Worry about yourself, tough guy, and your girlfriend. She doesn't have much time left."

Tereza pushed past Tomas, and he was tempted to follow her back into the hall and remove her once and for all. While he hesitated, a pair of enforcers rounded a nearby corner, wrecking his chance. Tereza was a facetaker in good standing, so killing her would make him a priority target. He wouldn't add enforcer blood to his hands, not for Tereza.

"Your time's coming," he called after her as the doors closed, but the threat sounded weak even to him. Unless he found a way to undermine Mai Luan's hold over the council, Tereza's position was secure.

As he rode the elevator up, he tried to prepare his mind for the meeting. Shahrokh was the leader of the council and used to be his boss. Asoka ran most of the enforcer units, but Shahrokh maintained an elite force assigned directly to him. With his physical and mental health deteriorating so badly, he left most of the actual leading to his subordinates.

Tomas's current cover was a special investigator reporting directly to Quentin. The post gave him tremendous autonomy and was the only reason he managed to spend several months under cover with Alterego helping Gregorios hunt for Eirene. It also ensured he avoided much contact with Shahrokh.

Shahrokh's office was located in the corner of the building, with spectacular views of St. Peter's Basilica. His secretary waved Tomas through.

"How is he?" Tomas asked softly.

"Grumpy."

Shahrokh sat in an overstuffed chair situated close to a gas fireplace cranked all the way up. The spacious office was stifling, but the elderly councilman sat wrapped in a thick blanket. Two medical staffers attended him.

More importantly, Anaru stood leaning against the mantel. The huge Maori enforcer looked at ease despite the sweat dripping down his dark-skinned face. He was captain of the central command enforcer squad known as the Tenth, which reported directly to Shahrokh.

The name referred back to the elite Tenth Legion of Julius Caesar that Shahrokh had led for a time while cementing his alliance with Caesar. Anaru's expression remained neutral, but Tomas noted the slight clenching of his massive hands. The man was a brutal fighter and a decent strategist. His massive size personified the bull that was the company standard, just as it had been the standard of the original legion. He had inherited the post as captain after Tomas vacated it.

The two had not parted as friends.

Tomas saluted. "Reporting as ordered, sir."

Shahrokh waved the hovering medical staffers aside and motioned Tomas closer. Anaru hovered nearby, within easy striking distance. On a good day, Tomas could take Anaru, but he wasn't feeling himself yet and the big man would snap him in two if it came to a fight.

"I heard rumors you were dead," Shahrokh said without preamble.

"It's not the first time wishful thinking's failed to kill me," Tomas said, meeting Anaru's glower.

Shahrokh blinked a couple of times but seemed to be looking straight through him. After a few seconds he started. "What was I saying?"

"That Tomas should be dead, sir." Anaru supplied.

The old man's eyes focused again. "Yes, exactly. I heard rumors you were dead."

"It'll take more than wishful thinking to end this life," Tomas said.

Anaru leaned toward him, but refrained the urge to turn his wishful thinking into action. Tomas was grateful that his discipline held.

The man was smarter than he pretended, but sometimes he got stuck on an idea. He had hated Tomas for leaving the company and always considered it an act of betrayal. Worse, it was only after Tomas resigned as captain that Anaru won that coveted position.

"I've been on special assignment in recent months." That much was true. "My investigations have unearthed clues that might help lead to Gregorios."

Shahrokh hissed at the hated name, but it was Anaru who spoke. "The Tenth is assigned to hunt down the rogue. What were you doing on our turf?"

"It was not my primary objective. I ran across a heka cell that turned out to be connected with Mai Luan."

"Leave her alone," Shahrokh said harshly, destroying any chance Tomas could draw the conversation around into a warning of Mai Luan's intentions. "Her research is of paramount importance."

"Of course, sir."

He swallowed the next words he planned to speak as Shahrokh's gaze wandered to the fireplace and his eyes drooped closed. Tomas and Anaru stood silent for three minutes before Shahrokh shook himself out of the stupor and looked up at him.

"Tomas, I'm glad you're here. I need whatever information you gathered about Gregorios."

"It's our job to catch him," Anaru interjected.

Shahrokh frowned at the big man. "You haven't been able to find him. Time is short and we need that rogue terminated."

"I'd be happy to pass on the information I have to the Tenth," Tomas offered.

"No. The legion has never been disgraced by failure before. As of now, your other duties are on hold. You will resume command of the Tenth with Anaru acting as your second. You are ordered to find and terminate Gregorios. Am I clear?"

"Completely." Tomas maintained his calm expression only with effort. This was a change he hadn't expected, and it complicated his position immensely.

"We can take him without any outside help," Anaru protested.

"I cannot afford to take the risk." Shahrokh huddled lower in his chair and his voice dropped to a hissing whisper. "Asoka's teams failed. All of them! He was too close to the traitor. Might be compromised."

"But sir—" Anaru tried again.

"No. You've all failed and now he returns just in time to threaten our very existence. He must be removed. Tomas was your greatest commander and I need him again."

"Yes, sir." Anaru spoke without hesitation but the glare he directed toward Tomas over Shahrokh's back could have melted holes in solid stone.

Great. If Anaru didn't spark a riot and lynch him, they would kill him for sure when his intel failed to produce Gregorios.

"I'll put everything on hold and report to the barracks first thing in the morning," Tomas assured the old man.

"Good. Now suit up. You have work to do."

"Yes, sir."

He should just leave, should give Anaru time to cool off, but that glare could not be ignored. So he met the angry giant's glare and ordered, "Make sure the roster and status reports are ready for my review, and I'll see if I can get you boys up to speed."

"Excellent," Shahrokh said, completely oblivious to the seething fury of the man standing right behind him.

Tomas left and tried to look unhurried as he beat a hasty retreat toward the elevator. Anaru probably wouldn't attack him outright, but he needed to give the man a little time to deal with the insulting demotion.

Besides, Tomas needed his battle suit.

He was in such a hurry that the fact that Shahrokh's secretary was not at her desk didn't bother him. He barely glanced at the slender figure seated in a plush chair in the corner of the waiting room.

Instincts honed from years of fighting heka and rogue face-takers kicked in and snapped his thoughts into focus. He stopped in his tracks and turned toward that slender figure as she rose to her feet.

"Hello, Tomas," Mai Luan said with a hint of a smile.

CHAPTER FORTY

A crowned queen was never treated with more reverence than I was by those whole-souled western boys. . . . And for seventeen long years I was just their little sister, sharing both their news of joy and sorrow from home. They didn't care that I'd got a better rune, and I didn't rub in the fact none of them could manage another.

~Annie Oakley

Tomas, aren't you full of surprises?" Mai Luan asked as she slowly approached.

"You have no idea." Tomas resisted the urge to retreat. He could never outrun her anyway. He considered going for the pistol concealed at his hip, but she was too close. Even if he managed to draw it before she ripped his arms off, a simple handgun wouldn't do more than give her justification for killing him.

"Where did you find a doctor with the skill to patch that wound?" She looked genuinely curious. "I thought I'd covered all the bases."

"You're not as clever as you think you are." He lacked the proper weapons to beat her, but that didn't mean he'd cower.

"On the contrary, I'm far more clever than a simple mortal like yourself." She spoke it as a simple truth. "You ruined my first torture for Sarah. The next one won't end as quickly for either of you."

"I will kill you," Tomas said evenly. Her words sparked a blossoming rage.

"Save your bluster," Mai Luan said, patting his cheek. "I hear we're going to be working together."

"Never."

"We're not so very different," Mai Luan teased. "You want to keep the council locked in the downward spiral that's killing them. I'm just taking a different path, one that will actually grant them new life. For a time."

"As slaves to you?"

"They'll be alive," she hissed, dropping her facade of good humor. "That's more than they deserve, and more than anyone else is offering, isn't it?"

"I won't let you do it," he promised.

Mai Luan leaned closer, her voice a fierce whisper. "Try to stop me, and I'll denounce you to the council. How long do you think you'd last once they learned you're allied with Gregorios?"

"What about Gregorios?" Anaru asked as he exited Shahrokh's office.

Mai Luan smiled and Tomas forced down his anger. He needed to pick his battlefield, and this wasn't it.

"We need to find him," Tomas said.

Mai Luan winked. She started to turn away, but paused and frowned down at his shirt. "You have a new rune."

Tomas retreated, but Mai Luan snatched him back. He stood several inches taller and weighed at least forty pounds heavier, but she didn't struggle to haul him close. She lifted his shirt to inspect the healing rune.

Tomas pushed at her hand with all his strength, but couldn't budge it.

"That's how you survived, but where did you find one with a rounon gift in time? And one skilled enough to compose a higher healing rune?"

Anaru approached with a frown. "You marked Carl's body?"

Mai Luan laughed and released Tomas. "That's how you fooled me for so long. You're wearing another mortal's form."

"What did he fool you about?" Anaru asked, his already suspicious mind latching onto the phrase.

Tomas groaned inwardly. He hadn't wanted Mai Luan to know the truth about him. Now she held his life in her hands again. Any more information she shared with Anaru could easily lead him to find the truth.

"You speak with a forked tongue," Tomas growled at Mai Luan, smoothing his shirt.

"Name the rounon," Mai Luan countered.

"You consort with rounon unknown to the council?" Anaru asked.

"In time of great need. If I hadn't, the rumors of my death wouldn't have been just rumors."

"Who?" Mai Luan pressed.

The council regulated anyone with rounon gifts. Those who embraced the heka practices were eliminated. Hunters were tracked, and news of hunters in Rome would create a stir that might lead the enforcers to learn of Gregorios's recent visit to Jerusalem.

Any mortals possessing a rounon gift who had not yet embraced a heka cult might be recruited to serve the enforcers, but everyone needed to be registered and monitored. It seemed Mai Luan hated the idea of unknown mortals with soul powers outside of her control as much as the council did.

When Tomas didn't respond, Mai Luan said, "Speak before I lose my patience. Sarah's too new to have any useful contacts."

"Who's Sarah?" Anaru demanded, looking angrier about being ignored.

"A useless mortal. One I will soon eliminate," Mai Luan said, still grinning.

Tomas snapped, "Leave her out of this. You have work to do for the council."

"Oh, that's well in hand. Sarah owes me a debt, and I'll collect every ounce of it in blood."

"We'll see about that," Tomas said. He yearned to throw himself at her, but she'd only beat him to a pulp.

Mai Luan gave him a patronizing smile, as if she could read his thoughts. "Say hello to Sarah for me. I expect to see her soon."

She headed for the exit, and Tomas watched her go, filled with hot fury and towering frustration.

Anaru stepped between him and the retreating Mai Luan. "Tell me about this rounon, and this Sarah."

He wasn't about to do that. "Sarah's a private matter. We'll deal with the rounon after we find Gregorios. He's priority number one. Stay focused on that mission."

They were running out of time at every level. Mai Luan held every advantage, and soon she'd become unstoppable. There had to be a way to block her. As he pushed past Anaru and headed for the elevator, he considered possible options.

He had to strike now, while Mai Luan considered him cornered and helpless.

CHAPTER FORTY-ONE

I sometimes feel that I live the life of an actor more than any who perform in the companies throughout London. Every war, every treaty, all present a false front. The extremes of negotiation I must embrace are concealed from even my closest counselors. But it must needs be, for I am eager for my second life and the truth must be protected. The superstitions of the commoners, fueled by the hated hunters, would trigger civil chaos should they learn that facetakers move among us.

~Queen Elizabeth I

Tomas took the elevator to the second basement level. It emptied into a long storeroom crowded with shelves piled high with boxes, bags, and other containers. Half of the long fluorescent lights strung above the shelves were out, leaving the room in twilight. It smelled of dust and of mold. The air was probably older than most of the items waiting to be cataloged.

Tomas threaded through the piles of artifacts, antiques, and historical treasures to a small office at the very back that had once been a broom closet. A tall young man whose short-sleeved shirt barely contained his heavily muscled form sat squeezed into a swivel chair behind the desk. Papers and invoices crowded every available space, nearly overwhelming the old, blocky monitor. Almost hidden by the clutter, he typed with frantic speed on a hidden keyboard.

"Hey, Carl," Tomas called.

The young man started in surprise and upset a tall stack of papers. Only by a lucky grab, fueled by superb reflexes, did he manage to salvage the stack. He glanced up and the smile that was starting to form on his face crashed into an expression of dismay.

"Please, not yet," Carl whined.

Tomas leaned over the desk and displaced another pile of papers. As Carl scrambled to prevent them from triggering a general avalanche Tomas said, "I thought you'd be happy to see me."

"I am," Carl insisted as he rebuilt the disrupted papers into unsteady mountains. "But your timing is terrible."

"You've already gotten way more time than we planned."

"That's the problem. Just last week I met this super-hot doctor, fresh in town from Sweden."

He swiveled the monitor, knocking a teetering stack off the desk.

Tomas peered at the close-up photo through the swirling paper blizzard. "I see what you mean, but I've got a new mission and I need it back."

"Can't you give me the weekend? You can have it on Monday," Carl begged.

"I don't have that much time."

"Come on, man. Give me something. She'll never go out with me if you take it back."

"I got you a scar." Tomas lifted his shirt high enough to show it off. The solid scar looked a month old already. The smooth lines of the healing rune encircling it magnified the rough outline of the knife wound.

Carl winced, but then his eyes bulged in wonder. "No way! You got me a rune?"

"It was a knife wound. Would've killed me otherwise."

"That's awesome, but I was told I couldn't handle any runes. It wouldn't take."

"Probably true, but I've bonded with them before and it worked for me. If it hadn't, I'd be dead."

"Wow. Think it'll work for me too?" Carl prodded the rune with a finger.

"It should. Now that it's sealed to the body, you should be able to get it to attune to you. Might take a while, but I think it'll work."

"Awesome! I can't believe you got into a knife fight wearing just my wimpy frame."

"I've been working out."

"Me too. Just like we agreed. I've got to admit though, I'm not looking forward to the switch. I can do things now I never dreamed of."

"Try. Now that my muscle memory taught your mind what's possible, you can train your own muscles to do some of it."

"Really?"

"It's actually a training technique we use to speed up learning new moves."

"Thanks." Carl pumped his hand but his enthusiastic smile faded after a moment. "It won't be enough though. Not at first."

"It's the best I can do."

"Come on. I'll do anything!"

That was exactly what Tomas was waiting for. "All right. Do me one favor and I'll arrange another loan some time soon."

"Yes!"

"Just for a few hours."

"I'll take it. What do you need?"

Tomas rose and led the way toward the door. "Come on. You're going to help me fetch something. Bring your keys."

CHAPTER FORTY-TWO

Mortals annoy me. So busy scurrying around in desperation as their pitiful single lives run out.

~Asoka, facetaker council member

"No," Alter commanded. "Harder. You have to want to hurt me or you're wasting our time."

The two of them stood where he had caught her fist before she could hit him in the nose. He pushed Sarah hard and sent her stumbling.

She settled back into the stance he had taught her. He was annoying her enough that she really did want to hit him and wipe that smug look off his face. The two of them had trained hard for a couple hours and she was feeling exhausted but thrilled at the same time. Tomas was right. Alter approached training in a very different way and focused his teaching on brutally direct tactics.

They had jumped right into sparring, and every move was aimed to disable opponents in the most painful way possible. Every blow drove for soft spots like groin, throat, knee, or nose.

Alter had said, "You don't have the luxury of trying to fight anyone. You're not big enough or well trained enough to beat most normal men, let alone an enhanced kashaph. Your only hope is to surprise and hurt them enough to escape."

The moves made sense and Alter was a surprisingly good teacher, although he was enjoying the workout with her a little too much. It wasn't her fault that the only exercise outfit she could get was a too-tight loaner from one of Quentin's staff. The biggest hindrance was that if she ever really connected with any of the punches or kicks he urged her to throw at him, she could do some serious harm.

Not that she had hit him yet.

She decided that needed to change. So she launched herself at him with determination to bring the pain. He noticed the change and grinned as he swatted aside or dodged her blows.

"Good. Harder."

Sarah lunged, trying to close the distance and slap his grinning face.

Alter abruptly changed directions, grabbed her hand and twisted her around, off balance. Before she could recover, he had locked her arms around her own torso and held her trapped with her back pressed against him. His powerful arms held her tight in an almost-embrace.

"Stay balanced," he said softly into her ear as she struggled in vain to free her arms and break away. "Or your opponent can gain the advantage."

She stomped on his instep and he yelped. His hold loosened just a bit and she yanked her right arm free. She spun and tried to punch him in the throat.

He caught her fist. "Good improvisation, but you should've made a clean break so I couldn't trap you again."

Sarah tried to knee him in the groin.

Alter caught her knee and stepped close, too close to hit effectively. With his hold of her fist in one hand, and her leg with the other, he pulled her against him to keep her off balance and vulnerable.

He started to make another condescending comment so Sarah threw her weight against him. As he stumbled back, she wrapped her other leg around his and tripped him to the ground.

They hit hard but he flipped her over like a child and ended up on top, pinning her.

"Nice move," he said.

"Not good enough. Let me up." She struggled to push him off but he held her in place a couple seconds more, his gaze intent. He started to lean in closer, clearly tempted to kiss her.

So she head-butted him.

She didn't really expect to connect, so she threw every ounce of strength into the move, hoping to get him off. She did connect, and actually felt his nose break under her forehead. She felt a little ashamed at how good that felt. Her forehead stung from the impact, and she cringed to feel his blood dripping down her face.

Alter yelped and rolled off, hands clutching his bleeding nose. "I can't believe you did that."

"I thought you wanted me to hit you," Sarah said as she rolled to her feet. "Remember, don't let your opponent distract you."

Alter grabbed up a towel and pressed it to his face. His voice took on a distinct nasal tone when he spoke. "Good move."

"Thank you," she said, but her smile faded. "Did I hurt you bad?"

"I'll be fine. Just give me a minute."

The two of them moved to a pair of simple wooden chairs situated near the windows overlooking the pool. Sarah really needed to find a suit so she could test the water.

"Where did you learn to fight?" she asked him.

Alter shrugged. "We train all our lives to destroy the kashaph."

"Didn't you do anything fun?" She imagined little Alter pummeling a practice dummy at age six.

"Training is fun."

He had so much to learn.

"What do you do for fun now that you're an adult?"

"What do you mean?"

"You know, when you're not training and not studying runes or whatever other work you do. What do you do to relax?"

"I go shooting."

He couldn't be real. "Don't you ever go out on dates or just do things not connected with hunting?"

Alter looked a little unsure of himself for the first time. "Not really."

"Well after we're done with all this fighting and saving the stupid council, we'll do something fun to celebrate."

He actually blushed. "Are you asking me on a date?"

"No," she said quickly. "Nothing like that. I just think you should try something fun."

His look of disappointment almost made her laugh. Time to change the subject. "I know your family doesn't like what the facetakers do, but you seem to hate Gregorios especially."

"I've sworn a blood oath to destroy that demon for what he's done to our family."

"But didn't he just restore your brother?"

"For that I am grateful," Alter admitted reluctantly. "But his torment of my brother was just the most recent of his crimes."

"Tell me."

"I don't think you'll believe me."

"Why not?"

"Because you've fallen under their influence." He took one of her hands in his. "I worry for your safety."

"That's why you're training me," she reminded him, slipping out of his grasp. His earnestness was sweet, but she couldn't encourage his interest.

"Not just that. You're a good person. I see that, but you've fallen in with some of the most dangerous people on the planet," he added.

"No. I've seen enough of the real dangers to know. That's why you fight the heka just like they do. That's why everyone agrees Mai Luan is the worst danger. Don't let your hatred for them blind you. They're not as bad as you think."

"And they're not as good as you hope," he growled.

"You're right. I don't believe you."

"Just try to keep an open mind. You'll see the lies eventually. Then we'll talk."

The door opened and Quentin came in. He nodded toward the bloody towel. "Having fun, I see."

"Alter was teaching me some fighting moves," Sarah said as she rose and donned her jacket.

"Good. Looks like you learned a few things." He joined them by the window. "I verified Tomas made it into the headquarters without any major issues."

"Were there minor issues?" Sarah asked quickly.

"Perhaps." His expression gave nothing away.

"What? Is he going to be all right?" she pleaded.

"I believe he will be fine," Quentin said.

"Shouldn't you have stayed there to help, just in case?" she asked.

He shook his head. "I felt it better to keep my distance. He should be back by this evening. If your training session here is concluded, may I step in?"

"What do you have in mind?" Sarah asked, reluctant to leave the topic of Tomas's safety.

"Have you ever fired a fully automatic rifle before?"

"I knew I liked you for a reason," Sarah said, linking arms with him. "Show me the way."

CHAPTER FORTY-THREE

Our common country is in great peril, demanding the loftiest views, and boldest action to bring it speedy relief. Reports that General Lee has employed and, in fact, aggressively recruited channellers and enchanters, is at every level disconcerting. Enslaving a man's body is morally wrong and, by the clear edicts of our eternal God, enslaving his soul cannot be tolerated. Let us renew our trust in God, and go forward without fear, and with manly hearts. We must abolish all practitioners of this evil and preserve this commitment throughout all time. If we do this, we shall not only have saved the Union; but we shall have so saved it, as to make, and to keep it, forever worthy of the saving.

~Abraham Lincoln

E levate the barrel a little more, my dear." Quentin's voice was soft but commanding.

Sarah angled the M4A1 rifle up into the air. The compact assault rifle fit her extremely well, and she'd just finished firing several magazines of 5.56 ammo with the firing selector set to full automatic. The recoil was very manageable, and with the suppressor screwed onto the barrel, she almost didn't need the advanced ear protection Quentin had provided.

"Are you sure no one will call the police when we start shooting grenades?" Sarah asked.

The ear protection blocked all sounds above dangerous decibels, but didn't impede regular conversation. She was eager to fire the M203 grenade launcher attached under the barrel of the rifle, but worried that neighbors would notice the explosions.

Mature stands of trees shielded the shooting range situated behind Quentin's mansion from observation. A series of earthen mounds held pop-up targets at fifty yard intervals, and a massive berm blocked off the end of the range at over four hundred yards. With suppressors attached to the various handguns and rifles Quentin had guided her in shooting, she hadn't worried about the sound causing an issue, but they were still pretty close to the city.

"Not to worry, my dear," Quentin said, hefting a fat, blue projectile. "We can only shoot practice rounds at this range."

Sarah had already loaded one of the 40 millimeter rounds into the launch tube. She'd really hoped to see it explode big, but wasn't surprised by the answer.

"Hold it steady there," Quentin said, helping her sight through the raised flip-up sight. "For some deployments, we can attach a better sighting system, but for today's purposes close is all we need."

When all looked right, he nodded to her. He was as genteel as always, but while acting as range master, he spoke in crisp commands, with a voice that demanded exact obedience and strict adherence to his range rules.

Sarah pulled the trigger situated just beyond the long magazine. The gun bucked in her hands, the kick less than a .20 gauge shotgun. The grenade shot from the gun with its characteristic whumping sound.

A second later, an orange cloud exploded a little short and to the right of the target she'd been aiming for.

"That was awesome!" Sarah laughed. She used to think she knew how to shoot, but Quentin had taught her a lot in this first training session. She'd never fired military weapons like these, and she was enjoying herself.

Quentin gave her an approving look. "Not bad. The grenade launcher is a powerful weapon. Sometimes it's preferable to destroy targets from a distance."

"Too bad you can't shoot things close-up with these," Sarah muttered, thinking about Mai Luan. She'd love to wipe the terrifying woman's smile off her face with one of the high explosive rounds Quentin had shown her.

"Sometimes we can," Quentin said, hefting an olive drab round with black markings. "This is a buckshot round. Like a giant shotgun. Great for room clearing or slowing down a pesky cui dashi."

Sarah hefted the fat projectile. He hadn't said it would kill Mai Luan, but it'd do more than regular bullets. "Can I keep this one?"

"Of course, my dear. In fact, I'll have a properly cleaned rifle sent to your rooms, along with a selection of ammunition if that would help you feel more comfortable."

Sarah kissed his cheek. "You're a rare gentleman."

She fired off several more practice grenades and got the hang of the crude sights. The last two rounds concealed the targets she aimed at with billowing clouds of orange smoke.

Eirene joined them as Sarah ejected the last spent shell.

Sarah stripped off her ear protection and gave Eirene a hug. The facetaker provided a source of steadying strength for Sarah in the frightening world of soul powers and superhuman threats she'd become a part of.

"How's the training going?" Eirene asked.

Sarah grinned. "Great. Quentin's got a lot of cool toys."

"You haven't seen the good stuff yet," Quentin said with a smile.

"I can't wait."

"Perhaps later. It's almost dinner time," Eirene said.

Quentin sent the women ahead, promising to join them as soon as he saw to his weapons. Sarah fell in with Eirene and the two of them returned to the mansion.

"Eirene, tell me what it's like," Sarah said, voicing curiosity that had been building within her since she learned about the vast age the facetakers lived.

"What is what like?" Eirene asked.

"Everything?" Sarah laughed. "History. You've seen it all. Kings and queens, the Middle Ages, Rome. Tell me about famous people you've met."

Eirene settled onto a couch in a nearby salon and motioned Sarah to join her. "Every life is unique. At least, that's the way I approach it."

"How can it be? You've lived for centuries. Doesn't it get boring sometimes?"

Eirene said, "Any life can be boring, but that's often a choice of the individual. Not all facetakers look at their lives as Gregorios and I do. For them, the lives just run together and they begin to stagnate. I believe that leads to rapid progression of mental dissipation. To me, each life is a new adventure, and each of the lives I've led leaves a different mark."

Sarah found that hard to believe. Her own parents, who she saw only rarely, looked bored with their lives except when they were accusing her of consorting with the devil. She shuddered to think what they'd say if they knew the truth. "Which life was the most fun?"

Eirene settled back and her eyes drifted toward the ornate ceiling, a little smile flickering across her lips. "Gregorios would insist it has to be the one in which he finally convinced me to marry him. That was a very good life, probably the one I'd consider the most romantic, but perhaps not the most pure fun."

Sarah wanted to ask her about that romantic life, but Eirene was already continuing.

"I think the most fun I had was the life I spent as a privateer, sailing the Caribbean in the sixteen nineties."

"You were a pirate?" Sarah exclaimed, thinking of Blackbeard and Henry Morgan, and the Pirates movies.

"Not a pirate. A privateer. I carried a letter of marque from the Dutch crown to hunt enemy ships."

"That's amazing." Sarah tried to picture Eirene on the deck of an ancient sailing ship, cutlass in hand, tropical wind blowing her hair.

"It was a lot of fun. The council assigned me to scope out the New World, investigate potential investment opportunities, and hunt down renegade heka operating as pirates."

Sarah said, "Let me guess, Blackbeard was an occultist."

"No, he was a channeller. That's why he was so hard to kill. Gregorios finally put him down during the assault by Lieutenant Robert Maynard's squadron."

"So did you and Gregorios sail together?" Sarah asked. The thought of facing the two facetakers as pirates scared her more than a little.

Eirene smiled. "Occasionally. I captained my own ship for a decade, helped bring in the notorious pirates Anny Bonny and Mary Read, who were occultists, and accumulated a fantastic amount of Inca gold from plundered Spanish gold ships."

"I thought you said you weren't a pirate?" Sarah asked.

Eirene pulled from her pocket a gold coin whose faces were so worn that Sarah couldn't distinguish the symbols on them. "I've carried this doubloon ever since, as a reminder to enjoy life."

"I thought we can't take anything out of our lives?" Sarah joked as she inspected the coin.

Eirene laughed. "Always memories are the most precious baggage we bring, but bank accounts that have been growing for several hundred years are pretty helpful too."

Sarah handed the coin back, and Eirene extracted another coin, this one silver, from her pocket. "This is one of the famous Spanish silver pieces of eight. I took this one from a heka enchanter in Nassau at the end of my privateer life."

A maid appeared to announce dinner would be served shortly.

Eirene handed the piece of eight to Sarah. "Hold onto this for me, my dear. We'll talk again soon."

"Thank you!"

Sarah gave Eirene another hug and rushed upstairs for a quick shower before dinner. She considered the glimpse she'd gained into a piece of Eirene's history, and the sense of wonder helped hold at bay the constant fear of facing Mai Luan again soon.

She met Gregorios outside the art gallery dining room. He was dressed casually in a leather jacket and jeans.

He greeted her with a smile. "Good timing. Tomas is back."

CHAPTER FORTY-FOUR

Of course I deserve victory. I am a better general, my troops are better disciplined, and we possess superior runes. Let them come with their facetakers and their hunters and I will defeat them.

~Napoleon Bonaparte

The art gallery dining room had become their central meeting place and as usual, the table held more of its inexhaustible supply of food. This time, formal place settings were prepared on one side of the long table, and the mouth-watering aromas would normally have drawn Sarah in like a tractor beam.

She paused in the doorway and breathed deep, but when she glanced around the room, she forgot all about the delicious-smelling dinner. In the middle of the room, not far from the table, stood a gleaming machine so similar to the ones she had seen at Alterego that she instantly realized it had to be Mai Luan's machine.

"How did you get your hands on that?" Sarah cried, advancing toward it. From what she'd heard from Tomas and Eirene, the machine was the key to Mai Luan's plan and was certainly well guarded after Eirene's escape.

Tomas was crouched on the far side, mostly hidden by the bulk of the machine as he fiddled with some cables. Gregorios moved to one side. His face already looked better, the bruises almost gone, and his grin lacked any hint of pain.

"Tomas proved more resourceful than even we expected," Eirene said from the far side of the machine.

"It was actually easier than I expected," Tomas said, rising to his feet.

"Whoa!"

Sarah stared. He wasn't the Tomas she knew. Gone was the average, unremarkable guy. He rounded the machine and approached as a tall, muscular young man. His face, which had always looked rather plain, fit the new body perfectly and somehow looked a lot more handsome, even though the features were the same.

Alter growled, "Demon handler. Whose life did you sacrifice?"

"No one's," Tomas replied, but his eyes stayed glued on Sarah. He lifted his arms a little. "This is me. The form you saw before was a loaner."

"How is it possible?" Sarah asked as she slowly advanced. "I can usually tell when someone's having an out-of-body transfer."

Gregorios spoke. "With a little extra effort, we can smooth most of those telltale wrinkles away. I made sure Tomas looked genuine so no one would realize what he was."

Tomas took her hands. "Do you like it?"

"You look great."

He did. He really did, and part of her was thrilled with the change. It all made sense finally. This was the reason he hadn't wanted to get physical. The shock would have been far worse had they really begun exploring a closer relationship while he lived a lie.

But that was only part of how she felt. "Why didn't you tell me?"

"I planned to."

Alter passed close behind them, scowling. He muttered, "First of the lies."

Sarah ignored him. He was wrong about Tomas. He had to be.

The young hunter wandered over to the table. "Unholy demons."

"That's why you wanted to come to Rome," Sarah said to Tomas.

"Yes."

"You could have warned me," she told him.

He looked down, for the first time unsure. The expression didn't fit those sculpted good looks very well, but it helped erase the flash of mistrust Alter's words had triggered. "I wasn't sure how you . . ."

She touched his face and drew his gaze back to hers. "You were worried I wouldn't come?"

He shrugged. "You just went through so much, fought so hard to regain yourself. I knew you wanted to get away from soul transfers and everything to do with Alterego, so yes, I was nervous."

"Next time, trust me," she said softly.

"I will," he promised, looking relieved.

She let her hand trail down to his muscled shoulders and chest, then slide down one iron-hard arm. He really was in amazing shape.

"Enjoy him later, dear. We have work to do," Eirene said kindly.

"Sorry," Sarah said, but didn't take her eyes off Tomas's face.

He gave her a quick kiss, and if the others hadn't been watching, she would've insisted they take more time getting it right. He touched her face with one strong hand and she leaned her cheek into it. It felt good.

He said softly to her, "I'm sorry I waited so long. I couldn't infiltrate Alterego looking like this. Even if they had bought the lie that a simple technician really liked to work out, my runes would've tipped them off."

"Runes? You mean like that healing rune?" She grimaced at the memory of cutting into his skin, at how nearly she had lost him.

"Sort of. These are better."

He lifted his forest-green t-shirt. The first thing she noticed was his fantastic set of abs. He also sported half a dozen runes inked across his torso. She reached out to trace the healing rune he wore right where she'd carved the new one into his last body. There were some slight differences and she sensed that the rune he wore on his real body was more powerful.

"Not bad," Alter said. He approached, still looking upset by Tomas's change. "For basic enhancements anyway."

"These aren't basic. This is top of the line work," Tomas insisted.

Alter shook his head. "Top of someone's line, maybe."

He pulled off his own shirt with a flourish and pointed at his gorgeous torso. "This is why you came to me for help with runes."

He was not as heavily muscled as Tomas, but every muscle stood out, sharply defined. He could easily have made the cover of a men's health magazine. Well, he could if his torso and upper arms weren't covered with runes. Tomas's runes were more advanced than the crude one she had helped carve into his side, but Alter's runes were an entirely different level of sophistication. The runes were far more elegant and intricate, works of art that made Tomas's runes look like the crude constructs of a child.

"Wow." Sarah could not help but reach out and trace one along his bicep. It was beautiful and its power seemed so apparent. She didn't know the characters but she felt she understood the overall rune.

"This one increases strength, doesn't it?"

"How could you possibly know that?" Alter demanded. He had been grinning openly at her attention, but his smile faded. "You said you were new to runes."

"I am, but it just makes sense."

"I was right about you," Eirene said as she too approached Alter. "You have a natural sensitivity to runes." She touched an intricate rune just below Alter's sternum. "These are masterpieces, Alter."

"Thank you," he said, blushing under the scrutiny.

To Sarah she said, "Runes are like anything. There are levels of expertise, different levels of craft."

Eirene gestured at Tomas. "The ones he wears are tried and effective, proven over the centuries."

"Unimaginative," Alter said.

"Standard," Tomas countered. He was doing a decent job of trying to conceal his displeasure at how interested Sarah was in Alter's runes. "They work on anyone with the strength of soul to handle the drain."

"What do you mean? I thought you had to have some kind of natural gift to wear a rune."

Alter said, "No. The rune must be etched and activated by one possessing at least the equivalent of a channeler rounon gift. But to actually bond to a soul is all the responsibility of the person wearing the rune. If their soul, the force of their life, is sufficient to fuel the rune they can bond to it."

Tomas added, "Most people can't. One of the tests to become an enforcer is for a soldier to prove they can handle at least one rune. If they can't, they don't have the inner strength to face the heka."

"Your runes are personalized," Eirene said to Alter.

"So no one else has runes just like that?" Sarah asked.

"Perhaps, but perhaps not." Alter put his shirt back on before continuing.

"Remember how we discussed the ability to search memories for powerful moments in a person's life? Training and strength of soul, coupled with the right memory can reveal personalized runes that reflect pieces of a person's character, their strengths. Those runes are built upon some of the basic power runes. The resulting rune can become a personalized soul map that taps deeper into the power of that individual soul. With it they can access far greater power."

"So they're super enhancements?"

"In a way. They draw from the power of that soul and also from the power of the inner truths revealed through those memories, which serves as a multiplier. The greater the purity of soul, the clearer the self-knowledge, the greater the effect."

"How do you build them?" Sarah felt a hunger to understand. The power of that interest startled her.

Alter lifted his shirt again to show his own healing rune.

Sarah could look at those abs all day. She needed to get a photo of him and Tomas standing together shirtless.

He took her hand and traced her finger along the inner markings of the rune. Tomas shuffled his feet, a little frown on his face, but didn't voice his opposition.

"Look closely. We start with the same fundamental symbols used to construct the standard runes used by the enforcers and the heka." With his guidance, she isolated the basic strokes of the same healing rune within the outer marks built upon them.

"I see it," she said with a grin.

"Very good." He traced her finger along some of the other marks. "I've incorporated a couple other symbols into this rune and wrapped it all inside a powerful personal memory rune. The final product increases my healing rate ten times over what the standard rune might accomplish."

Gregorios said, "Impressive. That's a significant memory you're drawing from."

Sarah noticed for the first time that Alter's nose had not only stopped bleeding, but looked completely normal. There was no indication she had smashed it flat barely half an hour ago.

"Can I get one?" she asked.

Alter said, "Perhaps. I'm a leading runesmith, and you have an amazing natural sensitivity to runes. With a little study, we can fashion a rune specific to you. Then we can see if you have the strength for it."

"She has the strength," Eirene said with confidence.

"Later," Gregorios said. "Right now, we need Alter studying this machine."

CHAPTER FORTY-FIVE

Some truths are eternal. Others last a lifetime. Know the difference.

~Gregorios

How'd you get this?" Sarah asked again, turning to the shining steel machine. The rune discussion had distracted her from Tomas's startling accomplishment. He'd stolen Mai Luan's machine!

The gleaming stainless steel base of the machine was identical to the one used at Alterego. The main difference were the helmets and their thick cable umbilicals. The machines at Alterego had sported an articulating arm like those found in most medical offices, but it had connected to bulky life support units placed over the heads of faceless bodies awaiting new souls. Mai Luan's machine, with its cable-linked helmets sporting jagged faceplates looked more menacing.

"She couldn't have been stupid enough to leave it unattended," Eirene added.

Tomas said, "She wasn't, and it wasn't. It was locked in the vault."

Gregorios and Eirene exchanged a surprised look.

Sarah asked, "So that's supposed to be pretty secure, right? Like a bank vault?"

Tomas nodded. "Exactly. No one gets in there without the code or the key. I got both from Carl."

"Carl?" Sarah asked.

"The old me. He's thrilled with that rune you carved."

"I'm glad he liked it."

She tried not to think about how she had hugged Carl's body, held his hand. She didn't even know who he was. He might be a weirdo. He might be . . .

"Carl's not married is he?"

"No," Tomas said quickly. "He's just a single guy. Doesn't even date much."

That was a relief. The thought of what renters might have been doing with her body had been one of the reasons she had longed to get it back and leave Alterego. She didn't want to face the same worries about Tomas.

"Regardless of how you got in, the council will figure out it was you," Gregorios said.

"Eventually," Tomas conceded with a slow shake of his head. "And right after getting that big promotion too."

"What are you talking about?" Sarah asked.

Tomas explained about his meeting with Shahrokh and appointment as captain of the task force hunting Gregorios. Sarah expected Gregorios to look worried, but he actually laughed.

"You're captain of the Tenth again? Just brilliant."

"What's the Tenth?" Sarah asked.

Tomas explained a little about the elite enforcer unit and their ties back to the original, famous Tenth Legion of Julius Caesar.

"You're kidding."

They weren't.

Although Tomas had warned her about how old they were, it still came as a shock to think they had lived in the times of ancient Rome. To think, Shahrokh had spent time with Caesar. Hearing them speak of events from over two thousand years ago with such casual acceptance drove home the wonder of it all.

"Were you in the legion too?"

Gregorios shook his head. "I was usually busy elsewhere. Never liked the legions."

She glanced at Tomas but he shook his head. "I wasn't born yet."

Sarah still didn't know how old Tomas might be, but she didn't trust herself to ask yet. Finding out she was dating an old man would be one too many truths for a single day.

Eirene glanced up from her work with Alter. "Shahrokh didn't say anything about me?"

"No. Sorry. The entire mission is focused on Gregorios," Tomas said.

"Pity. You'll have to correct that oversight. I'm at least as much of a threat as he is."

"I'll make sure to add you to the hit list."

"Thank you, dear."

"This isn't the time for levity," Quentin said as he entered the room and joined them. "I just got off the office network. The alert's already been generated and spread to all forces. Tomas has been labeled a rogue and his capture ordered."

Tomas sighed, looking depressed, so Sarah wrapped her arms around his waist.

"It'll be all right," she whispered.

"I knew it'd happen, but I had hoped they wouldn't figure it out yet."

"What were you thinking?" Quentin asked, looking from Tomas to the machine. "You've compromised your position."

"I had to do something," Tomas snapped. "Mai Luan held every advantage. She was going to use it on the council and enslave them. I can't let that happen."

Eirene said, "Don't be too hard on him. If I'd thought we could get to the machine, I'd have voted to steal it too. We've got her now."

Quentin shook his head. "Don't break out the bubbly yet. It was a bold move, but you accomplished less than you expected."

"What do you mean?" Tomas asked.

"She has more machines," Quentin said.

"When did you learn this?" Gregorios demanded.

"Just now. Security's been tightened throughout the head-quarters and enforcers stationed inside the vault. I need to head into the office shortly to open the magic shop and distribute some of the bigger toys."

"They're taking it badly," Tomas said.

Quentin asked, "What did you expect? This is the promise of salvation, and you stole it. To them, this is worse than if you had tried to shoot up the council chamber."

"I did it to protect them. I swore an oath," Tomas protested.

"That I understand," Quentin said. "And if there had only been one machine, it would've been a good idea."

"Tell me about the other machines," Gregorios said.

"It sounds like there are at least three more. Due to arrive by secret courier in the next few days."

"Three?" Eirene echoed.

"She plans to submit the council to them after one final test," Quentin said.

Gregorios frowned. "She's done testing. Who's the subject of the next session?"

"Asoka."

Gregorios' expression turned grave. "Not good. Asoka was there with me in Berlin."

"That's the memory she's after. The fall of Berlin definitely qualifies as a pivotal moment in history," Alter said.

Gregorios nodded. "She's not wasting time. She tested the concept with Eirene, and proved she could access Berlin with me. She's ready to move on the master rune, and Asoka won't resist her like I did. If there's a master rune, she'll get it."

Eirene frowned. "Then why call it a test?"

Alter suggested, "She must want the master rune first. Then she can submit the council members to the machines and, with the power of that master rune, she can enslave them all."

"She's launching a coup and they're helping her do it," Gregorios growled.

Alter added, "With so many machines, she'll have many more people in her team."

Tomas said, "All the excuse she'll need. She can bring in a strike force and remove anyone who objects to new management."

"That's it, then. Once she controls the council, she'll be ready to move against world leaders," Gregorios said.

"Not to mention, hunting us down," Sarah added.

Eirene grimaced. "We can't let this happen. Our lives hang in the balance, along with the future world order."

"She really wants a rune tied to the fall of Berlin? That was such a terrible time," Sarah said.

Alter nodded. "From such a pivotal moment she can hope to command a particularly destructive master rune."

"We need to review our options. We have to devise a plan to block her before she can get into that memory," Eirene said.

Gregorios gave his wife a thumb's up signal, then blew her a kiss. "Agreed. I always think best on a full stomach. Let's eat."

Sarah couldn't believe her eyes when most of the group headed for the table. She wasn't sure she could eat, with such weighty matters to consider. Alter ignored everyone else and crouched over the machine, studying the many runes engraved on the helmet.

Tomas stood close beside her, holding her hand in his new, strong one. She felt powerfully attracted to the new Tomas and relieved to know his secret, but couldn't deny the change also made her uncomfortable.

He was right to have worried. What she thought she knew of him now rested on a shaky foundation. How much was true? How much of the Tomas she cared about was just part of his undercover persona?

He had saved her life more than once. That should be enough. Was it?

The little doubt implanted into her mind from Alter eroded her confidence. She needed to figure it out, but she needed time to understand her own heart too.

He squeezed her hand. "Ready for dinner?"

"I don't know if I can eat," she admitted as he drew her toward the table.

"Eat," he insisted as he held her chair out for her. "You're going to need your strength when we face Mai Luan."

She'd bring along her grenade launcher too.

CHAPTER FORTY-SIX

We shall defend our island, whatever the cost may be. We are not without runes of our own, and the strength of our souls will prevail. We shall fight on the beaches, we shall fight on the landing grounds, we shall fight in the fields and in the streets, we shall fight in the hills; we shall never surrender.
~Winston Churchill

The central fact to all this trouble is Mai Luan," Gregorios said around a mouthful of fillet mignon. "We need to isolate and remove her."

"Ideally," Eirene agreed. While Gregorios set to the feast with more gusto than good manners, Eirene ate with poised dignity. She looked like she'd feel just as comfortable eating a fancy meal in the presence of European royalty, with all their rules of etiquette.

Sarah realized she probably had done just that on many occasions. She'd have to ask Eirene about it. Did she know Queen Elizabeth?

She had selected only a fruit salad and small piece of marinated chicken, not expecting to each much. The first bite changed her mind. The chicken fell off the bone, and was soaked in a delicious sauce that tasted like heaven. She still felt nervous about the situation, but her stomach rumbled and she served another, much larger helping.

Tomas gestured with his fork. "Isolating her will be difficult. The only place we know her location is at Suntara."

"We could tail her when she leaves, find her main base of operations and take her there," Gregorios offered.

Quentin said, "More difficult than it sounds. The council provides full screening service for her. Enforcers monitor all traffic patterns around her vehicle for several blocks. They pull back eventually, but she takes a different route through the city each time. We'd never keep her under surveillance without being spotted."

"For the first time, I wish my team wasn't so good at what we do," Tomas muttered.

Sarah reminded them, "We have the machine. That should count for something."

Eirene nodded. "It does. If we could remove Mai Luan, we could use this machine to restore the council. Once their mental faculty is restored, they'll understand the danger."

"We don't even need to kill Mai Luan right off," Gregorios added. "If we can drive her off and restore the council, they'd bring their full resources to bear."

"Even she wouldn't last long then," Tomas agreed, spearing a slice of roast pork harder than necessary.

"We could call in my family," Alter called from where he crouched beside the machine, studying the runes and copying them onto a pad of paper.

"Perhaps, but I still consider them a last resort," Gregorios said

"We could make it a family affair," Eirene suggested.

"I've considered that," Gregorios said. "But most of our resources are positioned poorly for a quick response."

"We may need them."

"Who?" Sarah asked.

Gregorios said, "A security force we control. If we call them up, it'll take too long, and it'll escalate the situation into full-blown war."

"We might not have a choice," Eirene said.

Gregorios considered that while he chewed. "We'll start positioning them just in case. But hold that option in reserve. If possible, we should deal with Mai Luan ourselves."

"I'm not sure we're positioned to do so," Tomas said.

Sarah asked, "How do you even kill a cui dashi? I've seen her shot, stabbed, blown up, and all it does it distract her a little."

"She is unusually powerful, even for a cui dashi," Gregorios agreed. "She has to have been around longer than most. That makes her dangerous, but not immortal."

Eirene added, "She'll regenerate from even normally-fatal wounds, but only to a point. The strength of her nevron is mighty, but it's not infinite."

"So what does that mean?" Sarah asked.

"It means we hurt her a lot, and keep doing it," Tomas said. "Eventually we overwhelm her resistance, wear down her soul strength."

Quentin said, "That's the trick. We can ambush her, but she's faster than we are, stronger, and she's bound to regenerate from any initial damage we inflict. We need to hold her long enough to deal more damage than she can heal from."

"What can do that?" Sarah asked, thinking of her grenade launcher.

"High explosives help," Quentin said, as if reading her mind.

Tomas added, "Fire. Fire's difficult to heal, even for cui dashi. If we could trap her in a hole and drop a couple tons of napalm on her head, we'd be off to a good start."

Sarah paled. Tomas didn't look like he was joking, but she couldn't imagine anything surviving that kind of bombardment, let alone healing from it.

"Not a bad idea," Quentin said thoughtfully.

"You have napalm?" Sarah asked.

"Well . . . not officially, and not that exact recipe."

Gregorios said, "Napalm makes too much of a mess. It might draw authorities before we could finish her off."

"We could mix up some Greek fire," Eirene suggested.

"I thought the recipe for that was lost back in the Middle Ages," Sarah said.

Eirene tapped her head. "I might be old, but my memory's still fine."

Gregorios said, "Might not be a bad idea. We haven't used it in centuries. She wouldn't expect it, and that stuff is awesome."

"I'll whip up a batch," Eirene said.

Quentin rubbed his hands together. "I'll help."

Eirene shook her head. "This is a secret recipe. No sharing with anyone else."

"You don't trust me?" he asked with mock offense.

Gregorios leaned back, sipping a drink, his brows furrowed as he considered the puzzle. "We need to lure her out of the city. It'd be easier to trap her, and the noise from explosions, fire-bombing, and heavy machine guns wouldn't attract a response as quickly."

None of them seemed worried about where or how they'd acquire all those weapons. Sarah started to wonder what else Quentin might have offered to let her shoot if Eirene hadn't interrupted their practice session.

Tomas said, "I don't see how we'll lure her anywhere. She's too focused on tying up the council."

"Sarah could do it," Eirene said.

They all turned to her, and Sarah managed a weak smile under all the attention. "Uh, I object."

"Me too," Tomas said immediately. "Sarah's not an enforcer or a hunter."

Quentin said, "But she's managed to capture Mai Luan's ire. Did she not stab you only to torture Sarah?"

"She did," he admitted. "And in the headquarters she promised the next time she'll hurt us both a lot more."

"All the more reason to use Sarah to draw her out," Eirene said.

"Hold on. Can't we think of a better idea?" Sarah wanted to see Mai Luan destroyed as much as any of them, but getting Mai Luan to chase her couldn't be a good idea.

Gregorios raised his glass in a little salute to Sarah. "It might just work. I'm sorry, Sarah, but you might be our best bet to getting a crack at her."

"How am I supposed to get her to chase me without having her just run me down in the street?" Sarah demanded.

"Motorcycle," Quentin offered.

Tomas shook his head. "Unless she hits a traffic delay. There are too many variables."

Eirene said, "We could work through those. I hate to place you at risk, Sarah, but it's an option we can't ignore."

"I can," Sarah objected.

Gregorios asked, "What would you have us do? We don't know where she's staying, so we can't attack her in her lair. We can't launch a frontal assault on Suntara."

"That would be a suicide mission," Tomas agreed. "And even if we could overwhelm their defenses, Mai Luan might just bolt before we locked down the building."

"Or use it as an excuse to take over ahead of schedule," Gregorios suggested.

Quentin added, "Worse, it would mean shedding enforcer blood when they're not the enemy. Something I am loathe to do."

Tomas said, "Me too. Those are my men. Killing them can't be on the table."

"It can if there are no other options," Eirene said.

Sarah paced away from the table, all too aware of the building pressure. Many lives hung in the balance beside her own, and she was starting to accept the fact that risking hers might be the best way to prevent many more from dying.

She stopped beside the machine where Alter had removed one of the steel panels on the chassis and was crouched beside it, head shoved completely inside. "We have her machine. I wish there was some way this could help."

"I don't see how we can," Gregorios said.

Alter popped out of the machine and jumped to his feet. "Actually, it might be the key to destroying her."

"Really?" Sarah asked.

"I'll need to do some more work on this, but from what I'm seeing here, I think this machine might be the one way to get to Mai Luan that no one will expect."

"How could it possibly do that?" Eirene asked. The entire group rose from the table and approached the machine.

"She wants a master rune, most likely from the fall of Berlin. Gregorios and Asoka both share those memories, right?" Alter asked.

Gregorios nodded. "The important parts. That's when he tried to kill me and first labeled me rogue."

Alter nodded enthusiastically. "From what I'm reading in these runes, and from what I know of memory walking, this machine offers a unique possibility. We know what memory she's going to, and it's a shared memory. If you return to it at the same time via this machine, I believe you'll both be drawn to that same shared memory."

"Like we could face each other in there?" Gregorios asked. "Yes."

Sarah frowned. "How's that possible? I mean, they're both just going back into their own heads, right?"

"Yes and no." Alter turned to a blank sheet of paper in his pad. He drew a couple of overlapping circles. "Imagine these are the pooled memories of Gregorios and Asoka."

"Imagine, the accumulated experience of all my lives enclosed in that circle," Gregorios said with a rueful smile.

Eirene kissed his cheek. "I always said you were too shallow, dear."

Alter drew another circle that intersected the other two. "This is where it becomes guesswork. This circle represents true history. Think of it as a lingering shadow of time, linking to all the souls that touched upon that moment."

Eirene started to nod. "Brilliant."

To Sarah the three circles didn't mean anything yet.

Alter pointed to the intersection of the three circles. "Powered through this machine and the runes it brings to bear, we won't just visit an isolated memory in there. Drawing upon your nevron and that of the one working the machine, I suspect that your memory walks brush against the true fabric of history."

"And since they're both visiting the same moment, that'll link them," Eirene said with a nod of approval. "What an amazing possibility."

"Are you saying we can time travel through this thing?" Sarah asked. She loved science fiction stories, but this was real life.

Alter said, "In a manner of speaking. History, particularly those pivotal moments that might spawn master runes, is infused with unrivaled amounts of soul power. That's a real power source, the only true spiritual one in the world. Master runes are a manifestation of that power, focused into a single point. The resulting force remains potent even though the world has rolled beyond its moment. Through these machines, I believe we'll be able to reach back and touch those moments, to reconnect with the actual fabric of history."

Eirene grimaced. "If there's any chance you could be right, that makes it even more imperative to stop this. Messing with history is fine in dusty archives, but we could unleash all sorts of unanticipated consequences if what you're saying is true."

Alter glanced from her to Sarah. "I believe I'm right, but this is unique. In the past, individuals walking memories usually only found personal enlightenment runes. Only twice were possible moments of accessing master runes recorded. In both cases, one a hunter and one an enchanter, the memory walkers involved possessed exceptionally powerful rounon gifts."

"What happened to them?" Sarah asked.

"The enchanter was killed the next day in the battle for Constantinople."

Gregorios grunted. "I remember that. Always wondered how they breached the wall there."

Sarah yearned to ask more about that, but Alter continued. "The hunter was my second great grandfather."

Eirene said, "Ronen's father. He was an unusually powerful man."

"He never spoke in detail of what he learned from his dreams," Alter said. "But he never visited them again. He hinted that he knew of a rune so powerful he didn't dare record it in our rune lore for fear someone might try to use it."

"So we don't really know," Tomas said.

"No. Actually obtaining a master rune is really uncharted territory. I can guess some of what might happen, but there's no way to know for sure."

"Simply amazing," Tomas said as he paced around the machine. To Sarah, the jagged faceplate looked more ominous than ever when she thought of Mai Luan using it to gain access to so much power.

Gregorios said, "Let's try to nail down whether or not you're right about this. We'll have to test the theory soon."

Eirene warned, "Not too soon. If we tip off Mai Luan, we'll lose the element of surprise."

"Good point. We'll wait until we're ready, then we'll test it prior to the assault. That'll give us time to prepare for the memory hunt."

"With contingency for a real-life assault if this doesn't work," Tomas said.

Gregorios nodded. "Absolutely, but let's hope Alter's right."

"I am," Alter assured them. "This battle will be fought in 1945 Berlin."

CHAPTER FORTY-SEVEN

The danger of living too long is in failing to live each life as if it matters. Too many facetakers grow complacent or arrogant. One road leads to boredom and soul fragmentation. The other impels them to see mortals as sheep that need ruling. Both end in destruction.

~Eirene

The next two days passed in a blur of activity. Gregorios was often off doing mysterious things he never explained. When Sarah did see him, he moved with intense purpose. Eirene shared his dedication, but those moments they spent together softened their expressions. Witnessing the depth of their obvious love helped ease some of Sarah's own worries.

Quentin spent a lot of time at the Suntara headquarters, filling his role as the arms master there, and listening for clues about when Mai Luan and her machines would arrive. Sarah wanted to train with him some more, to shoot some of the bigger guns he hinted he had available. He promised to spend time with her again soon, but couldn't dedicate the proper time yet.

Tomas tried to conceal how much being labeled a rogue and stripped of command affected him, but Sarah could tell. The only good thing that came of his need to keep a low profile was that she got to spend a lot of time with him. She grew accustomed to his new form very quickly and wondered how she'd never realized he didn't belong in Carl's mediocre body.

The two of them spent a great deal of time sparring in the training room. Sarah trained hard, driven by the knowledge that the confrontation with Mai Luan was fast approaching. She needed every scrap of knowledge and skill she could acquire.

So she also trained with Alter twice a day. Tomas tried to object, but she overruled his concerns. Alter approached training differently. While Tomas tried to impart to her a solid foundation of self-defense that she could build upon, Alter pushed her to learn to hurt, to disable as fast and brutally as possible. He praised her for how fast she took to fighting. She was already in top shape, but she fell into bed exhausted at night, muscles aching from the long workouts.

On the second day, Tomas took her to an intimate lunch near the Spanish Steps. She enjoyed the quiet hour with him, but kept worrying that someone would spot them. She scanned the crowds, looking for heka or enforcers. Tomas looked outwardly calm, but when he wasn't looking at her, his eyes moved constantly.

Sarah tried to draw him out about the Tenth, but he dodged the questions. The time passed all too quickly while they chatted about places they wanted to see after the mission was over. It helped Sarah to talk about their ultimate victory as a foregone conclusion. Although everyone kept a positive attitude, she was no fool. If Gregorios and Eirene worried, she knew she should be terrified.

In his new form, Tomas turned heads nearly as often as she did. The spike of jealousy she felt when unknown women flirted with him or openly drooled over his fantastic physique nearly made her laugh. She had been falling for his honest soul when he still looked plain, so she found herself wanting more of his time than ever. The best part was that he acted more relaxed, more confident. He seemed far more willing to explore a romantic relationship now that the lie no longer kept them apart.

As soon as they finished the mission, they needed a real vacation.

All that stood in the way was Mai Luan.

Only Alter seemed unaffected by the gravity of their endeavor. He actually grew more and more energized the closer they approached the upcoming conflict. He really looked forward to fighting Mai Luan. He had never faced her in person. That experience would have tempered his enthusiasm.

The evening after their wonderful lunch date, Tomas entered the sparring room just as she and Alter were wrapping up a session with some grappling moves. Alter had taught her several new techniques, but he tended to get distracted by the close proximity the moves demanded.

Tomas look displeased to see her locked in a wrestling hold with Alter. She pretended not to notice as she disengaged and ran over to give him a kiss.

"How is the training going?" he asked.

"Great. I can't wait to show you what I've learned." She punched his rock-hard abs lightly. "I'll take you down to the floor for sure."

Alter interrupted before the conversation could take the turn she hoped it would. "Sarah has great aptitude. I think you should accelerate her training."

"You've mentioned that," Tomas said, his voice holding too much challenge for Alter not to notice. They'd argued that point twice already. Alter claimed Tomas was wasting too much time focusing on the basics, while Tomas countered that Alter was moving too fast, forcing her into training positions she couldn't fully apply yet.

"I know what she can do better than you," Alter retorted.

Before the argument took off again, Sarah said, "You're both teaching me a lot. I think we should spar, just to prove it's working."

"Great idea," Tomas said, eyes locked onto Alter.

Alter grinned. "Yes. Let's go a round."

"No, I meant I should spar with each of you," Sarah said. She didn't want them fighting. They were too eager to hit each other. She worried they'd lose control and really start fighting. She knew enough about their capabilities to know they'd both probably end up badly hurt.

Tomas said, "This'll be good for your training. Show you what you'll be able to do eventually."

Alter nodded, "All for education."

The two men faced off, despite her attempts to dissuade them. Alter made a minute bow, which Tomas mirrored.

Then they attacked.

Both men flew at each other and they met with a flurry of kicks and punches too fast for Sarah to follow. They flowed around each other in a stunning display of speed, skill, and acrobatics. She had never seen anything like it. Their enhancements increased their speed, agility, and strength to astonishing levels.

She had been studying runes in the evenings with Alter and Eirene, but still had too much to learn.

Sarah worried her fears would prove all too true as they both landed solid blows, any of which would have sent her flying across the room. The men shrugged off the hits and kept fighting, their faces locked into expressions of utmost concentration.

Tomas stood a little taller and had the advantage of extra muscle, but Alter moved with the grace of a mongoose. His limbs blurred with speed, an advantage he leveraged to the fullest as he rained blows across Tomas's face and torso.

Tomas might lack the speed that Alter brought to bear, but he still moved faster than any non-enhanced fighter ever could. He maintained his balance despite several blows that slipped past his blocks, but still retreated steadily from Alter's blazing fast attack.

Then he made his move.

With an abrupt reversal, he stepped right through a heavy kick and landed a mighty blow in the center of Alter's chest. The force of the impact threw the lighter man right off his feet. Alter slid halfway across the room before he flipped back upright in an impressive acrobatic move.

The two men faced off again, both breathing hard, both looking more than a little battered.

Clapping from the door interrupted the match. Sarah had been so caught up in watching the fight that she hadn't noticed Eirene arrive.

"Excellent performance, gentlemen, but I'm afraid I need Alter back at the machine."

"Good bout," Tomas said with grudging respect as he rubbed his jaw.

Alter didn't look like he wanted to concede anything, but after a glance at Sarah he mumbled, "Not bad."

After he left with Eirene, Sarah threw her arms around Tomas's neck. He was sweaty, but his breathing had already recovered. Some men smelled awful when they sweated, but not Tomas. She kissed him and he held her tight for a long moment.

"You were amazing," she said.

"Thanks. Keep training and you'll get there."

He released her, but she held onto him, gripping his face in her hands. "But Tomas, I don't want you thinking of Alter as a threat to you in any way."

"I don't know what you mean," Tomas said, trying to back away.

She held him. "I know you don't like me training with him."

"The way he looks at you . . ." Tomas began.

"Is my problem. Alter's helping me. I'll keep him in his place, but I need you to trust me. Can you do that?"

Tomas sighed and took her hands in his. "I only want to protect you."

"Then worry about Mai Luan. I can handle Alter."

"I trust you, Sarah," Tomas said, and she read simple sincerity in his eyes. That trust sent a shiver of warmth flowing through her.

"Then it's settled." She kissed him again. "I'll see you at dinner."

After showering, she returned to her rune studies. Alter had been working with Eirene to decipher the full meaning of the runes on the machine. They drew on assistance from his father via emailed photos and phone conversations. Melek had confirmed that many of the runes were previously unknown and he dedicated the vast experience of his runesmiths to help decipher them.

The project seemed to energize the hunter enclave. With their help, Alter confirmed that the inscribed rune sequence granted the person wearing the second helmet the ability to ride along inside the memories of the person wearing the primary helmet. It also granted them the ability to exercise control over the other person's memories.

When Melek learned that Mai Luan might be seeking a master rune, he was at first furious that Alter would share that secret with Gregorios. He soon realized the overriding need however, and reiterated Alter's offer to send a full contingent of hunters to Rome to assist in tracking down and eliminating Mai Luan.

Gregorios admitted the offer tempted him, but he couldn't risk it. The facetaker enforcers routinely tracked hunter movements and a bunch of hunters coming to Rome would definitely be noticed and make the work all the harder. The plan they were developing depended on surprise.

Through it all, Sarah absorbed everything she could about runes. The subject called to her like nothing in her life ever had. Runes just made sense. She realized the location on the body where runes were placed played a key role in proper sealing and in unlocking specific attributes. When she mentioned the suspicion to Alter, he again regarded her with astonishment.

"Help me create one for myself," she urged.

He gave her some pointers and Eirene added some comments, but they lacked a lot of time to work with her on it. So she worked on it alone and found she loved the process of exploration and discovery.

She convinced Alter to get his father to send a listing of basic runes. He acted like the fact that his father agreed to do so was a huge victory, so she took that as an encouraging sign. As the hours of study quickly slipped by, she began to draw sections of various runes in the margins of her notes and an image began to take shape in her mind.

The team worked through much of the next night as they feverishly teased out the full story of the runes. Sarah couldn't go to bed while everyone else stayed up to work on the project. That was the excuse anyway. The reality was that she didn't want to stop. So she brought her work up to her room and continued piecing together the bits and pieces of runes that called to her the loudest.

She lost track of time as she worked, and was startled out of her focused effort by a soft knock at the door. When she opened it, she was startled to see Sofia, the doctor who had helped treat Tomas standing in the doorway. The sight of her triggered a rush of fear.

"What's the matter? Is someone hurt?" Sarah demanded.

"Nothing like that," Sofia said in a soothing tone. Her voice was rich, with barely a hint of an Italian accent. Her black hair hung loose around her oval-shaped face, giving her a more relaxed look than when Sarah had seen her in the hospital wing.

"Then what can I do for you?" Sarah asked, not sure why else one of Quentin's doctors would visit her.

Sofia held out a small piece of paper. Sarah caught sight of a rune on it, and eagerly accepted it. Sofia said, "Alter asked me to share this with you?"

"Really?" The rune was more complex than most of the other runes Alter had shared with her so far. It combined the central components of the basic runes for health and strength.

It was exactly what she needed, and she inhaled sharply as a new image sprang with startling clarity to her mind.

Sofia smiled at her reaction and added in a conspiratorial tone, "Be sure not to mention to Alter that you received this."

"Why not? This rune feels important."

Sofia shrugged. "I know little of what you are all doing, but I know it's important. Alter suggested that his family would not be pleased that he had shared this with you."

Sarah nodded with understanding. Alter was showing unusual subtlety. This way he could share more knowledge with her, but easily deny he had done so. "I see. Don't worry, I'll pretend I figured it out on my own."

"Good luck," Sofia said before leaving.

Sarah plunged back into her work. She wished she could find a way to thank Alter, but if he felt the subterfuge was necessary, she'd play along. Besides, she had too much work to do. With growing excitement, she pulled out a fresh sheet of paper and began drawing as fast as she could, eager to get her ideas down before forgetting anything.

She started with that combination rune and added the bits and parts of several other runes that she had marked in her notes. The pieces fit together remarkably well as a new, customized rune took shape. She finished the new greater rune with several connecting lines that intersected and joined the basic runes. The completed rune was far more complex than any she had studied. It looked more like the ones tattooed on Alter's torso and arms.

It felt right.

She copied it carefully to a second piece of paper and hurried downstairs to show it to Eirene, who was taking a break at the long table in the art dining room.

Eirene took one look at the rune and said, "Oh, my."

"What? Is it that bad?"

"No, dear. It's . . . unexpected."

Alter dropped into a chair nearby and reached for a pastry coated in chocolate. He glanced over at the paper and his eyes bulged with surprise. He snatched the paper out of Eirene's hand and ripped it into tiny pieces.

"Hey!" Sarah protested. "That was my rune."

"Where did you steal that from?" he demanded.

"You need to work on your people skills!" Sarah left the room in a fury.

She was new at runes. She had no idea if she had broken some etiquette rule he hadn't bothered explaining yet, or if the rune was somehow a bad thing. Only, it still felt so *right*.

Ten minutes later while she was beating at a punching bag in the exercise room, Alter entered. She ignored him and punched harder.

"I am sorry," he said and actually sounded humbled.

"You should be."

"It's just . . . where did you find that rune?"

Sarah glared at him. "I didn't find it. I designed it, just like you told me to."

"I didn't teach you that."

Sarah faced him, hands on hips. "It's my first rune, all right? Just spit it out. What did I do wrong?"

"You don't understand. That was the signature rune of my great grandmother."

"This isn't the time to start teasing," she growled.

"I'm not. At first I thought somehow it got included in the list my father sent, but I double-checked the file and couldn't find it."

So Sofia was right. He'd never admit he'd sent those last pieces to her. Fine. She'd keep up the façade too. "Because I built it. It felt like the pieces should fit together."

"They do. Greater runes are often personal, but sometimes runes are . . . rediscovered." He paced away before continuing. "You really just designed that all by yourself, using only the basic runes we shared with you?"

"I did."

"Those pieces do fit together exceptionally well. They did so first for my great grandmother. She was a special woman, beloved by the entire clan, but murdered by a kashaph assassin shortly after my grandfather was born."

"That's terrible," Sarah said, her anger draining away.

"More than you know. Evidence later revealed that she was in league with them. She seduced my great grandfather in order to kill him, but when she didn't do it, they killed her instead."

"Why?"

"Because they're monsters!" Alter snarled. "The scandal disgraced my great grandfather and even though the family destroyed several powerful kashaph enclaves in revenge, the toll was terrible."

Sarah pulled out her first draft of the rune. "This was her rune?"

"Yes, it was her signature contribution. She pioneered several important ideas about combining multiple runes and personalizing them."

"Really?" Sarah studied the rune again. The pattern still felt intuitively right. "It seems so obvious to me."

"Then it is yours."

"What do you mean?"

"You've earned your first rune."

CHAPTER FORTY-EIGHT

I've decided to contract with the facetakers, despite the death threats by the hunters should I do so. I will learn all I can in this life, love my family, and prepare for the future. Now that I know how to live again, why wouldn't I wish to do so?

~Grace Kelly

Sarah stood in the dining room, surrounded by the entire team, filled with nervous excitement. Apparently getting your first rune was a big deal, even at three o'clock in the morning.

Tomas had been thrilled to learn she was getting a rune, and very impressed by the design she came up with. Even the fact that Alter would be inscribing the rune didn't dampen his good spirits.

Tomas had said, "I figured you'd start with a basic healing rune, not some customized greater rune."

"Do you think I should wait?" Sarah asked. It made sense to get a healing rune. She should've thought of that.

"It's up to you. The only problem is that most souls can't handle too many, so you have to choose what you get carefully. The first rune can take a little while to bond, so it's not recommended you get a second one for a few weeks."

"Then I want this one," Sarah said.

The part where someone would cut into her skin to create the rune made her nervous, but Sarah tried not to show it. Alter surprised her by holding up a permanent marker.

"For first time runes, we start with this. The resulting rune won't seal as deep or produce such powerful results, but it also poses far less risk."

He turned a bit so he also faced the gathered group and began speaking of the importance of runes, of the grand history held sacred by runesmiths throughout the ages.

Sarah couldn't believe it. He was launching into a prepared monologue.

Tomas interrupted before he got too far. "We're kind of pressed for time, you know."

Alter shushed him. "This is important. We'll make the time."

He continued his speech as if the interruption never happened. Sarah exchanged an incredulous look with Tomas, but it was clear Alter wouldn't stop until he finished his message. It was endearing, in an annoying sort of way.

He discussed the great importance associated with runes, their connection with history, and of the commitment shared by all who took upon themselves that burden. He stressed the responsibility to use them only to help others, and to fuel them only with the strength of her own soul.

"All others are abomination," Alter proclaimed. "And they will be hunted down and destroyed."

Tomas tried to interrupt again, but Sarah shushed him. Alter was really on a roll, and she was fascinated by the glimpses into the hunter culture that slipped past his normal reticence. He was very earnest and probably didn't realize how much he was sharing with them from an actual hunter first-rune ceremony.

Tomas eventually protested, "She's not a hunter. You don't need all the pomp and circumstance."

Alter said, "Don't belittle it. At least one person here will appreciate their runes as they should."

He eventually drew to a close and approached Sarah.

"Do you accept this responsibility?"

"I do," she said, feeling the weight of the moment. This was not just a game, a cool trick to try. It was not just important to Alter. It was very real and very serious.

"Do you accept the consequences?"

"I do," she said with more conviction.

"Do you accept the risks?"

"I do."

He held up the marker. "You will wear this rune until the mark wears away completely. If you prove to have the strength of spirit to fuel it—"

"She has plenty of spirit," Tomas said. He gave her a wink.

Alter continued, "And unless the design of the rune proves faulty for you—"

"It's right," Sarah insisted.

"Then and only then will you be ready to wear the permanent mark."

He pointed at her side just above her right hip. "With the mark here it will—"

Sarah stopped him. "Wait. Not there."

Alter frowned. "That's where my great grandmother wore hers."

"It doesn't feel right," Sarah insisted. She had worn her jacket over a tank top for a reason. She removed the jacket and gestured at a spot on her left shoulder blade.

"Place it here."

Alter shook his head. "Sarah, you don't know what you're asking. The position matters as much as the design. Placing this rune there would be very dangerous."

"Why?"

Alter frowned. "Why do you always push right into the gray areas we don't discuss outside of the runesmith circle?

"It's a gift."

Tomas said, "You can't stop now. Not after that beautiful speech."

"Fine. But—"

"We know. Don't share the secret," Gregorios interrupted.

"The left shoulder blade is the wrong place. When placed on the right hip, which is what I still recommend, this rune fosters a general improvement of all positive attributes. It will improve your health, help you heal, make you stronger, faster. It is one of the best all-around runes you could have come up with."

That sounded pretty good. He made a convincing argument, but the location still didn't feel right. "So what's wrong with putting it where I want it?"

"There is only one rune we mark onto the left shoulder blade. It's a powerful rune, but risky, and has been successfully sealed by only the most experienced hunters."

"What does that rune do?"

"That's a discussion for another time," he said with an obstinate set to his chin that she recognized. He wouldn't relent on the point, at least not without more persuading than she was willing to do. He kept glancing from Gregorios to Tomas, who both looked intrigued. There was something about that mystery rune he didn't want them to know.

Well, if he could be obstinate, so could she.

"That's where I want it. It's my rune and I'll put it where I feel it should go."

"It's a bad idea," Alter said.

"It's not permanent," Sarah reminded him. "You said yourself the danger is lessened and it'll wear off."

"You don't understand."

"Because you won't explain it to me," she snapped. "Just do it."

Before he could argue further, Eirene interrupted. "Alter, she has the right."

"You're meddling in things beyond your knowledge."

"I know more than you imagine," she said softly. She took Sarah's hands in hers. "There is danger, my dear. I feel it's slim in this case, but it does exist. The most common reaction is that the soul lacks the required force to bond a rune and power it. In those cases, nothing happens, but I have no doubt you possess the soul force required."

"So what's the danger?" Sarah asked. She planned to get the rune, regardless of the risk. She hungered for it in a way she couldn't explain, but also couldn't deny. She'd designed this rune, so she refused to believe it might harm her.

Eirene said, "In rare cases, a rune might partially bond. The danger is increased the more complex the rune."

"And magnified by the fact she's never bonded a rune before," Alter added.

"A partially bonded rune draws upon the strength of the soul, but lacks the full sealing. The effects vary, depending on which symbols activate and which do not," Eirene explained.

Alter nodded. "Exactly. This rune contains pieces from several basic runes. We call partially activated runes outbreaks because they can trigger any number of dangerous complications, from severe pain to disability, and even death."

If they were trying to scare here, they were succeeding. Sarah looked from Alter to Eirene. "Do you really think this rune will produce an outbreak on my shoulder blade?"

Alter nodded at the same time Eirene shook her head.

"That's not helping," Sarah complained.

Eirene said, "It depends on the strength of your soul. I am convinced you possess a mighty soul. If you're really sure, then this rune placed in that spot could prove incredibly powerful."

Alter continued grumbling and Sarah faced him. "I understand the dangers now, and I agree with Eirene. This is my rune. So either spit out the secret you're choking on, or get to work. We have other things to do."

"Fine. Maybe when you recover you'll trust me."

His obstinate worry nearly swayed her. He had never knowingly hurt her and he was the expert. Maybe she should listen to him?

She glanced at Eirene, who had stepped back beside Gregorios and clasped his hand. She looked close to tears. She knew something she wasn't saying too, but she supported Sarah's choice.

"Do it," Sarah ordered, embracing the decision, no matter the outcome.

With surprisingly quick, sure strokes, Alter marked the intricate design into her shoulder blade. It had taken her ten minutes to draw it. He completed his work in sixteen seconds.

Alter stepped back and said, "Your first rune. May it serve you well and enhance all the best in you."

Eirene gave her a hug, followed by Tomas.

"I don't really feel different," Sarah said.

Gregorios hugged her too. Behind his often gruff façade, she had sensed a far more sensitive core. He met her gaze and gave her an approving nod. "First runes seal more slowly. It'll probably take a day or so for it to begin linking to your soul."

Tomas said, "It won't take her that long. I wager she bonds fast."

Gregorios said, "Unlikely. Sometimes for the first one it takes even longer, and usually it manifests by degrees over time."

"There is one way to test it," Alter said.

"No, wait!" Tomas cried, but Alter moved too fast.

He snapped a punch toward Sarah's face.

Her body reacted before she really understood what was going on. Instead of recoiling or screaming, she slipped into one of the forms he had taught her. She shifted a fraction to one side and lifted her left arm to deflect his punch. His fist flashed so close to her face she could smell the marker on his fingers, but it didn't quite touch her.

She rolled under his fist, her hips and torso twisting together to place her right shoulder in perfect position. With all her weight concentrated into her right fist, she punched him in the stomach.

The impact rattled her arm all the way up to her shoulder, but she felt no pain. Alter clutched his stomach, startled.

Tomas laughed. "Awesome!"

Eirene pulled Sarah into a hug and whispered into her ear, "Well done, my dear."

Gregorios looked from Sarah to Alter and grunted. "Huh. We're going to have to discuss the placement of this rune in more detail, boy."

Alter nodded absently. "I still don't believe it."

Tomas grinned. "You're the one who proved it. Did you actually mean to punch her?"

"No, I just wanted to prove my point before the rune sealed and hurt her. This shouldn't have happened."

Eirene patted his arm. "There are some secrets even you don't know yet."

Quentin interrupted. He had returned to the table to check a laptop. "My friends, I received a tip from one of my staffers at the headquarters. The council have kept the details of Mai Luan's next visit secret, but there are hints she's coming today or tomorrow. I'll head into the office at first light and see what I can find."

Gregorios said, "Good. That'll give us time to finalize the plan and run our test."

"After breakfast." Eirene gave Sarah another hug, then dragged Gregorios out of the room.

As the others filtered after, Sarah pulled Tomas aside. "I'm not sleepy. How about you?"

"Not really," he said through a yawn.

"My new swimsuit arrived yesterday. I'm going to swim some laps. Join me?"

"You do realize it's three-thirty?"

"Wimp."

He grinned. "Fine. Let's do some laps. First one to give up pays for dinner tomorrow."

"You're on."

CHAPTER FORTY-NINE

I can't go back to yesterday because I was wearing a different person then.
~Lewis Carroll

The chime of the elevator drew Quentin's attention from the recently completed project on his workbench. The expansive research lab where he worked was situated in the first basement level, next to the armory. He was alone in the fun shop, as he liked to call it, and expected to see one of his assistants returning from lunch break.

Instead, a burly man dressed as an enforcer stepped from the elevator. Quentin had never seen the swarthy-skinned man before.

"May I help you?" he called, while slipping a slender device off his workbench and into his pocket.

"You are Quentin?" The enforcer asked in heavily accented English. The accent matched his Turkish dark coloring.

Quentin had known many Turks, and both friend and foe had commanded respect.

"Indeed I am," he replied.

"Master Shahrokh requires your presence immediately."

The enforcer's hand dropped to his waist as he spoke, caressing the hilt of a long, forward curving knife Quentin recognized as a traditional Yatagan, a Turkish blade popular back in the Ottoman Empire.

He had to be new, or he'd never enter Quentin's domain and make any kind of threatening move, especially not with a simple knife.

"I don't think we've met," Quentin said, shifting along the bench and stowing a pair of automatic pistols. He knew every enforcer stationed in Rome, and would have wagered that he knew every enforcer employed by the council. Did Shahrokh expect him to miss the import of having a man he'd never met bear the summons?

The enforcer declared, "I am Behram. Shahrokh doesn't like to be kept waiting."

"Of course not," Quentin agreed, catching up his jacket. "Lead on."

"Leave your sidearm here," Behram ordered, pointing at Quentin's shoulder holster.

Quentin was tempted to ask the curt fellow to make him, but then he'd have to explain to Shahrokh that he'd been delayed carrying the broken enforcer to the infirmary. He slipped off his shoulder rig and placed it into a locking cabinet. It fit inside better after he palmed a couple more toys.

"Let's move along, son," Quentin said, leading the way to the elevator. "I've got work to get back to."

Behram didn't respond, but punched the button for the third floor. He remained silent all the way to Shahrokh's office. The secretary looked nervous as she motioned Quentin into the inner office. He knew the council were fading fast, but the timing for this foolishness was simply terrible.

Shahrokh sat behind his massive mahogany desk in a padded leather executive chair that was far too big for his wizened frame. He wore a dark suit, but the powder blue fleece blanket draped around his shoulders lessened the hoped-for intimidating effect. Quentin had known Shahrokh for over two decades, and he'd never known the man to need to try intimidating his visitors.

"How are you feeling today, sir?" Quentin asked.

"Terrible, and I'll remain that way until the machines are proven effective," Shahrokh growled

"We're all hoping for successful tests," Quentin said. He stopped before the massive desk, but Shahrokh made no motion for him to sit.

Behram positioned himself a couple paces behind Quentin and to his right.

"You seem to have taken a particular interest in the upcoming test," Shahrokh said, his watery gaze fixed on Quentin's face. "I've received reports that you've been trying to learn the time of Mai Luan's expected arrival."

"Of course," Quentin said, keeping his expression calm. He had thought he'd been quite circumspect in his inquiries, but the council must have added additional security layers he hadn't been informed of. "For such an important event, I want to be prepared to supply the men with every tool they might need."

"A plausible explanation," Shahrokh said, nodding his wrinkled head with his shriveled neck. "If not for recent events, I would believe you."

"You've never had cause to doubt my loyalty," Quentin protested.

"Nor did I doubt Tomas," Shahrokh shouted, climbing shakily to his feet. "And he served with greater distinction than you, and ten times as long!"

"I am not Tomas," Quentin said carefully.

"No," Shahrokh agreed, dropping back into his chair. "And yet Tomas worked for you, and you alone, for the past many months. Is it beyond the realm of possibility that the two of you have colluded against me?"

"Tomas did what he did to protect you against a cui dashi," Quentin said, unable to restrain himself. Seeing Shahrokh brought so low saddened him and enraged him at the same time. This man had always been such a mighty force in the world, and now he was reduced to a pathetic, suspicious husk.

"She alone promises salvation, and by your own words, you condemn yourself."

The outer door opened and another enforcer entered. Domenico was an Italian who loved to laugh, although at the moment he wore a solemn expression.

"My loyalty has not wavered," Quentin said, slipping his right hand into his pocket.

Shahrokh said, "Perhaps. Perhaps not. But we can take no chances this close to success. You will remain in holding until after the machines are proven."

"And if I object?" Quentin asked.

Behram's hand slid to his Yatagan. "Don't."

Domenico approached. "Quentin, sir, please. This is only a precaution."

Even he didn't look like he believed his words, but Quentin acquiesced. "Very well. I will submit to your command. Perhaps you'll reconsider."

Shahrokh said, "I look forward to reinstating you soon. You are dismissed."

Quentin left the office, with Behram and Domenico falling into step on either side. Behram extracted a pair of steel handcuffs.

"Put those away, or I'll drop you right here," Domenico snarled.

"He's a prisoner," Behram objected.

"Quentin's won the respect of every man in this building," Domenico said evenly. "So I guarantee anyone seeing you leading him anywhere in handcuffs will shoot you first and ask questions second. Your call."

The Turk tucked the handcuffs away with a scowl.

When they stepped into the elevator for the trip down to the third basement level holding cells, Domenico muttered, "I'm sorry about this, sir."

"Don't converse with the prisoner," Behram snapped.

Quentin said, "Always follow orders. Discipline is the foundation of success."

Behram nodded, looking even more cross that he was forced to agree.

"I regret we've met under such difficult circumstances," Quentin said, extending a hand.

Behram looked at him like he was crazy.

"You don't have to be cross," Quentin said with a warm smile and patted the enforcer on the arm.

Behram's eyes bulged as every muscle convulsively locked under an electric burst delivered by the device in Quentin's hand. The color of skin, and molded to his palm, the device was kind of like a super-charged buzzer. It was all but invisible before it delivered thousands of volts of shock effect.

"Uh, sir, I should probably object," Domenico said.

"Duly noted," Quentin said, jabbing a pair of tranquilizer darts into the still-stunned Behram. As the man slumped to the floor, he pushed the elevator stop button.

"What are you going to do?" Domenico asked.

"Try to resolve this mess we find ourselves in."

"That would be welcome, sir, but how?"

"You obviously see that the council is on a fatal course."

"There's nothing I can do," Domenico lamented.

Quentin met his gaze. "Actually, there is. There's only one man who can lead the Tenth through this trial."

"Captain Anaru's a good man," Domenico said.

"Of course, but we both know who we need in command right now."

"He's been labeled rogue."

"Labels can change," Quentin said, gripping Domenico's arm. The enforcer tensed just a little, but then relaxed when no electric shock assaulted him. "Notify my home of what's going on, and pass along a message for me. Will you do that?"

Domenico hesitated only a moment. "I will."

"Good man. I'll be in my shop, and I will not be accepting visitors."

"I'll spread the word," Domenico said, his ready smile breaking forth for the first time.

"Excellent. Then I'll need only one more favor."

CHAPTER FIFTY

The alternate domination of one faction over another, sharpened by the spirit of revenge natural to party dissension, which in different ages and countries has perpetrated the most horrid enormities, is itself a frightful despotism. But allowing enchanters to gain a foothold within this fledgling nation would lead at length to a more formal and permanent despotism.

~George Washington

Tomas approached the side entrance to the Suntara building with an unhurried stride that concealed his keyed-up nerves. At every step, he expected a heavily-armed squad of enforcers to swarm from the building, or a sniper to fire from a concealed outpost high above.

He accepted the risk. No other path lay open to him. He'd departed immediately upon receiving Quentin's message, despite strenuous objections from Sarah. Their plan to take Mai Luan required careful timing, relying upon information only Quentin could obtain. Even though his position had been compromised, Tomas was honor-bound to respond.

The message had provided a long-shot chance, and Tomas seized upon it. Even if that chance was little more than a lie, wrapped in hope, he'd take the risk. Tomas paused outside the wooden entry door and checked his concealed weapons. After a deep breath, he typed in the key code and pushed open the door.

Domenico waited for him inside. No one manned the inner security booth.

"It's good to see you, Captain," Domenico said with a grin.

Tomas clasped hands with him in the traditional Roman manner, hand to forearm. Despite the passage of the centuries, the Tenth still greeted each other the traditional way. "I appreciate your faith in me."

"I hope it's well-founded, for both of us."

"It is," Tomas assured him, despite his own doubts. "Take me to Anaru."

Domenico led Tomas into the headquarters, down halls he knew better than any home he'd ever lived in. Almost immediately they encountered a trio of enforcers from the Tenth, men Tomas had known for years, men he had hand-picked to join the elite unit.

"Fall in," Tomas ordered, without slowing.

After only a brief hesitation, they did so.

By the time Domenico led the way into the Tenth's barracks in the rear of the building on the ground floor, their party had swelled to a dozen men. Twenty more men fell in behind, open curiosity on many faces. Tomas was relieved to see few showed open resentment toward him. Maybe he had a chance after all.

Anaru's office was a simple room, the decorations even more spartan than when Tomas had occupied the space. Anaru sat behind a desk that looked too small for his massive frame, eyes fixed on his computer monitor.

He glanced up when Domenico and Tomas entered the office, then surged to his feet, his expression angry.

"How'd you catch this traitor?"

"Catch isn't the way I'd put it," Tomas said, stopping beside Domenico. The rest of the enforcers clustered around the doorway, silently watching. "We need to talk."

"We're beyond talking," Anaru said, rounding the desk. He seemed even bigger than Tomas remembered, his natural giant Maori genes enhanced to the uttermost. He stood several inches taller than Tomas and weighed at least eighty pounds of dense muscle heavier. "Domenico, why didn't you deliver him to Shahrokh as ordered?"

The much shorter Italian enforcer stood proud. "Because you have to hear what this man has to say."

"The words of traitors mean nothing to me," Anaru said, stopping a couple paces away from Tomas.

"The council's in danger," Tomas said

"And you've been declared rogue," Anaru reminded him. "You no longer hold sway here."

"Listen to the captain," Domenico insisted.

"I'm the captain! Don't you ever forget it!" Anaru shouted.

Tomas snapped, "Then act like a captain, and deal with the real threat."

"You are the threat," Anaru said, taking a menacing step forward. "You're in league with Gregorios, and you stole the machine that would have restored the council's strength."

That generated a ripple of low murmurs from the watching enforcers.

Tomas kept his gaze locked on Anaru's. "And yet, here you stand, working with cui dashi and heka, granting them free access to the council. Who's the greater traitor?"

"I've kept my honor. I've obeyed every command."

"Some commands are wrong," Tomas replied, trying to keep calm. He needed to sway Anaru to his side, but the big man's long-standing resentment was a high hurdle Tomas wasn't sure he could overcome. "A good captain knows the difference and knows when the deeper oath has to supersede."

"Some decisions are not in my hands," Anaru said a little less belligerently. "You know that better than anyone."

"I do," Tomas agreed. He turned toward the watching enforcers. "But this is a critical moment. You all know me. You know my heart and my honor. Do you really think I'd risk coming here if I didn't feel this situation required all of us to stand together like never before?"

"You left us. You abandoned your command, the post you held longer than any other captain, as if it meant nothing," Anaru accused.

His anger was back. Tomas didn't blame him. He'd personally recruited Anaru years before, oversaw the mighty warrior's training, groomed him for eventual command. Anaru had grown impatient when he realized he'd never win the coveted captain's post, and had challenged Tomas for the position. Only weeks after defeating Anaru, Tomas had received the call from Gregorios and made the difficult decision to leave the Tenth to help hunt for Eirene.

Tomas said, "You see how bad things are. I saw the council fading, saw them instituting policies that would destroy everything they'd work so hard to implement. I left to help Gregorios, who was the one man who might set things right."

"By your own confession, I'm within my rights to execute you right here," Anaru said, hand dropping to his pistol.

"Don't let your personal feelings cloud the issue. You swore an oath, and it wasn't an oath to hate me."

"I swore an oath to serve and to protect, and I've kept my honor."

"If you turn me in, if you support the council's decision to submit to Mai Luan, you'll be making a mockery of that oath, and helping the very enemies we've sworn to stand against destroy the leaders we've sworn to protect."

A fresh ripple of murmurs ran through the assembled enforcers. Everyone understood the danger, although perhaps not as clearly as Tomas. They all knew enough to realize welcoming cui dashi and heka into the headquarters could only end badly.

Anaru was the key. The other enforcers would obey his command, despite personal reservations. The captain made the decisions and carried the weight of responsibility.

Anaru dashed his hopes when he declared, "My orders are clear. I cannot countermand them."

"Then I'll have to," Tomas said.

"You challenge me?" Anaru asked, his eyes lighting with anticipation.

"I do."

This was the final gamble. He'd hoped Anaru would realize the need to act, that the captain might set aside his bitterness, but hadn't really expected him to.

Anaru had clearly understood where the conversation would end up, had allowed it to take them to this point. Had he wanted to, he could have managed the situation differently and blocked Tomas's ability to make the challenge.

He'd allowed a chance, but Tomas wasn't entirely sure why. Did Anaru secretly yearn to break with orders and destroy the hated cui dashi? That would break with orders, tarnish his carefully honed honor, but stay true to their deepest oaths. Or did he position Tomas to make a challenge because only by defeating Tomas could he remove any lingering doubts as to his right to command?

It didn't matter. Even if Anaru secretly supported Tomas's stance, his honor would never allow him to throw a fight. He'd fight to win. His honor was as firm as steel, and just as unyielding.

If Tomas lost, his life was forfeit, and no doubt Mai Luan would succeed in enslaving the council. Tomas accepted the risk. He'd fought for this command more than once. The Tenth was his legion, and he welcomed the chance to fight to redeem them, no matter the cost.

With deliberate motions, Tomas drew his two concealed pistols, turned them barrel-down, and passed them to Domenico. Anaru did likewise.

The challenge was given and accepted.

The enforcers broke into excited conversation and betting grew heated as Tomas and Anaru together led the assembled company down one level to the practice room. Fashioned like a gladiator arena, the circular, sand-floored room spanned forty feet in diameter. This was the sparring room, where the enforcers trained for hand-to-hand fighting.

Tomas crossed the sand, every step triggering hundreds of memories. He'd personally trained most of the men now climbing into the spectator seats above the eight-foot wooden wall. This arena, built seven centuries ago, had housed the Tenth ever since. It held a rich history that permeated every inch of the aged wooden wall.

He dropped his coat, stripped off his shirt, and kicked off his shoes. A challenge for leadership was a hand-to-hand contest. More than one contender had died in this arena while battling for dominance, but that was fitting in a contest of strength. The Tenth was an organization steeped in tradition, and the requirement that the captain defend his post against any and all challengers with fist and heart had remained constant for nearly two thousand years.

Anaru had paused near the entrance and was already stripped to the waist. His hugely-muscled torso rippled with strength, and the many tattoos he sported would have done his Maori ancestors proud. The big man stepped into the sand, feet moving quickly, hands beating against bicep and chest in a rhythmic war dance his ancestors had chanted for centuries.

With each step, he shouted in Maori, chanting the war cries of his people. The whites of his bulging eyes gleamed against his brown skin, and his muscles quivered with growing battle frenzy. He stuck out his tongue while he chanted, the ancient Maori threat to consume his fallen victims.

Tomas had seen the war dance many times, and had to admit it was still impressive. His muscles tensed with anticipation and adrenaline burned through him, filling him with eagerness to close in battle.

Anaru maintained perfect balance, gliding forward with intricate footwork. His balanced center allowed him to strike or block, adapting with great speed.

Breaking through Anaru's daunting defenses had always been the key to victory. The man could strike like a cobra, his huge fists falling with overwhelming force. Naturally possessing incredible strength, he bore more runes of strength than any other enforcer. Tomas had seen him bench press a Suburban.

Tomas advanced cautiously, closing to ten feet, just outside of striking range. He expected the two of them to circle each other, probing one another's techniques, and eventually building to a full tempo. That's how they had usually sparred, and how their two serious duels had progressed.

Not this time.

CHAPTER FIFTY-ONE

How the early priests came into possession of these secret runes does not appear, and if there were ever any records of this kind the Church would hardly allow them to become public.

~Harry Houdini

Anaru lunged into a rush that surprised Tomas.

He managed to fire off a couple of jabs that did nothing to slow the Maori, who bulled through the blows, anticipated Tomas's last-second dodge, and drove a mighty fist into Tomas's sternum. The hammer stroke catapulted Tomas across the arena. If not enhanced, the blow would have crushed his chest. It still rattled him, driving the air from his lungs.

He rolled smoothly back to his feet, but struggled to breathe.

The assembled enforcers shouted encouragement for their captain, and the betting intensified. Whatever their personal doubts about the rightness of the council's current directives, the enforcers loved a good fight, and Anaru was giving them one.

Anaru rushed across the sands in another reckless charge, shouting in Maori. Tomas could imagine meeting a man much like Anaru leading a surprise Maori attack on an unsuspecting village, and the sight would have instilled paralyzing fear on the hapless villagers.

Tomas embraced the fear, but it couldn't rule him. He magnified the apparent effort required to breathe, as if Anaru had hurt him badly, encouraging the big man to rush in for a quick kill.

Anaru fell for the ruse, and with a mighty cry closed the distance, his huge fist poised to deliver the knockout blow.

At the last second, Tomas dropped to the sands, barely avoiding Anaru's deadly hands, and kicked the side of Anaru's leading knee. The leg buckled and Anaru tumbled to the ground with a howl of pain.

Tomas rose, but waited for Anaru to return to his feet, which he did slowly, favoring his wounded leg. Tomas had hoped to break the knee, but Anaru still managed to support some of his weight with it.

With Anaru reduced to a hobble, Tomas circled him, throwing punches and kicks, probing Anaru's defenses and forcing him to constantly turn. Anaru tried launching a counterstrike, but his wounded leg slowed him down and Tomas easily avoided his grasping hands and punched him a couple of times on his meaty head. The blows had no visible effect, but they served to enrage him. Anaru prided himself on his fighting ability and considered any punches to the face an insult to his honor.

Anaru lunged, catching Tomas in a tackle. They rolled over each other, pummeling with fists and elbows. Tomas tried to slip away, but Anaru pressed Tomas against the sand and reared his torso above him, raining blows with his heavy fists like sledgehammers.

"You're weak," Anaru cried as he beat Tomas into the sands. "This time no one will doubt my right to command."

Rattled by the brutal beating, Tomas tried to protect his face and avoid the worst of the blows, but he needed to break free or Anaru would beat him to a pulp.

He couldn't punch as hard, but he was faster, so he changed tactics. He stopped playing defense and despite his weaker position, he threw fists and elbows into Anaru's midsection as fast and hard as he could. The intensity of his attack surprised Anaru, who drove his torso down to render Tomas's leverage ineffective.

Just what Tomas needed.

He clapped both hands across Anaru's ears.

The huge Maori howled and reared away, clutching at his head.

Tomas kicked him off and tripped Anaru before he could regain his balance. Then Tomas straddled Anaru, pinning the man's massive arms with his knees and pounding his face.

"You lack vision, and you've gotten fat!" Tomas shouted.

Anaru bucked under him, shouting Maori curses, and threatening to knock him flying.

Tomas punched him twice in the throat. As the giant gagged, Tomas rolled off and retreated a step. He waited for Anaru to haul himself to his feet. The two faced off, and Tomas maintained a calm expression, despite the aching of his body from Anaru's beating.

His healing runes were already easing the pain, but more importantly he needed to command the psychological aspect of the fight. That would be a key in defeating Anaru and in proving to his men that he was worthy to lead them.

As soon as Anaru was set, Tomas closed in and launched a blistering attack with feet and fists, elbows and knees, drawing upon every fighting trick he'd learned in his long career. He could have choked Anaru when he'd recently knocked the big man down, but he needed to beat him soundly, fist to fist.

The two fought across the sands in close hand-to-hand combat, striking, parrying, and absorbing hit after hit. Tomas managed to avoid the worst of Anaru's overwhelming punches, but even glancing blows rattled him. He didn't let up, didn't show the pain, and drove Anaru all the way to the far wall.

Anaru's earlier confident shouting faded to panting and growling, but he kept fighting, his massive arms still posing a deadly threat.

A well-placed kick from Tomas knocked Anaru into the wooden wall. He lunged back at Tomas, his arm sweeping out in a haymaker that would've knocked Tomas's head off.

Tomas slipped under the deadly swing and launched himself at the nearby wall. He jumped, kicked off the wall to reverse course, and soared high, coming down with all his momentum focused on his right elbow. He drove it into the base of Anaru's throat just as the big man turned to face him.

Anaru's collarbone snapped and Tomas's elbow drove deep into the soft tissue beneath. He crashed against Anaru, but bounced off the bigger man. Anaru stumbled but didn't fall. His face was contorted with pain and rage.

Tomas's elbow throbbed from the impact, and he stared in amazement. That hit should've knocked even the gian Maori out of the fight.

Anaru lunged, hands reaching for Tomas's throat.

Tomas stepped between his grasping hands and threw every ounce of strength into a right cross at Anaru's jaw. The blow snapped the big man's head back, then his body followed. He toppled backward and crashed into the sand, where he lay unmoving.

Tomas's hand burned. He was sure he'd just broken at least one finger, so he kept his fist clenched. Panting from exertion and pain, he carefully circled the fallen giant, but Anaru didn't move.

From the nearby stands, Domenico leaped to his feet. "Captain Tomas wins!"

The rest of the enforcers broke into a cheer and several of them rushed out to treat the unconscious Anaru. Domenico approached Tomas and offered an ice pack for his broken hand.

"Thank you," Tomas said through bruised lips, trying to hide how much he hurt and how badly he wanted to lie down in the sands and sleep.

Domenico grinned. "Good fight. For a while, I thought you were done for."

"So did I."

He turned to the rest of the enforcers gathered onto the sands. More than half of the Tenth had assembled to witness the duel. "Does anyone else challenge my right to command?"

Tradition required he make the offer, but he worried someone might actually take him up on it. If any of them shared Anaru's long-held resentment, this would be their best chance. Tomas didn't think he could win another duel, but he'd be honor-bound to accept the challenge.

When no one spoke up, he smiled. "All right, then. It's good to be back."

The enforcers, his men, cheered and surrounded him clapping him on the back and congratulating him. Their support filled him with soaring joy. These were his men. Leaving his command had been one of the hardest decisions he'd ever made. Being labeled an enemy had hurt deeply, but it all washed away under the simple joy of again being part of this company.

"We're honored to have you back. What are your orders?" Domenico asked.

"See that Anaru's patched up. I need him functional."

At Domenico's surprised look he added, "Anaru served as captain with honor. He's now my second. You're now my first lieutenant."

"Yes, sir." Domenico saluted.

Tomas hoped Anaru would accept the appointment as second with good grace. It was the best honor Tomas could offer, and better than most fallen captains received. Most were stripped of rank and, if not kicked out of the legion outright, were often transferred to remote posts where they couldn't undermine the authority of their usurper. Tomas needed Anaru's knowledge of current operations, and he needed the Tenth united. If Anaru embraced his new role, together they could take Mai Luan apart.

"Someone inform Quentin he can come out from behind his barricade. I need his help. And someone find out when Mai Luan's expected to arrive with her new machines."

"She's already here," Anaru said, sitting up with the help of two other men. His face was pale and his eyes weren't entirely focused, but his voice sounded clear. "The council's assembled. They're planning to begin the final test within the hour."

Tomas cursed. Quentin's last report had suggested they had at least until evening.

"Domenico, assemble everyone on the double! Battle array. This is an alpha level event. The council's in grave danger."

As his lieutenant began barking orders and men rushed to gear up, Tomas grabbed his phone and dialed Gregorios. He cursed again while he waited for it to ring.

The memory hunt was about to start, and he was out of position.

CHAPTER FIFTY-TWO

The Liberal State is a mask behind which there is no face; it is a scaffolding behind which there is no building. Upon this truth I will stake my upcoming lives.

~Benito Mussolini

A re we ready?" Gregorios asked without preamble when he entered the dining room.

Sarah hovered near Alter and Eirene, absorbing everything she could of their discussion. They had drawn all of the runes they'd found marked onto the machine, and the table was covered with the drawings.

"As near as we can be with so little time," Alter said, gesturing toward the table.

"We're out of time," Gregorios reminded him.

"When will Tomas get back?" Sarah asked. Her relief at the news that he'd survived the crazy return to his company and regained his position as captain had been eclipsed by renewed fear at the news of Mai Luan's imminent test with Asoka.

Gregorios declared, "He won't be back. Not in time for it to matter to us."

"But he's part of the plan," Sarah protested.

Over the past couple of days, the team had worked out the framework of a plan to block Mai Luan's attempt on the master rune. It relied upon Tomas and Alter working together to fight her while Gregorios defeated Asoka and terminated the memory before it reached the point where the master rune would be revealed.

Gregorios grimaced. "The plan's going to have to change. This is our only shot, and we can't wait. It's now or never."

Eirene patted Sarah's arm. "We'll figure it out, but at least Tomas is there. With a little luck, and lots of muscle from the Tenth, he might be able to remove Mai Luan while she's sleeping."

Gregorios nodded. "He suggested the same thing already. It opens up an entirely new front she can't have foreseen. If we can block her in time, he can take her out."

"We haven't solved the entire mystery of these runes yet," Alter warned. "There are just too many unknowns and we're not even going to get to test our ideas before jumping right into the memory hunt."

"That can't be helped. Can we or can we not fire this thing up?" Gregorios asked.

"Yes," Alter said after a slight pause. He gestured at the many runes on the table. "I've already modified the runes on our machine to grant you more control of the memory. It should allow whoever's in the secondary helmet to actively interact with the memory without being able to take over like Mai Luan did."

Eirene said, "I still don't understand how she pulled that monster into your dream. That part worries me, and I haven't found any evidence among these runes that speak to that."

Gregorios said, "I'm not sure she did it on purpose. I've been thinking about that. She seemed surprised by it, and that creature attacked Asoka and his squad. That couldn't have been part of her plan."

"You fought her," Alter said with a snap of his fingers. "That changed things."

"It's my mind. I should be able to change what I want."

Alter shook his head. "This is a memory, not some random dream. The runes work by driving you back to a specific point in history in search of a master rune. For it to work, you must walk the memory with great care and approach a pure truth of that moment in history. Changes threaten the memory's integrity. I suspect it produces gaps that are filled with negative energy."

"Monsters?" Sarah asked with a shiver.

"It appears so. Drawn from the subconscious mind of the dreamer."

"Fascinating as this discussion is, we're out of time. We'll just have to be careful," Gregorios said.

Eirene added, "I believe the additional helmet is ready. The runes are in place anyway. It should allow two passengers into the memory with you."

Sarah asked, "But who's going? Tomas isn't here."

"I can take Mai Luan," Alter declared with customary zeal.

"Maybe." Eirene didn't sound convinced. "But distracting her first was the plan, and that approach still offers us the best chance of victory."

"You've got to power the machine, love." Gregorios told her. "And I'll be busy with Asoka. If Quentin were here, we could ask him."

Sarah spoke, offering the most logical solution, but the one no one had suggested yet. "I'll go."

Alter protested. "You can't. It's going to be very dangerous."

"That's why I have to do it," she insisted.

Eirene hesitated. "You've made wonderful progress in your training, but this isn't going to be a stroll down memory lane. This will be war. Injuries suffered while locked into the memoryscape transfer to our sleeping forms. Gregorios and I both experienced it. You could get hurt."

"Or killed," Alter added.

"I know," Sarah said. The thought of facing Mai Luan terrified her, but she believed in the plan. For it to have any chance of success, for Alter to get his chance to defeat Mai Luan in the memory, or for Tomas to kill her in her sleep, they needed another person.

"Like Gregorios just said, this is our one chance. She hates me, so I'll try to draw her out, keep her distracted. Then Alter can hit her when she's not expecting it."

"That could work," Alter admitted grudgingly.

"Are you sure?" Gregorios asked, his gaze intent.

Sarah steeled herself against the rising fear, trying to instead infuse herself with the burning rage she'd felt right after Mai Luan had stabbed Tomas. "I'm going with you."

He clapped her on the shoulder, knocking her a startled step. "Good girl. You spit in her eye, and Alter will do the rest."

They had already dragged three recliner chairs into the room. While they positioned the chairs around the machine, Gregorios reviewed the plan. "Remember, don't do anything stupid. Sarah, distract her, but don't try fighting. Just let her gloat. People like her always enjoy that, so let's count on it. Alter will hit her when she's not looking."

"You bet," Alter agreed, cracking his knuckles.

"Even if you can't kill her, just slowing her down should be enough," Gregorios added. "Asoka won't resist her, and he'll oppose anything I try to manipulate in there."

"You don't think he'll turn on her when he learns what she's after?" Sarah asked.

Gregorios said, "I doubt he'll care. Once he learns he can break with the memory, he'll be eager for a re-match. Once I prove that history got it right the first time and remove him, I should gain full control over the memory and either wake us up, or at least shift us away from the pivotal moment. Either way, we'll block her."

"Hopefully Tomas can get into position and take her out," Eirene said.

Gregorios nodded. "I'm counting on it. He knows what he's doing. We just need to prevent her from getting that master rune."

"Don't stray too far from the memory," Alter advised. "With all the forces in play, everything will drive us toward the moment that'll trigger the master rune."

"I believe I know the moment," Gregorios said, his expression grim.

"What is it?" Sarah asked.

"Something I have to deal with. But if we stick to the plan, we should have plenty of time to get out of there before we hit it."

"You might have the hardest job," Alter told Eirene. "From our calculations, I expect the strain of maintaining the connection for all three of us will be severe."

"Can you guess how severe?"

"Unfortunately, no. That was one of the key elements we needed to test. There's no way to tell until we try it out, but if we tarry too long it could prove dangerous."

"We could find an external supply," Eirene suggested.

"No!" Alter looked horrified. "I'm the only rounon here, and I'm oathbound never to draw from the soul force of another. That is abomination."

Eirene asked, "Even if we used a heka? You'd just kill them otherwise."

"Death is honorable. Turning to their wicked ways would destroy me along with them," Alter insisted.

Gregorios considered the earnest hunter for a moment before saying, "We may have to consider it eventually, but we don't have an external supply today anyway."

He took Eirene's hands in his. "She consumed an entire soul powering the machine through my memories. I don't know if the added strain came from the fact that I fought her, but be careful. It all depends on you, love."

"Be quick, and I'll be fine. We're all taking risks."

The group turned to face the machine and Gregorios reached for the primary helmet. He grumbled, "I hate Berlin."

CHAPTER FIFTY-THREE

I have the benefit of patience. It took Gregorios centuries to become the man I could commit my heart to. Most women don't have that luxury. I am sometimes surprised by how many of them still manage to find worthy men in their first lives.

~Eirene

Gregorios awoke in Berlin.

He stopped on the Wilhelmstrasse despite the pull to keep walking. The all-too familiar dream memory was slightly different. The sky looked strangely indistinct and some of the buildings looked less damaged than they should.

Someone was messing with his memory.

He focused and forced the details back the way they should be. The sky sharpened into distinct billowing clouds of smoke and the buildings deteriorated before his eyes. Instantly he felt the mental strain as another will attempted to block the changes and overlay his memory with details of their own.

It was a strange feeling, like a mental tug-of-war, made stranger by the fact that he couldn't yet see Asoka. At least it proved Alter's theory. Both he and Asoka had traveled to the same common memory, and despite the physical distance between them in the real world, the rune-powered machines were linking them to the shadow of that historical moment.

He rarely felt fear any more, but the magnitude of what Mai Luan had crafted scared him. Asoka and Mai Luan were already here somewhere, and he had to stop them before she gained the master rune, or they'd never stop her.

Alter materialized beside him. The hot-blooded young hunter looked around and asked, "Where are they?"

"They're here somewhere. I can feel them. Look sharp."

A mortar exploded less than a block away from them. Sarah, who had just materialized nearby yelped with fright.

Gregorios wore the same SS uniform he preferred in this memory and Alter had appeared wearing a German infantry uniform. As soon as Alter noticed the outfit, his face reddened and he rounded on Gregorios.

"Change this now!"

"It doesn't matter," Gregorios said.

The uniform actually looked pretty good on him and it blended well with the location. The invisible battle of wills was distracting. If he had not survived countless duels with rogue facetakers and mastered the art of drawing upon and directing his will, he wouldn't have been able to maintain the integrity of the memory. "It's just a dream."

"It's a memory, isn't it?" Sarah asked.

Gregorios said, "For me. For you, it's more a living dream."

"A nightmare. I will not wear the uniform of the men who slaughtered my people," Alter growled.

Oh, right. So many details.

Gregorios concentrated, and Alter's uniform changed into a turban and robe.

The young man glared, and Sarah laughed. She wore a nurse's uniform and it looked fantastic on her, like pretty much everything did. How Tomas had caught her eye, Gregorios still couldn't imagine, but she was proving to have a soul as interesting and profound as her looks. That was an incredibly rare combination. She broke the traditional look by pulling her hair out of the tight bun and rolling it into a simple ponytail.

Gregorios concentrated again, and Alter's robe faded into a black Jewish rabbi outfit.

"Best you can do?" Alter demanded.

"Kind of busy here. Asoka and Mai Luan are messing with things."

"Don't let them."

"If you stop interrupting."

"Of course." The boy actually looked contrite for a second.

"So they know we're here?" Sarah asked.

"No doubt."

Alter clenched his fists and looked down meaningfully at his empty hands. "How about some weapons?"

"What did we just talk about?"

Sarah was peering through the clouds of smoke down the rubble-filled thoroughfare at the squad of soldiers passing like wraiths. "Can we just make up anything we want?"

Alter said, "He can. It takes effort, and if it breaks with the memory too much, bad things could happen."

"Avoid bad things. Keep the monsters under the bed tonight," Gregorios agreed.

Sarah closed her eyes and her brow furrowed in concentration. A second later, a semi-automatic pistol appeared in her hands.

Alter gaped. "How did you do that?"

Sarah shrugged and displayed the piece. "Tomas's gun."

A low growl spun them around. A dog-sized creature all covered in black scales, with long fangs and burning orange eyes pulled itself out of the ground. It lunged toward Sarah.

She shot it in the head and it dissolved into dust.

"What was that?" she gasped. It was a good sign she reacted emotionally only after killing the beast.

Alter grimaced. "Bad things. You broke the integrity of the memory, so the gap was filled with negative energy."

Gregorios said, "Enough with the lectures. We have to get to the bunker before they do."

Just then the woman with the little girl and baby boy scurried past as they always did, fear in their eyes. Gregorios grabbed for her, hoping to direct her into the gardens where they might live a little longer, but she yelped and ran faster.

"What are you doing?" Sarah exclaimed.

Gregorios turned to watch the little family running toward their doom, frustrated that he could do nothing to save them.

Wait a minute. This was his memory.

As the fatal mortar whistled down from the sky, Gregorios willed the memory to change.

One hundred feet above the family, the mortar exploded into a shower of rainbow lights that drifted down around them. The woman gaped in astonishment while the little girl laughed and clapped her hands.

A pristine white china doll dropped into her hands.

Gregorios turned back to the others with a satisfied smile. "Finally."

The appearance of a creature that looked like a man wearing an octopus on his head didn't dampen Gregorios's good humor. He grabbed a jagged piece of steel from the street and beat the creature to dust.

"What was that?" Sarah asked.

"Doesn't matter. It was worth it."

In a much better mood, he led the way up the street at a run and turned into the Reich Chancellery. He pointed southeast through the smoke toward the distant Reichskanzlei. "That way."

Sarah, who had paused to survey the gardens said, "We've got company."

A platoon of Russian soldiers came swarming around the far end of a heavily damaged government building to their north and started shooting at them. Most of the bullets went wild at that distance but the trio still ducked and ran.

"This isn't right," Gregorios shouted above the clatter of small arms fire. "The Russians never made it this far so fast."

"Focus!" Alter shouted as the three of them rounded a thick hedge that provided a little concealment, and ran hard.

He was right. They were on Gregorios's turf. He didn't need to play by other peoples' rules. He needed to keep that fact front and center in his mind. So he slowed and used his imagination instead.

A squad of German soldiers poured into the gardens from a nearby alley, followed by a tank. They opened fire on the Russians and the two groups engaged with brutal intensity.

"Nice touch with the tank," Alter said.

They ran south again but paused at the top of a low hill so Gregorios could survey the back door of the bunker to see if any other surprises awaited them. Sarah, whose face had paled at the sight of the killing and the screams of wounded soldiers, risked a glance back in the direction they came.

"Look!"

The soldiers who had been butchering each other moments before, were united to fight a bunch of demonic monsters. The creatures sported horns and fiery eyes and were roughly man shaped, but far more muscular. Gunfire seemed to only anger them and they ripped through the soldiers with terrifying ease. One of them roared, and a flurry of tiny white specs burst from its maw and enveloped a pair of soldiers who fell screaming to the ground.

The tank fired into the midst of the demon creatures and three of them disintegrated.

"What are those things?" Sarah cried.

"More bad things," Alter said. He cringed at the sight of several of the fallen soldiers rising to their feet and trying to eat their comrades.

Sarah shouted, "What does that mean? And how are there zombies in Berlin?"

Gregorios said, "Those aren't zombies. Skin's too pale and they move too fast. Those are ghouls."

"So you're a zombie expert?" she asked, her eyes wide with fear.

He shrugged. "Zombies were always a waste of time, but we're in a memoryscape here. Ghouls are stuff of nightmares. They fit better."

She gave him a skeptical look and he decided not to explain further. She wouldn't believe him unless he showed her in the real world. Most people didn't react well to seeing actual undead.

"I think the demons are horerczy," He said as he led the others down the hill toward the distant bunker. "The white specs look like butterflies close up. They're alps, a type of German vampire shape shifters."

More screams from the north, and it sounded like tearing metal. Gregorios didn't bother turning.

As they ran, Alter said, "Breaking with a true memory is inherently dangerous. We discussed it."

"We didn't talk about this," Sarah said.

He said, "I don't know much more. Reuben's the one who preferred studying this kind of theoretical stuff. It never interested me."

"What do you think now?" Gregorios asked with a raised eyebrow. "I didn't summon the monsters, and I'm thinking neither did Asoka."

Alter said, "You brought in the troops. That created the holes through which the monsters formed."

"So the more we break with the memory, the worse the monsters?" Sarah asked.

"Something like that," Alter confirmed.

"Okay then," Sarah said, looking worried, but determined. "Try not to change too much."

They rounded a pile of rubble. The bunker lay barely a hundred yards ahead through shifting smoke, torn up lawns, and the shattered trees of the gardens. A group of SS soldiers advanced from the south out of a thick stand of timber. Asoka led them, and Mai Luan jogged at his side.

Mai Luan spotted him, raised a German Luger pistol, and started firing. She didn't look surprised to see him, so either she had felt him tampering with the memory, or Asoka had warned him.

She was a fantastic shot.

The first bullet missed by only a couple inches, and Gregorios felt the air of its passage. He ducked and ran for the cover of a nearby fallen tree.

"Fighting out here in the open gives them the advantage," Gregorios said as the others crouched beside him. "I've got to get into the bunker. I might be able to break the memory stream in there, since those events are the critical ones."

"Then shouldn't you avoid the bunker altogether?" Sarah asked.

He shook his head. "If Asoka breaks through, that's where he'll go. I need to get there first. You two hold the rest of them off."

More bullets tore into the fallen tree and sent splinters flying.

"How are we going to do that with just one pistol?" Sarah asked, cringing lower.

Gregorios winked. They were playing in his mind, after all.

Sarah's pistol morphed into a shotgun. A fifty-caliber machine gun with a long belt of ammunition appeared in Alter's hands.

The young hunter grinned as he yanked back the bolt to rack the first round into the chamber. "This'll do."

CHAPTER FIFTY-FOUR

History is the version of past events that remains after we write out the important parts.

~Napoleon Bonaparte

Gregorios rushed toward the bunker and left the din of battle behind. Stray bullets tore into the earth behind him, but Alter and Sarah were providing enough covering fire to keep Mai Luan and her soldiers distracted.

Asoka had led the force of SS soldiers scrambling east for cover behind some buildings just south of the Old Chancellery building. From cover of the rubble, they returned fire and forced Alter and Sarah to change position and dive behind piles of concrete and broken wood, all that remained of a once-beautiful gazebo.

The SS would eventually drive the two back with the weight of numbers. Alter, with his hunter training, should be able to keep the attackers busy long enough for Gregorios to break the critical moment.

His biggest worry was that Mai Luan might hurt Sarah, but he had to take the risk. As much as he cared for her, he couldn't stay to protect her. They all risk much in this fight, and they all had come prepared to make the required sacrifices.

He still hoped Asoka and the cui dashi would be the ones to make the ultimate sacrifice in the end.

To the north, the Russian and German soldiers were still battling ghouls. It looked like the tank had destroyed the demonic horerczy, but a giant snake had wound around the armored vehicle and was trying to rip it apart.

Gregorios always detested Berlin, and now he hated it more than ever. The memory was threatening to fly out of control. He wasn't sure what would happen if it did. Would it just force them awake or would their minds die? The fact that injuries sustained in the memory affected their sleeping forms motivated him to keep it together. He didn't need much time.

He paused at the bunker door and glanced back. The firefight between the SS soldiers and Alter and Sarah was still raging, and looked like it could continue for a while before either side gained the advantage. He didn't see Asoka or Mai Luan, and that worried him. Were they circling around to attack Alter and Sarah? More likely, they'd left their men behind just as he had and were moving toward him around one of the nearby buildings.

Either way, he held the advantage. Hopefully it would be enough.

He entered the bunker, slammed the heavy door behind him, and locked it. Mai Luan could break through, but it would slow regular soldiers for a while. Mai Luan was linked to this historical moment through Asoka, so she didn't lie in wait for him in the inner room. She was stuck outside, hopefully for a couple more minutes.

Gregorios headed down the stairs.

The memory pulled him down and he allowed himself to go with it. The less resistance to it, the better. He had caught Mai Luan by surprise. She had undoubtedly assumed she would control Asoka's memory and gain her prize without opposition. That mistake would cost her everything. Gregorios hated re-visiting this memory for so many reasons, but he would go through it one more time if it meant thwarting her plans.

At the bottom of the stairs, he knocked on the oak inner door. When the voice summoned him through, he stepped inside.

Adolf Hitler awaited him, flanked by his long-time companion and recent bride, Eva Braun. A handful of staffers hovered nearby.

"Leave us. See to the defenses," Hitler commanded his aids.

They all filed past except for one. The young man was tall and strong, a perfect example of Hitler's Aryan race. He was also Hitler's favorite transfer vehicle.

Some people fell to addictions faster than others. For some it was smoking, for others alcohol or pornography. For Hitler it was soul transfers.

As soon as he had learned of facetakers, he had demanded a soul transfer. Once he tasted life in a perfect Aryan body, he could never go back. Had he lived in times before modern communications, it would have been a simple, if still expensive, process to affect the transfer and send him on his way. Unfortunately the world knew what he looked like so he couldn't just assume a dramatically new body, a fact he bewailed often in private.

So he had contracted for ongoing facetaker presence. Between major public appearances he would transfer into the body of an Aryan man. Gregorios was assigned his facetaker, and he grew to know the man far too well. At first it was just another job, one that guaranteed fantastic new wealth for the council and for Gregorios personally. Hitler pillaged Europe not just to fund his war machine, but to fund the staggering cost of transfers.

Over time, as the number of transfers mounted, Gregorios noted the telltale signs of mental dissipation. He tried to warn the dictator of the dangers, but Hitler insisted they continue. Some souls resisted soul fragmentation, and his will was strong enough that he could do so for a while, but no mortal could maintain that pace for long.

Gregorios made the mistake of trying to frighten Hitler by explaining that his soul was fracturing and bits of the souls from the bodies he inhabited would filter into the cracks.

Hitler loved the idea.

Most souls rejected foreign contamination just as bodies often reject organ transplants. It was a natural reaction. Hitler was the only client Gregorios ever met who longed for those bits of soul to fuse to his. He hoped that over time he could assimilate enough from the souls of those perfect Aryan specimens to become one himself.

Delusions were a sure sign of mental dissipation.

Gregorios had planned to put a stop to it before Hitler became too unstable, but the council commanded him not to intervene. At the time he hadn't understood their purposes but now, standing again in the Fuhrerbunker, it finally made sense.

Ordering Asoka to attempt to dispose of Gregorios was a preemptive measure to conceal the truth of their growing mental disability, but it was not their only action in Germany. They were using Hitler too. He was their test case. If he, a mere mortal, could successfully assimilate external souls, then they could do the same. If he could somehow beat the soul fragmentation and become something greater, they could find a way to extend their lives. In the days prior to Mai Luan's fantastic machines, it was their best hope for staving off death.

The truth only fueled Gregorios's anger.

So many lives destroyed in their quest to thwart their fate. Even if Mai Luan's machines helped reverse their soul fragmentation, Gregorios vowed to terminate them, just as he should have decades before.

Hitler beckoned Gregorios deeper into the warren of small rooms. They stopped in a bedroom stripped bare but for two cots. Hitler and the young soldier both lay down.

The dictator gestured toward his face. "Proceed. There is not much time."

"No, time is run out."

Gregorios positioned himself above Hitler's face and a wave of revulsion set his hands shaking. In the memory, Asoka would break in within minutes. In this dream, he might have even less time.

This man had committed so much evil.

Gregorios had allowed him to do it.

He had tried to stop the Fuhrer, but had not tried hard enough. He had sent intelligence to the hunters to help turn the tide in Stalingrad, and had even executed the enchanter who had convinced Hitler to launch the attempted genocide of the Jews. Gregorios had learned the entire holocaust was crafted in an attempt to destroy the hunters by eliminating the nation within which they hid. Of course, they were far too clever to get caught and sent off to the concentration camps, but that did not prevent the attempt.

The slaughter of millions of innocents had sickened Gregorios more than anything since the atrocities committed during the fall of ancient Rome. He had removed the architect of the plan, but had not been able to stop the implementation of it.

With an effort, Gregorios forced the tumultuous thoughts away and willed the memory into sharp detail. He embraced his nevra core and drove his fingers through the skin under Hitler's jaw. Purple fire burned in his eyes and along his hands as the dictator's face began to lift free. He hated the thrill that filled him as he took another soul, but could not quite block it out.

Just as the soulmask began to pull free, a weight slammed into Gregorios's left shoulder and sharp pain took his breath away. The unexpected assault staggered him two steps, broke his concentration and his grip.

Hitler began to scream. Being left suspended in a partial transformation was incredibly painful.

He deserved it.

A small, implike creature clung to Gregorios's shoulder, its little talons driven through his muscles. The little monster bit at his face and dug its rear claws into his back. It smelled like dead fish and rotten fruit burned on a barbecue.

Eva screamed and the young soldier lying on the next cot lunged to his feet. Gregorios grabbed the little monster by the neck and ripped it off. It brought chunks of his shoulder with it, and blood sprayed across the room. The pain would have toppled him had he not blocked the sensory input from those nerves.

He threw the little beast at the soldier.

The man screamed as it chewed on his face, and struggled in vain to pull it off. Gregorios drew his pistol. He had not been armed a moment before, but he summoned a colt fort-five 1911-style pistol, his favorite gun of all time. He shot the little demon and it exploded into black mist.

The bullet also blew a gaping hole through the soldier's head.

Eva Braun kept screaming, so Gregorios shot her too. She'd be dead in minutes anyway, and a quick bullet was a mercy.

He paused to concentrate. His wounds closed and a sense of strength and health returned.

He could get used to that.

It took only a few more seconds to finish removing Hitler's soulmask. Gregorios ignored the whispered questions and demands from the dispossessed despot as he exited the room and headed for the deepest corner of the bunker. He passed conference rooms, a communications center, and plush living quarters but didn't pause. Anywhere he tried to hide the soulmask, Mai Luan could find it easily. He could think of only one place he might keep it concealed long enough.

At the deepest part of the bunker, he turned into a long storeroom. The air smelled of dust and mold, and hung still and heavy. The long shelves of the storeroom held nothing of interest. Just stacks of unimportant documents, barrels of water, and some spare linens. None of it was meant to be used, but served a vital purpose of disguise.

In the back corner, he fumbled behind a broken wooden box full of propaganda pamphlets until he found a concealed lever that felt like nothing more than a splinter-riddled shard of the box. When he pulled it, the shelving beside him swung away, revealing a cleverly concealed door.

Time to finish it.

CHAPTER FIFTY-FIVE

The court of Cyrus the Great embodied majesty in a way lost to the world ever since. Today we live in such luxury, and yet the world grovels in mediocrity. I am starting to think there will never be another great king.

Perhaps it is time I offer myself for this service.

~John, facetaker council member

Eirene panted for breath and her body quaked from the strain. She stood over the helmet that held Gregorios, her hands clasping the jagged mask that blocked sight of his face. She didn't need it. She had memorized his features centuries ago, but she still longed to see him.

The drain had started high, but manageable. Over the past minutes it had increased until she could barely maintain the connection for all three of them. She was not sure what was going on, but they needed to finish soon. If not, she would be forced to try to pull one of them from the memory.

Who would she choose?

Alter was a hunter, trained to fight heka and cui dashi from birth. She knew the strength of his family, the depth of his commitment.

Sarah was untrained, inexperienced, but she had designed that particular rune. Had she learned in the memory to tap its powers, unknown even to Alter's family? If she did, she might be the best choice to help Gregorios.

The drain spiked again in intensity and Eirene sagged over the machine as she bent all her will to maintaining the connection. When her vision cleared, she noticed blood pouring down Gregorios's shoulder, and icy fear chilled her.

If he died in there, he couldn't sever contact with his body to save his life. If he tried, she wasn't sure what might happen. Would he awaken? Or would he lose contact with her and be trapped in that shadow of history forever?

The skin closed a moment later, but that triggered another severe drain. Eirene recovered more slowly that time. She leaned her face against the welcome coolness of the faceplate and whispered, "Hurry, love."

CHAPTER FIFTY-SIX

In every generation without fail, someone discovers the idea of world domination. They think it's new or that they're uniquely suited to rule. I used to try to convince them they were wrong.

Now I just remove them.

~Gregorios

The entire floor?" Tomas demanded.

"I'm afraid so, Captain," Domenico said.

The two stood in the Tenth's main muster hall, a low-ceilinged, concrete room filled with folding chairs and a round table dating back to the final crusade. Troop roll calls, a map of the building, and documents detailing a history of each of Mai Luan's previous visits to the headquarters covered the table. Twenty-five enforcers clustered in groups nearby, awaiting orders.

Tomas turned to Anaru, who stood at attention nearby, despite Tomas's urgings that he sit. "How is it possible the council's safety was entrusted to a squad outside of the Tenth?"

"Shahrokh's orders, sir," Anaru said crisply. His left arm was in a sling, and his jaw still looked bruised. He'd be mostly recovered in the next half hour, but rest would help accelerate the process. "After your defection, Shahrokh said he couldn't trust the Tenth."

"Guess he was right about that," Domenico muttered.

"Right that we'll protect him even from himself," Tomas added. "What do we know of the men up there with him?"

Anaru said, "Eight men. All personally recruited by Shahrokh over the past two years, and stationed in Iraq and Indonesia."

"What do we know about them?"

Domenico gestured toward the papers on the desk. "We're missing their personnel files, so very little."

Anaru said, "They were classified. The squad's called the Eagles. I met their leader, a man named Behram."

Domenico grimaced. "I did too. Turkish. Grumpy. Gave Quentin a hard time."

That was all Tomas needed to know.

"We'll try for non-lethal take-downs for the enforcers, but what of the heka?"

Domenico scowled and muttered an Italian curse.

Anaru maintained his stoic expression. "On Shahrokh's orders. Mai Luan was allowed to bring several assistants and seven security guards."

Tomas frowned. "That's fifteen men holding the fourth floor and essentially holding the council hostage."

Domenico said, "I doubt the enforcers would allow anything to happen to the council. They're Shahrokh's new personal guard."

Tomas said, "Don't count on it. Mai Luan's planned this too perfectly. I guarantee those men are either already somehow in her employ, or she has a plan to take them out as soon as she gets what she wants from Asoka's mind."

"What's she after?" Domenico asked.

The existence of master runes was too important a secret to entrust even to his men. "Information to help her take over the council's minds. Details are classified, but if she succeeds, she'll destroy them and we won't be able to stop her."

Anaru protested. "With all due respect, sir, the Tenth can take down a cui dashi."

Tomas said, "We've done it in the past, but she's changing the playing field. We need to remove her now, or we may never get another chance."

Domenico said, "The fourth floor is sealed. They've blocked open the elevators, and they've got men stationed at the stairs."

"What orders did Shahrokh give you?" Tomas asked.

Anaru said, "Keep the perimeter secure, and keep everyone away from the fourth floor."

"Do we have video feeds?"

"Of the hallways, yes," Domenico said. He pulled a laptop around and typed a few commands before turning it toward Tomas. The screen was split to display four simultaneous video feeds that showed armed enforcers stationed near the stairs, and heka positioned by the doors.

"That's Behram," Domenico said, pointing to a swarthy-skinned enforcer standing near the closed door to the stairwell.

The man turned and Tomas got a good look at his face. He didn't like the man's surly expression. He was a good judge of character, and he never would have recruited a man like that.

Tomas muttered, "They've ceded the council room to the heka. Not a good sign."

"We might be able to talk our way past the enforcers," Domenico offered.

"If we can, we'll need to storm the council room fast, before the heka can turn on the council," Tomas said.

Anaru said, "I don't like it. We can traverse that hall in three seconds, but not while running into enemy fire. Even if we make it that fast, there are five heka in the room. They could execute every council member in that much time."

Tomas studied the situation for another minute. "No video of the council room?"

"Negative. There's usually a camera, but it's out of service today," Domenico reported.

He reached a decision. "Where's Quentin?"

"Distributing some of his new equipment," Anaru said.

"Get him on the phone. I have an idea how to even the odds, but it'll take a few minutes to set up."

He pointed at Anaru. "You've met Behram. Take four men with you and see if you can talk your way up to the fourth floor. Try to get into the council room as extra security, but even reaching the hall would be a good start. Position the rest of the company on the third floor."

Anaru saluted. "Yes, sir."

Tomas said, "We'll watch your progress on the video. If you succeed, I'll join the rest of the company and we'll make our move."

"If they don't let us up?" Anaru asked.

"Then we fall back to plan B, and things get ugly." Tomas hoped it didn't come to that. Enforcers hadn't battled enforcers since the heka infiltration of 1453, and Tomas hated to think they might have to break that streak today.

CHAPTER FIFTY-SEVEN

Don't forget what I discovered that over fifty percent of all national deficits from 1921 to 1939 were caused by payments for past, present, and future soul transfers.

~Franklin D. Roosevelt

This isn't working," Sarah shouted as she crouched behind a pile of broken concrete. German bullets whined as they ricocheted off the stone inches away.

Alter fired a long burst from his machine gun and dropped back down beside her. Although the belt hanging from the gun didn't look that long, it didn't seem to run out of ammo.

Her shotgun did. She'd have to ask Gregorios about that. She had fired all the buckshot it had originally been loaded with and switched to slugs. Every time she pulled one from the wide leather belt she had draped over her shoulder, a new one materialized to take its place. Why didn't her shells reappear inside the shotgun and save her the trouble?

"What?" Alter shouted as bullets smacked the far side of the barrier.

Although Sarah knew there were six inches of cement protecting her, the angry buzzing of ricocheting bullets sounded too close. Still, she was a little surprised by how well she was coping with her first big firefight. She kept telling herself it was just a dream and tried not to think about how Gregorios had brought injuries back the last time.

"This isn't working," she repeated.

"We've got to hold them off until we get a clear shot at Mai Luan."

"I haven't seen her."

"You can't see anything down here," Alter said with a wild grin. He rose again and began firing, but pitched backward with blood spurting from the right side of his chest.

Sarah forced herself to rise and fire several shots at the SS soldiers before gaining a clear target. A couple of them had started to charge when they saw Alter fall, and she focused on them.

Time seemed to slow as she drew a bead.

Her finger pulled the trigger, and the first soldier tumbled to the ground, his chest a mass of blood. She had already switched to the second target and fired again. Her recent training with Quentin had helped sharpen her skills, and she barely thought about the movements as her hands pumped round after round into the chamber and her finger squeezed the trigger.

In that moment, she barely felt the kick that usually rattled her. Was it Gregorios's doing or the adrenaline of battle, or maybe another effect of her new rune?

She didn't care. She only wished she'd caught a glimpse of Mai Luan and got a chance to pump a slug through the cui dashi's skull, but Mai Luan never appeared.

After firing the gun dry, she dropped behind cover and shoved more shells into the loading port while checking on Alter. She pulled aside his black jacket and white shirt but found the wound already closing. The bleeding had slowed to a trickle.

Alter said, "Don't worry about it. I have more healing runes than just about anyone."

"Just don't get hit in the head."

Alter grinned, lunged to his feet, and fired off another long burst. When he crouched beside her again he shouted, "We need a new plan."

"Like I just said."

"Well now they shifted position. Some of them are dug in to hold us off but I can't see the rest."

Sarah glanced around, but saw only smoke. Did that mean Mai Luan was flanking them, or was the cui dashi chasing down Gregorios? She wiped dirty hands on her clean apron, then rubbed at her eyes. The haze was starting to get really irritating.

She smelled nothing but gunpowder, and her ears rang from the shooting.

"Together!" Alter shouted.

They rose at the same time. Alter led the way, firing controlled bursts from his machine gun at any visible target, and he handled the heavy weapon with ease. His accuracy forced the enemy soldiers to duck away from the bullets tearing into their positions.

Sarah followed, but didn't fire because she lacked a good target. He was right, the SS soldiers had scrambled a little farther north. They had taken shelter in a burned-out shell of a building just south of the bunker Gregorios had disappeared inside. She saw no sign of Mai Luan or Asoka, and worried the two had slipped out the far side. Sarah wouldn't be able to see them until they nearly reached the bunker door.

"We need to find Mai Luan," Sarah shouted.

"Find cover first," Alter replied, continuing to pour bullets into the burned-out building. One controlled burst caught a soldier just rising to fire and knocked the man off his feet, his chest covered in blood.

Sarah picked out a pair of soldiers firing off quick bursts from behind half-broken walls. She anticipated one of them and fired just as he popped into the opening. He took the slug to the stomach and fell back out of sight.

Her satisfaction with the successful shot was dampened by the feeling of bile rising in her throat. This might be a memory, but it felt like a nightmare. Normal people didn't shoot other people and feel happy about it.

Loud moaning wails drew her attention. Three undead soldiers crawled out from a nearby building and rushed the SS squad's position.

"Eww." Sarah cringed at the sight. She'd lost count of the number of zombie movies made in recent years, but seeing undead in this sort-of real life dreamscape was nasty.

"Now's our chance," Alter shouted and led the way out of the gardens toward a building just south of where the SS were fighting the ghouls.

Sarah still didn't see the difference between them and zombies, and only wanted to shoot them dead, well, more dead. Why didn't broken memories fill with happy thoughts? She could totally handle unexpected visits from unicorns.

They raced across the open area without getting shot. Alter kicked open a door in the four-story building and crashed through without slowing. They found a set of steel stairs and pounded upward. Sarah glanced down the long corridors branching off at every level but saw no one.

"How did you know these stairs would be here?" Sarah called.

"Faith."

When they reached the top, they crossed the flat roof covered with small stones, and crouched behind the half wall that encircled the outer edge. The air was filled with the clattering of small-arms fire and then with the booming of a bigger explosion. Sarah risked a glance over the edge, and from that height could look right down into the burned-out shell of the building where the SS soldiers had been hiding.

A couple of ghouls were feeding on a dead soldier, but the rest clustered around the far side of the building, shooting east toward the main street. Sarah crossed the length of the roof to the eastern edge where she could see some of the street. A large company of Russian soldiers and another tank were stationed around and atop piles of rubble.

"Think that's more of Gregorios's doing?"

Alter shrugged. "Doesn't matter. Gives us the chance we need to find Mai Luan." He ran back to the western side of the roof overlooking the SS soldiers' position.

With a whooping yell, he jumped off.

Sarah rushed after him and peered over. Alter had fallen four stories and landed in the open bed of a long truck whose tires were missing. Instead of screaming in pain from broken legs, he was blasting the surprised SS soldiers.

Movement drew her gaze farther to the north. Mai Luan and Asoka broke from cover behind a burned-out troop transport and led a small force at a run toward the bunker. Moving to the building had positioned Sarah and Alter against the SS soldiers, but granted Mai Luan the chance to get past.

The tank in the street fired, and the building shook under Sarah's feet. The eastern side of the roof where she had stood a moment ago buckled upward with a squeal of twisting steel and snapping timbers. Then a twenty foot hole appeared as debris fell away in a thunderous avalanche.

Something howled inside the building directly below the hole. It sounded like a wolf that had swallowed a PA system.

Time to go. She had a sudden, inexplicable urge to leap off the roof after Alter.

That was crazy.

A furry arm as thick around as her waist shot through the hole in the roof. A giant paw with wicked-looking claws capped the huge arm. The claws, already dripping with blood, dug into the roof and started pulling something massive and black and hairy up through the hole.

Sarah jumped.

CHAPTER FIFTY-EIGHT

I've never understood why men love the filth and hunger and exhaustion of war. From my luxurious palace, I've launched more revolutions than any general. Toppling economies may not seem so dramatic, but it's the results that count. No head of state ever defies me twice.

~Aline, facetaker council member

The fall off the roof seemed to take forever. Maybe she just fell slower than in the real world?

She hit just about as hard though.

Sarah landed in the bed of the truck beside Alter and rolled with the impact. She managed to not break her ankles somehow, but rolled the length of the truck before slamming to a jarring halt against the steel cab. Every part of her body ached and for a few seconds she couldn't breathe.

Maybe jumping had been as stupid as she had feared.

The pain bled away faster than it had any right to. After eight seconds she took a deep breath and hauled herself to her feet.

"Glad you're not dead," Alter shouted. Then he cursed and swung his gun around to shoot east toward where the Russian soldiers had been stationed.

Sarah looked that way and swallowed a lump of terror. The Russians were coming, but they weren't shooting. Instead two dozen soldiers shambled forward, moaning with hunger, bloody fingers extended like claws.

Zombies, ghouls, didn't matter. Why did it have to be creepy undead monsters?

She began firing as fast as she could, pumping slug after slug into the charging gang of undead. Only after the last one fell did she realize she hadn't needed to reload even once. Her leather belt of extra shells was gone too.

"What's up with the bullets?"

Alter shrugged. "Perk of the memory world, I guess."

"Mai Luan's gotten past us," Sarah cried, remembering their real mission.

Alter muttered a curse. "Come on!"

Together they vaulted out of the truck, and Sarah led the way around the building until they could see the bunker. Several soldiers were just charging out the back door toward Asoka's small squad.

Mai Luan appeared in their midst, moving so fast it almost looked like she had teleported. The soldiers tried to shoot her, but they looked to be moving in slow motion compared to her.

She destroyed them.

"Useless," Alter grunted and ran for the shelter of the circular guard tower just south of the bunker.

Mai Luan led her small team through the door into the square bunker.

Alter paused at the guard tower to check for an ambush, but Sarah ran past without slowing. "Hurry! We're late."

Alter caught up and pulled her to a stop just outside the doorway into the box-like bunker. She wondered how extensive the underground complex might be. Gregorios and now Mai Luan and Asoka had all disappeared into it.

Alter lofted a grenade through the doorway.

"Where did you get that?" Sarah asked as they both scrambled away from the door.

The ground shook from the explosion, and a gout of flame and smoke erupted from the door.

"One of those dead guys." Alter pointed at the men who had put up such a pathetic defense of the bunker.

A blur of motion out of the corner of her eye turned Sarah around, but Mai Luan reached her before she could bring her shotgun to bear. The cui dashi ripped the weapon out of Sarah's hands and tossed it aside.

"Hello, Sarah," Mai Luan said with false cheer. She wore a tightly fitted German military uniform that accentuated her slender figure, but a bluetooth earpiece nestled into her ear, breaking with the consistency of the ensemble.

Alter tried to shoot Mai Luan, but she pushed the barrel aside, aiming it toward Sarah's head and forcing Alter to release the trigger.

She grabbed him by the collar and slammed his own gun into his face again and again, striking so fast Sarah could barely count the blows.

Alter sagged in her grip, his face a bloody pulp. Mai Luan tossed him away. He soared thirty feet and rolled out of sight behind the sentry pillbox.

"You impress me a second time," Mai Luan said conversationally as she leaned close to wipe bloody hands on Sarah's nurse uniform. "I never imagined to find you here."

"Life's full of surprises," Sarah said, trying not to look as terrified as she felt.

The plan was falling apart. Asoka had already descended into the bunker with a squad of soldiers. Could Gregorios fight all of them off? Alter was supposed to kill Mai Luan, but she'd beaten him with frightening ease.

Sarah lacked any weapons, couldn't possibly fight Mai Luan, but she wouldn't cower.

Mai Luan smiled, just a brief upturning of her lips. "You shouldn't have come, Sarah. I was hoping for an interesting hunt."

"Give me my shotgun back and I'll make it interesting."

"You have to think bigger," Mai Luan said, brushing a strand of her silky hair out of her face.

"I could shove a grenade in your mouth," Sarah suggested.

Mai Luan clenched a fist and considered it. "You know, I could kill you so fast you wouldn't even feel death coming."

Sarah retreated a step. "I'd rather you didn't."

"But that wouldn't begin to cover the debt you owe me," Mai Luan continued, ignoring her comment. "You've got spirit, Sarah, but that's not enough. You didn't even bring Tomas in here with you. At least then I could've had some fun torturing him again."

"I healed him once. I'll do it again if I have to," Sarah retorted angrily.

"You?" Mai Luan asked, looking intrigued.

"Well, he showed me how to mark the rune, and he bonded to it himself," Sarah said. She didn't want to explain anything, but at least they weren't talking about which way Mai Luan planned to kill her.

"Indeed?" Mai Luan considered her. "Again, a surprise. You owe me an honor debt for the trouble you've caused, but perhaps there's another way to resolve this."

Sarah shrugged. "Sure. I shoot you once for every soul you've destroyed."

Mai Luan laughed. "Don't be a fool. They were only mortals. Their sacrifice was a small price to pay."

"Not to them."

"You are so naive. You waste so much effort on the undeserving. You could accomplish so much more if you spent your talents helping those who will shape the world."

Sarah wasn't sure how to respond to the abrupt change in the conversation. Was the woman actually offering her a job? Was this the first torture? Lots of people claimed to work for soul-sucking bosses, but she couldn't imagine actually signing on to work for Mai Luan.

"You think you're more important than everyone else?"

"Of course," Mai Luan said, looking surprised by the question. "I am a higher form of life. Even among mortals there are some more important than others. You perhaps are one. You've gained wealth and influence, and you've proven you're resourceful. You are one who could do much good."

"Stopping you is the best good I could do."

"Don't be dull," Mai Luan said, pacing around Sarah slowly, inspecting her as if considering a new possession. "If you even could stop me, what would you accomplish? You'd guarantee only that nothing gets better for anyone."

"Better? How are you making things better for anyone?"

"That's my ultimate goal. The world is chaotic, filled with war and suffering, and yet you defend the status quo. Think of the good we could do, working together. With the power of history at our command, we can remake the world into a better place."

"Better for you."

"Better for everyone. Think about it. I could end warfare between the nations by uniting everyone. I could end poverty, guarantee all mortals equality."

"Sounds great, except equality in chains is not an improvement."

"You are more than a common mortal Sarah. You have tasted many lives, glimpsed real greatness. Ally with me and I will place you over the rest of the mortals. You control them, you define their conditions. You care for them, guarantee they're treated fairly."

Sarah hesitated. Some of what Mai Luan offered could actually improve the lives of much of the world if she could believe anything Mai Luan said.

"You could be the saving queen of the world, my global administrator."

Sarah cringed to think of that level of responsibility. She hated balancing her checkbook. She wasn't world-administrator material.

"You make a compelling argument, but what of those who choose not to bow to you."

"Every new world order must remove the corruption of the last before it can rise. But we could make the transition as painless as possible." Mai Luan spoke with a passion Sarah had never seen before, as if she actually believed the crazy plan.

"Leaving you the ultimate dictator of the world."

"Stop fixating on titles," Mai Luan said with a roll of her eyes. "The world is already corrupt. I can correct so many things."

"I wish I could believe you," Sarah said, although in a way she didn't. It was easier to hate Mai Luan when she was simply an evil person trying to destroy the world.

"I speak in earnest," Mai Luan said.

"And yet, even your name's a lie," Sarah pointed out.

"How could you possibly know that?" Mai Luan looked startled, and for a second even vulnerable.

"Does it matter? What's your real name?" She yearned to grab up her shotgun and shoot Mai Luan in the face, but that would only end the conversation. The glimpse she'd gained into Mai Luan's thoughts was fascinating in a freaky sort of way, but at least the woman was still talking. Sarah believed Gregorios could beat Asoka and his soldiers. She had to. Every minute she kept Mai Luan talking gave him a little more time to wrest full control over the memory and wake them all up.

Mai Luan snapped, "You haven't earned the right to know my name. For Chinese, a name has deeper meaning than westerners comprehend. In my family, one must earn a proper name."

"So your family thinks your plan stinks too?"

Mai Luan grabbed Sarah by the throat, lifting her off the ground. "I'd have earned my new name by now if you hadn't interfered."

She shook Sarah like a terrier shaking a rat, but instead of ripping her head off, she dropped Sarah to the ground. Mai Luan leaned close and Sarah shrank from her angry gaze. "I could just kill you like I had planned, but if you serve me, we both benefit. You can work to restore my honor, and I'll let you keep Tomas."

Without warning, a hole appeared in Mai Luan's neck. Hot blood sprayed across Sarah's face as Mai Luan shrieked with surprise. More holes tore into her, stitching across her torso. The roaring of Alter's machine gun close behind Sarah thundered in her ears, and she rolled away.

Alter had snuck up on them while they talked, exactly as they had planned. He advanced on Mai Luan, firing on full auto, shouting with every step.

Mai Luan reeled back under the brutal onslaught, her slender body shuddering as bullets tore into her. Sarah felt sick from the sight, but refused to turn away. Alter was doing it. He was killing her.

Then Mai Luan leaped straight up. She soared impossibly high, and disappeared behind the building. Alter started rushing around the boxlike building, but a rumbling sound echoed from inside.

Alter frowned. "Sounds like she's broken through the back wall. She's inside." He rushed toward the door, but it burst off its hinges and collided with him, knocking him down.

Mai Luan emerged from the building, bloody but no longer bleeding. Sarah stared, awed anew by the woman's superhuman healing ability.

Mai Luan snatched up the broken door, and as Alter climbed to his feet and brought his machine gun around, she swung the door like a huge bat. The blow caught him with such power that it sent him tumbling right over the nearby sentry pillbox.

"You keep annoying friends, Sarah," Mai Luan said.

"Not as annoying as my enemies."

"Don't try my patience," Mai Luan snapped.

Gunfire sounded from inside the building behind Mai Luan. She cocked an ear to listen. "My destiny awaits. Prove your loyalty and remain here, and you'll be richly rewarded."

Sarah opened her mouth to reply, but Mai Luan silenced her with a raised finger. "Only once do I make the offer, Sarah. If you choose to enter the building, I will destroy you and everyone you've ever loved."

Mai Luan turned and rushed into the building.

Sarah watched her go, terrified to follow, but horrified to think what might become of her if she chose to obey.

"Sarah, are you all right?"

Alter jogged around the sentry pillbox, looking battered but determined. He stumbled once and winced, clutching at his ribs.

"You're one to talk," Sarah said, running to his side to offer support. "That hit would've killed most people."

"It hurt," he admitted. "But I'll be fine in a few minutes. Where'd she go?"

"Inside after Gregorios."

"We have to hurry." He scooped up his machine gun and Sarah retrieved her shotgun. She shook off the temporary hesitation from Mai Luan's twisted words.

Together, the entered the building and started down the stairs into darkness.

CHAPTER FIFTY-NINE

Learning the truth of the facetakers was the pivotal moment of my life. To think I can not only carve out the perfect society, and purge lower forms of human life, but live again as the perfect man and enjoy the fruits of my conquest. This is the truth all great men have learned. It is not enough to take the world, one must have a plan to keep it.

~Adolf Hitler

Gregorios stepped through the concealed door and carefully closed it behind him. Asoka knew how to find it, but Gregorios didn't have to make it easy for the man. He descended a long concrete stairway into darkness. At the bottom he faced a blank iron door, illuminated only by the tiny bit of light that leaked under the bottom edge. This was the most secret part of the bunker, the area that the allies never discovered in the long years after the war. It was where the real work was done.

The door opened to reveal a long, low-ceilinged room completely sheathed in gleaming stainless steel, and brightly lit by thirty-seven naked Mazda bulbs. Gregorios marched through the room without glancing at the medical beds lining both sides of the central aisle.

He had seen enough of the swollen, mutilated corpses to last several lifetimes. He had witnessed many atrocities over the centuries, but nothing compared to the cold brutality of the Nazis. The clinical approach they took to exploring the human body and to experimenting on both the living and the dead was unique. They tested the limits of human endurance through various forms of torture that took brutality to an entirely new level.

The room smelled like a charnel house and he gagged on the stale air. The approaching Russian troops had finally forced a termination to the work performed in the chamber. Racks of knives, picks, hooks, and electric prods stood in gleaming rows in their custom-built toolboxes that loomed near each of the beds, waiting for fresh victims. With a thought, he removed the bodies. The room needed to be hosed down or, better yet, fire-bombed. Sometimes the only answer was cleansing by fire.

On the far side of the room, he pushed aside a tall rolling cabinet. The vials of carefully labeled blood and other fluids clinked together but he was careful not to knock them off the shelves. The cabinet had been concealing a simple wooden door.

He pushed it open and stepped into a small room paneled in unfinished wood and paved with ancient stone. In the center of the floor gaped a hole nearly five feet in diameter, covered with a heavy, iron grate.

Gregorios heaved the grate aside. It squealed on rusted hinges before falling aside with a boom that reverberated through the small room. The ancient pit fell away into blackness. He had dropped a stone down it once and listened for five long seconds before the echoes of it splashing into water reached back up.

He figured the hole had to extend at least four to five hundred feet down. The Germans had rediscovered the pit during excavation of the bunker. Hitler's chief medical researcher, who headed up the torture division, had been thrilled with the find. So many possibilities.

Against the back wall rested several old-style soul coffins. Gregorios appropriated one and flipped open the lid to reveal a simple, lead-lined interior. He lifted the psychopathic dictator's soulmask, and for the first time listened to the indignant prattle and useless commands spouting in a constant stream from that whisper-voice. Sometimes not being able to run out of breath could be simply annoying.

"You will do my bidding," the whisper-voice shrieked.

"No, your bidding has done enough damage. Now you pay the price."

He shoved the soulmask into the coffin, latched it, and turned toward the grate. In the true memory, he didn't bother with the coffin. He had re-lived the memory many, many times, although he usually tried to wake up before reaching this point. Even so, he had stood above the hole and dropped that soulmask enough times for the moment to forever burn into his mind. Floating on its rainbow mist, the soulmask fell more slowly, forcing him to wait more than a full minute before the soft echoes of the eventual splashdown climbed back out of the hole.

Hitler had stood in that very spot on quite a few occasions and watched as personal enemies requiring special deaths were pushed into the hole. The sides were mostly smooth, with just enough jagged points to guarantee hands and feet were shredded to the bone. The condemned always scrambled to halt or at least slow their fall, and their screams were particularly pathetic. Several of them survived the splashdown only to suffer a lingering death.

Apparently the water was pretty deep, but there must have been at least one spot on the rock wall to cling to. A couple of those poor souls had lingered for days treading water and clinging to the side, bleeding out slowly into the uncaring waters. Eventually exhaustion beat them down and dragged them under.

Gregorios had disposed of countless enemies through the years, but dropping that fractured soul down that hole might just have been the most perfect condemnation he had ever devised. He hated Berlin, the lingering sense of responsibility for not having acted sooner, and all the associated memories, but the moment he dropped the soulmask atoned for much of what he'd allowed to happen through those years.

The dispossessed soul didn't breathe so it couldn't drown. Hitler would languish among his victims for many years, driven mad—well, more completely mad—by the solitude of dispossession. Eventually his soul force would dissipate and he would die, but it would take a very long time.

A fitting end for that monster.

Gregorios fought the current of the memory that drove him to complete his task. He knew deep down that it was that moment that would reveal the master rune. Instead, he turned from the pit and shoved the coffin against the far wall, piling the other empty coffins around it.

The lead casing inside the tiny coffin would make it harder for Mai Luan to sense the location of the soulmask. She'd expect him to hide it as far from the hole as possible, so that too should buy them some time until he defeated Asoka.

With his task completed, he turned to leave, planning to ambush Asoka in the warren of rooms above. Before he could reach the door leading back into the torture chamber, the wall in front of him rippled and dissolved into smoke. Another will assaulted his control over the scene and he clutched his head against a stabbing headache.

Mai Luan and Asoka stood in the center of the torture room, barely forty feet away. Asoka had already forced a different reality upon the large room. People hung on racks or bled out on the many tables, although no staff worked those moaning victims. They were just window dressing for the deranged mind that had wrested control. Either Asoka or Mai Luan appeared to want to twist the reality of the memory into something darker, even more evil than he remembered. He wasn't sure if that would affect the master rune by seeking a darker truth, but he didn't know it wasn't possible either.

He wouldn't allow it.

Mai Luan could drive Asoka's memories, but it was Asoka's will that held sway over their connection to this historical moment. His was the mind that Gregorios had to fight. Gregorios had beaten him before. He would do it again.

As he bent his will to fighting Asoka for control, his old friend-turned-enemy staggered and his face paled with the strain. The bleeding bodies flickered and disappeared.

Gregorios snarled with the effort as he battered aside Asoka's will. He could feel the memory firming around him, linking more and more to his will alone.

Then his control slipped.

Asoka fought back with far more strength of will than before. It felt like Mai Luan was somehow fortifying Asoka's mind. She approached several steps, a smile of victory on her face. She wore the same German uniform she had the first time he saw her there, but also sported a bluetooth earpiece.

"Where's the soulmask, Gregorios," she asked.

"Where you'll never find it," he lied.

"I'm glad you decided to join us. My research suggested your memories would prove the most accurate and the best source to find the master rune."

Gregorios had no idea where Alter and Sarah had ended up. He hoped they weren't dead. He'd never fight off both Asoka and Mai Luan alone.

"I wouldn't miss it," he said with false confidence. "You've worked so long to get here, seeing you fail means so much more."

"Finish it," she snarled.

The force of her will, driven by that command and buttressed by the natural current of the dream forced him to turn toward the pile of soul coffins. He took one halting step in that direction before he could stop himself. Gregorios stood there, every muscle quivering with the strain of not moving. It was like trying to stand against an avalanche.

In a direct nevron confrontation in the real world, Mai Luan would sweep aside the strength of his soul as easy as brushing away a fly, but Gregorios actually managed to hold his ground. It required every ounce of will power, honed over thousands of years, but he managed it.

It took a second for him to realize how he did it. This was his memory. Mai Luan could apply her will upon it only through the umbilical rune link to Asoka. Her connection was far more tenuous than his, and it must limit her influence over the memoryscape.

She was a passenger here. He was the driver.

Gregorios snarled and ever so slowly twisted away from the rear wall.

Mai Luan charged, her expression a mask of seething fury. She closed with terrifying speed while he turned to meet her with the reflexes of a frozen slug.

This was going to hurt.

CHAPTER SIXTY

First they ignore you, then they ridicule you, then they fight you with sword or rune or nevra core. And then you win.

~Mahatma Gandhi

"Captain, Anaru and his team are approaching the fourth floor landing." Domenico spoke softly from his position in the stairwell below the third floor landing. He carried a portable video camera with a wireless connection that fed the tablet in Tomas's hands.

Tomas watched from Quentin's workshop where the two of them were preparing the equipment he'd need to initiate his backup plan if Anaru's insertion failed. He silently urged his men to succeed, wishing he could lead them. No doubt Behram and his enforcers would recognize him, so he was forced to watch while his men walked into danger.

"Halt." Behram stepped into the fourth floor doorway when Anaru began ascending the last flight. "No unauthorized personnel are allowed up here."

Anaru said, "I know my orders, but we've received word of an increased threat level. My men and I will supplement your forces."

"Negative. This level is secure. Distribute your men throughout the rest of the building, but leave this area to us," Behram said.

Anaru continued his slow approach. He was tantalizingly close. A quick rush, and he could reach Behram. "The rest of the command is already deployed. The Tenth has always protected the council. I mean to do so today too."

Behram raised his rifle and Tomas clearly heard the click when he switched off the safety. "Take one more step, and I will shoot you down, Captain."

"You don't want me for an enemy," Anaru growled.

"My orders are clear," Behram said, looking unaffected by the giant angry Maori ten steps below him. "No one passes."

Another enforcer stepped into the doorway beside Behram and spoke quickly, but so soft Tomas couldn't hear.

He tapped his earpiece to activate it. "Anaru, hold position until we hear what they're talking about."

Behram nodded once and the second enforcer disappeared. "You can do something useful for me after all. We need a medical team up here ASAP."

"Are council members in danger?" Anaru asked.

"Negative. Send the team now. We'll free up an elevator for them. Have them bring a full trauma treatment kit."

"Do it," Tomas ordered.

Anaru nodded and retreated down the steps. Only when he reached the third floor hallway did he speak into his tactical throat mic. "I could've taken him, sir."

"Perhaps, but he offered us a chance. Order up the medical team, and find me a pair of enforcers that Behram and his men haven't met."

Domenico said, "Good idea. We'll slip them in with the medical team."

"The council will recognize them," Anaru said.

Tomas said, "It's possible, but order them to wear surgical masks and keep their heads down."

"I volunteer," Domenico said.

"No. You're too well known to them," Anaru countered.

"Anaru's right. Get a couple of volunteers they won't recognize. Get them into that medical team," Tomas said.

Quentin added, "I'll send up a few miniature video cameras to attach to the gear. That'll get us a live feed from the council room."

"Good idea."

Tomas passed the information along and left his men to organize the insertion team. He guessed Mai Luan or Asoka were the ones requiring medical assistance. That meant the memory battle had commenced. He needed to stack the situation even more in his favor.

"Anaru, position a team on the roof of that elevator when it comes down for the medical team."

His second said, "Already thought of that. I've got two more squads preparing to scale the other elevator shafts. They can blow sections of the floors and get inside fast when we make our move."

That was the kind of creative thinking Tomas loved from his teams. "Good thinking. Domenico, I want you and five men down here on the double. We're going to initiate plan B at the same time and hit them from as many directions as possible."

Quentin handed him a black helmet with the letters SWAT stenciled in white letters across the back. "This will keep the population in line."

"Excellent. Once we get the teams outfitted, I need you back at the mansion."

"My place is here," Quentin insisted.

"I know, but the memory fighting's started and they're a man short."

Quentin grimaced. "Right. I'll take the helicopter."

Tomas turned back to the contraption on the table. "First, show me how this thing makes me Spider Man."

CHAPTER SIXTY-ONE

Modern weapons are a marvel. The Tenth, fully armed, could defeat any historical army. And yet, sometimes I worry that it's too easy to kill now. It takes a strength of character lacking in many first-life soldiers to value the soul of an enemy even when forced to take their lives.

~Tomas

Gregorios refused to die at Mai Luan's hand, frozen in place, a helpless victim. He threw himself against the restraint of her will and took a single step.

The movement broke her hold over his actions and he stumbled forward with the abrupt lack of resistance. She slowed, one hand pressed against her head, distracted for a precious second by the mental defeat.

His hand flashed down to his hip and he drew his pistol and shot her in the head just as she focused on him again.

Mai Luan cursed and clutched at the bloody wound.

So he shot her seven more times in the face. The moment Gregorios's pistol ran dry, Asoka charged.

"This time, you die!" he shouted as he tackled Gregorios.

The two of them tumbled across the small room, barely avoiding the deep pit as they beat on each other. Gregorios could have reloaded the pistol, but he preferred beating Asoka senseless with his fists.

Mai Luan's wounds healed almost instantly, but instead of ripping Gregorios's arms off, she paused to watch the fight, a little smile on her lips.

That was fine with Gregorios. He'd deal with her next.

In the memory world, Asoka was again young, and as head of the enforcers he was fit and well trained. Gregorios had worked with him for centuries and they had known each other's fighting styles intimately.

The two traded fast blows and hammered at each other with hands, feet, elbows and knees. Asoka howled his hatred with every blow, but Gregorios withstood the barrage. He released his own long-simmering anger and embraced his fury. During the past decades while Asoka aged and his mind faltered, Gregorios had continued to train and add to his skills.

The life of a rogue had some advantages.

With a blinding combination of moves adopted from twelve different fighting schools that he had merged into his own unique style, he drove Asoka back across the small room. As Asoka's confidence faltered, Gregorios wrested control of the memory.

He re-formed the wall between the two rooms just in time to drive Asoka's face right through it.

The wall wavered, then disappeared. Mai Luan was helping Asoka again.

Gregorios's headache flared again, so fiercely he stumbled and nearly fell. He fought against the crushing weight of the two wills trying to break him and managed to hold his own. The wall between the rooms did not reappear but the screaming, bloody bodies did not return to the tables.

He would take the small victories.

Gregorios surged back to his feet just in time for Asoka to try gouging out his eyes. He broke Asoka's hold and spat on him. They had both fought several facetaker duels over the centuries, and going for the eyes broke tradition.

"You've abandoned honor twice over," Gregorios snarled.

"To destroy you, I'd make a deal with the devil," Asoka cried.

"You've already done that."

The two of them launched simultaneous attacks, but hissing growls began echoing in the room. Gregorios glanced behind him in time to see four emaciated creatures climbing out of the pit.

The creatures looked roughly humanoid but their skin was a sickly gray color and it hung loose over their bones. Their hands and feet had long fingers and toes capped with filthy, curled nails. Their eyes were black, and their mouths filled with fangs.

They smelled like all the athletic socks left in all the high school lockers in the world had been gathered into a single room, left to rot for a year, and then released. They were known as pagkamatay and they were the one thing Asoka feared above all else, for they represented violent, eternal death.

They were also incredibly hard to kill.

Asoka actually shrieked when he saw the monsters, howling with hunger, crawling out of the pit. He sprinted away and dove past the rolling cabinet that had concealed the little room. The movement drew the attention of the first two monsters, who rushed right past Gregorios and chased Asoka. Although they looked emaciated, they moved with terrifying speed and would run him down in seconds.

Gregorios silently urged them on as he lifted his hands and willed a pump shotgun into them. It was already loaded with one of his all-time favorite exotic rounds.

He shot the next pagkamatay out of the air at a distance of two feet, just as it leaped at him. The boom of the shotgun pealed with fantastic echoes through the steel-sheathed room. The death shriek of the monster nearly ripped out his ear drums.

He had fired a magnesium pyrotechnic round known as Dragon's Breath that could blast fire up to one hundred feet. It punched through the monster's sternum and filled its chest cavity with boiling, magnesium fire. The impact blasted the creature back across the floor with three thousand degrees of final judgment melting it from the inside out.

Gregorios dodged the second pagkamatay as it leaped from the lip of the pit at him. He pumped the shotgun as the creature reversed direction and came at him again. It howled as it charged, so he fired a round through its open mouth. Even in that blood-streaked torture chamber, the resulting scorch marks were spectacular.

Whistling to himself, Gregorios pumped the shotgun again and followed Asoka into the torture chamber. He found his enemy fighting one of the other monsters. Asoka was so terrified, he'd forgotten he could summon weapons to hand.

Mai Luan held the last beast in her hands and was calmly breaking each of its limbs. The pagkamatay howled in pain and struggled to escape, but she broke its final leg, ripped off its jaw, and crushed its head under her stiletto heels.

Gregorios raised his shotgun, but a paw attached to a limb as thick as his waist swatted his feet out from under him. He hit the ground already rolling. Another paw cracked stone behind him. He came back to his knees to face the snapping maw of a wolf-like creature he hadn't even notice exit the pit behind the pagkamatay.

He fed it his shotgun and pulled the trigger.

The monster burned like a torch.

Gregorios kicked it and sent it rolling right back to the pit. It tumbled over the edge, leaving scratch marks on the lip, before dropping out of sight.

They needed to be more careful. They were messing with the memoryscape too much and nightmares were working in through the cracks.

Mai Luan was bludgeoning to death the pagkamatay that had been savaging Asoka, who had suffered several deep lacerations and looked dazed from having to face his worst fears.

Asoka's distraction allowed Gregorios to gain the upper hand in their wrestle over the memory. The wooden wall materialized between the torture chamber and the pit room.

Gregorios charged, planning to tackle Asoka and rip his face off before Mai Luan could intervene. Hopefully that would end the dream and block her goal of gaining the master rune.

Asoka had other ideas. An antique wooden baseball bat materialized in his hands and he smashed Gregorios to the ground with it.

The timing for remembering he could summon weapons was really annoying. Gregorios groaned. He should have expected that weapon to appear at some point. Asoka had loved American baseball with a passion, and kept a replica of this exact bat in a glass case in his office.

Asoka jumped on top of him and grasped his face with glowing hands. So much for hand-to-hand combat settling the fight.

"You cheated," Gregorios growled as he embraced his nevra core and blocked Asoka's nevron from slicing his soul from the body. The two struggled for dominance and Gregorios slowly pulled Asoka's hands away.

Then Mai Luan dropped to her knees beside them. Her uniform again looked spotless, her face smooth, and her hair glistening as if recently washed.

Who had time for details like that?

She placed her hands onto his jaw. "I've got this."

Her nevron struck like fifty of Asoka's baseball bats. The sheer immensity of her cui dashi core drove his will into a corner of his mind where it whimpered in fear.

Pure, unfiltered terror filled him.

He couldn't stop her.

CHAPTER SIXTY-TWO

I'll never admit it to them, but perhaps the council was right. Their warnings of revolt and political chaos resulting from my activities are proving all too accurate. I cannot be blamed for wanting to embrace my soul power can I? With my heka lover, I am a god and will not be ruled by them.

~Rasputin, rogue facetaker

Mai Luan shouted in victory as her fingers began slipping under Gregorios's skin, despite all his efforts to stop her. Her fingers seared his face while her nevron burned his soul. He had not lost a life-fight like this in eighteen centuries, but she was going to destroy him. There was nothing he could do to stop her.

Then her fingers stopped and a look of confusion etched her smooth face. Some other power was blocking her ability to completely remove his soul.

Then he understood.

Eirene.

Her soul was still engaged in the real world. That must amplify her power in the dream world because although Mai Luan struggled with renewed determination to finish him, she could not sever the tie between him and Eirene.

Once again his wife stood between him and destruction. He really loved that woman.

"Tag." Sarah spoke from right behind Mai Luan, out of Gregorios's view. "You're it."

A shotgun roared, and Mai Luan sprawled sideways, spurting blood from a ghastly hole in the side of her head. Asoka lunged, but Sarah shot him in the chest and side-stepped his clumsy charge. She shot him again in the back, sending him stumbling into the small pit room. He fell, rolled twice, and tumbled headfirst down the ancient well.

She turned her gun back to Mai Luan and fired, but the cui dashi shot off the floor in a fantastic, convulsive move, landing on her feet like a cat.

Alter apparently didn't like cats.

He opened up with the fifty-cal at point blank range on full auto. Bullets ripped into Mai Luan, shaking her like a puppet on a string in a high wind. The noise was a marvelous din that continued to grow as echoes built upon echoes. Gregorios laughed despite the deadly rain of lead passing over him and shredding Mai Luan.

She retreated under the onslaught, spurting blood from dozens of wounds and screaming so loud that Gregorios hoped Alter would puncture a lung to quiet her down.

Gregorios rolled out of the line of fire, and Sarah helped him stand.

"You arrived just in time," he shouted above the constant dine of Alter's machine gun.

She gave him a dazzling smile, then joined Alter shooting slugs into Mai Luan's already bloody torso. The onslaught shook her so badly she couldn't escape. She tried dodging, but the two kept up such an intense rate of fire, she couldn't break free. The terrible damage she was absorbing began to take its toll and she dropped to one knee in a pool of blood.

Then Alter and Sarah both ran out of ammo.

"Hey," Sarah exclaimed, shaking her shotgun. "What gives?"

Gregorios's headache intensified, and he winced. "One of them is messing with things again."

Mai Luan rose to her feet, her riddled body already healing. "I warned you, Sarah."

"I choose not to accept your offer," Sarah said, and threw the shotgun.

Mai Luan swatted it out of the air and brushed back her hair. "I grow tired of your lack of vision."

Alter tackled her. Normally she could have dodged his enhanced speed or punched him out of the room, but she seemed a little rattled by the incredible trauma she'd just suffered. He knocked her off her feet and the two slid through pools of blood for a dozen feet.

Alter came to his knees beside her and clubbed her repeatedly in the head with his empty machine gun.

Gregorios summoned a Husqvarna chainsaw with a twenty inch bar and an aggressive chain. It was already running, and when he pulled the trigger, it revved up to a hungry roar.

Sarah cringed away. "What are you doing?"

"We're going to have to take off her head."

He advanced, but Mai Luan caught the gun as Alter brought it down for yet another blow. Shooting her with the machine gun had slowed her down a bit, but hitting her didn't deliver nearly enough damage.

Gregorios rushed forward. He only needed a few seconds to get into position and tear that monster's head off.

He wasn't going to get that much time.

Mai Luan surged to her feet, lifting a struggling Alter. With a snap of her elbow, she threw Alter into Gregorios. He tried to dodge, but was too close. He managed to twist the chainsaw out of the way and release the trigger before hurting either of them as they crashed to the floor in a heap.

Before he could extricate himself, Mai Luan snatched Alter off of him and tossed the young hunter over her shoulder. He sailed across the room, shouting and flailing his limbs, and crashed into the wall on the far side hard enough to dent the steel.

Gregorios swung the chainsaw around, but Mai Luan had regained her super speed. She plucked the weapon out of his hands and kicked him in the ribs.

He felt two ribs break, and the shocking pain rattled him for a second before he could sever connection to those nerves. The blow tumbled him across the floor, through the broken wooden door in the dividing wall, and into the well room. He clutched at the smooth stones of the floor, and slowed his slide enough so that when he passed the edge of the hole and began to fall, he managed to catch the lip with one hand.

Dangling over the edge, his feet scrabbling against the slick stones above hundreds of feet of empty space, he clutched that lip of stone with all his strength. Echoes of banging, like steel on stone, reached him from far below in the darkness of the well. He had known Asoka had survived the fall, for the man's resistance to his control over the memory had faded initially but then returned as strong as ever. If he had time, he'd drop rocks down on his old enemy, but he needed to deal with Mai Luan first.

From the direction of the torture room, the chainsaw began to rev.

Only Sarah stood against Mai Luan out there.

CHAPTER SIXTY-THREE

Without a doubt, Napoleon fields enhanced troops. Their superhuman battle prowess turned the tide against us. I recommend contracting with the hunters to counter those rounon powers. Without their assistance, we cannot defeat Napoleon. As to the rumors of a cui dashi advisor to the emperor, I could gather no concrete facts. One informant did offer the name of Xiao but who or what they may be is unclear and the informant died trying to learn more.

~Holy Roman Emperor Francis II in a letter to British Prime Minster William Pitt after his defeat by Napoleon at the Battle of Austerlitz

Sarah rushed for the idling chainsaw, but Mai Luan reached it first. She picked it up and revved the engine, holding the throttle wide open for three long seconds.

Sarah backed away, feeling terribly vulnerable. She wished she hadn't thrown her shotgun. She might be out of ammo, but facing Mai Luan with empty hands was worse.

Mai Luan grinned and advanced slowly, continuing to rev the chainsaw. Sarah retreated. She didn't run, because that might encourage Mai Luan to run her down and rip her apart with that terrifying weapon.

As she retreated, a strange numb sensation rippled through her, beginning at her left shoulder blade where her new rune was located. Sarah couldn't imagine what it meant, but hoped Mai Luan wasn't somehow messing with her rune. Cui dashi possessed rounon powers as well as nevra core, so it might be possible.

"Sarah, Sarah. I've decided what to do about you," Mai Luan chided.

"Don't jump to conclusions. Feel free to take your time."

"I've wasted enough time here, and your time has run out," Mai Luan said with an evil smile.

Sarah glanced toward Alter, but couldn't see him past a row of cabinets holding implements of torture. She looked toward the well room, but the angle was wrong to see the hole in the floor, so she couldn't see if Gregorios had risen yet.

She was on her own.

Mai Luan revved the chainsaw again. "I'm going to remove your hands and your feet." She spoke in a conversational tone, as if discussing what she planned to wear for the evening. "The pain will be excruciating, but you will survive, at least for a while. In that way, you can witness my ultimate victory."

Sarah shuddered, her eyes glued to the spinning chain as Mai Luan advanced. She had always refused to watch any of the B horror movies like the *Texas Chainsaw Massacre* for good reason. She wondered if Mai Luan had seen them as a small child. It might explain part of why she'd turned out so badly.

Sarah backed into one of the empty steel torture beds, still streaked with dried blood. She jumped over it, placing the bed between her and the advancing chainsaw.

Mai Luan shook her head. "That's all you've got, Sarah?"

"Give me a minute!"

"You don't get a minute." Mai Luan slammed the chainsaw blade onto the bed. The chain sparked and made a horrible racket as it scarred the steel surface.

Sarah dodged away and snatched up a metal tray from a table next to the next bed, scattering knives and picks and pliers whose use she didn't want to think about.

Mai Luan vaulted the last bed and came on fast, swinging the chainsaw in slow arcs. She could have moved the heavy weapon much faster, but appeared to enjoy taunting Sarah with it.

Sarah dodged the first strike, but ran into the nearby torture bed. With nowhere to run, she brought up the steel tray to block the next strike. The tray bucked and rattled in her hand, and the screeching of the chain as it skittered against the tray sent shivers of fear rippling up her arm along with the powerful vibrations. Again she felt the strange numb sensation spreading from her new rune, and wondered if she'd made a mistake forcing Alter to inscribe it there.

Mai Luan struck again, this time knocking the tray right out of Sarah's hands.

When she raised the weapon to strike again, Sarah lunged, closing with the smaller woman and grappling for control of the saw. She pulled with all her strength, but barely shook Mai Luan's arms.

The smaller woman laughed. "Way to go, Sarah. Showing spirit to the bitter end." The woman wasn't even struggling. She looked calm, unworried by Sarah's close proximity.

Sarah kneed Mai Luan in the ribs as hard as she could. With her greater height, she got great leverage, but the blow caused no visible effect.

Mai Luan's lip curled into a mocking smile, then she head-butted Sarah in the face.

The blow knocked Sarah off her feet, and for a second she saw nothing. Her mind went blank, overwhelmed by the sharp pain. She blinked her eyes open and found herself lying on the floor, with Mai Luan standing over her, chainsaw already descending toward her left hand, engine roaring on full throttle.

Then the terrifying machine tumbled out of Mai Luan's hands. The cui dashi spun, and only then did Sarah notice Alter standing behind Mai Luan, a heavy pipe in his hands.

He tried to club Mai Luan with it, but she snatched it away and grabbed him by the throat, lifting him off the floor. "I'm tired of your interruptions. Tell me your name before you die."

"I am Alter, son of Melek," he grunted through the pressure on his throat as he kicked her ribs repeatedly. "And I defy you."

"I've killed several of your relatives. They had better taste in clothing, but I found them just as pathetic."

He struggled harder, squirming against her grasp even though she could snap his neck any time she chose.

Sarah used the distraction to roll to her feet and snatch up the idling chainsaw. She revved the engine and the heavy tool shook with deadly power in her hands. She turned toward Mai

Luan, but felt sick by the thought of what she was intending to do.

Mai Luan slammed Alter onto a nearby torture bed so hard she drove the breath from his lungs. When Sarah rushed in, trying to drive the blade of the chainsaw into Mai Luan's back, the woman kicked it out of Sarah's hands.

She didn't even look worried.

"I'll finish you in a minute," Mai Luan said as she snatched Sarah off the floor by her shirt. She tossed Sarah away, sending her tumbling through the broken door into the well room.

Sarah collided with Gregorios, who had just climbed to his feet at the edge of the well, and they both tumbled over the edge again.

Gregorios managed to grab the lip, but Sarah slid right over the edge and began to plummet into the black hole. She screamed, but her scrambling fingers couldn't reach the stones of the far side.

Gregorios caught her ankle.

She crashed into the side of the well, striking her head hard enough to rattle her thoughts and leave her hanging limp in his hands. His voice helped her focus her scattered thoughts as he repeatedly called her name.

"I'm alive, I think," she groaned.

"Good." He sounded relieved. "I can't hold you forever. You need to help me."

"How?" She was hanging upside down in a slick-sided stone well. The cracks between the stones, if there were any, were too small for her to see, and when she slid her hands across the stones, she felt no joints.

Far below, she heard something banging, almost like a hammer against stone. She didn't want to find out what was making those sounds.

"You need to sit up. Reach up and grab onto my arm."

Mai Luan's voice reached her from the torture room above. It was faint, but clear. "Let's have a little fun, shall we, my little hunter?"

"Release me," Alter shouted.

"All in good time. You're fighting for Gregorios, really? I never expected you to forgive him and Eirene for what they've done to your family."

"That's none of your business," Alter cried.

"I'm making it my business. Did they tell you who really killed your great grandmother?"

"What are you talking about?"

Sarah frowned, trying to understand what Mai Luan was playing at. Why would she bring up that painful memory? How would she even know about it?

"You still think it was a kashaph plot, don't you?"

"It was." His voice didn't sound so sure.

Gregorios muttered, "Not good. Hurry, Sarah."

It took a couple of tries, but Sarah managed to do a vertical sit-up and grab Gregorios's arm. He released her foot and she righted herself.

"Climb up," he ordered. His face was beaded with sweat, and his arm quivered with the strain of holding her.

A new sound rose from the depth of the well below her. A hissing of gas and sound like rubber stretching. One more reason to get out of the well fast.

Sarah pulled against Gregorios's arm. The strain was intense, but with the recent training she'd been doing, and the enhancement of her rune, she found the strength to pull herself higher and grab his shoulder. He braced one foot against the wall and she wedged her foot against his hip and heaved again.

He wrapped an arm around her thigh and helped. With that extra support, she lunged and grabbed the lip of the well.

"I'm going to grant you a gift," Mai Luan said.

"I want no gifts from you but freedom to take off your head," Alter snarled.

"Perhaps you'll reconsider who the enemy really is after you see this."

"Come on!" Sarah helped Gregorios get his other hand onto the edge of the well, and together they pulled themselves up and out of the well. She rolled away from the dangerous edge, her muscles screaming from the abuse. The stone floor was cool, and this little room smelled less like old blood.

Out in the torture room, Mai Luan stood over Alter, who still lay on the torture table. She held his struggling form down with one hand, and was doing something with the other hand that Sarah couldn't make out.

He started to shout.

Sarah rose, but Gregorios shouted, "Get out of my line of fire!"

An automatic rifle with a scope had appeared in his hand. As soon as she moved, he sighted in on Mai Luan. "We need to stop this."

Just then, a bright red balloon rose silently out of the hole. It was long and slender, filling the five-foot diameter of the well. With one hand, Asoka held a chain attached to the bottom of the balloon. He looked wet and dirty and very angry.

With the other hand, he held a saber, which he raised to strike Gregorios's unprotected back.

"Look out!" Sarah cried, tackling Gregorios out of the way. The rifle fired, the sharp report painful in the small room.

Asoka released the helium balloon just as it reached the ceiling. He landed on the lip of the hole, wobbled for a second, before gaining his balance. He charged, sword high, and Gregorios rose to meet him, a Roman gladius short sword in hand. The two circled each other, blades flashing like living silver, striking so fast, Sarah couldn't follow the movements. The clanging of steel reverberated through the room, making it sound like far more than two men fought there.

"Help Alter," Gregorios shouted.

Sarah scooped up the heavy rifle, dodged around the fighting men, and rushed into the torture chamber.

Mai Luan still stood above Alter, and Sarah realized she was marking a rune onto Alter's wrist with her fingernail. He beat desperately against her arm, his expression terrified, but couldn't break free.

Sarah didn't need to see the rune to know it had to be bad. She brought the rifle up, took aim at Mai Luan's face, and pulled the trigger.

Click.

Only then did she realize it was a bolt action rifle.

"Really? Gregorios?" she muttered, cycling the bolt with frantic speed. Why couldn't he have summoned a semi-automatic? She brought the rifle back up just as Mai Luan raised her hand, her index finger capped with its bloody nail.

The new rune began to glow with blue-white light.

"No!" Alter shouted. "I refuse to . . ."

His voice faded away, and his body slumped motionless on the bed.

CHAPTER SIXTY-FOUR

Elizabeth has a depth to her that I have found in no other woman, not even enhanced girls I've known growing up. It's amazing to think she's gained so much wisdom while still so young. I find it refreshing to see that one short life can be enough, that runes or soul transfers are not needed to find happiness.

~Ronen

Alter stood in a comfortable bedroom beside a window overlooking his family's compound in Jerusalem. He recognized this room. It was his parents' bedroom, the room where each leader of his clan lived. His thoughts were fuzzy and his senses duller than normal. He realized he was watching the world through the eyes of another. He was peering into the memory of another person.

A shadow moved outside the window, which was three stories above the ground. Rune-marked hands grasped the windowsill.

Then time seemed to blur in a gut-wrenching twist of half-seen images. When his sight cleared again, he stood over the broken body of a woman whose face had been beaten into a bloody pulp. His own rune-covered hands held a blood-splattered fire extinguisher.

He moved to the window just as the outer door opened to reveal a strong man cradling a young boy. Alter instantly recognized the man from old family photos.

His great grandfather, Ronen.

Ronen screamed in anguish at the sight of his fallen wife. "Elizabeth!"

Alter turned for the window and caught sight of his reflection in the glass.

Eirene.

She was younger, wore a different body, but he recognized her face.

This was her memory.

Still trapped in Eirene's memory, Alter leaped out the window, chased by the echoes of Ronen's weeping.

Alter rocked against the steel bed, gasping with shock from what he'd seen in the memory. Tears he didn't remember shedding streaked his face.

Could it be true?

He sat up and turned to Mai Luan, who stood beside the bed, one eyebrow raised in silent question.

Behind Mai Luan, standing in the broken doorway to the well room, Sarah held a rifle pointed at Mai Luan's back. Behind her, he caught glimpses of Gregorios and Asoka battling with swords.

He waved Sarah to wait. She didn't fire, but didn't lower the weapon either.

"Why did you show that to me?" he asked Mai Luan.

"You call me evil. You strive to destroy me without knowing anything about what I'm doing other than what these facetakers have told you. And yet, they've lied to you, they've mocked your family for generations."

"The memory was a lie. Your ways are never the ways of truth."

"What you saw was real," Mai Luan insisted. "I discovered it when I walked Eirene's memories during the first test."

The explanation was plausible, but he didn't want to believe it. She was the evil one. She had to be lying.

And yet, what if she wasn't?

The murder of great-grandmother Elizabeth had rocked the family, dishonored Ronen, and triggered a fierce hunt for previously-unknown kashaph cells around the world. Before that time, the family had been fighting an escalating conflict against the facetakers. Could the demons have orchestrated the assassination to distract the family?

Alter rose and picked up one of the fallen torture knives.

"Are you all right?" Sarah cried.

"No," Alter said softly.

Mai Luan watched him calmly. She asked, "Will you fight me again, hunter, and die before wreaking vengeance? Or will you honor your family?"

"What's it to you?"

"We may have different purposes, but I prefer fighting someone who knows who they are and why they're fighting. Only then can you honor your family."

He couldn't argue against that logic, and that disturbed him as deeply as the recent memory had. Cui dashi were devils incarnate. Everyone knew that. And yet, for the first time in his life, a tiny doubt cracked his previously unshakable zeal.

Sarah approached cautiously, rifle still held at the ready. "What's going on, Alter?"

Gregorios had come to Jerusalem seeking help against the cui dashi, but Alter's goal had always been to bring vengeance upon the hated facetaker. Somehow the purity of his mission had become twisted, but now he had glimpsed a deeper truth.

He had to know. In that, Mai Luan spoke the truth. Only then could he know what to do next.

Alter began marking a rune into his arm with the knife.

Sarah cried, "Wait. What are you doing?"

"I need to know," he said, firm in his new resolution.

She held his gaze, her terrified expression tearing at him as she pleaded, "We need your help. Whatever lies Mai Luan showed you, I know we can work it out."

"No dear one." He would avenge his family honor and perhaps then she would allow him to show her the truth and set her free from the subtle chains they used to shackle her soul. "I will work it out. Right now."

"Wait, please."

For the first time, the pleading of her voice, those bright eyes that usually blanked out all thought held no sway over him. He knew his purpose and he would not deviate.

Alter completed the rune and it flared to life.

The dream faded to black.

CHAPTER SIXTY-FIVE

Do what you can, with what you have, where you are. The runes will do the rest.

~Theodore Roosevelt

omas stood outside the northwest corner of the Suntara building on the west side, directly below the council room window, wearing body armor and tactical vest dripping with weapons and equipment. Four enforcers in similar full battle array stood nearby. They all wore vests with SWAT emblazoned across the back. Other members of the Tenth had placed portable barriers across the street and were acting as crowd control. The disguises should gain them the few minutes they needed before the real authorities arrived.

"Sir," Domenico spoke into his earpiece. "The medical team was just inserted, including three enforcers."

"No issues?"

"Negative. They barely looked at our men. Just ushered them into the council room fast. Video link coming online now."

Tomas breathed a sigh of relief. He'd worried Behram would have intercepted the enforcers. They'd taken a terrible risk, and he would've carried a heavy burden of guilt had it not worked.

He remembered every man who had died under his command. The list was long, but he honored that burden and refused to allow the faces of those men to dim from his memory, despite the passage of the years. It was a weight that came with command, and embracing it helped him remember to never send his men into harm's way lightly.

Getting the enforcers into the room was a huge win. The elevators and the stairwell were situated on the east side of the building, closer to the main entrance. Once they launched the assault, it would take the Tenth precious time to secure the east side and advance up the central hallway, flanked as it was by several offices and two smaller conference rooms that might hold additional enemy forces.

Tomas tapped a small screen strapped to his left forearm. It came to life and video started streaming. They had secreted five of Quentin's mini cameras within the medical gear. A technician in the Tenth's dedicated communications room managed the feeds.

The various video angles revealed the council chamber in chaos. Shahrokh was present, as were Aline and Meryem. They all looked worried, and Sharhokh was standing, shouting at Tereza for explanations.

Another video showed the reason for the concern. Asoka and Mai Luan were connected to one of the machines. Asoka wore the helmet with the phoropter-looking faceplate, but Mai Luan's helmet sported a faceplate that barely covered her eyes, leaving her cheeks and jaw exposed. Both dreamers were covered in blood, and more had dripped to the floor.

They looked whole at the moment, although the medical teams were working with some of Mai Luan's white-coated technicians to clean them off and look for more wounds.

As the video continued to cycle through the various feeds, Tomas noted the other two machines Mai Luan had brought in for the council were positioned at opposite corners of the room. He had expected them to be set near the door, close to the first machine, and the placement seemed strange.

He didn't have time to worry about the oddity. The next video feed showed Tereza. She was not running the machine, as Tomas had expected. Another facetaker he didn't recognize, a woman with a wide face, powered the machine. Three soul-masks were strapped to it too.

Tereza stood at the table with a tall, slender, blond man with a pinched face and long nose. They had extracted seven more dispossessed soulmasks and the man was marking runes onto them. The angle wasn't great, but still showed that the runes were very complex. Tomas noted at least two of Mai Luan's people working with the medical team wore fanny packs.

"We've got enhanced for sure. I see at least a couple charlies."

Anaru said, "We spotted them too. So far we've counted four."

"Plan on the rest being occans or channelers. We've definitely got an enchanter in there," Tomas added.

Domenico said, "Has to be. He's fast."

Anaru added, "Our best rune expert is already analyzing the runes. He just suggested they're supporting Mai Luan and Asoka, fostering healing and keeping them alive."

"Try to capture that one alive," Tomas ordered.

"Roger," Domenico and Anaru said together.

Anaru asked, "What's going on? It's like they're in the middle of a fight."

"They are. Gregorios is fighting them in the memory."

"How is that possible?" Anaru asked.

"What's important is that he appears to be successfully stalling her," Tomas said. He worried that Gregorios might be in trouble. If Mai Luan and Asoka were getting so much extra help, Gregorios couldn't hold out for long. He silently urged Quentin to get home fast to send him an update.

He needed to get his men into position and end this before Mai Luan won past Gregorios. "Are the other teams in position?"

"Almost," Anaru reported. "We have teams ready to storm the stairwell, and others moving into position under each of the elevators. They'll have the floors wired in two minutes."

"Good. I'll be in position shortly. We'll move together."

Tomas faced the wall and adjusted the unique piece of equipment Quentin had helped him assemble before leaving for the mansion. The Suntara building lacked any external stairs or fire escape, so he needed to scale the four-story building. A gas-powered grapple could be launched, but Tomas had a far more elegant solution in mind.

With the push of a button, he fired up the specialty machine strapped to his back. At its core, it was a vacuum pack, supercharged, and customized to run virtually silent. It produced several hundred pounds of suction that ran through stirrups strapped to his shins. The stirrups included wide paddles with a soft, rubbery coating that could seal to almost any exterior building surface.

Tomas pushed one leg against the wall and it sealed in place. He stepped up, pulling himself off the ground, and pressed the next leg higher on the wall. By pulling up on his foot, he triggered the release that broke the pressure and allowed him to pull the paddle from the wall and take another step.

The revolutionary design allowed him to literally walk up the side of the wall with remarkable ease. The Tenth had taken a preliminary design originally developed by an American university working with grant money from the US military, and enhanced it.

With his legs locked into the stirrups, Tomas could walk up the wall, leaning back at a slight angle. The design allowed him to do all the work with his legs, leaving his hands free to fire weapons or use equipment as needed. Since no one was firing at him, he had also attached secondary paddles for his hands, connected to the main paddles with suction hoses and support wires. Using his hands allowed him to move faster, climbing the wall like a high-tech Spiderman.

The design was so new Tomas had only tried it once before. Even the militaries looking into the idea were years away from fielding a comparable model. As Tomas climbed the side of the building, he only hoped he'd get into position fast enough to make a difference.

CHAPTER SIXTY-SIX

*The beauty of a woman is not in a facial mode, but the true beauty in
a woman is reflected in her soul. It is the caring that she lovingly gives, the
passion that she shows. The beauty of a woman grows with the passing years.
With the right rune, a woman can let a little more of that beauty shine forth
than she might otherwise manage, but all things being equal, I still believe
happy girls are the prettiest girls.*

~Audrey Hepburn

Sarah stared at the spot where Alter had just faded away, but
could barely believe he had really left them.

Mai Luan laughed and turned toward Sarah. "One down.
I suppose I'll have to kill you after all, Sarah. Once Alter assas-
sinates Eirene for me, I'm not entirely sure what will happen to
you in here."

"You b—"

Mai Luan punched Sarah in the chest, driving the air from
her lungs in an explosive blast and sending her tumbling. The
rifle flew from her hands when she crashed into one of the heavy
steel torture beds.

"Watch the language," Mai Luan said with mock gravity.

Sarah groaned and rose, leaning on the table for support.
The pain bled away quickly, but she still felt rattled by the sheer
power Mai Luan possessed.

Asoka tumbled through the broken doorway from the well
room, but rolled back to his feet. A deep gash down the side of
his face disappeared. He'd lost his saber somewhere, but a pistol
appeared in his hands.

He opened fire on Gregorios, who was charging through
the door toward him. The bullets tore into him and he stumbled,
sliding across the slick floor.

Asoka dropped the spent pistol and an axe appeared in his hand. He snarled, "I own this dream. I'm a god here, and you're dead."

He swung the axe for Gregorios's neck, but a thick wooden shield appeared in Gregorios's hands. The axe sunk into the wood, and when Asoka raised it, Gregorios released it, leaving the shield stuck on the blade.

Another shotgun appeared in Gregorios's hands, and he blasted Asoka off his feet.

"I could get used to this," Gregorios said, rising. The gunshot wounds were already gone.

He tackled Asoka and the two fought with savage fury. With each strike, they summoned new weapons. Guns blasted into each other while knives slashed and stabbed. Both men took terrible wounds and their blood soon covered the floor. The air around them shimmered after each blow, and their bodies instantly healed.

Sarah watched with growing fear. They controlled the memoryscape, and thus could summon whatever they wanted and will their bodies whole again.

That didn't mean they should.

Alter and Gregorios had both warned her of the dangers of tampering with the dream world too much. Bad things responded immediately.

Shadows along the edges of the room drew deeper, and tearing sounds echoed out from the darkness. It sounded like claws ripping through the steel walls to get in. Growls and moans filled the room, and Sarah cringed. The two powerful facetakers might be fighting the duel of all time, but they were going to kill everyone if they kept it up much longer.

"You look scared, Sarah."

Mai Luan approached with an easy smile and a casual step. "You should be."

She looked healthy, her uniform spotless, a new bluetooth earpiece in place.

"I'm not scared," Sarah lied. "And I'm done with you."

She spun toward a nearby cart filled with torture implements and began snatching them up. Wicked looking blades and hooks and probes. She threw them at Mai Luan as fast as she could. She no longer cared about the stains marring many of them.

Mai Luan closed the distance between them faster than seemed possible even for her. She caught one thrown scalpel and slashed at Sarah's throat.

Sarah dodged and tried to punch Mai Luan. With her new rune, she was so much faster, so much stronger.

She never had a chance.

Mai Luan swatted her fists aside and punched her again and again with sledgehammer blows that drove her across the room, farther from Gregorios with every step. The pain slowed her, disrupted her thoughts, but she fought on. Giving up meant death.

She might not have a choice.

The beating paused for a moment as Mai Luan spun to catch a catlike creature out of the air and rip its head off with her hands. Sarah caught sight of Gregorios and Asoka. They had stopped beating on each other long enough to shoot, stab, and beat to death a swarm of nightmare monsters.

Some looked like goblins, others like the undead ghouls that had attacked the soldiers above ground. Some moved with blurring speed, like a pair of demonic cats similar to the one Mai Luan had just killed. Gregorios chopped the beasts out of the air with a huge battle-axe. Others were slower, heavier, like something that looked like a rock with arms that Asoka beat on with a heavy hammer.

Mai Luan slapped Sarah across the face and sent her tumbling onto a blood-soaked torture table. "Thanks for fighting with courage, Sarah. It's not much, but it helps a little."

Sarah noticed for the first time that the walls were beginning to look opaque. The entire memory was taking on a surreal feeling, as if it was beginning to fade. Either Gregorios and Asoka were destroying the memory from within, or Eirene was almost out of strength.

Would Alter really kill her?

CHAPTER SIXTY-SEVEN

Only a man who knows what it is like to be defeated can reach down to the bottom of his soul and come up with the extra ounce of power it takes to win when the match is even. My rune just formalizes the process.

~Muhammad Ali

E irene groaned under the strain of a sharp increase in the load. She sank to her knees beside Gregorios's chair and rested her sweat-soaked face against the cool metal of his helmet. For a moment she closed her eyes and focused on just breathing, just holding on a little longer. Her nevron was nearly spent, her soul drained to the point of utter exhaustion.

The drain eased a moment later. Not much, but even that little bit was a welcome relief. She opened her eyes and only then noticed that Alter had removed his helmet and risen from the couch where he had been slumped beside Sarah.

He approached, knife drawn, expression angry.

"You've lied to me from the beginning," he snarled.

"I had hoped to spare you," she said between panting breaths. Speaking was difficult, but she couldn't bear to see the betrayal reflected in his eyes.

"You're the demon who destroyed Grandfather Ronen's life!"

In a flash, Eirene understood what had happened in the memory, what Mai Luan had done to him.

He raised the knife but didn't immediately strike. Despite his anger, he was clearly torn. He was a good boy at heart, so much like his beloved ancestor. She hated that Mai Luan had twisted him so badly.

Eirene shook her head sadly. "You are playing into Mai Luan's hands. She will win the master rune."

"I can't fight her if I can't trust you. Tell me the truth."

She understood his point, but he was acting like an idiot. Eirene gave him an impatient look. "You already know you can't trust anything Mai Luan told you."

"She didn't tell me. She showed me a memory."

"An entire memory, or part of one?"

He frowned, and that was all the answer she needed. "Alter, we could have discussed this later. You've left the others in terrible danger."

"You deny you killed my great grandmother?"

Eirene sighed. "The woman who died that day was not Elizabeth. It was the kashaph assassin who came to kill Ronen."

Alter shook his head. "Stop lying! I saw enough. Grandfather Ronen recognized Elizabeth at his feet and I saw your reflection in the window."

She nodded weakly. The drain was growing steadily again and black spots began flickering behind her eyes. She had never drained her soul so dangerously low in all her years. She needed to break the connection or she would either pass out or die.

She was not sure she could extract them against their will.

What would happen to them if she lost connection before they got out?

"No, my boy," she whispered from where she sagged against Gregorios's inert form. "Mai Luan twisted the memory. Your great grandfather saw what he needed to see. He recognized a dead body on the floor."

Alter gasped as the truth finally penetrated that thick skull.

"Now you understand. I saved Ronen's life and the life of his son that day. I killed an assassin and I left in her body."

"You?"

"Yes."

He stared at her, thunderstruck. A storm of emotions flickered across his face. "You're Elizabeth?"

"I've wanted to tell you," she said. It was becoming increasingly hard to think, but she savored the warmth that flowed through her to know that he finally understood the truth.

"Why?" His knife fell to his side and he knelt beside her.

"I gave a life to him when I was supposed to remove him. He never knew, and I was never supposed to love him."

CHAPTER SIXTY-EIGHT

There are those who say what I do is abomination, but it is god who granted me these gifts. Like the saints of old, I can draw upon deeper powers of the earth. Why celebrate them as men of god, and denounce me as a heretic?
~Joan of Arc, Rune Warrior

Sarah tried to roll off the table, but Mai Luan pounded her so hard that ribs cracked. Sarah screamed and writhed against the uncaring steel, but Mai Luan held her down with one hand. With the other she hefted a long, wickedly curved knife.

Across the room, Gregorios and Asoka were still fighting each other while dispatching an ever-rising tide of nightmarish monsters.

"I don't have much time," Mai Luan said as she raised the knife. "But a little torture's called for. How about I start with the ears?"

A pistol appeared in Sarah's hands. She wasn't sure where it came from, but wouldn't waste the opportunity. She shot Mai Luan in the face as fast as she could pull the trigger. The cui dashi reeled back under the barrage of heavy bullets and Sarah twisted up off the table, still firing.

"How about you finally die!"

That strange numb sensation rippled out from her rune again, and her pain and bruises faded away.

The gun ran empty.

"Seriously? At seventeen?" That made no kind of sense.

Mai Luan spat out a bullet, her wounds already closing.

Sarah ran.

A hole opened up in the floor directly in front of her and a short, squat monster covered in green scales, with a mouth almost bigger than its fat head crawled through. It caught Sarah's ankles with long, too-thin arms as she tried to vault it, and she crashed to the floor.

The monster leaped at her, but Mai Luan swatted it aside so hard it exploded into green mist.

Mai Luan stood over Sarah with an executioner's axe in her hands and a grin on her flawless face.

"Good improvisation, Sarah! Let's see how you do with no arms."

"So you were supposed to kill him?" Alter asked.

He struggled to decide on the truth. The memory had felt so real, but part of it had blurred. Could it be the way Eirene suggested?

Who did he *want* to believe?

"My orders were to gather intel and ensure his attacks on facetaker interests ceased. The assumption was that I would kill him, but I didn't want to. He was a good man."

She leaned toward him as if to embrace, but her hands were stuck in the machine and she couldn't quite reach. Alter resisted an urge to wrap an arm around her shoulders. When he first met Eirene he had mistaken her for a much younger woman and felt instantly drawn to her.

At first, he had assumed he was just attracted to her, but that wasn't it. Sarah attracted him more than any woman he had ever met. He wanted to be near Eirene, but in a different way. Although he should hate her, she had slipped into his life, despite his reservations. He had instinctively trusted her, despite all reason. He still couldn't quite define why.

"When the assassin came I found another way, a way to complete the mission and still spare his life." Her voice was soft, weak. The drain was killing her as surely as his knife would have.

"I should kill you," Alter said as much to himself as to Eirene, but his anger had evaporated.

"Know that I shared something special with him, and he will always be dear to me."

A memory came unbidden to Alter's mind. Long ago, shortly before Granfather Ronen had died, they had spent a quiet afternoon together. They visited the park, ate a picnic, and grandfather had talked. His mind had drifted back to early days and he had spoken long about his beloved Elizabeth.

Alter had been old enough to feel moved by the depth of the old man's emotion, but too young to feel embarrassed by the showing of such emotion. The memory of that day had stayed with him and become a cherished source of strength and the source of one of his most powerful personalized healing runes.

As that afternoon had faded to an end, the old man had patted his hand and said, "My Elizabeth. She will always be dear to me."

Filled with a flood of emotion, Alter placed one hand over hers and spoke in a whisper.

"Grandmother."

Mai Luan struck before Sarah could imagine any weapon, any way to stop her.

She had to escape, had to run!

The rune on her shoulder throbbed, suddenly so cold it chilled her entire back. That strange numbness radiated through her body, but this time it continued to intensify until she couldn't feel her extremities.

The axe whistled down and sank right through her shoulder. It struck the floor and sank into the steel with a spray of sparks.

It had not made that sickening sound of steel striking flesh, and no blood spurted out of the wound. Sarah felt no pain, but only a vague pressure in her shoulder.

"By the forbidden runes, what devilry is this?" Mai Luan lifted the axe free. Sarah's arm looked unharmed. Not even a scratch where the blade had driven through the flesh.

It also looked hazy, like thick glass. Sarah could dimly make out the floor beneath her. The sight freaked her out. What was happening to her?

"You're fading," Mai Luan gasped.

"But I'm not gone!" Sarah twisted away, and her torso slipped right around Mai Luan's grasping fingers, like dense mist. She wanted to pat her skin, hug herself, maybe scream for a while, but the executioner's axe in Mai Luan's hands posed the greatest threat. She could freak out later.

Her body felt strangely light, and Mai Luan couldn't seem to quite grab her. She could feel the grasping fingers like distant flickers across her skin as she pulled out of Mai Luan's hold. Maybe Eirene's connection to the memory was fading. Maybe the duel between Gregorios and Asoka was pushing the memoryscape beyond its limits.

No, it was her rune. It had to be.

Sarah rolled to her knees beside Mai Luan and willed a knife into her hands. She plunged it to the hilt into Mai Luan's stomach and wrenched it sideways with all her strength. The slender cui dashi screamed and clutched her hand. Mai Luan's movements radiated up through the blade, and the feel of holding the steel into another person's guts disgusted her. She nearly puked right into Mai Luan's face.

Mai Luan yanked the knife out, despite Sarah's resistance.

"Not so happy about that one, are you?" Sarah panted. The smell of blood clung to both of them, but she noticed for the first time that Mai Luan was wearing a rose-scented perfume. She would have expected something more sinister.

"Keep fighting," Mai Luan urged. "Every wound you inflict helps restore more of my honor."

"Then give me the axe," Sarah suggested.

Mai Luan back-handed her all the way across the room.

Sarah cried out in pain, wondering what had happened to becoming insubstantial. She collided with the wall right next to a bloody spot where a body had hung from chains at some point. The impact rattled her and she slid limply down the wall to the floor. If her rune really had triggered that insubstantial ability, why had the effect faded? How could she get it back?

She focused, willing the rune to respond again.

On the other side of the room, Mai Luan threw the heavy axe.

Numbness again radiated out of her rune just as the axe struck. The huge weapon sliced right through Sarah's body and struck the wall behind. Sarah felt it pass through her chest, but felt no pain. The axe clattered to the floor, and Sarah rose shakily to her feet.

She should be dead.

She needed to know how the rune worked. She was in so far over her head, she couldn't imagine how to reach a safe shore.

Mai Luan cursed and snatched up a nasty looking hook. "Tell me how you did that, or I'll rip your eyes out."

"Come get some," Sarah shouted, hefting the axe. If she could maintain the insubstantial effect, she might just have a chance.

Just then, the numbness began to fade.

Eirene spat blood. Her entire body shook under an intense increase in the strain. The force of her nevron was flickering, dropping below the critical threshold as the machine dragged her toward oblivion. She needed to break the connection, or she would die.

If she did, they would die, or be lost to the memoryscape.

Through her connection, she caught whispers of images, barely-formed glimpses into what was happening. The little she saw only intensified her worry. Somehow Sarah still lived, despite what had looked like an axe driving through her torso. She wouldn't survive much longer. Gregorios and Asoka were still fighting, a battle like none the world had ever seen. The more they broke with the memory sequence, the greater the drain became.

On the reclined chair beside her, Gregorios looked battered, and blood soaked his clothing and dripped to the floor. On the couch, Sarah looked bruised. Blood trickled from under her helmet.

Alter lifted Eirene back to her knees and grabbed her by the throat. He leaned close to her, his gaze intent, but his expression strangely unreadable.

"Let her go, or you're a dead man."

Quentin stood in the doorway, pistol leveled at Alter's head. His dress slacks looked impeccable as always, with perfect creases, but he had shed his customary jacket and tie.

Eirene lacked the strength to feel much emotion, but she was grateful Quentin had come. She'd tried to reach Alter, felt like he understood the truth, but couldn't fathom what he planned to do next. She just wanted to lie down and sleep for a month.

"She will die unless you do exactly what I say," Alter stated.

Quentin lowered the pistol and advanced slowly. "Whatever happens to her, happens to you, boy."

"Move over to the couch."

He did so, and Eirene could only watch. She couldn't even speak. Her vision began to fade as Quentin settled onto the couch beside Sarah.

"You're killing them," Quentin said.

"This I do upon my honor."

The last thing Eirene saw was Alter's knife flashing down.

CHAPTER SIXTY-NINE

If people understood how much misery they endure so that their rulers can accumulate enough wealth to purchase another life, no government would last more than one generation.

~Gregorios

As Mai Luan closed the distance between them, Sarah struggled to focus, to will her rune to respond again, but felt none of the telltale numbness radiating from it.

She dropped the axe. She'd never hit Mai Luan with it without the protection of insubstantiality. She wanted to howl with frustration as the cui dashi closed. If only she'd learned more about the rune sooner.

She focused, and the short, ugly shotgun Tomas had used outside the safe house in Rome appeared in her hands. She didn't have to check the two feeder tubes to know they were already loaded with slugs.

She fired the first round when Mai Luan was barely ten feet away. The slug caught Mai Luan in the chest, and she stumbled.

The second shot missed.

Despite the gaping wound in her chest, Mai Luan dodged.

Sarah twisted and kept firing. Mai Luan continued to dodge, running around Sarah until she reached the wall and jumped off it, back the way she had come.

Sarah anticipated the move and shot Mai Luan out of the air. She charged the slender woman, firing as fast as she could. Somehow she knew that this time the gun wouldn't run dry of ammo until she blasted the hated woman into pieces that all the king's horses could never put together again.

Determination to see this evil creature eradicated burned away hesitation and fear. She would finish this once and for all.

Mai Luan rolled across the floor, trying to get a solid footing, but Sarah pursued, shooting her knees and then her head. Mai Luan still healed with impossible speed, but the wounds delayed her just long enough to keep her down.

She shrieked with fury, and hopefully some pain. She'd demonstrated that she wasn't immune to pain, and Sarah kept inflicting as much as she could.

Mai Luan's look of smug confidence faded under the barrage of lead and Sarah screamed too, pouring out all her rage, all her disgust at what she was forced to do here.

Then the entire room shuddered. The walls shook and the ground trembled.

All of the strength fled from Sarah's limbs and she dropped to her knees. The shotgun, suddenly too heavy to hold, clattered to the floor at her feet. She could barely hold her head up far enough to watch Mai Luan rise with renewed health. The room solidified again, but every table held a tortured victim. Cries of pain and pleas for mercy filled the room.

Sarah struggled to understand what had happened. She had been so strong. She could have done it.

On the far side of the room, Gregorios had also fallen. Asoka stood over him with a baseball bat, beating on his unmoving form and shouting a stream of profanities, mixed with words from languages Sarah couldn't understand.

Mai Luan took up the shotgun and pointed it at Sarah's face. It took all of Sarah's remaining strength to remain upright on her knees and meet Mai Luan's gaze.

"You proved a worthy adversary. I wish we had more time for proper torture. Oh well." Mai Luan shrugged.

And pulled the trigger.

In that instant, strength flowed back into Sarah like a dam had burst, and time seemed to slow. She watched the trigger depress and actually saw the flash of light from the initial blast of powder at the far end of the barrel.

Then the shotgun twisted out of Mai Luan's hand, tumbling onto a nearby table. The heavy slug passed so close to Sarah's head, it tore a chunk out of her hair. The booming report of the gunshot echoed painfully in her ears.

Quentin now stood beside Mai Luan, a bulletproof vest over his customary white shirt. He smashed a thirty-pound hammer into Mai Luan's chest. It shattered ribs and knocked the cui dashi off her feet.

Across the room, a renewed Gregorios caught Asoka's bat and used it to fling the other facetaker into a swarm of monsters. Asoka howled as the monsters tore into him, but he beat at them with a terrible fury.

Quentin offered Sarah a hand up. "Are you all right, my dear?"

"I could kiss you."

"Perhaps after we leave this unpleasant location," he said with a wink.

"Perhaps never," Mai Luan shouted, leaping to her feet even though her shattered chest was still healing. She grabbed a torture table and threw it.

Quentin pushed Sarah aside, and the table barely missed her. The chivalrous move delayed him, and the table caught him squarely, knocking him sprawling.

The table landed atop him, and he didn't move.

"Enough of this!" Mai Luan shouted.

Instead of attacking Sarah again, she rushed with her inhuman speed across the room toward Gregorios.

"Look out!" Sarah shouted.

Gregorios spun, but Mai Luan raced past, snatching him off his feet and dragging him along by the throat. She moved so fast, his body flew behind her, not even dragging on the floor.

Sarah gave chase, but Mai Luan moved so fast, she had no hope of ever catching her. The wall that divided the torture chamber from the well room dissolved, and Mai Luan rushed to the pile of soul coffins. She kicked the coffins aside and snapped open the lid of the bottom one, extracting a dispossessed soul mask.

Gregorios beat at her without effect, then kicked her knee, almost knocking her down. She shook him until his teeth clacked and he hung stunned in her grasp.

She turned to the pit and placed the soulmask in Gregorios' hand. "Enough play time."

She knocked the soulmask from his hand.

CHAPTER SEVENTY

I've lived long enough to see governments rise and fall. Most day-to-day worries that seem so important mean nothing in the long term. Perhaps once in each generation I find a person who stands above the rest, whose soul has the depth to matter.

Sarah is such a person.

~Tomas

Eirene crouched on one knee behind Gregorios, exhausted, but once more under control.

Alter knelt beside her, head bowed, sweat pouring down his strong, young face. His right hand still held her throat and she could feel his arm trembling under the strain. The rune he had marked across his hand and onto her collarbone burned with a blue purity she had rarely seen.

The boy was truly gifted. His blood leaked onto her skin and bound the two of them together. He had added his own life force to help fuel the machine.

He was taking the brunt of the load. Mortals, even those with such a strong rounon gift, should not be able to merge the force of their souls with hers like this. She was not sure how much longer he could hold, but she leaned her forehead against his and whispered to him.

"Hold on, dear boy. You can do it."

Sarah met Gregorios's gaze, and despite the thirty feet that separated them, she read the fear in his eyes. He tried to kick the soulmask as it fell into the pit, but Mai Luan pulled him back and shook him again.

He didn't want the soulmask to fall in there. In a flash, Sarah realized what it must mean. This was the pivotal moment.

She ran for the pit, knowing she'd never arrive in time to help.

The roof of the bunker faded away, revealing the sky filled with billowing clouds of black smoke. A complex symbol appeared in the air directly above them, burning with white-hot fire, back-lit by exploding bombs as it hung suspended above the doomed city.

Silence blanketed everything, and Sarah slowed to a stop. The monsters faded to mist and left them all standing as mute witnesses of the master rune. Sarah had felt drawn to runes since the very first one Tomas drew in blood on his side. Runes felt right, they made sense.

This one nearly overwhelmed her ability to comprehend it.

Its flaming lines consumed her vision and filled her with joy so bright she felt like she could fly. It assaulted her senses like nothing she'd ever experienced. It smelled like a crisp winter morning, and it sounded like a mighty chorus of brass instruments. It felt like silk against her cheek or the soft fur of a puppy under her fingers. Its twisting, complex pattern burned into her eyes and her mind. It sealed itself to her heart like a living brand.

It became a part of her, a piece she could never forget, no matter how many years might pass. The master rune took command of all of her senses for seven long heartbeats before it began to fade.

Then the roof snapped back into place above them and Sarah reeled as her senses returned. The room smelled of blood, and gunpowder, and sweat. Her ears rang from too many gunshots, and her eyes burned from the acrid smoke.

She held out her hand and the heavy axe Mai Luan had thrown at her earlier appeared in it. Quentin flanked her, his hammer again in hand. Blood matted his hair and he walked with a limp, but his expression was determined.

Mai Luan flung Gregorios into the back wall. Then she drew a knife and began carving into her own cheek.

Sarah gasped as the shape became clear.

She was branding herself with the master rune.

Tomas hung from a rope attached to the roof, feet braced against the wall just above the top of the huge council room window. After his quick ascent up the wall with the Spider-man wall climber, he'd lowered ropes that allowed his men to follow using fast winches. They'd planted explosives along both sides of the council room window, as well as the window to the next room on the fourth floor.

Now Tomas and two enforcers waited in position above the council room window, with the other two members of the team above the other one.

"Status?" Tomas spoke into his throat mic.

"All teams in position," Anaru reported.

"Show me the video feed on Mai Luan."

The tiny screen on his left sleeve came to life, showing Mai Luan in her chair beside Asoka. Asoka looked worse than last time, covered with cuts and what looked like claw marks and teeth wounds. Despite the extra support the enchanter was providing with those soulmasks, Gregorios must still be holding his own.

Then glowing lines began appearing on Mai Luan's face. Within seconds, a complex rune began to take shape.

Domenico asked, "What's happening in there? I've never seen a rune like that."

Tomas's blood chilled. Not good. He ordered, "Turn off that feed and delete the cached files associated with this one. No on records that rune."

"What does it mean?" Anaru asked.

"It means we're going in now," Tomas said. Gregorios had failed. Hopefully he still lived, but Tomas needed to move before Mai Luan awakened as an unstoppable force. "All teams, engage on my command. Now, now, now!"

Tomas triggered the detonator. The explosives pressed into the wall along both sides of the council chamber window detonated. The glass was made of high quality bulletproof material, but the blasts ripped huge holes in the walls. The glass, still intact but spider-webbed with cracks, fell away amid the cascade of splintered stone.

He kicked off the wall and rappelled down and into the window, landing in the room and unhooking his harness with a practiced twist.

The heka security Mai Luan had brought with her responded with remarkable speed. Even as Shahrokh and the surprised councilwomen were still reeling from the blast, the heka raised weapons toward Tomas.

Tomas shot the first man, while his three enforcers embedded in the medical team tackled others. He moved into the room, his IWI Tavor bullpup carbine at his shoulder. The suppressed rifle chattered as he dropped two more heka. The other men of his team landed in the room behind him and opened fire.

He shouted, "We're the Tenth. Eagles, stand down!"

Three of Behram's enforcers were in the room. Two of them pulled Shahrokh down out of the line of fire, but did not engage, so Tomas left them alone. The third one fired at an enforcer who had been disguised as a medical tech. The bullet caught the man in the side and he fell with a scream.

Tomas shot the Eagle in the shoulder, hoping the man stayed down. He hated to kill enforcers, but he would if he had to. One of Tomas's men, a Filipino enforcer named Isagani, who was routinely underestimated because of his slight build, moved around the table to cover the fallen Eagle.

The tall enchanter had fled the room even as Tomas landed. Sounds of gunfire echoed in from the hall through the open door. Anaru and Domenico and their teams were engaging. Hopefully they'd recognize the enchanter and take him alive.

Three more heka rushed into the room from where they had been stationed outside, firing before they could identify valid targets. One of them shot a fellow heka in the back. Another shot one of the real doctors on the medical team.

Tomas dropped one of them with a double-tap to the head. His men shot the other two. Tomas let them check the fallen to make sure they were really dead.

His eyes were drawn to Tereza, who was snapping a photo of the rune on Mai Luan's cheek with her phone. She glanced in his direction, then bolted out the door. Tomas was tempted to shoot her, but executing facetakers was a right jealously guarded by the council. He decided not to cross that line yet. She couldn't escape past Anaru and Domenico.

He needed to confiscate that phone, though.

Within five seconds of triggering the explosives, his team gained control of the room. Tomas left his men to tie up the wounded heka while he pursued Tereza.

The hallway directly outside the council chambers was empty. The men stationed there had either entered the room, or had moved to support Behram, who had been stationed on the east side of the building, close to the stairwell.

Behram had retreated down the central hall that ran east to west through the building, driven by Anaru and Domenico. The teams had tossed a dozen flash-bang grenades in the initial assault, and the entire floor was filled with smoke.

The assault was faltering as Behram's Eagles and the remaining heka security forces moved into the offices and smaller conference rooms lining the central hall. Anaru and Domenico would win through eventually, but it might take a few more minutes.

To Tomas's right, the two enforcers who had entered through the window in the office next to the council room lay groaning on the floor. Tereza was just stepping over them and slipping into the room.

Tomas rushed to his men. "What happened?"

"Tall guy," one enforcer said through bleeding lips. "Shot him twice, but didn't stop him."

"Protective rune," Tomas guessed. In the video feed, the enchanter had drawn complex runes fast on those soulmasks. Protective runes were difficult and time consuming, and only the most powerful heka could usually manage them. He really needed to interview that guy.

Tomas helped his men back to their feet and ordered them to flank him. Under most circumstances, he'd wait for heavier weapons, but he needed that phone.

The door was locked, so he kicked it open.

Tereza and the enchanter stood inside, near the window. She was tugging on the rope the enforcers had rappelled in with, clearly considering a climb to the roof to escape. The ropes wouldn't reach the ground, but from the roof she'd gain access to the ropes some of the men had used in their ascent.

Tomas shot her in the torso several times. At least one bullet struck her heart, and two others her lungs. She stumbled under the onslaught and nearly fell out the window. The enchanter grabbed her and pulled her back in.

Tomas shot him in the head.

The bullet ricocheted away, not even leaving a scratch.

"That's a good rune you've got there," Tomas said, advancing slowly into the room.

"Indeed. You would be Tomas," the man said. He spoke with a Chinese accent.

"And what do I call you?"

Tomas couldn't see the phone. It was probably in Tereza's pocket, but he didn't dare approach any closer. Protective runes were hard to breach while powered directly by a soulmask, and Tomas suspected the enchanter possessed several.

The downside of such runes was that they were very specific. A rune that shielded from physical damage probably wouldn't provide any assistance against getting tied up. Together, he and his men could probably subdue the enchanter, even if they couldn't directly harm him.

Tereza's soulmask suddenly became visible as she abandoned the dying host. The skin of her face sloughed away, allowing her translucent soulmask to slip free.

"You may call me Zhu," the enchanter said as he scooped up the soulmask.

"Well, Zhu, why don't you drop to your knees and place your hands on your head?"

Zhu laughed. "Because you have no power over me, enforcer."

He began drawing a rune right onto Tereza's soulmask with a finger. Few things affected soulmasks unless they struck with enough force to shatter them, but his finger trailed a glowing mark on its surface.

Not good.

Tomas rushed the man, planning to kick his legs out from under him, but Zhu hopped the sweep and lashed out, palm-striking Tomas in the chest. The blow knocked him back a step.

The two enforcers flanking Tomas opened fire, but their bullets ricocheted away, doing no harm.

"Cease fire," Tomas ordered. "We'll have to do this the hard way."

Zhu completed the new rune with a flourish. It was a complex rune, one Tomas didn't recognize. "Too late for that."

Tomas took a step forward as the rune blazed with blue-white intensity. Tereza's high-pitched whisper voice screamed.

Before Tomas could close on Zhu, the building shook, and the room filled with silver mist. Instantly, Tomas's energy drained away. His enhancement runes burned against his skin, but the strength he normally enjoyed faded and he stumbled to one knee. The other two enforcers followed suit, and the sound of distant gunfire faded to silence.

"What did you do?" Tomas asked, fighting to remain upright as his men toppled to the floor.

"You know so little of runes, you who suppose to judge us. No one even thought twice about the placement of the other machines."

"I don't understand," Tomas whispered. Breathing was becoming difficult and his vision was narrowing. His muscles quivered with the strain of just kneeling.

"Of course you don't," Zhu laughed. In his hand, Tereza's soulmask had darkened, the rainbow mist fading to gray and its healthy shimmer turning opaque. "They make up the key points of a rune web of my own design. My mistress will awaken shortly to find everyone on this floor reduced to a catatonic state."

Tomas collapsed to the floor, but fought to remain conscious. He tried to think of a way to fight the effect, but he possessed no rounon gift. He couldn't even lift his gun and fire a useless shot at the enchanter. All he managed was to shift it a little.

Zhu leaned over him. "You probably won't awaken again, Tomas. If you do, it's only because Mai Luan wishes to prolong your death."

Tomas tried to curse the man, to threaten him, but only managed the barest whisper. "I . . . Kill . . . You."

"Good-bye, Tomas."

CHAPTER SEVENTY-ONE

The world is full and waiting to be enslaved. History itself will bow to me. Maybe then I'll finally get some respect.

~Mai Luan

Gregorios stood, shedding soul coffins, and a heavy machine gun appeared in his hand. He opened fire, the sound deafening. Sarah's shotgun appeared in her hand again and she fired at the same time. Quentin held a bullpup-style assault rifle and poured a steady stream of lead toward Mai Luan as well.

She stood unharmed in the center of the deadly storm.

Bullets ricocheted in every direction, and Sarah ducked when one buzzed past her head, sounding like a score of angry hornets. Gunfire trickled off as the two men realized their weapons were having no effect.

Mai Luan threw her arms out wide, grinning with ecstasy. The master rune blazed with blinding glory on her cheek. The brilliant, sapphire glow flowed from it to encase her body, and a shock wave of energy exploded in every direction. It swept them all away, and blew the roof right off the bunker.

Sarah's ears rang, and she blinked against the light, staring in open-mouthed awe at the hole ripped through tons of poured concrete. Unlike the moment when the master rune appeared and the roof just faded to nothing, this time Mai Luan had torn a gaping hole through it. The bunker could have withstood a mortar barrage.

"Finally!" Mai Luan shouted in a voice so loud it beat through Sarah's damaged ears and shook her. The light around the cui dashi grew brighter and she seemed to swell with power. "Let them try denying me a new name now."

"If that's all you wanted, I could've gotten you a new name, freak," Sarah said. "Fifty bucks and a visit to the town clerk, and done."

Mai Luan advanced, her eyes filled with silver light. She flowed right over the pit without falling. "You dare insult the honor of my new name?"

"Not much honor if you can't even pick your own name," Sarah said, backing away and trying to hide her mounting terror. "Who's going to pick it for you?"

"She who has the right to do so," Mai Luan said. The executioner axe appeared in her hands.

"What if she chooses something you don't like?" Sarah asked. She stopped retreating because Mai Luan was closing the distance anyway, and she couldn't bring herself to turn her back on that axe and try to run. "Like Meg or Eunice or—"

Mai Luan covered the floor between them in a rush and slapped Sarah so fast she never saw the blow coming. It snapped her head around so far her neck creaked. She spun to the floor with a groan.

As Mai Luan raised the axe for a blow, Quentin crashed into her, a slender knife in his hand. He drove it into her throat.

Mai Luan tossed him aside, and Sarah could read the pain in her silvered eyes. The rune was granting her tremendous power, but she wasn't immortal.

Before Mai Luan could remove the knife sticking from her neck, Gregorios arrived with a wide-bladed spear. It looked like he had also realized they might have more of a chance hurting her with bladed weapons at the moment.

Mai Luan knocked the spear aside with her axe and shouted, "Bow to me, fools! Can't you see I've won?"

Sarah leaped to her feet beside Mai Luan and yanked the blade from her throat. Mai Luan gasped and blood gushed from the deep wound.

That was the opening Sarah needed.

Sarah slashed Mai Luan's face, aiming for the blazing rune. The rune was the key. It provided the overwhelming strength Mai Luan was enjoying, but it wasn't right. The master rune was seared into Sarah's soul and she could never forget it. The one Mai Luan had drawn on her cheek was similar, and yet different. It burned with malevolence absent in the rune Sarah had witnessed. Somehow Mai Luan had corrupted it, twisted it to evil designs.

Most of the rune was the same, but two marks on the right side of it drew Sarah's attention. One looked Egyptian, like a bent sword. The other looked like a pictograph of a bird. She aimed for these symbols.

Her knife cut into the rune and slowed, as if the flesh had turned denser.

Mai Luan screamed and grabbed Sarah's arm.

She twisted the knife, cutting a new mark through the two runes, bisecting them and forming a new symbol.

Mai Lun collapsed, clutching at her face. The rune changed color, now blazing with dark green light. It began melting into her face. Mai Luan screamed, pawing at the rune.

"What have you done?" she shrieked.

Even though she felt sickened by the sight, Sarah said, "I have no idea, but I'm glad I did."

The wall of the office that faced the council chamber exploded. Shards of wood and steel pelted Zhu, knocking him stumbling into the outer wall, bleeding from a dozen cuts.

The shaking of the floor roused Tomas. He'd drifted into a deepening haze, only conscious through dogged determination. He'd never felt so exhausted in his life.

Then he wasn't.

The drain on his strength and will evaporated. He blinked a couple of times and looked around, clear-headed for the first time since falling into Zhu's web.

The wall had exploded. Billowing dust obscured everything, so he couldn't see what had blown up, but it smelled wrong. He knew the smell of just about every explosive material, but this one stumped him. It smelled sharp, like burning plastic, but with a sweet undertone, like charred sugar. Then another smell registered.

Burning soulmasks.

Soulmasks didn't decay normally. If left dispossessed, souls deteriorated slowly over time, breaking from within. They could be destroyed, usually by smashing with blunt force, but other ways worked.

He'd smelled a burning soulmask once when they'd eradicated an entrenched heka cell in the mountains of Siberia. A channeler had led that cell, and they'd somehow acquired two precious soulmasks. When Tomas entered their compound to mop up after blowing the place with several high explosive mortar rounds, he'd found the burning soulmasks.

Soulmasks were burning nearby, and the stench was increasing.

Zhu pushed off from the wall, coughing. Tereza's soulmask had disintegrated in his hand, and he looked confused and afraid. He bent over Tereza's corpse and pawed through her pockets until he found her phone. He lifted it in triumph.

He turned to find Tomas again kneeling, rifle tucked into his shoulder, aimed at his head. The look of dismay on his face was priceless.

"Good-bye, Zhu," Tomas said, and pulled the trigger.

Whatever had shattered the wall and lifted the rune web had dissipated Zhu's protective spell too. This time the bullet had no trouble punching through his skull.

Tomas would have preferred taking Zhu in for questioning, but he didn't dare leave the man alive while some unknown threat was blowing up the building. He pocketed the phone. Maybe they could glean some useful numbers from it.

That minimal effort left him panting. He rested for a minute, breathing through his sleeve to minimize the amount of smoke he inhaled. As soon as his strength returned, he moved into the hall, keeping low.

He discovered the council chamber was the source of the explosion. The inner wall was gone, the huge conference table reduced to rubble, and a much bigger hole blasted through the outer wall.

A shimmering yellow light rippled between the three machines that formed a triangle around the perimeter of the room. Everything within that triangle had evaporated except for the council members. Enforcers, heka, and the medical team were all dead, reduced to piles of charred bones.

Mai Luan and Asoka still lay in their reclined chairs, but their skin had blackened. The rune on Mai Luan's face looked broken, and bled huge drops of crimson light, like glowing blood. The facetaker fueling their memory journey slumped over Asoka's chair, and the purple fire of her nevron flickered only weakly.

Shahrokh and Meryem lay on the floor in the center of that deadly triangle, their hair singed off, their clothes charred, and their bodies blackened. They still lived, for their faces were locked into grimaces of pain.

Aline lay beside them, her body melting into the floor. It was her soulmask that he smelled burning. It was already blackened and cracked, the rainbow mist burned away. It had to be some kind of rune that had destroyed the powerful facetaker, but he'd never heard about anything like this.

He could shoot the facetaker, which would destroy the memoryscape Asoka and Mai Luan were traveling through, but that might wake up Mai Luan, and he lacked the strength or the weapons to take down a fully conscious cui dashi.

So Tomas shot Mai Luan in the head.

As Mai Luan writhed on the ground, suffering from the broken rune, Sarah retrieved the fallen axe.

Quentin joined her, limping and dirtied, but determined. "Would you like me to do that for you, my dear?"

"Thanks, but I've got this."

"You unworthy mortal," Mai Luan shrieked, and staggered to her feet, hands outstretched to grab Sarah again. The silver light had fled her eyes, and she seemed to have trouble focusing, but no doubt she still possessed the strength to rip Sarah apart.

Sarah swung the axe, but Mai Luan knocked it aside.

The cui dashi took one angry step forward, then stopped, her body rigid in shock.

Sarah took advantage of the momentary distraction and struck again, shouting, "I've got a new name for you!"

The blade tore through Mai Luan's cheek, shearing the rune away before plunging into Mai Luan's shoulder.

Mai Luan screamed and snatched for the fallen rune, real fear in her eyes for the first time. Her skin burst into flame and she screamed again.

Sarah released the axe, leaving it driven into Mai Luan's burning torso, and focused. Her M4A1 rifle appeared in her hands, with the grenade launcher tube already loaded with the room-clearing giant shotgun round. Sarah pressed it against Mai Luan's chest.

Their eyes met and Sarah said. "Scarface. Suits you perfect." She pulled the trigger.

The blast threw Mai Luan backward, her chest vaporized. She screamed one final time, a long, tortured sound, then simply disappeared.

Glorious silence filled the now-empty torture chamber. The air that had been smoky, filled with the stench of death and blood and gunpowder changed, becoming crystal clear.

Gregorios stood and laughed. "The least I can do."

Quentin, limping and dirty, swept Sarah into a hug.

"My dear, as you Americans are fond of saying, that was awesome!"

For a second after Tomas shot Mai Luan, nothing happened. Her skull didn't explode like it should, and only a little blood trickled out. So he shot her again. For good measure, he emptied the magazine.

He dropped the empty and reached for a replacement, planning to keep shooting until something happened.

The machine exploded.

The other two machines exploded a split second later.

The blast catapulted Tomas down the long central hall and he slid all the way to the elevators on the far side. He lay stunned for a minute, staring up at the expensive chandelier hanging above the foyer. He wondered how it had survived the devastation, apparently undamaged.

A huge hand grabbed his arm and hauled him to his feet.

"You all right, Captain?"

He hadn't seen or heard Anaru approaching. He recognized the signs of being shell-shocked, but tried to focus his thoughts.

"I think I'm alive. You?"

"Barely functional, sir," Anaru said with a frown. "How'd they disable us?"

"Some kind of rune web. The enchanter's dead, so I have no idea how he did it."

Anaru frowned. "I started waking up in time to see most of the heka run. Didn't have the strength to kill them."

Tomas glanced at the elevators. He hadn't heard the heka make their run for it. "They're the least of our worries. We'll track them down once we clean up this mess. Come on."

He led the way back to the council chamber. More of the enforcers began emerging from the side offices or rising from where they'd collapsed in the hall. The machines were destroyed, the little that had been left of the chamber reduced to rubble. Shahrokh and Aline had succumbed in the final explosion, their bodies broken, their soulmasks cracked and smoking.

"What could do this to facetakers?" Domenico asked, poking the disgusting remains.

Tomas felt bone weary as he surveyed the destroyed council chamber. His gaze fell on the corpses of his men, and he felt the far-too familiar feelings of anger, sorrow, and thirst for vengeance. "We'll find out when we track down those heka. For now, let's find survivors and treat the wounded.

Behram pushed through the enforcers to face Tomas. "You made a mess of this, Captain. All you had to do was follow orders."

Tomas punched him in the jaw. Behram collapsed.

"Tie that idiot up before I shoot him."

A voice-ripping scream turned Sarah around. For a second she feared Mai Luan had somehow returned to the memory, that she'd actually survived.

It wasn't Mai Luan.

It was Asoka.

He stumbled into view from behind an overturned cabinet. Bloody wounds covered him, but instead of healing, he was beginning to melt into the floor.

"What's happening to him?" Sarah cried, sickened by the sight.

Asoka staggered toward them, dripping hands held out in a plea for mercy.

Gregorios said, "Something's happened in the real world. Their bodies just died."

"How do you know?"

"I just do."

Asoka whispered, "You were supposed to die this time."

Then he collapsed into a crimson pool on the floor.

That was gross. Shivering from the amount of horror she'd had to endure, Sarah turned her back on the dead man. The three of them clasped hands, and the bunker reassembled. Gregorios led them upstairs and outside where a pair of bodies burned in a nearby ditch.

"Who's that?" Sarah asked with a grimace.

Gregorios said, "Memory's back on track. Those were the bodies of Hitler and Eva Braun that the allies discovered.

"I'm done with bodies," Sarah said.

Gregorios nodded. "Me too. I really hate Berlin."

Then he looked up into the sky. "We're done, love. Bring us home."

The memoryscape faded.

Sarah awoke to the sound of distant sirens.

CHAPTER SEVENTY-TWO

What keeps me going after so many lives? The same thing that drove me in the first. The love of a special woman who I know I can kiss for centuries without getting bored.

Don't ever tell her I said that. It's more fun to show her.

~Gregorios

One week after the nightmare battle with Mai Luan, Sarah entered the art gallery dining room at Quentin's mansion. She had healed quickly from the bruises and physical effects of the confrontation, the process accelerated by her healing rune, but she was still struggling to cope emotionally.

She felt almost normal today, having actually slept well instead of suffering nightmare dreams filled with death and torture. What they'd done had been necessary, but it had been ugly.

Gregorios and Eirene sat at one end of the table, just finishing a late breakfast. Sarah hadn't seen Gregorios much in the past week. He'd spent most of his time at Suntara, consolidating his new position as council chair, overseeing repairs, and dealing with government investigations into the explosions. The scene had been labeled a terrorist attack, and he had actually applied for government assistance to help fund repairs.

When Sarah had asked him why he bothered, since he was probably richer than any billionaire the world knew about, he had shrugged. "Need to keep up appearances, don't we?"

Sarah hugged Eirene, whose color had returned.

"How are you doing?"

"I'm fine, dear," Eirene said with a warm smile.

"You look a lot better." Eirene had collapsed as soon as they awoke, and had slept for four days. The strain of maintaining the connection so long, particularly after they'd strayed so far from the true memory, had nearly killed her. If Alter hadn't lent his strength, she would have died and probably destroyed their minds in the process.

Sarah had decided to forgive Alter for abandoning them in the memory battle. Mai Luan had actually strengthened their position when she'd tricked Alter into returning to Eirene.

It still blew Sarah's mind to think Eirene was Alter's great grandmother.

"And you look radiant, my dear." Quentin swept into the room, dressed in camouflaged military pants and a tight fitting black t-shirt that showed off his excellent physique. He wore the simple outfit with his usual style, making it seem somehow far more formal and elegant.

He bowed over her hand and kissed it lightly.

Sarah grinned at him. "It's not going to work. I'm still going to out-shoot you today."

"I applaud your optimism. Add me to your card as many times as you like."

"I'll do that," she promised. She had only resumed sparring with Tomas and Alter the day before, but she'd trained with Quentin nearly every day.

Under his tutelage, her shooting was progressing in speed and accuracy. They had begun running a gauntlet of moving targets, and yesterday she had posted her best score, only five points behind his.

She had learned that his reference to her card was an allusion to days long past when women would carry dance cards at formal affairs and men would jockey for chances to get their name onto those cards to secure a dance.

While Sarah and Quentin ate, Gregorios and Eirene discussed the ongoing repairs to the headquarters and the unsuccessful search for the remaining members of the heka cell.

Tomas joined them just as the conversation turned to Mai Luan and the final events of that deadly struggle. He wore jeans and a white t-shirt, the look Sarah loved the most. She kissed him when he sat beside her.

Gregorios pointed at Tomas with a sausage he'd just speared with his knife. "All the evidence we've found supports what Zhu told you. That web he triggered had been pre-staged via additional runes marked into the machines."

"What do we know of those runes?" Tomas asked. "I've never experienced such a powerful web."

Eirene said, "Very little. The machines were badly damaged, but Alter's working on them."

"I bet. He'll send every one of those runes back to his family," Tomas said.

Gregorios shrugged. "A small price to pay. We might actually get back onto almost cordial terms with the hunters."

"That would be a nice change," Eirene agreed.

"What exactly are these webs you're talking about?" Sarah asked.

"The most advanced spells enchanters can prepare," Tomas explained. "High level stuff. Rare to find an enchanter who's learned enough to master even basic ones."

"We haven't seen this level of sophistication since the fourth crusade," Eirene added.

"What a mess that was," Gregorios muttered.

Such casual references to long-ago historical periods still rattled Sarah. She planned to spend some quality time with Eirene soon and just talk. There was so much she wanted to know, although she was beginning to worry about what she'd learn. She'd seen enough to realize history as mortals knew it wasn't exactly right.

She needed to know, though. It left her feeling a bit lost, like a boat drifting on the ocean without a rudder. History connected people to the world, helped make sense of things. She couldn't make sense of the world or her place in it if her only references were lies.

Quentin sipped his drink and said, "Clever chap, that enchanter. That rune blast was as effective as high explosives, but the security sweep couldn't pick it up."

"He powered it with those soulmasks," Tomas said.

Eirene nodded. "And probably by Mia Luan's master rune. I need to ask Alter about that."

Tomas shook his head. "It was crazy. We had no defense against it. Just drained everything and dragged us down to the floor, helpless as kittens."

Gregorios said, "Brilliant plan. Once she woke up, she could've taken the soulmasks of every enforcer and assumed control over the headquarters in one fell swoop."

"Any idea yet what broke it?" Tomas asked.

Gregorios nodded and pointed his fork at Sarah. "Your girl there cut Mai Luan's face and broke the master rune."

"I'm still amazed that worked," Eirene said thoughtfully. "Usually a simple cut across a rune won't affect its properties."

"Maybe because it was a master rune?" Sarah suggested.

"Perhaps."

Tomas squeezed her hand. "You saved my life, Sarah."

"Saved everyone," Gregorios said as he speared a large piece of melon. "That move corrupted the web and broke Zhu's enchantments."

"And you removed him before he could recover," Quentin said.

"I still wish you'd taken him alive," Gregorios said.

Quentin said, "On the contrary, he did the right thing. Zhu was too dangerous to leave alive without a full containment team."

"I know, but I can still wish, can't I?" Gregorios asked.

"We'll track down the surviving heka from Mai Luan's cell. We may yet learn something useful from them," Tomas said, then turned back to Sarah. "I wish I'd been in the memory with you."

"No you don't," she said with a shudder. "It was a nightmare."

Gregorios said, "You performed brilliantly. Turned out to be a lucky break that Tomas ended up in the headquarters and you in the memory. He shot Mai Luan and you finished her off."

"We make a pretty good team," Sarah agreed.

Tomas had insisted on a detailed report of everything that had happened in the memory. Sarah hadn't wanted to revisit the terrifying ordeal, but talking through it had actually helped ease some of her nightmares. Mai Luan should have destroyed her, and yet somehow she'd survived.

She still struggled with the feeling of lingering guilt to think she'd survived while so many others had died. They'd stopped Mai Luan, but at a terrible cost.

"Mai Luan was one twisted woman," Tomas said.

Sarah nodded. "No doubt about it, but I wonder how she might have turned out if she hadn't felt driven to prove herself and hadn't felt so unappreciated."

Tomas shook his head. "Everyone needs to feel validated, but she took it to psycho extremes."

"She nearly succeeded," Quentin said.

Eirene nodded. "Even in death, she destroyed four council members."

"What triggered that final explosion?" Tomas asked. "At least Shahrokh and Meryem were still alive until then."

Eirene said, "The best we can figure is when Mai Luan died, the backlash from all the power she'd concentrated through that master rune did it. Nothing short of that would have overpowered the council members. They were old, but their nevra cores were still potent."

Gregorios grunted. "Made a mess. Most of them would've had to be put down anyway."

"Couldn't they have used the machine to restore themselves?" Sarah asked.

"No," Gregorios said, his expression grim. "They endangered the entire world order with their stupid alliance with Mai Luan. That crime's unpardonable."

Eirene took his hand. "Well now you're in charge, and we can set things right again."

"We do have a lot to do. Speaking of which, I need you to respond to the queen of England today. She's looking for assurances that we'll be ready for her next transfer," Gregorios said.

The two of them began discussing operational matters, so Sarah rose and pulled Tomas to his feet. She still felt uneasy about some aspects of the facetaker activities, but she didn't want to deal with any of that today.

"We'll catch up with you later," she said. "Tomas and I are heading into the city." She was thrilled to finally get a chance to visit the sights without worrying about Mai Luan chasing them down, or heka assassins attacking without warning. It would be so nice to just be a tourist for a day.

She'd keep the supercharged Taser Tomas had gifted to her in her handbag, though. Just in case.

"Have fun, kids," Gregorios said.

CHAPTER SEVENTY-THREE

I have not failed. I've discovered the great secret of a second life.
~Thomas Eddison

Sarah sat at an outdoor cafe with Tomas, truly relaxed for the first time since arriving in Rome. She leaned against his hand as he cupped her face in the same way Gregorios and Eirene did. It felt wonderful, and the deeper meaning of the simple gesture thrilled her.

She eventually leaned back in her chair and gave him a dazzling smile. "You know, I'm still getting used to the new you."

"Take whatever time you need. I plan to stick with this life for a long time."

"I know it's not your first one. How many lives have you had?"

"A few." He looked nervous, but she kissed him.

"I don't mind dating an older man, especially one who looks this good."

He did look great. She was just glad neither of them would have to change bodies again. Tomas leaned across the table for another kiss, and she met him half way.

They took their time getting the kiss just right.

Now that they had some time, she planned to get to know the rest of this man she was seriously falling in love with. She didn't know what tomorrow might hold, but after what they'd just survived, anything would be an improvement.

From an elevated vantage point just inside a third story window of a nearby building, Alter sighted on Tomas with a sniper rifle just as he kissed Sarah. Alter paused for a moment to watch her face. She was enjoying herself.

He'd spent much of the past week studying the charred remnants of the broken machines, hunting for runes and clues regarding the high-level enchantments that had been employed. He'd already sent several encrypted emails to his father, who was thrilled with the progress, but who expressed worry about what the demons could do with such knowledge.

Alter hadn't shared the information he'd learned regarding Eirene being his great grandmother. He didn't think his father would believe it. Even if he did, he wouldn't receive the news with joy.

Alter didn't want to trigger a new war between the hunters and the facetakers. The demons had suffered great loss, but he'd learned enough about their forces that he recognized his family would pay a terrible price should the two groups launch renewed hostilities.

That left him in a precarious position. He needed to get to know Eirene, to explore this newfound relationship that connected them. And yet, the more time he spent with her, the more that relationship complicated his resolve to remove Gregorios.

Then there was Sarah. She was falling deeper into the demons' world, led into the valley of death by Tomas. If only she'd allow Alter to help her see the truth. She was a special woman, and he would not leave her to this fate.

He allowed his finger to slip to the trigger as he considered his options.

I know, that's a cliff-hanger ending. Sorry about that.

But I've got a present for you—more exclusive content!

I know you want to dive right into the next book in the series, and you definitely should! But it's okay to take a moment to read a really cool short story that takes place between the two novels. It's called Cyphers of Gold.

Castles, gold, and precious art . . . .

These are a few of Gregorios's favorite things. And finding a lost treasure is just the sort of adventure Sarah needs to restore her love for the memoryscape.

Exploring ancient castles for Nazi gold and lost artwork through facetaker memories offers a unique treasure hunting experience.

And with Tomas along, they might just create a new memory in the midst of the old.

Get your free copy here: https://BookHip.com/GFPWGJ

And if you still haven't checked out *Face Lift*, the exclusive short story available after *Saving Face*, you can still get it here: https://BookHip.com/GWHZMS

To make the download process as easy as possible, I use BookFunnel, the best site for downloading book conent safely and easily. You'll need to provide your email address for Book-Funnel to send you the story. (You will not get added to any lists. If you want to join my newsletter, there's a link on a following page.)

WHERE'S THE NEXT BOOK?

Right here. I know you're eager to dive into the next chapter of this thrill-ride. It's called *Rune Warrior*, and you'd better hold onto your hat, because this book is seriously awesome.

No girl likes a stalker.

Especially if they even chase her into the memoryscape.

Sarah loves exploring history, especially the glories of ancient Rome. But a mysterious man in a wide-brimmed hat threatens to enslave her soul and destroy the facetaker powers.

Think again, pal.

Sarah might just have a rare soul power of her own. That could give her the tools to fight. If she can convince iconic historical figures from the Middle Ages to teach her. One is a martyr, the other a mass murderer.

But her enemy has his own historical trump card.

His name is Spartacus.

And there is a reason his body was never found.

Get *Rune Warrior* here: https://smarturl.it/1rms8q

THUMBS UP?
OR THUMBS DOWN?

How did you like *Memory Hunter*?
 Are you willing to take 5 seconds and share your thoughts with the world? Now, while it's still fresh?

Post a review of *Memory Hunter* here: https://smarturl.it/sp55pq

Reviews help more than you imagine. How many times have you looked at reviews of books or products before buying?

If you've never posted a review before, it's super simple. Just two steps:

1. Rate the book 1-5 stars. Be honest. Be generous.
2. Write a short review. One or two sentences is plenty.

What goes in those sentences? Here are a few suggestions:

- Something you loved about it. (no spoilers please!)
- The fact that you couldn't put the book down all night.
- Who is your favorite character?

It's that simple. And it helps a ton.
Thanks!
Frank

AUTHOR'S NOTE

The entire concept of the Facetakers started as a really freaky dream. I awoke thinking, "Whoa, that was awesome!" The basic idea of the dream centered around the character who became Gregorios, the guy I still consider the ultimate facetaker. That dream eventually spawned *Face Lift*, the short story exclusive content I've shared links for already.

But Gregorios wasn't enough. He's such an epic, mysterious character, I needed someone else also. As I explored other possibilities associated with the concept of facetakers, the character of Sarah stepped out of the shadows and demanded attention.

Exploring the idea of selling body transfers to the public—sort of like Hertz rent-a-car meets *Invasion of the Body Snatchers*—led to the creating of *Saving Face*, the perfect way to begin the story.

But *Saving Face* was just the launch pad for the rest of the series. The Facetakers couldn't meet the full extent of their potential without diving into history.

As I dug into the series, I realized that Gregorios could not take the stage as the main character. That spot belonged to Sarah. She was the one who grew the most, the one who had to be the center of the action. It's not always easy to change directions, but in this case it was the right choice because *Memory Hunter* shines so much brighter with Sarah as the central protagonist.

We still get lots of Gregorios, as well as the rest of the excellent cast of characters, and they return for an even wilder adventure in *Rune Warrior*.

ABOUT THE AUTHOR

F rank Morin is a storyteller, an outdoor enthusiast, and an eager traveler. He is the author of fast-paced grab-you-by-the-eye-balls-and-don't-let-go adventures, including *The Petralist*, his epic teen fantasy series, full of explosive magic, huge adventure, and brilliant humor. Frank also writes *The Facetakers* fast-action historical fantasy thrillers you've been enjoying.

When not writing or trying to keep up with his active family, he's often found hiking, camping, Scuba diving, or traveling to research new books. Find out more about his novels and his shorter fiction, or join his readers group at: www.frankmorin.org

Made in the USA
Coppell, TX
21 September 2022

83481886R00240